# <u>Acknowledgements</u>

A lot of work goes into making a book like this and I have many people to thank for the final product. First and foremost, I'd like to thank my wife and kids for their encouragement and support during all the hours I spent writing and revising. I love you guys more than you could know! I'd also like to thank my beta readers (Mary Ann Okomski, Jen Campbell, Sean Quinn, Lisa Okomski, Chris Coxen, and Charlene Okomski) for helping me smooth out some of the rougher edges of the story. I'm also indebted to my editor, Elizabeth White, whose editing wizardry not only tightened the prose, but also improved elements of story and character. I also owe a big thanks to Officers Ed Campbell III (Boston Police, retired) and Ed Campbell IV (Danvers Police) for their insights on criminal investigations and police policy and procedures. I also want to thank the folks at Damonza.com for the fantastic cover design and Marissa, Hannah, Meghan, and the rest of the staff at JKS Communications for helping to spread the word about this book.

*Dedicated to law enforcement officers everywhere*

# THE ART OF DYING

## A RAY HANLEY CRIME THRILLER

## Derik Cavignano

© 2019 by Derik Cavignano

ISBN-13: 978-1733873307

ISBN-10: 1733873309

Library of Congress Control Number: 2019911089

# Praise for The Art of Dying

A 2019 American Fiction Awards Winner for Horror: General

"An edge-of-your seat detective thriller that crackles with gore and wit before delivering a stunning knockout blow. Fans of *The Silence of the Lambs* should flock to Derik Cavignano's new series debut."
*–BestThrillers.com*

"Boston gets gory in this enjoyable, horror-tinged crime tale."
*–Kirkus Reviews*

"The Art of Dying blends drama and horror for a disturbing and gripping thriller."
*–Foreword Clarion Reviews*

"Cavignano artfully misdirects the plot with family dramas and subtle clues, while keeping the cat-and-mouse conflict between Hanley and his quarry on track—all while the terror of the story's victims ratchets up the tension between chapters."
*—BlueInk Review*

"A highly suspenseful and delightfully twisted thriller with one of the creepiest villains in recent memory!" –Jeff Strand, four-time Bram Stoker Award nominee and author of MY PRETTIES

## Other books by Derik Cavignano

**THE RIGHTEOUS AND THE WICKED**

A sci-fi suspense thriller featuring Jacob and Ray Hanley

**COLONY OF THE LOST**

An ancient evil returns to the site of a lost colony

# CHAPTER ONE

Detective Ray Hanley shielded his eyes from the sun as he exited the Moakley Courthouse and gazed across the channel toward the steely peaks of Boston's financial district. Today's testimony had lasted longer than he'd expected, and as he hurried past the rusting steel girders of the old Northern Avenue Bridge, he knew he'd never make his appointment in time.

His cell phone chirped as he squeezed his broad frame into his unmarked Ford Explorer and fired up the engine. He was expecting his brother, but the display registered his partner, Billy Devlin, instead.

"You gotta get down here," Billy said.

"Can't. I'm supposed to meet Jacob for a charity golf tournament."

"You'll want to see this."

"What is it this time? Prostitute? Junkie? Another dead gangbanger?"

"It's Danny the Mule."

Ray sucked in his breath. Danny was a foot soldier for the Irish mob who'd vanished more than a month before. "Where'd they find him?"

"The quarry."

"Christ," he said. "I'm on my way."

\*\*\*

The Granite Rail Quarries hadn't been used to mine granite since the '60s. Since then, the sheer cliffs and onyx waters made it a favorite dumping ground for stolen cars, shopping carts and, of course, the occasional body. Teenagers from the city's South Shore neighborhoods considered it a rite of passage to leap from the treacherous ledges, some of which measured over a hundred feet high. Eventually, local politicians wised up and converted the area into a park, filling in the deepest quarries with dirt excavated from the Big Dig. But some of the smaller quarries still contained water.

Ray headed to the first of the water-filled quarries and found Billy standing shoulder to shoulder with a pair of state troopers on a rocky ledge scrawled with graffiti. An Underwater Recovery Team truck idled on a gravel path nearby, the winch on the flatbed whirring as it wound the cable back up.

Billy turned at the sound of Ray's approach, folding his arms across his rumpled sports jacket. He reminded Ray of a 1950s wise guy, both in attitude and in appearance. At forty-five, he was thirteen years Ray's senior. He seemed out of touch with the new millennium, and the fact he was rocking the graying pompadour of an aging doo-wop singer didn't help.

"Glad you could carve some time out of your busy schedule," Billy said.

"This better be good."

Billy exchanged a glance with Ty Garrison, one of the state troopers they'd come to know very well over the years. Garrison was in his early thirties and resembled a mocha-skinned Mr. Clean with his shiny bald head and a muscular frame that always seemed on the verge of tearing his uniform.

Garrison snickered—a funny sound coming from that giant's body. "Wait till you see this." He stepped aside to give Ray a look at the bloated corpse strapped to an inflatable rescue stretcher.

In his eleven years on the force, Ray had seen his share of bodies fished out of the water. They all had the same waxen pallor, their skin and nails tinged with blue. But he'd never seen a body come out looking quite like this.

The last time Ray had seen Danny the Mule was five years ago on the Southie docks. As part of the city's Organized Crime Task Force, Ray had taken part in a sting operation that netted a hundred pounds of heroin off a container ship originating from Hong Kong. They caught Danny unloading a container full of toy pandas stuffed with fifty million dollars' worth of smack.

When Danny saw the cops closing in, he retreated into a maze of brightly colored shipping containers, a cuddly panda flopping under each arm. Trooper Garrison was at Ray's side and he doubled over in hysterics at the sight of Danny waddling away like a petulant child. Ray resisted the giggles bubbling up in his own chest and chased after Danny, ultimately taking him down with a shot from his Taser. Danny wound up serving three years of a seven-year sentence but had disappeared without a trace just over a month ago.

Ray stared down at Danny's corpse and shuddered. "What in the hell is that?"

Except for a ragged purple scar, Danny's pelvic area was as bare as a Ken doll. Oddly, the missing organ had migrated to his face, grafted dead center over the space his nose had once occupied… and hanging just a bit to the left.

Billy shook his head. "Reason number twenty-three why you don't cross Sal Giabatti."

"What's that on his ear?" Ray asked. "It looks like stitches. Why would he have stitches on his ear without an obvious wound?"

Billy shrugged. "I think the better question is why is there a dick on his face?"

Garrison chuckled as the medical examiner's van rolled up beside them. "You don't see that every day."

"No," Ray said, "you don't. But I think the new look suits him."

"Sort of reminds me of an aardvark," Garrison said.

Ray folded his arms. "I feel like we need a new nickname. You got anything?" he asked, turning to the rookie trooper standing beside Garrison.

The young trooper, whose name he could never remember, shook his head, lacking either imagination or the confidence to offer a response.

"How about Danny the Tool?" Billy asked.

A curt clearing of the throat drew Ray's attention and he looked up to see Tina Bolton from the medical examiner's office approaching to collect the body. Equal parts brilliant and beautiful, Tina had a no-nonsense reputation.

"I'm sorry," she said. "Am I interrupting your frat party?"

Ray grinned at the other officers. "Make way for the fun police."

Tina pushed past him. Her curly brown hair tickled his cheek as she strode by with her forensic tech, Luis, who was biting back laughter.

"What's with her?" the younger trooper asked.

Garrison smirked. "Ray used to date her."

"That was nine years ago," Ray said. "And I'd hardly call it dating."

"Oh yeah?" Billy said, arching a bushy eyebrow. "What would you call it?"

Ray ignored the remark and turned to watch Tina conduct her field exam, which included the customary poking and prodding that went along with testing the degree of rigor and liver mortis, as well as getting a core temperature read from Danny's liver. When she was finished, Luis zipped Danny into a body bag, slid him onto an ambulance gurney, and loaded him into the van.

Ray approached Tina as she walked toward the passenger side of the van.

Tina stripped off her latex gloves and wheeled on him. "Don't ever belittle me like that again, Ray. Do you understand? This job's hard enough without you cutting me down in front of your buddies."

"What the hell are you talking about? You're the one who started it with your frat boy comment. And I know it may

4

seem callous, but humor's the only thing that keeps us sane with this job. You should try it sometime."

"Is that supposed to be an apology, Ray? Because it sounded an awful lot like an insult to me."

"Are you still fishing for an apology? Is that what this is about?"

"Don't flatter yourself, Ray. You threw away your chance a long time ago." But the intensity in her hazel eyes hinted at a deeper truth. "Why'd you come over here, anyway? Just to piss me off?"

Ray motioned to Billy and Garrison. "They think this is a Giabatti versus Flaherty dispute. Just your classic territorial battle between crime families. But something about this seems off. Whoever did this wanted Danny to suffer. They wanted to hurt him, to emasculate him, so I get why they cut off his junk. But why go through the trouble of grafting it onto his face? It doesn't make any sense. It's too elaborate for a crime family dispute. It feels more personal, like someone was trying to shame him. You know what I mean?"

"It's certainly not your typical gangster-style execution."

"Let me know if you find anything else unusual during the autopsy. I have a feeling we might only be seeing the tip of the iceberg."

"Oh, I definitely saw the tip of something," Tina said, and winked at him before climbing into the van.

Ray shook his head at her sudden change in mood and watched the van pull away, the cloud of dust spiraling up from its tires hanging in the air like an unformed question.

# CHAPTER TWO

Ray strode across the fairway and tried to shake the image of Danny the Mule's freakish corpse from his mind. He spotted his brother teeing off beside a dense stand of pine and yelled into his backswing. "That's a terrible shot, Jacob. You realize the fairway's that way, don't you?"

Jacob lowered his club as Ray crossed over the cart path. People were always saying he and Jacob looked alike. Same liquid brown eyes, same pale skin, same smattering of freckles around the bridge of the nose. If it wasn't for Ray's three-inch height advantage and his broader frame, they could've passed as twins.

"I'm very familiar with the course," Jacob said. "Seeing as I've been here for an hour already."

"So how come you don't know where the fairway is?"

Jacob turned to the other two partners from his CPA firm. "Wes, Gary, you remember my obnoxious brother, Ray, don't you?"

"He's hard to forget," Wes said, raking his hand through a crop of salt-and-pepper hair.

Ray nodded a greeting. "Looks like I got here in nick of time."

"How so?" Gary asked.

"Three accountants on a golf course? Another minute and you would've bored yourselves to death."

Jacob grabbed a Heineken from the cooler on his golf cart and tossed it to Ray. "Are you going to play nice in the sandbox today?"

"I play to win, little brother. You should know that by now." He watched Gary and Wes climb into their cart and speed off down the fairway. "We playing best ball?"

Jacob slid behind the wheel of their cart. "Yes, and I don't want to hear any complaints about my driving."

"Alright, but you'll never improve without the proper coaching."

They finished the hole with a birdie but had to wait for an older foursome to tee off ahead of them before moving on. Ray could see them shuffling around the tee box, all white hair, plaid pants, and labored movements. He leaned against the golf cart and rolled his eyes at Jacob. "I got a feeling we're gonna be here awhile."

"Whatever gave you that idea?" Jacob asked.

"Oh, I don't know, maybe because that one guy is wheeling around an oxygen tank."

Jacob took a swig of Heineken and glanced at his colleagues, who were taking practice swings in the distance. "How'd it go at court today?"

"A whole lot of grandstanding, not a lot of evidence."

"What do you mean?"

"The DA's running for governor and I get the feeling he wants to use this case to make a name for himself."

"What was it, a murder trial?"

Ray shook his head. "Grand jury hearing. You've probably seen it on the news."

"It's not the Coleman case, is it?"

"That's the one."

The news outlets were salivating over the story. It had all the trappings of a made-for-TV-movie: a thirty-year-old man wakes up covered in his wife's blood. She's missing but he claims he was asleep the whole time. So far, there's no body, no murder weapon, and no witnesses, but the DA wants to charge him with first degree murder.

Jacob adjusted his glasses. "You think the DA's jumping the gun?"

Ray finished his beer and tossed the empty into the back of the cart. "I don't think they can get a conviction with the evidence they have so far, so yeah, I think he's jumping the gun.

Right now, we've got Coleman locked up for possessing a firearm without a permit. Unless they charge him with another crime, he's set for release in a few days. And that won't look good for the DA, the mayor, or the chief."

"But if they charge him now," Jacob said, "they could deny bail and hold him until the trial, which could drag on past election day."

"Exactly. And at that point what do they care about the outcome of the trial?"

"But how can they charge him with murder without a body?"

"The doctor who testified said there was enough blood to conclude Coleman's wife probably died from her wounds. Also, they found blood in the trunk of Coleman's car, which is strange considering the car needed a new starter and wouldn't even turn over. A tow truck showed up while we were out there investigating. Turns out Coleman had called the dealer the day before to arrange a tow."

"So why would he put a dead body in a car he knew wouldn't start?"

"That's a good question, little brother. The way I figure it, he either forgot the car wouldn't start or someone really is trying to frame him."

"We're up," Wes called, motioning to them from the tee box.

Jacob exchanged a glance with Ray as they selected their clubs. "Do you think he did it?"

"Let's just say I've got a lot of unanswered questions. And I don't think the DA liked my testimony."

"Why not?"

"Because I think there's more to this case than meets the eye, and I said so in court. You've got to remember, these grand jury hearings are conducted in secret, without the defense present, so a lot of times they end up returning a rubber stamp indictment."

"But you got in the way of that, which I'm guessing pissed off the DA."

"You got that right," Ray said, clapping Jacob on the back. "Now hike up that skirt of yours and hit a decent shot for once."

# CHAPTER THREE

Ray navigated the Explorer through the cobblestone streets of Boston's North End, where the narrow thoroughfares and maze-like alleys dated back to 1630 and seemed better suited to horse-drawn carriages than SUVs. For the past century, the neighborhood had served as Boston's little Italy, and the brick row homes crowding the streets housed the largest concentration of restaurants, cafes, bakeries, and groceries of anywhere in the city. Measuring less than a half square mile, it was home to over ten thousand residents and more than one hundred restaurants, which put the odds of finding a parking spot on par with winning the lottery.

After circling the block more times than he could count, Ray wedged the Explorer into a resident permit space on Hanover Street, then hoofed it several blocks to the restaurant owned by the neighborhood's most notorious son, Sal Giabatti. The restaurant's darkly tinted windows showcased a sputtering neon CLOSED sign to discourage unwanted guests, and as Ray opened the door and stepped inside, a row of thugs swiveled their heads in his direction.

Two men at a back booth rose to their feet, their hands dropping to their hips, and Ray found himself staring into the coal-black eyes of a pair of Glocks. He raised his hands slowly and unfurled a dollar bill between his fingers. "Any of you boys got change for the meter?"

The bigger of the two mobsters—a roided-out twenty-something with a fake-and-bake tan and more veins than brain cells—muscled up to Ray and pressed the Glock's muzzle against his forehead. "You just made a big mistake coming in here."

Ray lifted an eyebrow. "How about I buy a cannoli and you validate my parking?"

A few of the made men in the back of the room started snickering, and Mikey Quick Trigger Maroni slapped a hand against the table, sending a splash of cappuccino onto the crisp, white tablecloth. Across from him, Jimmy the Weasel howled with laughter, his facing turning a shade darker than Giabatti's house marinara.

The door to the kitchen swung open and Sal Giabatti sauntered into the room. For a diminutive man in his early seventies, Sal possessed a surprising amount of style. He wore retro-cool glasses and an expensive suit, his white hair meticulously arranged into a perfect state of disarray. At first glance, he could've passed as an elder movie star or someone's ultracool grandad, but one look at the intensity in his dark eyes and you knew you were dealing with a dangerous man.

Sal turned his palms up in a gesture of disbelief. "No wonder we never get any customers." He signaled to the goon holding Ray at gunpoint. "Ease up, Tony. What the hell's wrong with you?"

Tony lowered the gun, confusion clouding his Neanderthal face.

Ray pocketed the dollar bill and suppressed a grin. "New recruit?"

Sal shrugged. "He's a little overeager."

"You think?"

Tony slunk toward the back of the room, his shoulders slouched in defeat.

Sal winked at Ray. "You've got some stone *coglioni*. Better be careful it don't get you killed one day."

"Is that a threat?" Ray asked. He meant it as a joke, but Sal's expression turned icy, and Ray imagined it was the same look Sal's enemies saw right before their skulls opened up to let in some fresh air.

"Don't try my patience, Ray. Just consider it sound advice."

"We need to talk."

"So let's talk. But how about something to eat? Today's special is linguine al vongole."

"Sounds tempting, but I'll pass."

"You know some cultures consider it a slap in the face to refuse a meal. Is that what you want to do, Ray? Slap me in the face?"

Ray donned what he hoped was a disarming smile. "I can't eat a big meal this early in the day, especially not with those extra ingredients Vinny mixes in just for cops."

Sal's lips peeled back into a grin—the predatory smirk of a great white. "Someone had to teach your partner about respect. I see you didn't bring him."

"I figured we could have a chat with just us gentlemen."

Sal motioned to an ornate mahogany bar that looked custom-made and insanely expensive. "Have a seat."

Ray settled onto a leather barstool and swiveled to face Sal. "What do you know about Danny the Mule?"

"I hear he went for a little swim."

"Is that all?"

"I understand he got some interesting cosmetic work done."

"How'd you know that? It's not exactly public knowledge."

"I hear things."

"Your boys have anything to do with that?"

"I got no beef with Danny."

"You mean not since you and Flaherty arrived at your business understanding a few years ago?"

"That's right."

Jack Flaherty ran the Irish mob in South Boston, and after years of bloody territorial disputes with the Italian mafia, Flaherty and Giabatti agreed to specialize in different businesses. Giabatti concentrated on gambling, loan sharking, and prescription drugs, while Flaherty concentrated on heroin, cocaine, robberies, and sex trafficking.

# THE ART OF DYING

It was a win-win for everyone. No one stepped on anyone else's toes, which meant less violence between organizations and less innocent people killed in the crossfire. The mayor attributed the declining violence to his tough stance on crime and the establishment of an interdepartmental Organized Crime Task Force. What he didn't want his constituents to know was that he'd brokered the peace deal himself. After all, he'd spent years distancing himself from his estranged brother, the notorious Jack Flaherty, whom he claimed he hadn't spoken with in twenty years.

It was a story everyone in Boston knew well—two kids from a broken home growing up in the blue-collar Irish neighborhood of South Boston. There was Tom Flaherty: altar boy, Eagle Scout, war hero, city councilman, and now, mayor. And then there was his older brother, Jack: neighborhood hooligan, high school dropout, alleged rapist, drug dealer, and murderer. Mayor Flaherty wanted nothing to do with his notorious brother, but only a fool believed their paths didn't sometimes cross.

Ray studied Giabatti's face, but his expression was unreadable. The guy must be one hell of a poker player. "You sure Danny didn't cross some line, break some unwritten rule, do something to disrespect one of your guys?"

"If something like that happened, I'd know about it. And I don't know nothing about nothing."

Ray decided not to press him on the double negative.

Giabatti stood up. "We done here?"

Ray nodded. "Yeah, we're done."

# CHAPTER FOUR

"What the hell do you mean you already talked to him?" Billy said.

Ray sipped his coffee. "You realize your eyebrows scrunch together like two caterpillars humping when you make that face?"

Garrison nearly choked on his latte in the middle of the crowded Dunkin' Donuts. He held up a hand and turned away, taking a moment to swallow around his laughter.

"You're lucky I don't slap that mocha latte right out of your hands," Billy said. "What the hell kind of grown man orders a drink like that anyway?"

Garrison dabbed his lips with a napkin. "Don't hate on us younger cops for having a more sophisticated palate than you old-timers."

"Old-timers?" Billy barked. "Forty-five is not old."

"It is to us thirty-two-year-olds," Ray said. He pointed to Billy's rockabilly hair, which had receded well north of his temples. "I swear you're going grayer by the hour."

"You would too if you were married to my ex."

"You gotta let go of the negativity," Garrison said, "and stop being such a grumpy ass old man all the time. That shit will eat you up."

Billy pitched his cup into the trash and wiped his mouth with the heel of his hand while flipping Garrison off with the other. "I'm serious, Ray. Why'd you go without us?"

Ray glanced over his shoulder to make sure none of the other customers were within earshot. "You really need an explanation?"

"You ditched me, Ray. You don't ditch your partner. Ever."

"I needed Giabatti to talk. And he sure as hell wasn't going to do that with you around."

A year ago, Billy had made a big spectacle of arresting Giabatti outside of church on charges he knew wouldn't stick and Giabatti had never forgiven him for it.

"He gave you jack shit, didn't he?" Billy asked.

"I'm building a rapport. It takes time and finesse."

Billy held up a fist. "This is the only finesse I need."

"Exactly my point."

Ray followed Garrison out of the Dunkin' Donuts and looked across the road at the Broadway T Station, where an early wave of businesspeople returning from the financial district spilled off the buses and emerged from the Red Line subway tunnels. To the left of the station was A Street and the chrome-colored walls of Mul's Diner, which was a local favorite for breakfast. Flaherty's hangout loomed a couple doors down from Mul's in a two-story brick building with no windows and a battered steel door painted emerald green.

Flaherty's bar was officially listed with the city as the Golden Shamrock, but the building lacked even a single exterior sign. Most locals knew it simply as The Rock, and it was a place few dared enter. Those who did risked forfeiting their souls to Southie's resident devil, Jack Flaherty.

Flaherty had a reputation as a ruthless thug with a violent temper, which was why this visit required nothing short of a team effort. As they approached the building, Ray eyed the security camera perched above the front door. He laid a hand on the knob and looked at Billy and Garrison, who had taken up position behind him. "You boys ready?"

Billy grunted.

Garrison grinned.

*It's go time*, Ray thought, and shoved open the door.

\*\*\*

Flaherty and his gang were seated around a hexagonal poker table, their hands folded neatly on the green felt top. No cash, drugs, or weapons in sight thanks to the security camera's early warning.

Flaherty flashed them a grin. "Afternoon, officers." His silvery-blond hair was cropped close to the scalp, his eyes ice blue and calculating. His rugged good looks had served him well over his fifty-one years, and legend had it he could charm a snake out of its skin.

"We're here about Danny," Ray said. "You got anything for us?"

Flaherty leaned back in his seat, the room so quiet that the squeak of the chair leg sounded like a scream. "No, detective, I don't *got* anything for you, though I might suggest a basic course in grammar."

Billy chuckled. "Strong words from an eighth-grade dropout."

"When you realize you're smarter than your teachers," Flaherty said, "who needs school?"

"Your mama must've been real proud," Garrison said.

Flaherty's lips drew into a sneer. "You'd better watch your mouth, boy."

Billy seemed like he was about to say something threatening, but Ray quieted him with a stern look. "We didn't come here to insult you," Ray said.

"How very civilized of you."

"But a man is dead," Ray continued, "and we've got procedures to follow. So I got to ask, do you know who killed Danny? Or why someone would want him dead?"

Flaherty leaned forward. "I don't need your services, detective. Those greaseballs killed my cousin. Plain and simple. And if it's a war Giabatti wants, I'll give him a war."

"I talked to Giabatti," Ray said. "I don't think he was involved."

"Then you're dumber than you look."

16

"You'd better think this through," Ray said. "If you start a war, you'll draw more heat than you can handle. Every cop in this city will be on your case. So be my guest and do something stupid, because it just might trigger your own demise. And in the meantime, I'll be watching you."

Flaherty shot to his feet and thrust a finger into Ray's face. "Don't tell me what to do, detective. You want to watch my every move? Go ahead. Because I'll be watching you right back. You and that pretty family of yours."

Ray seized Flaherty by the shirt and drew him so close he could smell the hot stink of his breath. "If you come near my family, I will end you. Do you understand?"

Flaherty's lips spread into a grin. "Every man has his weakness, detective, and it looks like I just found yours."

# CHAPTER FIVE

Ray mounted the stairs to his three-bedroom townhouse in Charlestown and fumbled in his pocket for the keys. Behind the sapphire blue colonial door, he could hear the stomping of footsteps and the slow-building chant that had turned into a ritual these last couple of months.

When the door swung open, Jason, Allie, and Petey stood in the foyer pumping their fists, jumping up and down, and chanting: *Dad-dy. Dad-dy. Dad-dy.*

Ray tossed his keys onto the foyer table and caught a glimpse of Michelle in the kitchen. She brushed a wavy blond lock behind her left ear and smiled that dazzling smile of hers. He couldn't ask for anything more than this—coming home to a gorgeous wife and three adorable kids who still thought he was the greatest dad in the world. Even without the benefit of hindsight, he knew these were the moments he'd treasure long after the kids grew up and had families of their own, moments he'd reminisce about as an old man.

He crouched down and wiggled his fingers, giving the kids the signal to begin their running leaps. They lined up in order of age, another part of the ritual. First came Jason, his potty-mouthed, Hot Wheels-loving six-year-old. In one fluid motion, he caught Jason midair, spun him around, and set him back down. Next came Allie, his fearless, five-year-old animal stalker. And then came Petey, his diaper-wrecking, two-and-a-half-year-old slobber machine.

As soon as he set Petey down, their Boston Terrier, Sparky, bounded into the room, claws scrabbling against the hardwood, a tennis ball lodged in his jaws. Sparky dropped the ball at Ray's feet, hindquarters twitching with excitement, but as Ray reached for the ball Sparky snatched it back up again.

"When will this dog learn how to play fetch?" Ray asked.

"As soon as he learns not to poop in my shoes," Michelle said.

"You sure that's not Petey?" Ray said, heading into the bedroom.

"I haven't ruled him out."

"Is Mr. Snuggles also a suspect?"

Michelle grinned. "As a matter of fact, he is."

Mr. Snuggles was the fluffy white Persian that Allie had begged him to buy from the pet store. *You're not exactly acing Parenting 101*, Michelle had said. *Rewarding the kid for her relentless badgering? Next thing you know she'll be asking us six million times for a pony.*

It was a fair point, but Allie had always had a knack for manipulating him. A skill she'd no doubt inherited from her mother. *Understanding men is not exactly rocket science*, Michelle had told him once. *Ninety percent of the time men are thinking about sex, food, or sports, and the other ten percent of the time they're just scratching themselves.*

He could have argued with her, but she'd pretty much nailed it. And, lucky for him, most criminals were men. It was much easier to deduce a man's motives than to crack the code of the female psyche, especially since the female brain was obviously encrypted with an advanced form of alien technology.

Once inside the bedroom, Ray peeled off his work clothes—what Allie called his costume—and tossed them onto the bed: sports jacket, tie, holster, dress shirt, Kevlar vest, and undershirt. He'd never understood why detectives had to wear a jacket and tie in the first place. Was the superior fashion supposed to intimidate criminals into submission? Scare them straight with a paisley tie?

He drew his weapons from their holsters and placed the Taser and the Glock .40 caliber pistol into the safe in the closet. After slipping on a pair of basketball shorts and a worn Red Sox T-shirt, he returned to the kitchen and wrapped his arms around Michelle.

"How was your day?" he asked, kissing her on the cheek.

The kids swarmed in shouting, "Family hug!" and threw their arms around them. Michelle met his eyes with a wry smile. They hadn't shared a hug without at least one kid swooping in for the last five years.

Michelle rolled her eyes. "It's like having my very own rape whistle."

"Let's see how well protected you are after the kids go to bed."

Michelle furrowed her brow. "Don't get any ideas."

"Oh, I've got plenty of ideas."

Allie tugged on Ray's shorts and stared up at him with her bright hazel eyes. "Daddy, what's a rape whistle? Can I have one?"

He mussed up her hair and turned toward Michelle. "What's for dinner?"

"I'm glad you asked," Michelle said. "What are you making?"

\*\*\*

After surviving another exhausting bedtime routine, Ray and Michelle grabbed a bottle of wine and climbed the narrow staircase to the roof deck. Dusk had settled over the city and a pregnant moon hung low in the cobalt sky. From the patio table, Ray could see the gleaming lights of the Boston skyline toward the south and the granite obelisk of the Bunker Hill Monument to the east.

More than two decades of gentrification had transformed Charlestown into a hot real estate market, especially for neighborhoods like Ray's that were within walking distance of Monument Park and the shops and restaurants of the Gaslight District. Ray had purchased the townhouse when he first joined the force, back when prices were still reasonable and the scars of the Irish Mob Wars hadn't completely healed. These days, you couldn't touch a three-bedroom home in his neighborhood for less than $600K, and if you wanted to live a block or two from the Monument that would run you a million easy.

It was a warm May evening, one of the first of the season, and the vibrant scent of spring flowers from rooftop planters permeated the air. Ray loved coming up here after a long day to unwind, but he felt no relaxation tonight.

Michelle gazed at him over her glass of sauvignon blanc. "What's wrong?"

"Rough day."

"You want to talk about it?"

He shook his head. She worried enough about the dangers of his job. She didn't need to know he'd confronted the city's most dangerous men on their own turf, let alone that Flaherty had made a veiled threat against their family. The last thing he wanted was to allow Flaherty into his head, but there he was in the back of his mind, grinning like the Cheshire cat.

Michelle reached for his hand. "Are you okay?"

"Fine." He sipped from his glass. "How'd the PTA meeting go this afternoon?"

"Not good. They're moving ahead with the tuition hike for next year."

Ray groaned. "A ten percent increase? Just like that, no room for argument?"

Michelle tapped a manicured nail against her lips. "Let's see if I can remember the exact quote. 'The tuition increase is meant to compensate for the general rise in operating costs.'"

"What the hell is that supposed to mean?"

"You got me."

"Christ. Last year was five percent and this year is ten percent? It's ridiculous."

"I know, but there's not much of an alternative."

"No kidding," Ray grumbled.

Public school wasn't a viable option. Boston city schools received a boatload of state funding, but too many of the kids came from shattered homes and ended up involved in drugs or gangs at an early age.

"I guess I could pick up some extra details," Ray said.

"I don't want you to do that. You work long enough hours as it is. Maybe it's time I go back to work, get a little adult time during the day. Put something else in my mind besides songs from the Wiggles." She sat back and sipped her wine. "Why are you making that face?"

"I'm not making a face."

"Yes, you are. Your caveman face. The one that says, 'Me no like.'"

Ray chuckled in spite of himself. "Part-time teaching will barely cover the cost of daycare for Petey."

"That might be true, but I heard Shelia is looking for babysitting work. We could probably get her for ten bucks an hour."

"Sheila Morrison? The girl who dropped out of community college to spend more time with her loser boyfriend?"

"Come on, Ray, she's a nice kid."

"Her boyfriend deals drugs and runs errands for Jack Flaherty."

"Are you serious?"

"Why would I joke about something like that?"

"I can't believe you're just telling me this. He gave Jason a lollipop the other day."

"What?" He slammed his fist against the patio table and nearly overturned their wine glasses. "I'm gonna kill him."

"See what happens when you keep stuff from me? No secrets, Ray. I mean it."

"Fine, no secrets. But Tommy made me swear I wouldn't say anything. He's embarrassed his daughter's dating that scumbag."

Michelle glanced at the Morrisons' roof deck. "Does Pauline know?"

"She's taking it pretty hard. You know they had high hopes for her."

"What will they do?"

"Tommy wants me to catch him in the act."

"How will you do that?"

"I asked Frank to tail him, figure out when his next deal will be so we can tip off Donovan from Vice."

"Wait a minute, Frank from down the street?"

"No, Frank Eastman. He's got his own private investigator's business now."

"Why can't you just tell Donovan and cut out the middle man?"

"Because the lieutenant's not willing to waste police resources investigating a small-time dealer like Darren Boyle."

Michelle considered this for a moment and then grinned. "But if Frank does all the work, gives Donovan the time and place…"

Ray finished his wine. "Exactly."

"I like it," Michelle said. "Cleaning up Charlestown one dirtbag at a time." She leaned over and kissed him.

It was meant to be quick, but the moment their lips met Ray felt an intensity reminiscent of their early days together, and he kissed her back long and hard. Michelle moved onto his lap and wrapped her arms around the small of his back.

"Have you ever done it on a roof deck?" Ray whispered.

Michelle tucked a lock of hair behind her ear and grinned. "There's a first time for everything."

# CHAPTER SIX

The Artist stood in the center of the gallery and basked in the glow of his own genius. He was a pioneer. A savant. A visionary who dared to be different. They would write books about him one day, referring to him not as an artist but as *The Artist*. And there would be movies too. He'd be played by someone dark and brooding and handsome. Someone like a young Christian Bale.

The process of creating an entirely new art form was nothing short of euphoric. His art spoke to him, quite literally, and he liked hearing their screams in the dark. From that first shriek of horror to the silence elicited by the mocking echo of their own voices, it was a hauntingly beautiful metamorphosis—terror blossoming into acceptance.

A surveillance camera monitored the converted survival bunker, and although shadows draped the cavernous room, a handful of picture lights produced a sufficient glow to capture his exhibits in dramatic detail on film.

"The newbies always scream the loudest," he said, addressing the camera. "This sound meter registers every scream uttered in the gallery. Incidentally, Mrs. C is the reigning champion at 103 decibels. She may not possess many redeeming qualities, or any, really, but my goodness can that woman scream. Isn't that right, Mrs. C?"

He pointed the sound meter toward her and cocked his head. "Are you still with us, Mrs. C, or do I need to remind you of your manners?"

A disembodied voice, barely more than a whisper, croaked the appropriate reply.

"Good. I'm not sure you'd survive another session of behavioral therapy and I'm looking forward to spending more quality time together." He turned back to the camera. "It seems Mrs. C has lost her usual fire. Interesting." He whirled toward her and yelled, "Starting to taste that humble pie now, aren't you, Mrs. C?"

He smoothed out his dark hair and heaved a sigh. "Today, we unveil our latest exhibit, featuring our very own Barry Finkleton, curator of the prestigious Finkleton Gallery of Art. He's been in a bit of a coma these last few days, but let's see if we can wake him."

The Artist stalked to where he'd mounted Finkleton to the wall. A burlap sack muffled the sound of his moaning. The Artist climbed a stepladder and removed the sack with the flair of a magician, letting it glide gracefully to the floor.

Finkleton's head lolled to the side, his eyes rolling back to expose the veiny whites. The Artist slapped his pudgy face. "Come on, sleepyhead. Wakey wakey."

Finkleton's eyes snapped open—bright blue and brimming with terror. The Artist slipped a pair of glasses onto the bridge of Finkleton's nose. "Remember me?"

Finkleton shook his head, the picture light illuminating golden beads of sweat glistening on his brow.

"You called me a talentless loser. You told me to crawl back into whatever dark corner I hailed from and never set foot in your gallery again."

Finkleton's lips, still cracked and swollen from a recent blunt force trauma, quivered.

"Sound familiar?"

Finkleton didn't answer.

The Artist clucked his tongue. "Where are my manners? I seem to be blocking your view." He stepped off the ladder and gestured beyond Mrs. C to his other exhibits.

"What... what have you done to them?" Finkleton blubbered.

The Artist grinned. "Do you like it? It's a revolutionary new style. I call it the Art of Dying."

Finkleton made a guttural sound and spewed vomit onto the floor.

The Artist laughed. "I'll take that as a compliment. But you haven't seen the best part." He raised a handheld mirror to Finkleton's face. "Behold, your metamorphosis."

Finkleton screamed until he hyperventilated. The Artist brought him to attention with a sharp slap to the cheek. "That's better. I honestly wasn't sure where I was headed with this project until after I amputated your arms and legs, but when I saw all that black hair on your belly, together with your vile personality, my inner muse blurted out, 'By God, he's a tarantula!' And voila!"

The Artist stepped back to admire the prosthetic appendages he'd implanted into Finkleton's torso—eight gnarled limbs bristling with coarse, black hair. "Did you notice the egg sac attached to your rear? Symbolizing the artists you've discovered over the years, the careers you helped birth. It's genius, right? I'd appreciate your honest opinion, Mr. Finkleton. Do you recognize my talent now?"

The Artist winced as Finkleton screamed. "My goodness, 119 decibels. I believe that's a new record." He slipped the sound meter into the back pocket of his jeans and chuckled. "I'm afraid I might need to cut those vocal cords sooner than I thought. Now be a chum, Mr. Finkleton, and tell me... have you seen where I put my scalpel?"

# CHAPTER SEVEN

Ray swung by the medical examiner's office on his way to the precinct, circling the block until he found a metered spot on the east side of Mass Ave, where he was surrounded by the trendy shops and meticulously restored Victorian brownstones of the South End. Had he parked one block to the west on the grittier streets of Roxbury, the odds of his car being there when he returned dropped to about fifty-fifty.

After a brief walk down a tree-lined street, he arrived at the ME's office, an old industrial building with a half-brick, half-concrete façade. He rang the bell and waved to the camera, pushing through the door as Mrs. Granderling buzzed him in. She'd worked reception for the past few years and greeted everyone she met with the same measure of partially concealed contempt. Doc Death liked to joke that the stiffs in the morgue had more personality than she did.

Mrs. Granderling frowned at Ray from behind the reception desk, her gray-blond hair looking especially puffy—the kind of hairstyle that could conceal a small family of raccoons. "Can I help you?" Her voice was flat and nasally, more a sigh of resignation than a question.

"Doc Weintraub around?"

"He's very busy today."

"Can you just tell him I'm here?" he said, and favored her with his trademark smile.

Her lips pulled back into what could've been a smile or a sneer. It was gone so quickly it was hard to tell. She pressed a button on the phone and mumbled something into the receiver.

After a moment, she nodded and hung up. "He'll see you," she said, sounding disappointed.

Ray rapped his knuckles against the desk. "Always a pleasure, Mrs. G."

As he strode down the hall toward Doc's office, he felt the stench of the place seeping into his skin, smothering him in a noxious cloud of death, formaldehyde, and antiseptic. He wrinkled his nose and breathed into the crook of his arm, trying to stifle his gag reflex. The last thing he wanted was to blow chunks all over the hallway like some rookie cop.

"What's the matter, Ray? You don't like our brand of fresh air?" Luis Durgin, Doc's forensic autopsy tech, grinned at Ray as he wheeled a cart full of tissue samples down the hall, sections of heart, brain, and lungs sloshing around inside plastic containers. He was dressed in green surgical scrubs and had a pair of Beats headphones slung around his neck, the speakers buzzing with the angry wail of heavy metal.

"I don't know how you guys stand it," Ray said.

Luis shrugged. "I don't even smell it anymore, man." He winked at Ray, then pulled the headphones over his ears and headed toward the storage lab.

Ray turned left at the end of the hall and found Doc Weintraub in his office sitting behind a cluttered steel desk with a pile of papers scattered around him. Doc glanced up at the sound of his approach and waved him in.

Ray settled himself into a sturdy metal chair opposite the desk. "How you been, Doc?"

"Well, most recently, I've been up to my elbows in intestines."

Ray gave Doc an obligatory laugh, knowing he would keep on cracking bad jokes until one triggered a chuckle... and Ray couldn't afford to sit there all day.

Doc's office was dark and cramped, but thankfully the smell of freshly scrubbed death was a tad less nauseating in here. The blinds were drawn tight against the glare of the morning sun and a fluorescent light above the desk sputtered frequently enough to be annoying, but not enough to induce an epileptic fit. A *Far Side* calendar hung on the wall beside a shelf of medical texts, this month's cartoon explaining the real reason dinosaurs went extinct.

"So what's the word on Danny the Mule?" Ray asked.

Doc Death blinked behind his glasses, his hazel eyes clouded with confusion. "Danny the Mule?"

"Danny McDougal. The guy we fished out of the quarry."

"Oh yes, him." Doc rifled through the papers on his desk. "I've got the transcript from the autopsy somewhere in this pile." After a brief fishing expedition, he held up a stack of papers. "Tina and I both attended to this one given the unusual circumstances of the body."

"You mean the fact that he had a penis attached to his face?"

"I would certainly call that unusual, wouldn't you?"

"I'd say it qualifies."

"Tina's taking the lead on this one, so I'll let her debrief you on the autopsy."

Given their history, the mention of *Tina* and *debrief* in the same sentence could've been construed as an innuendo, but he didn't think Doc realized what he'd said. Doc dialed her extension and Tina appeared in the doorway a few moments later, her curly brown hair flowing over her shoulders like she just stepped out of a shampoo commercial, when, in all likelihood, she'd just finished gutting a corpse.

She met Ray's gaze and held it, her eyes reflecting a sea of emotions. She was complicated, guarded, and intense, and he was gregarious, outgoing, and unapologetic. Together, they were like oil and water, which was why it never worked between them.

Tina settled into the chair beside Ray. One of her knees brushed against his thigh and lingered for a moment. A test to see how he would react? Typical Tina. Always treating people like the subject of an experiment.

"What are we looking at?" Ray asked.

"Well," Tina said, "we didn't find any water in Mr. McDougal's lungs, so that means he didn't drown in the quarry."

"Not surprising," Ray said, "given the penis rearrangement surgery. Somebody obviously tortured him to death before dumping the body. You see any evidence that he was weighted down?"

"We didn't find any chafing on the wrists or ankles, nothing that would suggest he was wrapped in ropes or chains. But we did find bruising around his neck from what appeared to be ligature marks that had mostly healed."

"What do you mean?"

"I believe Mr. McDougal had some form of restraint around his neck while in captivity, but I can't pinpoint the source."

"Is that what killed him?"

"No, he didn't die from asphyxiation."

"What was the cause of death?" Ray asked.

Tina glanced at Doc Weintraub. "We don't have anything conclusive at this point, but we should know more when the tox screens come back."

"How about time of death?"

Tina fidgeted with her notes, looking uncertain for the first time in her debrief. If she were testifying at an actual trial, the defense attorney would be salivating at the chance of cross examination.

"It's hard to say at this point. The cold waters of the quarry would've slowed down the rate of decay, but there are a host of other variables to consider."

"Such as?"

Tina ticked off the points on her fingers. "Such as the temperature and humidity at the actual place of death, how much time elapsed before the body was disposed of in the quarry, not to mention the types of microorganisms in the water. It'll take quite a bit of lab work to pinpoint a precise range."

Ray shifted in his seat, drawing his leg away from hers. "What's your gut feel?"

"Judging from the degree of decay in his intestines, and taking into consideration the water temperature, I'd say the murder took place between two to four days ago."

Ray turned toward Doc Death. "What do you think?"

"I agree with Tina's assessment. A lot depends on how long he was in the water. We'll narrow the range with the lab results, but hopefully that gives you something to work with in the meantime."

"It does. Now, tell me about the castration."

"It was remarkably clean," Tina said.

"Meaning?"

"Meaning whoever did it likely had medical training."

"So we're talking a doctor, a nurse, or an EMT?"

"Possibly," Tina said. "Whoever did this nursed Mr. McDougal back to health. We found markings on his arms consistent with IV lines. The killer obviously wanted Mr. McDougal to survive. I can only guess to prolong his torture."

"Danny was missing a month," Ray said. "That's a long time for torture."

"I have to admit," Doc said, "it's rather impressive the killer succeeded in keeping him alive for so long."

"All the more reason to suspect a medical background," Ray said. "What about the stitches in his ear?"

"They were standard polypropylene nonabsorbable sutures," Tina said. "We found threads of it in both ears, but there was no evidence of an underlying laceration. Not even one that had healed."

Ray frowned. Why would the killer stitch an ear that didn't need stitching? "Anything else?"

"There is one other thing." Tina held up a Ziploc bag containing a sky-blue Hot Wheels car with white racing stripes. It looked like a 1970s Dodge Charger.

"Where'd you find that?" Ray asked.

Tina brushed a lock of hair from her eyes. "Halfway up Mr. McDougal's rectum."

***

Ray walked into the precinct just as Lieutenant Spinonni kicked off morning roll call. At the sight of Ray, Spinonni halted his opening remarks and folded his arms across his barrel of a chest. "What's the matter, Hanley, couldn't drag yourself out of bed this morning?"

Ray settled into the seat next to Billy. "I had to make a pitstop at the morgue."

"What the hell were you doing there?" Spinonni snapped.

"Visiting your sense of humor," Ray said, unable to resist.

The room erupted in laughter, running the gamut from discreet snickers to full-on belly laugh. Detective Duncan landed in the latter camp, cracking up with such violence that a wave of coffee sloshed out of his cup and soaked his chinos.

Twin bands of red lit up the lieutenant's cheeks like the rouge of a twenty-dollar hooker. "You'd better mind that mouth of yours," Spinonni said through clenched teeth, the hairs of his mustache bristling.

The room quieted, but Detective Duncan couldn't stop giggling.

"Enough!" Spinonni bellowed. He pointed at Ray. "My office after the briefing."

Ray wasn't surprised that Spinonni had singled him out. A few years ago, he'd arrested the lieutenant's nephew for playing a role in a drug deal turned homicide, and because Ray refused to look the other way, the lieutenant's nephew got ten years at the state penitentiary. The lieutenant had been making Ray's life miserable ever since.

Spinonni drew a deep breath, still fuming. "We've got a lot to cover this morning, so try to remember this is a precinct and not a preschool. Are we clear?"

No one said a word.

"First item of business, we've got a homeless guy bludgeoned to death on Boston Common. That's got your name written all over it, Duncan." Spinonni gestured to the door.

Taking the hint, Duncan rose from his seat and trudged toward the exit. "Have a nice time," Spinonni said. "And watch out for lice. I suspect the buggers will be looking for a new host."

Spinonni glanced at his notes. "Next up, we've got a match on a bloody print found at the scene of yesterday's knifing in Dudley Square. Benton, you and Eisberg take that one. See Sergeant Callahan for details."

Spinonni held up an official-looking envelope. "The arrest warrant for Julian Rogers. That's your case ain't it, Chang?"

Officer Chang nodded. "I'm on it."

"Next," Spinonni said, "we've got a report of another disappearance. Guy by the name of Barry Finkleton. Fifty-three years old, runs an art gallery on Newbury Street. His wife reported him missing yesterday. Foul play is suspected. Ridley, I want you to take the lead on that."

"Sure thing, boss."

"That brings us to the final order of business: the Coleman case. The grand jury ruled in his favor, so Jim Coleman was released from jail this morning. So now we've got a brutal murderer back on the streets thanks to the weak testimony of Detective Hanley. You got anything funny to say about that, Ray? Any off-color remarks to make us all chuckle about Coleman getting away with murder?"

Ray shook his head. *Christ.*

"Alright," Spinonni said. "That's it. Get your asses back to work."

***

Lieutenant Spinonni glared at Ray from behind his desk. Arms crossed, not saying a word. Ray figured the silent treatment was supposed to make him squirm, but all it did was piss him off.

33

"You got something to say, Lieutenant, or am I just here to look pretty?"

Spinonni slammed his fist against the desk. "I didn't spend thirty years in the service of this department to be disrespected in front of my subordinates. You pull that shit again and I'll suspend you without pay."

Ray didn't think the lieutenant could do that—either the union or the captain would intervene on his behalf—but he held his tongue. Spinonni was the type of guy you could only push so far, and he'd pushed enough for one morning.

"Coleman walked because of your testimony," Spinonni said. "And now a murderer is back on the streets."

"Coleman walked because there were too many gaps in the evidence. It's not my job to exaggerate."

"It wasn't a trial, Ray. It was a goddamn grand jury hearing. You didn't need to poke holes in the case."

"You got a body somewhere? Cause I sure as hell never saw one. Didn't see a murder weapon either. How do you expect me to testify around those facts?"

Spinonni's face flushed crimson. "I expect you to bridge the gaps in the evidence like any good investigator, but instead you got on the stand and sounded all wishy-washy. And now I've got the DA and the mayor with their panties in a bunch, wondering how the hell I let this happen."

"I don't like the outcome either," Ray said, "but we don't have enough evidence to hold him. And before the DA starts pointing fingers, someone ought to remind him that he's the one who rushed this case to court."

"Why don't you tell him that, Hanley? See what happens?"

"Just keep me on the case and I'll get the evidence to put Coleman away for good."

"You'd better deliver, Hanley, or else you'll spend the rest of your career pushing papers."

# CHAPTER EIGHT

Larry Reynolds was having a real bitch of a day. When men with names like Jimmy the Weasel and Mikey Quick Trigger Maroni drag you off the street and drive you to a deserted construction site in the back of their vintage Cadillac, it's understandable to feel a touch of despair.

No one likes falling short of a fundraising goal, and that's never as true as when you need fifty grand to pay off a gambling debt to the mob. If you're an optimist, which he wasn't, it was a useful way to determine who your friends really are. Unfortunately, his fundraising efforts yielded less than five grand and he'd already burned through a thirty-day extension.

It wasn't like he hadn't tried. If he hadn't gone all-in on four of a kind, only to lose to a straight flush, he would've strutted out of Mohegan Sun with fifty grand for the mob and a hundred for himself. He could've made that money last for years on a remote beach in Mexico, spreading it between cheap beer and cheaper women. But since Lady Luck was a fickle bitch, here he was instead getting hauled out of the car by his hair.

"Where's the money?" Jimmy asked. "Tell me you have my money, Larry."

"I'm working on it."

"You're working on it?"

"I just need—"

Jimmy punched him in the nose and Larry heard a distinct crunch before collapsing to the ground in a heap. The coppery taste of blood filled his throat, and as he rolled onto his side and spat into the dirt, the words of his brother drifted through his mind.

*I wish I could help, Larry, but the only liquid thing I've got is Ryan's college fund, and that wouldn't be fair to the kid, you know? And besides, I'd get hit with a tax penalty on early withdrawals. You believe that? Taxing you on your own goddamned money?*

The mobsters loomed over him, glaring down with murder in their eyes.

"You gambled it away, didn't you?" Jimmy said. "You stupid sonofabitch."

Larry sat up. "I'll get you the money. Just give me—"

Jimmy kicked him in the stomach, knocking him flat onto his back and expelling the wind from his lungs. "Shut your mouth and listen." He cocked his head at Mikey. "You believe this guy? Trying to give us orders?"

Mikey yanked him to his feet and slammed him against the Cadillac. "We warned you, Larry. Or did you forget our last conversation?"

Larry recalled that last conversation well enough, since most of it had occurred with the business end of Jimmy's gun in his mouth. The general theme had been pay up in thirty days or die.

"You ask me," Mikey said, "he's never getting that money. No matter how many chances we give him."

Jimmy folded his arms and stared at Larry. "I think Mikey's right, which isn't good news for you. I'd rather not have your death on my conscience, but I've got a job to do. And it's important not to forget that you brought this on yourself, Larry. If you think about it, it's almost like suicide."

Larry's eyes stung with the threat of tears. "Just give me one more week. I'll get the money, I swear!"

"I don't see it happening," Jimmy said. "We could give you another month and still never see that money. Business is business, Larry, and sometimes you gotta know when to cut your losses." He patted Mikey on the shoulder and motioned to the construction site, where a labyrinth of steel girders rose from a concrete foundation. "Take him to that trench near the backhoe. And make it quick."

Larry tried reasoning with them, but Mikey pressed a gun to the back of his head and marched him up a low rise toward the trench. In the distance, the black ribbon of the Mass Pike wound through the city, the drone of passing cars carried on the wind. Beyond that loomed the lights of Fenway Park and the iconic Citgo sign perched upon a building to the left of the Green Monster.

"How about them Sox?" Mikey said.

Larry closed his eyes and tried to slow his racing heart. "You don't have to do this."

"Stop talking," Mikey said. "You're making it worse."

"Oh, I'm sorry, do you prefer to murder in silence?"

A shot rang out and Mikey and Larry turned in time to see Jimmy the Weasel's head disintegrate into a fine, red mist.

A second shot hit Mikey in the shoulder and rocked him on his heels. The gun tumbled from his hand and Larry kicked it away, sending it skidding into the trench.

A figure emerged from the tall grass about fifty yards distant, a rifle slung over his shoulder. A moment later, a vintage black Camaro rolled down the drive and parked next to Jimmy's body. A middle-aged man climbed out and marched toward them, his eyes the color of blue steel.

Larry looked at Mikey, not sure whether to celebrate or to slither under the backhoe and hide. "Who's that?"

Mikey's voice was barely a whisper. "Jack Flaherty."

The burly man with the rifle nodded to Flaherty, then drew a handgun and shot Jimmy's corpse point-blank in the heart. "It only takes one bullet," he said, "but I like to shoot 'em *two* times."

The line sounded rehearsed, and Larry connected it to something he'd read in an organized crime exposé in the *Boston Globe*. Bobby Two Times, rumored to be Flaherty's most ruthless lieutenant.

"You've got to admire his thoroughness," Flaherty said, directing his gaze at Mikey. "What's he owe you?"

Mikey stood like a soldier reporting for inspection—chin up, back straight. Rivulets of blood ran down his muscular forearm and dripped off his fingertips, leaving crimson splotches in the dirt. "Fifty Gs," he said, his lips barely moving.

Flaherty whistled, his eyes locking on Larry. "Looks like I just saved your ass. Which means you owe that money to me now. Understand? You've got two weeks."

Larry nodded, avoiding Flaherty's eyes, which reflected the mad gleam of a cat toying with its prey.

"Just so we're clear," Flaherty said, "if you disappear without paying, your debt transfers to the person you love most. And since you look like a mama's boy, you should know I've got no problem collecting from little old ladies. But don't worry, I'm always willing to work out alternative payment arrangements, if you know what I mean." He slapped Larry on the cheek and grinned. "Believe me, the worst thing you could do is underestimate me. Am I right, Bobby?"

"Absolutely," Bobby said, his gun pointed at Larry's chest.

"What do you say, Mikey? Do you plan on underestimating me?"

"I don't think that would be wise," Mikey said.

"No," Flaherty agreed, "it wouldn't. Now call your boss and tell him the truce is over. And try your best to speak clearly, because Bobby's about to put a bullet in your kneecap."

Bobby Two Times winked at Flaherty and adjusted his aim. "What do you say, boss? How about I make it a double?"

# CHAPTER NINE

"You take your lumps?" Billy asked, climbing into the Explorer.

Ray arched an eyebrow and shifted into drive. "What do you think?"

"You know he can't take a joke, right?"

"Course I do. That's what makes it so rewarding."

"Be careful you don't push him too far. I've seen him ruin careers over less."

"You done lecturing me?"

"For the moment."

"Good, because I gotta catch you up on Danny the Mule."

When he finished telling Billy about his morning pitstop, Billy sat in silence, staring at the road and soaking it in. Somewhere behind those aging gray eyes, his mind was projecting a thousand scenarios, assigning probabilities, and distilling the results into a single theory. He'd seen Billy do it a hundred times and it was uncanny how often he nailed it.

"This was a revenge killing," Billy said. "Committed by some sick fuck who planned every detail, probably months or even years in advance. The castration, the nose replacement, the Hot Wheels car—it all has a very special meaning for the killer."

Ray nodded. "There's got to be something more about the car. I mean, Danny had a kid's toy parked up his ass. Think of the contrast—childhood innocence mixed with something so perverse. The way I see it, our killer was molested as a kid. And maybe Danny is the one who did it."

"Don't you think we would've heard rumors if Danny was a pedophile?"

"He was fifty-one when he died. Say he was diddling in his thirties or forties—that would leave enough time for his victims to grow up. And something like that can shatter a kid's psyche, leave him with the twisted wreckage of a broken mind. A kid like that might spend years planning his revenge."

Billy grunted. "It's a start."

"Let's see what we can pry out of the usual suspects."

"Right," Billy said. "Because they're such a talkative bunch."

"What about RJ?"

"Doubtful," Billy said, "but it might be worth seeing what he knows."

They were headed southwest on Washington Street, making their way from the Dorchester precinct to Coleman's house in suburban West Roxbury. Coleman lived in a two-story colonial near the wooded sanctuary of Stony Brook Reservation. It could've been a great starter home for a young family or an idyllic location for empty nesters, but instead it marked the scene of a horrific crime.

Ray pulled into the driveway and killed the engine, his eyes shifting to the porch windows, where the blinds were drawn tight against the outside world.

They climbed out of the Explorer. "What are the odds he's home?" Billy asked. "If I was Coleman, I'd disappear as soon as I hit the streets."

Ray shrugged, keeping his eyes on the windows and his hand near his gun. With Coleman just released from jail he didn't expect a struggle, but sometimes you just never knew. It was best never to let your guard down. That was a lesson he'd learned young, long before becoming a cop. Overconfidence had cost his father his life on a dingy subway platform when Ray was a freshman in high school. There were still times when he jerked awake in the dead of night, drenched in sweat, his ears ringing with the phantom echo of the mugger's laughter, his mind replaying the moment his dad slumped to the ground, blood spurting from his chest in arterial gushes.

Ray shrugged off the memory as he would a physical chill and ascended the porch stairs, chiding himself for dwelling on the past. A breeze coaxed music from a nearby windchime and he wondered if Suzie Coleman had heard the same metallic tinkling as blood ran from her body in the upstairs bedroom all those weeks ago.

He rang the bell and dropped back, his eyes shifting to the windows on either side of the door. One of the slats of the blinds lifted a quarter of an inch before falling back into place.

"Left window," Ray said, feeling his chest tense against his Kevlar vest. Ordinarily, the vest was a constant source of discomfort, but at times like this he welcomed its suffocating embrace. He used to slip on an exterior vest only for calls like these, but after the kids were born, Michelle talked him into wearing one underneath his shirt for the entire shift. But with the late spring days heating up, he was sometimes guilty of skipping it altogether.

The front door swung inward and Coleman appeared behind the storm door, visible from the waist up.

"Let's see your hands," Ray barked, drawing his Glock.

Coleman held out his palms like a mime trapped in a box. Dark scimitars underscored his eyes and Ray wondered if he'd been drinking. "My lawyer said I shouldn't talk to you."

"You got released from jail because of my testimony," Ray said. "Did your lawyer tell you that?"

"He said a detective poked holes in the prosecutor's case."

"That's right," Ray said. "Mind if we come in?"

"I should probably call my lawyer."

"Why?" Billy said. "You keep saying you didn't do it. Help us figure out who did."

Coleman settled his hand against the door, and for a moment Ray thought he might slam it in their faces. But instead he held it open and waved them inside. The place was decorated with high-end furnishings and accents of modern art, but it had the musty scent of a home that hadn't been lived in for a while.

"Are you here to make sure I don't skip town?"

"Something like that," Ray said. It'd been weeks since he'd last seen the place. He gestured to the dozen or so paintings he could see from the foyer, which had a sight line into the living room and dining room. "Are you an art collector?"

Coleman shook his head. "Those are Suzie's."

"She works in graphic design, doesn't she?" Ray said.

"Yes, but the paintings are just a hobby."

Ray pointed into the living room, where he could see an empty bottle of Tito's vodka lying on the floor beside the coffee table. "Mind if we sit for a chat?"

Coleman shuffled into the living room without answering, his gait clumsy enough to warrant a field sobriety test. He misjudged the height of the recliner and collapsed onto the cushion, his foot kicking the vodka bottle and sending it skidding across the hardwood.

Ray and Billy exchanged a glance and eased themselves onto a matching leather sofa.

Coleman's eyes shifted from Billy to Ray and back again. "I don't know what else I can tell you other than I didn't do it."

"Let's walk through the timeline again," Ray said. "The night Suzie went missing you were both at a bar with some friends. You had too much to drink and got into an argument with Suzie after she caught you hitting on a bartender."

"That's right."

"Why were you hitting on the bartender in the first place?" Ray said. "Didn't Suzie just catch you having an affair a few weeks earlier?"

Coleman averted his eyes. "It wasn't an affair. I got drunk at a conference in New York and had a one-night stand."

"How'd she find out?" Billy asked.

"She saw pictures on my phone. I don't even remember taking them."

Billy chuckled. "Rookie mistake."

Ray shook his head at the inside joke. Billy's own infidelity had unraveled in much the same manner a few years earlier. "You understand how bad this looks, don't you?"

"Yes, but I swear I didn't do it."

"Then who did?" Billy asked.

"You guys saw the lab results. They say I took a bunch of sleeping pills. Now, why would I do that? I was so wasted my buddy Ryan practically had to carry me upstairs. You don't need sleeping pills when you're half in the bag."

"Maybe you killed her and then tried to kill yourself," Billy said. "Alcohol and sleeping pills can be a lethal combination. Just ask any number of dead rock stars."

"I don't remember taking them and we don't keep sleeping pills in the house. Someone drugged me, someone set me up."

"It seems a little far-fetched," Billy said. "Especially since you never provided a single lead as to who might've set you up."

"I didn't do it. That's all I know."

"You'd better come up with a lot more specifics than that," Billy said.

"He's right," Ray said. "You may think you got away with murder, but this is just the beginning. We'll find your wife's body eventually, and I've got a funny feeling that all the evidence will point back to you. So enjoy this little taste of freedom while you can, because if you weren't fond of the city jail, just wait until you spend a night in the state penitentiary."

"It's a scary place," Billy said. "Especially for a pretty boy like you."

Coleman's face flushed. "Do you have any idea how this feels? My wife is missing and is probably dead. And as horrible as that is, I'm being treated like a criminal on top of it. I'm telling you, I was set up. I didn't do it."

Ray studied Coleman's face, trying to get a reading on his bullshit meter. "If you seriously believe someone framed you, then you'd better start thinking of people who might have done it." He handed Coleman a business card and stood up. "Call us if you think of someone we should check out, or if you suddenly feel the urge to confess."

# CHAPTER TEN

The gallery was eerily quiet in the predawn gloom, with only the restless moaning of the dying art permeating the semi-darkness. The Artist made his rounds among the three exhibits, slipping into the service area behind the display wall and replacing IV fluids, administering antibiotics, and cleaning the plastic chutes he'd rigged to catch waste.

An arrangement of scaffolding supported the exhibits from behind the wall, and holes cut into the sheetrock allowed the Artist to select which body parts to make visible from the gallery. Except for the display wall, everything in the gallery was constructed of concrete, and the twenty-by-twenty bunker itself was built directly into the bedrock.

When the Artist finished his rounds, he poked a finger into Finkleton's doughy belly. Finkleton flinched, exposing a raw wound at the top of his throat. "There's my Itsy Bitsy Spider. I'd better not catch you climbing up any waterspouts."

Finkleton's lips moved soundlessly in response.

The Artist chuckled. "Are you forgetting I severed your vocal chords? I'm afraid you'll have to snuffle from now on, Bitsy. In any case, it seems you've critiqued your last artist. Wouldn't you agree, Mrs. C?"

The Artist turned to where Mrs. C protruded from the wall like a statue of Aphrodite, her sandy blond hair wound up around a golden tiara. Twin lengths of chain secured her arms to an iron ringlet above her head, and a cushioned support beam kept her back inclined at a seventy-five-degree angle. Her legs were bent at the waist, her feet resting on a narrow shelf jutting from the wall. A liquid diet had melted away a few pounds and her twenty-eight-year-old body was now perfectly contoured, her milky-white breasts remarkably perky in the face of gravity.

The Artist stepped between her knees and stroked her baby-smooth inner thighs. She'd become much more submissive in the last few days, much more accepting of her place in the world. Even their lovemaking had become less adversarial.

The Artist offered her a sliver of meat from a ceramic bowl and she devoured it like a starving dog. He fed her another morsel, noticing how the hollow of her throat quivered when she swallowed, a line of drool dribbling from her chin. Traditional art forms lacked such intricate details, such nuanced expression, but his vision captured it all.

"You can thank Mr. Finkleton for donating the thigh meat."

Mrs. C chewed vigorously and nodded, but Mr. Finkleton just hung from the wall and pouted.

"Come on, Mr. Finkleton, don't be such a grouch. It's not like you have any use for your legs anymore. The least you can do is share them with your new friends." He gestured to Mrs. C. "What do you think, is he delicious or what?"

Mrs. C nodded.

"Well there you have it, Mr. Finkleton. What more could you ask for? Time to hold your egg sac high and embrace your inner spider." The Artist clucked his tongue. "I feel like we ought to dispense of the formalities, don't you? After all, Mrs. C *is* dining on your flesh."

He poked Finkleton in the ribs. "Doesn't get more personal than that, does it, Barry? Now, where are my manners? I never offered you a taste of your own meat. I believe that's considered the ultimate dining faux pas. What do you say, Barry? Snuffle once for wing and twice for thigh."

But Barry just clung to the wall like a smug little spider.

"Not hungry? Let's give it a few days, shall we? For your sake, I hope Mrs. C—I mean, *Suzie*—doesn't gobble up every last morsel first."

# THE ART OF DYING

"What about me?" his third exhibit croaked. "I'm starving."

The Artist turned toward the muscular form of Greg Cassidy, whose surgically-implanted bull's horns cast an imposing shadow on the gallery floor. Dressed in nothing but a loincloth, Greg had a red bull's-eye tattooed on his chest, a chain around his neck, and a golden ring through his nose. The piercing was horribly infected—that's what happens when you do it with a rusty nail—and everything he said came out in a nasally drone.

The Artist shook his head at his resident Minotaur. "I don't think you've earned a meal, Greg. You've done nothing but complain since you arrived."

Greg clamped his mouth shut, but his muscles tensed like springs.

"Don't you understand? You deserve to be here. You *all* deserve to be here. And the time to atone for your sins is now. Your deaths will usher in a revolutionary new artform, and the singular beauty of your suffering will capture the hearts and minds of the world and bring about your redemption. So, raise your eyes to the camera, bare your souls to the art, and become one with your destiny as the greatest exhibition of all time."

Greg thrashed against his chains. "Let me go!"

The Artist grabbed the chain dangling from Greg's neck and choked the insolent Minotaur into submission. "Say mercy and I'll let you crawl out of here like a dog."

Greg's face progressed through a spectrum of reds and purples before the Artist released the chain, leaving him gasping and wheezing.

"Wasn't that your catch phrase in elementary school, Greg? When you'd work me into a headlock in the boys' bathroom? You thought you were so strong, didn't you? Taking pleasure in torturing a kid half your size? Instead of sniveling about how I'm mistreating you, perhaps you should consider that I'm simply giving you a taste of your own medicine."

Greg made a gurgling sound, but his eyes were open very wide. "You?"

"Yes, me. The little boy you liked to kick in the balls during recess. Have you ever felt that agony, Greg? Ever cried at the sight of peeing out blood? A nine-year-old, peeing out blood. For no other reason than it gave a bully some sick sense of satisfaction. But the thing is, Greg, this is my playground now. And these are my rules. So, if you've never been on the receiving end of a bully's attention, then you're in for quite a treat. Because I've got years and years of payback planned. And, my oh my, won't it be a bitch."

# CHAPTER ELEVEN

"On the ground," Ray barked. "Hands over your head."

He groped behind him for the powder and the wipes, but Petey rolled onto his stomach and wriggled away, an Elmo diaper strapped to his backside and bursting at the seams.

Ray lunged across the hardwood and caught hold of a chubby ankle, but Petey thrashed his body like an alligator tucking into a death roll.

"Stop squirming."

"Lemme go!"

"You can't sit in a poopy diaper all day."

"I sit in my poop *forever*!"

Ray turned at the sound of giggling and saw Jacob and his wife, Megan, standing in the foyer.

"How is it that you can take down an armed suspect," Jacob asked, "but you can't hold on to Petey long enough to wipe his butt?"

Ray grunted. "Next time I'll use my Taser."

"I hear the people in child welfare services are real sticklers about that stuff," Megan said. "It might not be worth the red tape." She winked at him before heading into the kitchen with Jacob in tow, a bottle of wine hugged to her chest.

Ray called after them. "Not so fast, little brother. You and I have work to do."

Jacob pointed to Petey's bulging diaper. "I'm not going anywhere near that thing."

"Get over here and hold him down. Be a man for once in your life."

Jacob knelt beside Petey and pinned his shoulders against the floor. "I'm not sure I see the correlation, but—oh my God, what are you feeding him?"

Ray unfolded the diaper and Jacob gagged into his hand. "The horror."

After soiling a dozen baby wipes, Ray strapped a clean diaper onto Petey and released him back into the wild. "Go on now," he said in his best Steve Irwin voice. "In a few minutes, you won't remember a thing."

Petey crawled to where Allie sat on the living room floor wrestling a tennis ball from Sparky's jaws. Jason lounged on the couch behind her, his eyes glued to Michelle's iPad and whatever mind-numbing game he was addicted to this week.

Ray dangled the soiled diaper in front of Jacob's face. "What do you say, little brother, are you ready for parenthood?"

"I don't know, do they come with instruction manuals?"

"No, and the return policy is shit." He glanced over his shoulder to make sure the kids hadn't heard. "You guys still trying?"

"Yeah, but I'm not sure if I'm ready for what comes after."

Ray brayed laughter. "Trust me, little bro, no one ever is."

***

After stuffing the kids full of pizza and tucking them into an early bedtime, the adults tiptoed up to the roof deck for dinner and drinks. Megan gazed over Jacob's shoulder at the city skyline, the lights of the financial district glittering against a violet sky. "It's so beautiful up here. Have you used it much this season?"

"We came up here just the other night, didn't we?" Ray said, winking at Michelle. "Got some great use out of it."

Michelle kicked him under the table, catching him square in the shin—a move she'd perfected over eight years of marriage.

"Would you guys ever move back to the city?" Michelle asked, shooting Ray a dirty look.

"I don't know," Megan said. "It took me a few months to warm up to suburban life, but now it feels like home."

"I'm excited to start a family there," Jacob said, reaching for Megan's hand.

Ray shook his head. "You poor bastards have no idea how your lives are about to change."

"It makes you want to slap them, doesn't it?" Michelle asked, sipping her wine.

"Yeah," Ray said, "except I'm always in the mood to slap Jacob."

"Don't listen to them," Megan said, planting a kiss on Jacob's cheek. "They're just jealous."

"Let's see how cute you guys are when you're surviving on three hours of sleep," Michelle said.

"Yeah," Ray said, "or when you drag yourself out of bed at two in the morning, thinking it's just a routine diaper change and then—bam! Projectile diarrhea all over you."

"It's true," Michelle said. "I can show you the spot where Allie made a perfect profile of Ray on the wall."

"I was so tired I didn't even care."

"I don't know what you were doing," Megan said, "but I'm pretty sure you were doing it wrong."

"Speaking of doing it wrong," Ray said, "did Jacob ever tell you that when he was a kid he thought you could get a girl pregnant by squeezing her boobs?"

Megan raised an eyebrow. "That explains a lot."

\*\*\*

After the wine ran out, Ray and Jacob made a run to the liquor store for another bottle of sauvignon blanc. They walked through Charlestown's Gaslamp District, where the streets buzzed with the typical Friday night restaurant crowd and wannabe socialites spilled out of flashy cars dressed in designer clothes. A few blocks farther along, the crowds thinned out and the glitz receded into the night, leading them into a neighborhood where shards of glass glittered against the cracked pavement and junked-up cars lined the street.

They passed groups of Townies hanging out on their stoops talking trash and busting balls the way only Townies could. Farther down the block, Ray spotted Sheila Morrison and her drug dealer boyfriend loitering outside of the local pizza joint. She wore ripped jeans and a turquoise tank top that showed enough cleavage to make a hooker blush. Darren stood behind her with his tattooed arms looped around her body, his hands clasped underneath her breasts.

Sheila greeted Ray as he walked by, but Darren squinted at him like he was itching for a fight, his scraggly blond hair half obscuring his face.

*Yeah, I'm touching her boobs,* that look said. *What are you gonna do about it?*

"Hey, Sheila," Ray said, directing a menacing glare at Darren. "You kids behaving yourselves?"

She smiled and nodded, for a moment reminding him of the little girl who once played hopscotch in front of his house. That girl was still in there somewhere, but if she kept hanging out with Darren, she'd wind up just another Townie lost to the streets.

"Who was that?" Jacob asked once they were out of earshot.

"Girl next door."

"Her boyfriend seems like a loser."

"You think?"

Jacob shrugged, his face turning serious. "I've been waiting for the right time to tell you something."

"Let me guess, you're not sure how to make a baby."

"Come on, Ray. This is serious."

Ray stopped in front of the liquor store and folded his arms. "Alright, what is it?"

"A client I was supposed to meet this morning never showed. I called his office and the woman who manages his gallery said he's been missing since Wednesday night. It happened in the city, so I figured you might know something."

Ray thought back to the morning roll call. "His name Finkleton?"

"That's right."

"Why are you just telling me this now?"

"I didn't want to ruin dinner."

"How well do you know this guy?"

"Enough to know his finances and business dealings, things like that."

"It's not my case," Ray said, "but I can have Detective Ridley call you tomorrow, ask you a few questions."

Jacob held open the door to the liquor store. "Okay, sure."

The interior of Monument Liquors resembled a hoarder's apartment, with cases of beer and wine stacked haphazardly on the floor creating a maze of columns that forced customers to weave around the store like rats hunting for cheese. Since the place first opened, Sam Martinez had made due without a storeroom, though he still struggled with inventory management.

As Jacob negotiated his way to the coolers in the back, Ray lifted a hand to the stocky Latino man behind the counter, who was busy checking out a customer. "How you doing, Sam?"

Instead of his trademark response—*Living the dream, Ray, living the dream*—Sam flicked his eyes toward Ray without a word, tension evident in the set of his shoulders.

Ray reached instinctively for his gun, forgetting for a moment that he wasn't carrying. From his angle, he could only see the customer from behind, the man's right arm bent as if clutching a weapon, a Red Sox cap tipped forward on his head.

The register drawer rolled opened and Sam slid out stacks of bills one compartment at a time, the drawer's spring clips snapping onto bare plastic and echoing loudly. Somewhere in the back of the store, Jacob rummaged through the cooler, bottles clanking together as he searched for the brand of sauvignon blanc Michelle had requested.

Ray groped for a dusty bottle of champagne from a nearby rack, gripping it by the neck like a club.

The man glanced over his shoulder and pointed a .38 at Ray. "Put it down."

Ray returned the champagne to the rack and held out his hands, palms upturned like a priest giving a blessing.

"Get over here," the man barked, motioning with the gun. "Behind the counter where I can see you both." He glanced at Sam, his arm trembling. "Put the money in a bag."

Ray crept toward the counter, keeping his eyes on the gunman and hoping Jacob had done the smart thing and ducked behind a pile of boxes.

Sam fumbled open a plastic bag and dropped in what looked like a few thousand dollars. Ray stared at the gunman from behind the counter, observing the sweat glistening beneath the brim of his hat. "You seem nervous," Ray said. "This your first time?"

"Shut up," the man said, his eyes wild with panic. "Give me the bag."

Ray took the bag from Sam and slid it over the counter so that half of the bills tumbled onto the floor. When the man glanced down, Ray grabbed the gun with one hand and broke the man's grip with the other, using the technique he'd learned in the academy. Then he flipped the gun around and leveled it at the man's chest. "Boston Police, you're under arrest."

The man staggered back and collided with the rack of champagne, sending an avalanche of bottles crashing to the floor and exploding in a geyser of foam. He slipped in a fizzing puddle, arms pinwheeling for balance, but regained his footing and lumbered toward the exit with his head ducked, as if expecting a bullet in the back.

"Stop!" Ray yelled.

But the man in the Red Sox cap had already vanished into the night.

# THE ART OF DYING

Ray charged after him, the buzz from the evening's drinking now completely evaporated. The man hustled toward Monument Park, his arms flailing like the grownup version of the kid who always got picked last in gym class. Ray broke into a sprint, moving with the fluid grace of a wide receiver running for a Hail Mary. He'd always taken the physical demands of his job seriously, knowing that his life could at any moment depend on his speed, strength, and agility. And while there were plenty of guys scarfing down doughnuts at the precinct and getting softer by the hour, Ray wasn't one of them.

The man in the Red Sox hat rounded the corner and darted into the park, the Bunker Hill Monument looming over him like an ancient monolith. Ray weaved between a pair of wrought iron benches, startling a pair of horny teenagers making out near the foot of the obelisk. Ray closed the gap and launched himself at the assailant, tackling him at the waist and driving him face-first into the grass. The man rolled over and scrabbled away on all fours, but Ray kicked him in the side and laid him out flat.

Ray loomed over him, the .38 aimed at his heart. "You're under arrest," he said, and rattled off the Miranda warning.

The man's face contorted. "Please, I can't go to jail. They'll kill me."

"Who will kill you?"

"I can't, they'll know I talked."

"If you've got something to help your case, you'd better say it."

"But—"

"Let's start with your name."

The man drew a jittery breath. He seemed on the verge of hyperventilating. "Larry Reynolds."

"Why'd you rob the liquor store, Larry?"

"I owe people money. A lot of money."

"Let me guess," Ray said. "The mob?"

Larry nodded, his eyes welling up.

A warble of sirens approached from the south.

"Who's shaking you down? Jimmy the Weasel?"

"He was," Larry said, "but now he's dead. Him and Mikey both."

Ray arched an eyebrow. He hadn't heard any reports about Jimmy or Mikey getting whacked. "Did you kill them?"

"No," Larry said. "But I saw who did."

# CHAPTER TWELVE

"He looks like shit," Billy said.

"Let me see." Ray leaned forward in the driver's seat and peered into the binoculars, squinting as he adjusted the focus. He could see into the living room, where Coleman sat slouched on the sofa wearing nothing but a drooping pair of boxer briefs and a scraggly growth of beard. He seemed to be staring ahead at nothing, his eyes bloodshot.

"Doesn't look like a flight risk to me," Billy said.

"Seems more like a suicide watch."

"You really think he's innocent?" Billy asked.

Ray thought back to his first look at the crime scene. Something about the blood splatter had seemed off. It didn't match the patterns he was accustomed to seeing. Not even the splatter cards he carried for reference had anything remotely similar, and one arc of blood on the headboard had almost looked as though it'd been squirted from a syringe.

And Coleman was right—no sleeping pills were found inside the house. Not even a Ziploc bag with trace residue. Besides, if it was meant to be a murder-suicide, why bother hiding the body? And what about the hint of bruising on the inner crease of Coleman's elbow? Had someone injected him with a sedative?

"Do you think Suzie could've staged it?" Ray asked.

"What are you talking about? There was enough blood to be fatal."

"She could've drawn it in advance. They take a whole pint when you donate at the blood bank. You do that a couple of times, store it at the right temperature, then wait for the right moment and stage the scene."

"Okay, so she frames her cheating husband, but then what? She'd need to disappear forever, and her insurance policy is in Jim's name."

"They could be in on it together."

"I'm not feeling it," Billy said.

"Me neither. I'm just trying to lay out all the possibilities."

"What do you say we give him a little rope? Come back later and watch him from a more discreet location. See where he goes."

"Alright," Ray said, "but I want to be at the precinct when the feds have their turn questioning Larry."

"You think he'll cooperate?"

"We'll see. Flaherty has turned witnesses before."

"Yeah," Billy said, "or made them disappear."

"Let's hope not this time."

Ray's phone buzzed to life. He glanced at the display and hit speaker. "Tina, what's happening?"

"I've got an update on Danny McDougal."

"He still dead?" Ray asked.

"Did you expect it to be otherwise? We've determined cause of death."

"What was it?"

"Sepsis."

"That's an infection, isn't it?" Ray asked.

"Technically, it's a complication that occurs when a bacterial infection reaches the bloodstream. Without aggressive treatment, it can lead to organ failure."

"What do you think caused it?" Billy asked.

"There's a risk with any surgery, but maintaining a sterile environment reduces the chance of bacteria entering the body through an open wound. And while the surgical procedures performed on Mr. McDougal were surprisingly neat, the conditions may have been far from sterile. We're still waiting on several tests from the lab, but we're confident that sepsis caused him to suffer multiple organ failure. The bowel obstruction likely exacerbated matters. That alone might've killed him eventually."

"Anything else?" Ray asked.

"We submitted the Hot Wheels car to the crime lab for analysis. I expect the results are available by now."

"I saw the report this morning," Ray said. "It's a 1971 Dodge Charger. Tested negative for prints."

"Must've drove itself up there," Billy said.

"There's something else you should know," Tina said. "Mr. McDougal had a small wound on his throat that had partially healed around a foreign substance."

"What kind of foreign substance?" Ray asked.

"Calcium sulfate."

"What's that mean in English?" Billy said.

"It's more commonly known as plaster of Paris. It's used to make a variety of things."

"Like what?" Billy asked.

"Building material, casts, sculptures. Just for example."

"And you found that in his neck?" Ray asked.

"A couple grams of hardened material, yes."

Ray mulled it over. "Is that everything?"

"That's it for now," Tina said, "but I'll be in touch when we know more."

***

"What do you think?" Ray asked as they drove back to the precinct.

"The plaster of Paris in his neck could be something."

"Yeah, but how'd it get there?"

"Maybe he was tied against a stucco wall and cut himself on a rough edge."

"Could be," Ray said. "Based on the bruising, he might've been tied up by his neck."

"You still think Giabatti had nothing to do with it?"

"Why do you ask?"

"Flaherty gunned down two of Giabatti's goons in revenge for Danny's murder."

"Just because Flaherty thinks Giabatti killed Danny doesn't make it true," Ray said. "If Giabatti wanted Danny dead, he would've put a bullet in his brain, not perform reconstructive surgery. I think we ought to work the molestation angle. It's the easiest place to start."

"You know I like easy."

"Yeah," Ray said, "I've seen your girlfriend."

"What can I say, I like trashy women."

"Then you hit the jackpot with that one. What's your ex think?"

"I go through a lot of trouble to make sure those two never meet."

"Probably a good idea. How is Mary, anyway?"

"Still a pain in my ass. She won't stop bitching about Tyler's behavior, says he's disrespectful after spending the weekend at my place. Like I don't teach him manners or nothing. I mean, show me a twelve-year-old who isn't an asshole."

Ray steered the Explorer into the precinct's parking lot. He cut the engine and turned toward Billy. "There might be another angle here. The killer dumped Danny in the quarry without weighting him down. Hundreds of people walk those trails every day. It's obvious he wanted Danny to be found."

"He wanted to shame him," Billy said.

"Exactly. The papers could only run censored pictures, but all it takes is one rubbernecker to post cell phone photos online."

"Everything checked out with that guy," Billy said.

"Yeah, but did you see there's hundreds of comments on his post? The killer's got to be relishing in that. He's probably even commented himself. But even if he used different usernames, his posts would all originate from the same IP address."

Billy furrowed his brow. "You lost me."

"You really need to take a computer class."

"I know how to get to the porn sites."

"That's half the battle." Ray climbed out of the Explorer and grabbed his sports coat from the backseat. "My point is, our cyber guys might be able to identify the location he's posting from."

"Then why the hell didn't you just say that?"

"Because I forgot I was talking to an old man."

Billy shot him a dirty look and motioned to a bright orange spray of graffiti on the brick wall of the precinct.

*YOU HAVE THE RIGHT TO GO FUCK YOURSELF.*
*SO WHAT ARE YOU WAITING FOR?*

Billy shook his head. "I think RJ's losing his edge."

"I don't know," Ray said. "It's got a nice ring to it."

Billy touched a finger to the paint. "Looks fresh. Spinonni's gonna flip his lid."

Ray chuckled. "Good old RJ."

"We should pay him a visit."

"Exactly what I was thinking."

\*\*\*

Ray poured himself a coffee in the breakroom and overheard Lieutenant Spinonni bitching about the graffiti. It was obvious from Detective Ridley's expression that Spinonni had been blathering on forever, the lieutenant's cheeks getting ruddier by the moment. Ridley was backed into a corner, his exit blocked by the water cooler and by the swell of Spinonni's gut, which seemed a contraction away from birthing a litter of assholes.

Ridley gestured to Ray in an obvious plea for help.

"What are you smirking at?" Spinonni asked, turning toward Ray.

"Just enjoying my coffee. Got any leads on the weekly diss?"

"You think it's funny?" Spinonni asked.

"I find it amusing."

"It's an embarrassment," Spinonni said. "And if I ever get my hands on that punk, I'll give him an old-fashioned beatdown. Shit like that didn't happen when I was a patrolman. We would've gone out there and cracked some skulls."

"Ah, the glory days."

"Damn right," Spinonni said.

Ray caught a glimpse of Ridley slinking toward the door. "Hey, Ridley, where are you going? The lieutenant was just about to tell us about the glory days."

Ridley ran a hand through his Hollywood hair. "Um, I need to check on something." He darted through the doorway and vanished into the hall.

Spinonni stared after him. "He's a good kid—well-mannered and respectful. You could learn a lesson from him."

"I don't need to kiss your ass, Lieutenant. That's why I pay my union dues."

"Very funny. How's your buddy Coleman?"

"Best I can tell, he's a razor's edge from suicide."

"Good, it'll save the city some money. By the way, I'm assigning you the Finkleton case. Ridley just got called to active duty."

It took a moment for the lieutenant's words to register. He'd forgotten that Ridley was in the Army Reserve, although it did explain his unwavering respect for authority. "Afghanistan?"

Spinonni nodded. "Six-month tour."

"When's he—"

Captain Barnes poked his head into the breakroom and pointed at Ray. "They're ready for you in the interrogation room."

*\*\**

Special Agents Dearborn and Calhoun intercepted Ray in the hall. They were part of the FBI's organized crime unit and Ray had worked with them on cases like this in the past. Dearborn had a cowboy cockiness that Ray despised, but

Calhoun was a decent enough guy if you looked past the flashy suit and slicked-back hair.

"What's going on?" Ray asked.

Dearborn rolled his eyes and gestured toward the interrogation room. "That clown doesn't realize how good of a deal this is."

"What's the deal?" Ray asked.

"Full immunity in exchange for his testimony and participation in a sting operation."

"Wait a minute," Ray said, "what sting operation?"

Dearborn and Calhoun exchanged a glance. Calhoun said, "We need Flaherty to admit to extortion or murder on a wire."

"And you want to use Larry as bait? No wonder you two are standing out here talking to me."

Dearborn clenched his jaw. "You and I both know Larry's not worth shit if he clams up before the trial or if he mysteriously disappears."

"You need insurance," Ray said.

"Exactly."

"Can't you just hold him in protective custody until the trial starts?"

"That's one option," Dearborn said.

"Then why the operation?" Ray asked. "It seems extreme."

"The bureau has been burned before," Calhoun said.

Ray had been around long enough to read between the lines. The bureau had botched a similar case in the past and the director wasn't about to let it happen again. "So you need me to convince him to take your deal?"

"He asked for you," Calhoun said.

Dearborn thrust a finger at Ray. "You better not have made him a promise you can't keep. What'd you say to him last night, anyway?"

Ray locked eyes with Dearborn. "What I say to the people I arrest is my business. Now, put that finger away before it gets broken."

\*\*\*

Ray strode into the interrogation room and found Larry sitting at a scarred, wooden table with his hands cuffed in his lap. His court-appointed attorney sat to his left fidgeting with a pen and sweating under the lights.

After Ray shut the door, Larry turned to his attorney. "You can leave now."

The attorney blinked behind his wire-rimmed glasses. "Excuse me?"

"I said you could leave now."

"You sure you want to do that?" Ray asked.

Larry made a shooing gesture. "Off you go. Bye-bye now."

The attorney got up in a huff, making a big show of shoving his papers into a leather portfolio. He stormed across the room and shook his head at Larry before slamming the door behind him.

"That's the best the city had to offer?" Larry asked. "Even free of charge, I feel like I got ripped-off."

Ray squeezed himself into the tiny chair across the table from Larry. It was no accident that the chairs made for torturous sitting. The front legs were cut a half inch shorter than the rear to keep suspects feeling off balance. When combined with the bright fluorescent lights and the warm, stagnant air of a tiny room without ventilation, it made for a veritable chamber of discomfort.

"Why am I here again, Larry? You got something else you want to share?"

Larry shook his head. "I told you everything last night."

"You're in way over your head, aren't you?"

"You could say that."

"What's all the drama with your attorney?"

"The guy was a moron."

"Still, you probably need—"

"Please," Larry said, holding up a hand. "I ran circles around guys like that in law school."

"You went to law school?"

"Not just any law school, Yale."

"So how the hell did you end up here?"

"Cocaine, man. The song says she don't lie, but the truth is she will *fuck* you up."

Ray leaned forward. "Who hooked you, Larry?"

The fine art of interrogation often involved playing the roles of patient and shrink. He had to stay nonjudgmental if he wanted to gain Larry's trust and keep him from clamming up.

"This guy Stuart. He lived across the hall from me during first year. He swore by cocaine, said it kept him hyper-focused on his studies, let him pull all-nighters without losing clarity. Anyway, long story short, I got hooked and flunked out. After that, I started gambling to make money and ended up getting hooked on that too."

"Christ," Ray said, "that's a depressing story." He gestured to the interrogation room. "What's your angle here?"

"Honestly, I just didn't like those FBI guys."

"Yeah?"

"A couple of condescending pricks."

Ray brayed laughter. "You know they're listening, right?"

"Of course," Larry said, extending his middle finger to the two-way mirror. "I've got a question for you."

"Shoot."

"What do you think about this deal?"

"Why are you asking me?"

"Because I can read people and I think you'll give me an honest answer."

"Okay," Ray said. "It's a shitty deal, but I think it's all you're gonna get."

"So it's either that or prison?"

"That's one way of looking at it."

"What's the other way?"

Ray mimicked a throat-cutting gesture.

"What's that supposed to mean?"

"You're a Yale man, figure it out. Let's say you refuse to testify. After a couple months of hard time, you might still roll on Flaherty to get a reduced sentence. You think he's gonna take that chance? He's got a lot of friends in prison just itching to earn his favor. You'd be lucky to last a week."

Larry slumped in his chair. "You're right. I'm screwed."

# CHAPTER THIRTEEN

Jacob entered the bar and slid into the booth across from Ray. "Sorry I'm late. I've got this demanding new client and he—"

"Save the excuses for that pretty wife of yours." Ray swallowed the last sip of his beer and belched. "Drinks are on you tonight, little brother."

Jacob set his briefcase down on the bench and adjusted his glasses. "Looks like you've gotten a head start."

Ray gestured to the TV above the bar. "Blame it on the Sox."

"What's the score?"

"Sox are ahead by one, but the pitching looks shaky."

Jacob flagged down a barmaid and ordered a beer.

It was a warm spring night and Quinn's was teeming with college kids, Townies, and tourists fresh off the Freedom Trail, all crowded around the bar and mixing it up, their voices rising into the rafters in a raucous roar of conversation. The windows at the front of the bar were open to the night, inviting in the first whispers of summer and the salty scent of the harbor.

Ray stared across the table and had a flashback of his brother as a scrawny kid with a serious face, full of determination and eager to conquer the world. And here he sat looking so professional in his tailored suit and designer glasses, finally away from the office but still carrying it in his posture, and Ray couldn't help but wonder if, instead, it was the world that had conquered his brother.

Jacob sipped from a freshly delivered pint and looked at Ray. "Why are you staring at me like that?"

"Cause I'm worried about you."

"I thought you didn't worry about anything."

"You've been working too much."

"I'm building a business, Ray. I've got to work hard now so I can reap the benefits later."

"You gotta learn to relax."

"I am relaxed."

"Then why are you sitting like you've got a rod crammed up your ass?"

Jacob stared at Ray over his pint. "That's just how I sit."

"Because you've become accustomed to the rod."

"How many beers have you had?"

Ray thrust a finger at him. "You know I hate to be serious, but Dad's dead and Ma thinks hard work is the answer to everything. So I gotta be the voice of reason."

"That's a scary thought."

"Maybe so, but I'm telling you, when you and Megan have kids, you'll need to dial it back. No one goes to their grave wishing they'd worked more."

"Thanks for the unsolicited advice, especially coming from a guy who gets called away in the middle of the night to investigate murders."

"I still work less than you do."

"That reminds me," Jacob said. "I never heard from your police buddy about Barry Finkleton."

"That's because I'm handling the case now. I was gonna ask you a few questions tonight."

"You mean before you got sidetracked by lectures and insults?"

"Exactly."

"Well, what happened with Barry?"

Ray set down his beer and wiped his mouth with the heel of his hand. "Finkleton's wife said he never came home Wednesday night, but the security camera shows him leaving the gallery just after seven. He's got a parking spot in the service alley behind the building. Drives a nice, new Mercedes. No cameras back there, but the car was gone so we're assuming he got in it."

"What about the rest of the security footage?" Jacob asked. "Anyone suspicious coming or going during the day?"

"Nothing that raises any eyebrows. Detective Ridley interviewed the gallery staff, but none of them reported anything out of the ordinary. Neither did anyone else we met with."

"Who'd you talk to?"

"Ridley met with Finkleton's wife and some of the artists whose work he exhibits. And this afternoon, Billy and I spoke with residents from the brownstones neighboring the gallery."

Jacob frowned into his beer. "Maybe he skipped town without telling anyone."

"I don't think so," Ray said.

"Why not?"

"Because we recovered his car this afternoon. A patrolman found it in Roxbury up on blocks and stripped of anything valuable. Our crime scene techs said there were over a dozen sets of fingerprints inside the car. Basically, we've got a contaminated crime scene."

"What do you think happened?"

"I think someone carjacked him in the alley, except that Finkleton was the target instead of the car. There's been no demand for ransom, so I've got a hunch someone had a grudge against him. Probably drove him to a remote location, shot him dead, then ditched the car in the city to throw off the trail."

Jacob winced. "I hope you're wrong about that."

"Ridley got the sense that people didn't want to say anything bad about Finkleton, even though it seemed something might be lurking below the surface. You got any idea what that might be?"

Jacob adjusted his glasses. "He's not what I'd call a likable guy. He's opinionated, egotistical, and pretentious. I'm sure a lot of people dislike him, but I doubt someone would want to kill him."

Ray leaned his elbows on the table. "You'd be surprised what passes for motive these days. Was he in debt?"

"No, he's got a strong balance sheet. The gallery has a pretty good business model. New artists hungry for recognition will do anything to get their work displayed, so a lot of them agree to give Finkleton an enormous percentage of the sales. I'm talking they're left with pennies on the dollar. But a lot of times it pays off. Finkleton's clients are wealthy art collectors, and those people like nothing more than to discover the next great artist. It's bragging rights for the uber-rich."

"What happens when an exhibit's over? Do the artists owe anything else to Finkleton?"

"They could walk away if they wanted, but if their art generated enough interest, they could stay with Finkleton and negotiate a better margin on future sales."

"How about his employees? They like him?"

"They tolerate him. I see a bit of eye rolling, but they're a nice group of people. Most of them are grandmotherly types. I couldn't see them causing any harm."

"What about the artists he refuses to exhibit? Could be a big dream crusher for those guys."

"Yeah, I've seen artists walk in off the street carrying their portfolios with more care than a mom with a newborn. Sometimes, Finkleton seems impressed and tells them to come back with more samples, but most times he just scoffs at their work and points to the door."

"I'm guessing Finkleton doesn't keep records of the artists he turns down."

"I doubt it."

"What about the ones he invites back? He must set up an appointment, right?"

"You should check with Veronica, the gallery manager."

Ray drained the last of his beer and nodded, his gaze shifting to the TV as the Fenway Faithful uttered a collective groan. Another blown save.

"You really think he's dead?" Jacob asked, liquid-brown eyes filled with concern.

"I don't know," Ray said. "A case like this? I'd say the odds are a thousand to one that anybody ever sees Finkleton again."

# CHAPTER FOURTEEN

A crowd of mourners gathered at the base of the hill, huddled near a tranquil pond teeming with vibrant clusters of water lilies. A priest stood beside a shiny black casket, his hands clasped in prayer.

"To you, O Lord, we commend the soul of James Sorrento, your servant. In the sight of this world he is dead, but in your sight may he live forever. Forgive whatever sins he committed through human weakness, and in your goodness grant him everlasting peace. We ask this through Christ our Lord. Amen."

Jimmy's wife wailed at the sight of the casket descending into the ground, her face contorting beneath the shadow of her veil. Her stiletto heels had sunk halfway into the grass—as if in solidarity with Jimmy—and the crucifix wedged into her cleavage heliographed the sun with every hitch of her chest.

The priest prayed on, a pillar of strength in a sea of despair. "May his soul and the souls of all the faithfully departed, through the mercy of God, rest in peace. And may almighty God bless you, the Father, the Son, and the Holy Spirit. Amen."

Ray and Billy leaned against a Mercedes limo and watched the mourners disperse. Sal Giabatti headed their way, the white-haired patriarch of the Salerno crime family looking as dapper as ever in a designer suit and retro glasses. Giabatti didn't stop until he stood toe-to-toe with Ray, and for a moment, Ray wasn't sure if Giabatti was going to shake his hand or punch him in the face.

"Sorry to hear about Jimmy," Ray said. "You have our condolences."

Giabatti nodded, his lips pressed into a tight purple line.

"I know this is a difficult time," Ray said, "but Jimmy and Mikey didn't die of natural causes. You can't just retrieve their bodies and bury them without an investigation."

"I think it's a little late for that," Sal said.

Billy leaned in to say something but Ray waved him off. "We're not here to harass you, or to arrest you for obstructing justice. What we want is evidence to take down Flaherty."

"You know it doesn't work like that," Giabatti said. "We'll lick our wounds, bury our dead, and live to fight another day. This isn't a police matter; it's a family matter. And I'm asking you to respect that."

"You know I can't make that promise," Ray said.

Giabatti fixed them with an icy stare before opening the door to the Mercedes. He patted Ray on the shoulder. "You boys watch your backs. I've got a feeling this is gonna be one hell of a bloody summer."

***

"Well, that was a waste," Billy said. "I told you we should've done it my way."

"Your way would've ended in a shoot-out."

"At least we would've gotten some swift justice."

Ray shook his head. "You're starting to sound like Spinonni. Tell you what, next time you want to shoot up a funeral, I won't hold you back."

"I appreciate that."

They drove across town to Coleman's house and parked the Explorer where they had a view into the living room. After shooing away a news van, they took turns with the binoculars and spotted Coleman sitting on the couch wearing a pit-stained V-neck T-shirt with the remnants of his last meal smeared across his stomach.

"Christ," Ray said, observing the knots in Coleman's hair. "He looks even worse than yesterday."

They waited for Coleman to spot the Explorer, then gave it another hour before driving around the corner to Stony Brook Reservation. Billy climbed out of the truck and circled back to Coleman's house on foot to see if their departure had triggered any change in his behavior.

A few minutes later, Billy called to report that Coleman had put on jeans and a fresh T-shirt and was tidying up the living room. Not long after that, a silver Corolla pulled into the driveway and an attractive older woman got out carrying a casserole dish. Billy radioed the tag number to Ray, who ran it through the system and determined the car belonged to Coleman's mother. So much for their big break.

When Billy returned to the Explorer, Ray was leaning against the bumper staring through a screen of pine at the rippling waters of Turtle Pond.

"Either Coleman's innocent," Billy said, "or he's got no loose ends to take care of."

The midday sun accentuated the creases at the corner of Billy's eyes, and for a moment he really did look old. "What's the matter, Billy? You giving up on me? You know you've still got ten years until retirement?"

"Nine and a half," Billy said. "And, yes, I'm counting."

"I called RJ. He should be here any minute."

Billy nodded and they watched the road until a black Nissan sports coupe rolled up behind the Explorer.

RJ climbed out of the car and tipped them a nod. He had sandy-blond hair cropped close to his skull and wore a goatee long enough to braid. He looked lanky in his baggy Celtics shorts and oversized tank top that showed off the barbwire tattoos spiraling up his arms.

RJ grew up in one of Dorchester's roughest neighborhoods and was no stranger to Boston's underworld. A few years earlier, he had double-crossed a bookmaker with ties to Giabatti and came away with fifty grand and a price on his head. When Ray and Billy questioned the bookmaker as part of an ongoing investigation, RJ followed them to the precinct and asked for help getting the bounty lifted.

Armed with RJ's inside information, they succeeded in shutting down an entire branch of Giabatti's bookmaking operation, as well as uncovering evidence that the men had been hiding profits from Giabatti for years. Once Ray leaked that bit of information to Giabatti, the men lost their connections and the bounty got canceled.

Ever since then, RJ had become their most reliable informant, supplementing his income from building custom cars with the stipend he earned from the department. Over the course of a year, it amounted to a lot more than chump change, but being a rat in a place like Dorchester was a dangerous game.

Ray lifted a hand in greeting. "How you doing, RJ?"

"Surviving, man. Surviving."

"Sweet new ride like that?" Billy said. "Looks like you're doing better than just surviving."

RJ grinned. "This car's got so much power it's sick. And the best part is, you guys are making the payments."

"You'd better not be drag racing again," Ray said. "You get caught one more time, I don't think we can fix it."

"Relax, I got it under control."

"Yeah," Billy said, "I'm sure."

"By the way," Ray said, "we saw your recent handiwork at the precinct."

"What'd you think?"

"It was poetic," Ray said. "But I don't think Spinonni cared for it."

"How is that cranky old bastard?"

"One more weekly diss," Billy said, "and he'll blow a gasket."

RJ chuckled. "My art touches people in so many ways."

Ray lifted an eyebrow at the mention of art. It was like learning a new word—suddenly you started hearing it everywhere. Aside from RJ's reference, there was Finkleton's gallery, Suzie Coleman's paintings, and the plaster of Paris that

Tina said could be used to make sculptures. It was probably just a coincidence, but Ray filed it away for further examination. "We want to talk about Danny the Mule," he said. "You ever hear rumors of him molesting kids?"

The smirk disappeared from RJ's face, and for a moment he looked as if he'd seen a ghost. "Danny the Mule. Now, that's a blast from the past."

"He's dead," Billy said. "But you knew that, didn't you?"

RJ nodded. "I heard about it."

"You didn't answer my question," Ray said. "Did Danny ever molest any kids?"

RJ nodded. "I think so, yeah."

"You *think*?" Billy asked. "Or you *know*?"

"Let's just say I saw something a long time ago."

"How long ago?" Ray asked.

"I was twelve," RJ said. "I'm twenty-eight now, so you do the math."

"What did you see?" Ray asked. "I need you to be very specific."

"It happened at The Rock."

"Flaherty's bar?" Billy asked. "You went there when you were twelve?"

"My dad sometimes took me there when it was our weekend together. He used to do odd jobs for Flaherty. Messenger work, mostly. Picking up and dropping off packages. Shit like that. He liked hanging out with those guys. I think it made him feel important, like he was a tough guy, you know? Anyway, there was this stripper who used to entertain the guys. She'd walk around the bar with her tits hanging out, smoking a cigarette and wearing nothing but spandex and lace. She had her son with her, this skinny kid who looked to be around ten. He was kind of nerdy. You know, the shy, awkward type with nothing much to say.

"Anyway, he seemed okay when his mom was strutting around, chatting up the guys. But once a guy laid down a stack of bills and she got down to business, he would disappear into the back room. I wandered back there one time when a fight broke out up front, and I saw Danny coming out of the storeroom hitching up his pants and whistling. He winked at me as he walked past, and when I peered into the storeroom, I saw the kid standing beside a pile of boxes pulling up his pants and bawling. I didn't see him again for the rest of the afternoon. I think he holed up in the storeroom while Danny got drunk and groped his mom."

"Christ," Ray said. "Did Danny ever bother you?"

"If he ever tried to touch me, I would've ripped his dick off. And I think a guy like that knows it, you know? That's why they prey on the shy, quiet type."

"You remember the kid's name?" Billy asked.

RJ shook his head. "I only saw him a few times and we hardly spoke. The only conversation I remember having with him was about Danny."

"What'd he say?" Ray asked.

"He said if Danny ever offered me an elephant ride, I should say no."

"What the hell's an elephant ride?" Billy asked.

"The kid said it was like a horsey ride, except Danny called it an elephant ride. It's probably how Danny first got the kid alone. You know, parading him around on his back in front of everyone all innocent-like, then disappearing into the storeroom."

Billy shook his head. "Sick sonofabitch."

"Do you remember what the kid looked like?" Ray asked.

"Light brown hair, kind of skinny. I don't remember much else."

"What about the mom?" Billy asked.

"She had long black hair and a perfect set of tits. Her name was Amber. I remember that. My dad said she danced at the Puma."

"I'm sure she made a lasting impression," Ray said. "I don't suppose you caught her last name?"

RJ shook his head, a crooked grin tugging at his lips. "When I turned sixteen, I got a fake ID and went to the Puma to see her dance. I wasn't sure if she'd remember me, but she did, and we had a couple of drinks after closing. She was probably about fifty by then, but still hot in a slutty way."

"Fifty's not that old," Billy said.

"You keep telling yourself that," Ray said. He turned to RJ. "You remember what kind of car Danny drove in those days?"

"Yeah, that was the only thing I liked about the guy. He had a vintage 1971 Dodge Charger. Perfectly restored. Loved showing it off."

"Let me guess," Ray said. "Was it sky blue?"

RJ narrowed his eyes. "How'd you know?"

# CHAPTER FIFTEEN

Ray leaned against the headboard and stared at the spectral glow radiating from his laptop in a liquid crystal luminescence. Michelle lay curled up beside him, her chest rising and falling with the easy sound of her breathing. In this light, she appeared otherworldly, like a faerie creature sleeping in the glimmer of a moonbeam.

He rubbed her back and she nuzzled closer to him, uttering a sleepy sigh that made him smile in spite of the dark nature of his research. His browser was opened to a pseudo news site dedicated to bizarre deaths. The site attracted the underbelly of society, the hateful little trolls whose real character came out under the cloak of anonymity provided by the Internet.

The site's main page displayed a close-up of Danny on the rescue stretcher, his skin waxen and bluish. The angry purple scars of his castration showed up in stark detail, as did the dangling member attached to his face. A slew of comments followed the picture, the spiteful trolls flinging posts at the site like monkeys hurling feces.

*Reba99: LOL! I betcha that sumbitch cheated on his wife. You go, girl!*

*Mommabear: Damn straight! He gonna get some strange? Mommabear gonna rearrange!*

*JoeyT: Looks like that dude's hung like a Chihuahua... I think I'd drown myself too.*

*BigRex: Looks like the Great Gonzo!*

*Duff: What the hell's a gonzo?*

*SoxFan: Look it up, you moron.*

*Duff: Who are you calling a moron?*

*SoxFan: I thought I was pretty clear on that. YOU are a moron.*

*SteveyT: 10 bucks says Duff is a Yankees fan seeing as he's such a sensitive little bitch.*

*Lucy: I heard the dead guy was a gangster. I'd say he got what he deserved.*

*VinnyT: Yeah, sleep with the fishes!*

*TheArtist: Horrible people meet horrible ends.*

*MadMarksman: Amen to that.*

*TheArtist: His face is so expressive... even in death.*

*SoxFan: Yeah, I'd say he looks pretty bummed out. Hey Danny, why the schlong face?*

Ray stifled a laugh. Sox Fan had nailed it with that last comment. The remaining posts read like the others—mean-spirited and belittling. The only exception seemed to be The Artist, who came across as preachy and boastful instead of crass and insensitive.

So there it was, another connection to art. Coincidence? Or something more? He rubbed a hand over his stubbly cheek. What if it was a false lead? Something that risked dragging the investigation down a rabbit hole if chased too far, leading nowhere except for the cold case file.

The creak of a floorboard drew his attention and he turned to see Allie standing at the foot of the bed. She wore pink kitten pajamas and was clutching her stuffed rabbit, Mitsy, by the ears.

"What's wrong, Allie-cat? Another bad dream?"

She climbed onto the bed and nodded, her eyes brimming with tears. He set the laptop aside and drew her into his arms, feeling the flutter of her heart like a hummingbird's wings.

"What was it this time?" he asked, stroking her hair. "Dinosaurs? Bears? Momma's cooking?"

A haunted expression darkened her features. "A giant eyeball."

Ray wrinkled his brow. "How can that even be dangerous? Couldn't you just poke it with a stick?"

"It wanted to suck my eyes out. And it wasn't the only monster. There were more in the basement. They were coming for me."

"There's no such thing as monsters, Allie. They only exist in dreams, on TV, or in your imagination. Nothing's going to hurt you. I promise."

"Are you afraid of anything, Daddy?"

"Everyone's afraid of something." He scooped her into his arms and stood up. "Let's get you back to bed."

She rested her head against his shoulder and caught his eyes as they exited the room. "What are you afraid of, Daddy?"

"I don't know. Just the normal adult stuff, I guess." He climbed the stairs and padded down the hall past Jason's room, Allie's hair tickling his cheek.

"Like what?"

What could he say that wouldn't scare her? "Like worrying about keeping you guys safe."

Her eyes widened. "Safe from monsters?"

"Didn't I just tell you there's no such thing as monsters? I meant keeping you safe from accidents. Like falling and hurting yourselves. Stuff like that."

"Oh."

He tucked her into bed and drew the comforter around her shoulders, hoping she'd exhausted her questions for the night. The last thing he needed was for her to go digging around for more fears. She already had more than she could handle, and he preferred to keep his own buried deep where they belonged.

But as he sat on the edge of the bed watching Allie's eyes flutter under the spell of a little girl's dreams, he pictured himself struck down in a hail of bullets in some trash-littered alley and imagined his kids growing into adulthood carrying nothing but a few hazy memories of him. Like a faded figure in an old photograph, the passage of time slowly blurring him out of existence.

# CHAPTER SIXTEEN

The Artist disengaged the bolt to the survival bunker and pushed against the bloodred steel door, which swung inward with a reluctant screech of hinges. The stench of caged animals assaulted him as he wheeled a cart inside, and although he'd grown accustomed to such smells, it still took a moment to settle his gag reflex.

The door clicked shut behind him and he fumbled against the wall for the light switch. The exhibits stirred to life on the viewing wall, the sudden brightness wrenching them out of whatever shallow realm of sleep their bodies had allowed. Across the room, the red indicator light glowed on the security camera. The Artist relished in the knowledge that it would capture the delicate state of their rising.

He rolled the cart into the center of the gallery and parked it beside a hospital gurney equipped with nylon restraints and a vinyl cushion streaked with blood. The Artist leaned over the cart and stirred Bitsy's breakfast in a ceramic bowl.

"That IV may provide sustenance, but everyone knows a healthy spider needs his num-nums." The Artist approached the viewing wall and climbed onto the stepladder, tilting the bowl so Bitsy could see the juicy mound of flies, some of them still wriggling. He scooped a heaping teaspoon from the bowl and pressed it against Bitsy's lips, but Bitsy clamped his mouth shut like a stubborn little spider.

The Artist clucked his tongue. "Do you have any idea how difficult it was to peel your breakfast off the flypaper? And this is the thanks I get?"

Bitsy turned his head in a show of defiance and the Artist punched the insolent spider in the nose. When Bitsy opened his mouth in a silent scream, the Artist shoved a spoonful of flies into his gullet.

"That's it," he said. "Nummy-num-num, isn't it?"

Bitsy squeezed his eyes shut and nodded slowly, twin rivulets of blood trickling out of his nostrils and spattering the top rung of the stepladder.

The Artist grinned. "That's a good spider." He fed Bitsy another spoonful. "Now keep that spider hole open until you've slurped down every last morsel."

The Artist strode back to the cart and exchanged the empty bowl for a serving of oatmeal drizzled with brown sugar. "For my favorite goddess," he said, offering a spoonful to Suzie. "I know you're more of a carnivore, so I do apologize, but we are fresh out of roast leg o'Finkleton. You can thank our resident minotaur for that. He devoured more than his fair share at the last feeding."

"Where's my breakfast?" Greg asked. "I don't see a bowl for me."

"That's because you're having Rocky Mountain oysters."

When Greg failed to react, the Artist planted his hands on his hips and cocked his head. "Don't tell me you don't know what Rocky Mountain oysters are?"

Greg shook his head.

The Artist looked at Finkleton. "What do you think, Bitsy? Any ideas?"

When Bitsy didn't answer, the Artist chuckled. "I keep forgetting that I severed your vocal chords. How about you lip synch your answer instead? Give us your best Milli Vanilli?"

The Artist swayed his hips and spun in a slow circle, singing, "*Girl, you know it's true!*" He clapped his hands. "I can't be the only one feeling this. Bitsy, give me a head bob or something. And close your mouth. Nobody wants to see all those flies mashed in your teeth. Am I right, Suzie? Kind of a turnoff, isn't it?"

The Artist winked at the camera. He was killing it today. "Who remembers this old song? *I know an old spider who swallowed a fly. I don't know why he swallowed that fly... perhaps he'll die.*"

He sang the last three words in an ominous baritone. "Don't worry, Bitsy, I'm just yanking your egg sac. Those flies pack plenty of protein. Everything a healthy spider needs for building strong webs. Think of it like delicious chunks of chicken rather than dead insects with a nasty habit of regurgitating on their food."

Finkleton blubbered, his eyes turning bright and dewy.

"Come on, Bitsy, don't despair. You're much too spectacular to be cooped up in this dingy old bunker forever. Soon, it'll be time to venture into your natural habitat, where you can spin a web to catch your very own flies. And speaking of food, how about those Rocky Mountain oysters?"

The Artist turned to behold Greg's chiseled physique, the shadow of his bull's horns stretched long across the gallery floor. "Tell me what they are, Greg, and I'll give you a prize."

Greg's jaw gaped open, as if waiting for a spoonful of flies. "Um. I... ah..."

"Come on, Greg, take a guess. It's not rocket science."

Greg drew a shuddering breath and swallowed audibly, his Adam's apple bobbing on his throat. "Is it a shellfish? Like a clam or something?"

The Artist intoned the wrong answer buzz of a game show. "I'm sorry, Greg, but that is incorrect. The answer I was looking for was *bull testicles*, although I also would've accepted the slightly more vulgar *bull balls*. Unfortunately, that means you won't be taking home the grand prize today. But I am pleased to offer you our consolation prize—your very own back-alley castration."

The Artist yanked Greg's loincloth down to his ankles.

"What are you doing?" Greg asked.

# THE ART OF DYING

The Artist walked to the cart and slipped on a pair of latex gloves. He could see Greg in his peripheral vision, thrashing against his chains. The Artist reached for an alcohol swab and tore open the foil wrapper. "This might feel a bit cold," he said, crossing the room to swab Greg's scrotum. "But I'd hate to lose another exhibit to infection."

Greg's eyes bulged from their sockets. "No, please!"

The Artist brandished a scalpel, the blade reflecting the harsh gleam of the picture lamps. "I like the attitude, Greg. Really, I do. But there's no need to be nervous. I'm getting pretty good at this."

# CHAPTER SEVENTEEN

Sunlight glistened on the rippling swells of Boston Harbor, a distant cluster of sailboats skimming the surface, weaving around each other like dancers in a nautical ballet. Ray watched the display from the seawall at Waterfront Park, shielding his eyes from the glare and cursing himself for not remembering his sunglasses.

Located on the fringe of the North End, the park was a grassy area bordered by cobblestone and bisected by a tunnel-like arbor covered in wisteria vines. To the right, a pedestrian walkway stretched past the brick façade of the Marriott Long Wharf hotel and merged into a pier packed with sightseeing boats bobbing in the water.

As Ray scanned the crowd, he sensed someone approaching from behind. He turned around to find Frank Eastman standing there, the early morning light illuminating the deep creases that ran like fault lines across his brow. At five-nine and pushing sixty, Eastman didn't seem very formidable, but back in the day he patrolled the roughest neighborhoods of Dorchester, battling gangs and drugs and cracking just enough skulls to survive until retirement. These days, he ran a small PI firm and had recently won a bout with lung cancer.

As they shook hands, the pungent aroma of stale cigarettes wafted into Ray's nostrils and he had to clear his throat to keep from gagging. "Still ignoring doctor's orders, I see."

"Who needs doctors? You watch, I'll outlive them all."

Ray shook his head. There was no arguing with an old-timer like Frank. "You're a piece of work, you know that?"

"So I've been told."

"How'd you make out with the intel?"

Frank handed him a manila envelope. "See for yourself."

Ray fished out a stack of photos. "Still using the darkroom? You know it's the 21st century, right?"

"I got no use for that digital bullshit."

"What's the problem, you hate the convenience? I'll buy you one for Christmas."

"I'll smash it with a hammer as soon as I open it."

"Remind me never to buy you a kitten." He studied the first photo—his neighbor's loser boyfriend, Darren Boyle, standing on the deck of a fishing trawler next to Flaherty's chief enforcer, Bobby Two Times.

Ray sucked in his breath. "Something tells me this kid's more than just an errand boy."

"Take a look at the next one."

Ray pulled out the second photo—Darren and Bobby leading a group of teenage girls off the boat. The girls were dressed in miniskirts and skimpy tops, and the ones baring their shoulders had tattoos visible across their right collarbones.

Ray squinted at the picture. "You get a close-up of those tattoos?"

"What do I look like, an amateur?"

Ray flipped to the next photo and found the close-up. The tattoos were identical: three stars curved around a watching eye. "What's that, a brand?"

"The latest rage in human trafficking. Helps these scumbags keep tabs on the girls." He pointed to the tall brunette in the center. She wore a low-cut shirt emblazoned with a half blue, half yellow flag inscribed with a symbol resembling a dragonfly with its wings laid back.

"How's your knowledge of eastern European flags?" Frank asked.

"A little rusty. I'm gonna need a hint."

"It's Ukrainian."

"That's a hell of a hint, Frank. But there's no way that little fishing boat could make a trip like that."

"Turn to the next picture."

Ray slid another photo out of the envelope. It showed a massive container ship with Russian characters painted above the English translation: *Valkyrie*. "When did this reach port?"

"The log shows that it docked in Southie at five o'clock Thursday night. The picture of Darren was taken an hour later."

"So they rendezvoused in international waters and made a trade for what? Cash, drugs, weapons?"

"Something like that."

Ray gazed into the harbor, where a lone gull wheeled above the sailboats. Then he flipped to the next photo, which showed Darren loading the girls into the back of a white van. In the final image, Darren herded the girls through the tinted glass doors of the Purring Puma—the strip club where Flaherty was rumored to be a silent partner.

Ray slipped the photos back into the envelope and grinned.

Darren was going down.

***

Ray made a few calls before heading down to the Cape for a long weekend. As he and Michelle played with the kids on the beach, braving the shockingly cold New England water, a Coast Guard cutter carrying a team of ATF agents intercepted the Valkyrie on its return voyage to the Ukraine. The agents stormed the ship and seized a cache of weapons hidden behind a false wall in the engine room.

Meanwhile, the FBI raided the Puma, rescuing the girls and taking the owner into custody. Bobby Two Times evaded capture, but Darren Boyle wasn't so lucky. The feds arrived as he sat with Sheila Morrison on her family's stoop in Charlestown. He bolted at the sight of them, but Agent Calhoun chased him down and gave him an old-fashioned beatdown before slapping the cuffs on him.

# THE ART OF DYING

Tommy Morrison called Ray afterward and told him it was the best damn thing he'd ever witnessed. "I can't thank you enough."

"Sorry I missed it," Ray said, watching Jason run down the beach, his Buzz Lightyear kite refusing to take flight. "I wish I could've seen the look on Darren's face when they swarmed him. How's Sheila taking it?"

"She was upset at first. You know, screaming and crying at the cops. But once she heard the charges and saw the guilty look on Darren's face, she marched over there and kicked him right in the tenders." Tommy chuckled. "I think he cried a little."

***

From the moment Ray hung up the phone, it seemed like some cosmic prankster had hit fast-forward on the weekend. Before he knew it, it was Monday morning and he and Billy were sitting center stage at the Purring Puma, where a woman whose best stripping days were a decade behind her strutted around a pole and performed a routine of scissor kicks that resembled a naked rendition of *Sweating to the Oldies*.

At 6:30 a.m., the Puma didn't exactly have what Ray would call its star performers on stage. Despite a steady draw of traffic from the trucker breakfast crowd, the margins paled in comparison to the evening hours when men showed up in droves and drank until closing, raining down cash like confetti.

As the third-rate stripper spanked a dimpled ass cheek and favored them with a seductive wink, Billy flipped her a single and grinned at Ray. Under normal circumstances, it would've been damn near impossible to convince Billy to get an early start, but breakfast at a strip club was right up his alley.

After RJ's tip last week, Ray had reached deep into the department's files on Flaherty's known associates, and although certain documents from a dozen years ago made a few passing references to a stripper named Amber, they neglected to include her last name. Probably because she wasn't considered important enough to warrant further attention.

Trooper Garrison and Agent Calhoun reported similar findings with the State Police and FBI files, but Ray hoped more information would come to light after this weekend's raid of the Puma. According to Calhoun, the FBI seized a trove of electronic and paper records during their search of the premises. Calhoun promised to have one of his agents sift through the older documents for any references to Amber. It was the least he could do since Ray had handed the bureau such a buttoned-up case.

Despite Calhoun's promise, Ray knew the request would take a backseat to the trafficking case, so in the meantime, he figured he'd try his luck with some of Amber's former coworkers.

When the emcee announced the stripper's last dance, urging everyone to reach into his wallet and give it up for Natasha, Ray caught her eye and held up a five. And as Warrant's "Cherry Pie"—that timeless strip club classic—thumped through the speakers, she strutted across the stage, collecting singles as she went.

"Hey, sugar," she said, kneeling down to collect his five. There was no question she was pretty once—or even still—but smoking, drinking, or drugs had aged her face, and not even stripper's makeup could hide the creases around her eyes.

She arched her back and thrust a pair of silicone-enhanced breasts toward his face. "You like that, sugar?"

"I don't know about my friend," Billy interjected, "but *I* like it."

Ray lifted an eyebrow. "Then stop being such a cheap bastard and throw her a five."

Billy shot him a dirty look, but quickly folded a five over the six-inch glass partition that bordered the stage. An old pro, Natasha leaned over the glass and snatched the bill between her breasts.

"Bravo," Billy said, bringing his hands together in a clap.

# THE ART OF DYING

Natasha plucked the bill from between her breasts and tossed it into the crinkled pile of cash behind her.

"You been dancing here long?" Ray asked.

She touched a finger to the tip of his nose and giggled. "About half your life, sugar."

"Do you know a—"

The emcee's voice boomed over the speakers as "Cherry Pie" faded into Van Halen's "Hot for Teacher."

"Alright, alright, put your hands together and welcome Rosita to the main stage."

Natasha smiled. "Gotta go, boys." Then she blew Ray a kiss and pointed to a secluded corner in the back. "Meet me over there if you'd like a private dance."

\*\*\*

Natasha emerged from the dressing room looking like an aging Jessica Rabbit in a hot-pink minidress with matching stilettos. She guided Ray onto a vinyl banquet chair and began her routine, wasting no time as she teased down the neckline until her breasts spilled free. As she shimmied her hips, the dress sank lower until it dropped to the floor in a puddle of neon, leaving her wearing nothing but a lacy pink thong and a gold body necklace.

She wrapped her arms around his neck and danced so close that the exotic scent of her perfume washed over him like stripper potpourri. From the corner of his eye, he could make out the club's bouncer observing them from a distance, making sure Ray kept his hands at his sides.

He spoke to Natasha in a low voice. "I need to ask you some questions."

Natasha smiled and continued swaying her hips, as if she'd already heard every question a man could think to ask. "Alright, sugar. What is it?"

He noticed for the first time how striking her eyes were. Emerald green and luminescent, they erased years from her face, and it was easy to imagine her as a beautiful young girl

91

dreaming of a better future, instead of a middle-aged woman wishing for a better past.

He felt a pang of sadness for her, but quickly shrugged it off. "I'm looking for a stripper who danced here ten or twelve years ago, went by the name Amber."

"Sugar, I've danced with a dozen Ambers in my time. You'll need to be a little more specific."

"She was here eleven years ago for sure, but probably not long after that. She would've been about fifty at the time, had long dark hair. Used to make side money by entertaining Flaherty's crew at The Rock."

Natasha recoiled at the mention of Flaherty. "Are you a cop?"

Ray drew a finger to his lips. "How about we keep that to ourselves? She's not in any trouble, if that's what you're thinking. I just need to ask her some questions."

Natasha glanced in the bouncer's direction. "I don't know…"

"How about a fifty-dollar tip to help your memory?"

"Make it a hundred, sugar, and you've got a deal."

"What do you say we split the difference? But you've got to keep dancing so we don't attract attention."

She winked at him before turning around and bending over, the pink line of her thong dividing her ass cheeks.

"What's her name?" Ray asked.

"Angie."

"She have a last name?"

"It was hard to pronounce. Began with a T and sounded Italian. Around here, she was just Angie T."

"She ever marry?"

"That skanky bitch could never keep a man long enough." Natasha straddled him, her right breast brushing against his cheek.

"Where's she live?"

"She don't live anywhere, sugar."

"What do you mean?"

92

"She's dead."

"From what?"

"Accident, overdose. I don't remember."

"Where'd she live when she was working here?"

"Eastie."

"And after that?"

Natasha shrugged. "I don't know. We weren't exactly close."

"You ever meet her son?"

Natasha chuckled. "I get it, this is about her kid."

"I didn't say that. You remember his name?"

"I can barely remember what he looked like, let alone his name. He was skinny. And awkward. She sometimes brought him backstage when she couldn't find a sitter. But that had to be about fifteen years ago."

"What about the father? She ever say who he was?"

"Sugar, I'd be surprised if she even knew who—"

She broke off, and Ray didn't need to follow her gaze to know that someone had crept up behind him. He hopped off the chair and whirled around, coming face-to-face with Jack Flaherty, whose glacier blue eyes were brimming with rage.

"What the hell are you doing here?" Flaherty barked.

"Just enjoying the company," Ray said, and winked at Natasha.

"Spare me the bullshit, detective."

Natasha fumbled on the floor for her dress.

Flaherty looked her up and down. "You're not going anywhere, sweetheart. Not until we get this sorted out."

Ray looked toward the main stage, where Billy was chatting up a busty blond stripper wearing nothing but pigtails and the bottom half of a Catholic school uniform. He rolled his eyes. So much for his lookout.

"I'm getting tired of bumping into you around town," Flaherty said. "Why are you harassing my girls? Isn't Danvers out of your jurisdiction?"

"*Your* girls?" Ray said. "This place just got raided by the feds and you're too dumb to distance yourself?"

"I've got nothing to hide, detective. You know damn well that I'm an investor in this place. And if you had any sense, you would be too. It's what the Wall Street types call a cash cow with an inelastic demand. A fucking goldmine, in other words."

"Yeah," Ray said. "A cash business is perfect for someone like you. Wouldn't want to leave a paper trail, would you?"

Flaherty shook his head. "What kind of moron doesn't like cash? And what am I supposed to do when the chump who runs this place makes a bad decision and gets busted by the feds? I've got to protect my investment. And the last time I checked, that wasn't a crime."

By now, both Billy and the bouncer had caught wind of what was going down and stood on either side of them, eyeing each other nervously.

"You may think that you own this town," Ray said, "but you're nothing but a thug from the projects. And you may masquerade as the Robin Hood of Southie, but we both know that you're nothing but a sociopath who preys on the weak and the stupid."

Flaherty's face flushed crimson. "You'd better watch yourself."

"Or what, Flaherty? You want to make a specific threat? Go ahead, I'll haul your ass to the station just to ruin your day."

Flaherty thrust a finger at Ray. He was literally shaking with rage and Ray figured it would only take one more jab before Flaherty went mental. He'd heard stories of Flaherty delivering savage beatings to men twice his size and half his age. He was an experienced streetfighter who, even at fifty-one, was as lean and muscular as an Army drill sergeant.

"You listen to me, detective. I'm running this place while Sammy's in jail and you've got no right to barge in here and harass me without a warrant. So you can take that shiny gold badge of yours and shove it straight up your ass."

Ray stepped toward Flaherty. It was a tactic he often employed to assert his authority, since it forced the perp to draw back in an unspoken admission of weakness. But Flaherty refused to budge, and so they stood toe-to-toe, their faces less than an inch apart.

Ray poked a finger into Flaherty's sternum. "You may think you're untouchable, that you're smarter than everyone else, but you best watch your back, Flaherty, because I'm coming for you."

# CHAPTER EIGHTEEN

If Satan ever designed a highway, Ray figured it would look a lot like Route 1. With a glut of businesses lining both sides of the road and each parking lot bleeding into the next, it had virtually no onramps and forced motorists to merge directly into the path of enraged New Englanders speeding toward work, home, or Dunkin' Donuts. And if that wasn't scary enough, the stretch of road that ran through Saugus subjected drivers to several cheesy architectural landmarks, including a seventy-foot cactus, a life-size herd of fiberglass cows, a replica of the leaning tower of Pisa, and a bright orange Tyrannosaurus Rex, just to name a few.

As Ray peeled out of the Puma's parking lot and headed in the direction of the giant cactus, he glanced at Billy. "That went better than I expected."

Billy stared at him without blinking, his forehead creasing enough for his caterpillar brows to wriggle together for a brief reunion. He seemed at a loss for words, which for Billy was a rare thing indeed. "Are you out of your goddamn mind? Why would you mess with Flaherty like that?"

Ray strangled the wheel. "I'm done walking on eggshells around that sonofabitch. He's like a cancer spreading through this city, bringing death to everything he touches. Did you see how smug he was? Acting like he's above it all, when we both know he masterminded the whole sex trafficking operation."

"Of course he did, Ray, but so what? There are certain lines you don't cross."

"Yeah, like what?"

96

"Like making things personal with the head of the Irish mob."

Ray could've said the same for Billy's handling of Giabatti's arrest last year, but he didn't want to get off topic. "Flaherty's dodged conviction for twenty-five years. I think it's time to shake things up."

"You did a hell of a lot more than shake things up."

"Relax, Billy."

"Do you know what you just did? You made yourself a marked man."

"Come on, Billy. Not even Flaherty's crazy enough to target a cop."

"I'm telling you, Ray, you pushed him too far."

Ray stared at the road and fumed. Maybe Billy was right. But what was he supposed to do? Flaherty insulated himself with so many layers he was damn near untouchable, and the injustice of it all infuriated him. He didn't need to see the department's shrink to trace his anger back to the night of his father's murder on that dingy subway platform. Just knowing the punk was still roaming the streets as a free man filled him with rage.

It was almost twenty years ago, but Ray didn't think he'd ever forget a single detail. The punk would be in his mid-forties by now, but Ray felt sure he could pick him out of a lineup. If he closed his eyes, he could still see his greasy dark hair, his angular features, and the circular scar just left of center on his forehead.

Ever since joining the force, Ray had made a habit of talking to informants whenever he could, searching the criminal databases at the start of every week, looking through mugshots of men fitting the punk's profile, but without any luck. So, yeah, when Flaherty claimed to be nothing but a concerned investor, it touched a nerve. He thought about saying as much to Billy, but held his tongue. Some things were better left unsaid.

They rode over the Tobin Bridge, the city skyline looming in the distance like a range of jagged steel peaks. The

Mystic River flowed far beneath them, its murky gray waters glistening in the sun as a crane from a nearby loading dock plucked shiny, new cars from the deck of a container ship.

A short while later, as they approached the precinct, a call came in over the radio with a crackle of static. "We've got a report of a dead body at Stony Brook Reservation. Trail marker 226, near Turtle Pond."

Ray and Billy exchanged a glance. Stony Brook was just around the corner from Coleman's house.

Billy snatched the radio off the dash. "Unit 22. We're on it."

"Copy that, 22. What's your location?"

Billy glanced at the cross street. "Washington and Metropolitan. ETA under five."

Ray flicked on the sirens and accelerated toward Stony Brook, the Explorer's tires squealing as he cut the wheel and turned onto Enneking Parkway. A minute later, he steered onto the shoulder and brought the Explorer to a lurching halt opposite Turtle Pond, parking almost exactly where they'd rendezvoused with RJ days earlier.

"What are the odds?" Billy asked.

"I don't know," Ray said, "but I've got a feeling Coleman figures into this." He reached for the radio. "Unit 22 to Control. We've arrived on scene. Preparing to approach Turtle Pond on foot. Any other units on site?"

"Negative, 22."

"Copy that," Ray said. "I need a unit to check on a nearby residence. Suspect is under investigation for the disappearance of his wife. Last name Coleman," he said, and provided the address.

"10-4. Sending a unit now."

"10-4," Ray said, and climbed out of the truck.

After Billy retrieved a roll of police tape from the glove box, they headed toward the trailhead to secure the scene. They could see glimpses of Turtle Pond through gaps in the foliage, bright arcs of sunlight shimmering on the surface. The banks were reedy and choked with underbrush. The only accessible path to the water was a wooden dock that served as a scenic overlook.

They continued past the pond, traversing the glass-littered shoulder of the parkway, and came upon a steel gate blocking the trailhead. It consisted of two green posts connected by a triangular arm secured with a chrome padlock. Ray and Billy sidestepped the gate and turned onto the path, their eyes sweeping the area for clues. The earth was sodden from a recent rain and their shoes squelched in the virgin mud. Cattails lined the beginning of the path, giving way to scraggily pines as the ground rose toward a wooded ridge.

Billy gestured toward a section of old-growth forest in the distance. "Looks like we've got an audience."

Through the trees, Ray could discern a group of bystanders huddled together on an asphalt walking trail, their necks craned upward as they gawked at something beyond his line of sight.

Fifty feet farther ahead, the dirt path merged onto a paved trail. Ray stepped onto the asphalt and looked up at what dangled from the branch of an oak. "Christ," he said. "It's Finkleton."

Billy ran a hand through his rockabilly hair and exhaled sharply. "What the hell kind of freak show is that?"

Ray flashed his badge at the crowd. "Boston Police. I need everyone back. This is a crime scene."

The crowd begrudgingly dispersed and Billy secured the area, unravelling the spool of police tape and weaving it around more than a dozen trees until he'd created a wide perimeter with Finkleton at the center. When he was finished, he called out to the rubberneckers on the other side of the tape. "Nobody leaves. We'll need statements from all of you. You tell us what you saw, when you saw it, and give us your contact information, and then you can be on your way. Now, which one of you made the 911 call?"

A crunch of leaves drew Ray's attention and he turned to see Trooper Garrison striding up the path ahead of a contingent of crime scene techs. "Wait until you get a load of this," Ray said. "It makes what happened to Danny look normal."

Garrison shook his head. "I don't see how that's possib—" The words died on his lips as he reached the asphalt, his square jaw dropping open in cartoonish surprise.

Ray followed Garrison's gaze to where Finkleton dangled fifteen feet above the trail, turning slowly in the breeze like a slab of meat on a vertical spit. He was suspended by a slender rope connected to a harness that buckled around his torso, keeping him parallel to the ground.

The killer had amputated Finkleton's arms and legs, leaving him with raw, fleshy nubs protruding from his shoulders and pelvis. In their place were eight prosthetic spider legs—big, black, and bristly, like those of a tarantula. Beneath the harness, Finkleton was naked. Dark tufts of hair covered his rotund belly, the skin underneath so pale it was almost translucent.

A sheer white net the size of a beach towel hung near Finkleton's backside, a cluster of plastic eggs affixed to the center. It was hard to tell from this angle, but the four eggs he counted were either smeared with paint or had something inside them. When he craned his neck for a better look, he noticed the crown of a fifth egg protruding from Finkleton's butt cheeks.

Ray exchanged a glance with Garrison. "That's Barry Finkleton. He was reported missing a week ago. Owns an art gallery on Newbury Street."

Garrison removed his trooper's hat and wiped sweat from his brow. "You get all that just by looking at this sideshow?"

"Yeah," Ray said. "I'm that good."

"You and Billy been working it since the beginning?"

Ray nodded. "I'd prefer to keep it that way."

Since Stony Brook was a state park, it fell within Garrison's jurisdiction.

"You can have it," Garrison said. "Saves me the paperwork." He stole another glance at Finkleton. "What do you think this is about, anyway? Pretty elaborate way to kill somebody."

"I don't know," Ray said, although he'd already connected a few threads. "How many units do you have on scene?"

"Three."

"Let's get them on the park exits. I want to make sure no one's lurking around the woods watching us clean up their handiwork."

Garrison brought a radio to his lips, and as he relayed the instructions to his team, Billy walked toward them holding a spent roll of police tape.

"Good thing Finkleton's hanging out of reach," Billy said, "because he's the only part of this crime scene that's not contaminated."

Ray studied the rope securing Finkleton to the tree. "Someone used that limb like a pulley. Looks like the killer threw one end of the rope over, hoisted Finkleton up, and then walked over to the base of the tree and tied it around the trunk."

"Must be a pretty strong guy," Billy said. "Even without arms and legs, Finkleton's got to run a buck-twenty. He'd have to hold the rope with one hand while tying the knot."

"Didn't you ever make a rope swing when you were a kid?" Ray asked.

Billy scowled. "We had what I'd call a shortage of trees in Southie."

"Yeah," Garrison said, "probably to discourage lynchings."

"When I was a kid," Ray said, "I went through a phase where I carried a rope around the neighborhood so that I could climb different trees. I would throw it over a branch, sit in the loop I'd tied at the other end, and hoist myself up. I could even let go of the rope with one hand and just hang there as long as I held both sides in my other hand."

"Power of leverage," Garrison said. "Basic physics."

"What the hell do you know about physics?" Billy asked.

"Apparently more than you." Garrison looked at Ray. "Why's he so grumpy this morning?"

"I talked him into getting an early start."

Billy glared at him. "I didn't even get to finish my coffee before you got us kicked out of there."

"Kicked out of where?" Garrison asked.

"Long story," Ray said.

\*\*\*

The crime scene techs initiated a sweep of the perimeter. Ray flagged down one of the junior techs he'd worked with in the past, a muscular Latino kid with a neatly-trimmed goatee. "Hey, Hector, can I get a ladder over here? I want a closer look at that body before it's pulled down."

"Sure thing, Ray. Let me check the truck."

As Hector headed toward the path, Ray spotted Billy crouched at the edge of the asphalt. "You find something?"

Billy nodded. "Tire tracks."

Ray went over for a look and saw the distinctive imprint of a tire in the mud. The track was a few inches wide and appeared incomplete, as if the tire had only strayed partly off the asphalt.

"Someone drove the body up here," Ray said.

Billy called over Gary Wong, the ranking tech from the Crime Scene Services Section, who had shoulder-length gray hair and a no-nonsense demeanor. "We got a tire track," Billy said. "Let's get some photos and a cast."

Gary peered down at the track and frowned. "It's not enough for a positive ID. I'll have my team search along the path to see if we can find a better impression."

"Alright," Ray said. "See if you can also get a sense for where he rode in from."

When Gary left, Ray took a step back and surveyed the scene. There were at least a dozen investigators inside the cordoned-off perimeter, some snapping pictures of Finkleton, others recording video of the walking trails, and still others combing through the woods for trace evidence, picking up any trash that could be connected to the suspect—cigarette butts, soda cans, candy wrappers—and carefully placing them into paper evidence bags. Outside the perimeter, a trio of Boston Police detectives interviewed witnesses, scribbling notes on department-issued imitation leather pads. The entire scene required meticulous documentation. Ray would need to pull together everyone's notes and assemble a monster of a report. Garrison was right—this case was going to bury him in paper.

Ray rubbed a hand across his stubbly cheek and stared through the screen of trees at the ridge leading down to Turtle Pond. He could hear the distant traffic along Enneking Parkway, the drivers oblivious to the gruesome scene nearby. He stole another glance at Finkleton, whose body spun lazily in the breeze, the loop on his harness allowing for a full revolution.

The killer had chosen a well-travelled path to put Finkleton on display, everything carefully laid out to the smallest of details, like the harness loop ensuring a 360-degree view from the path, showcasing Finkleton like an exhibit. Yet another connection to art.

Ray had a hunch Finkleton wasn't his first victim. Or his last. Most likely, he'd practiced on others until he got it right, and Finkleton just happened to be his first statement piece, the first one worthy of prime time. Either way, his handiwork had all the hallmarks of a serial killer—the brutal and symbolic detail, the flaunting arrogance, the flair for the dramatic.

A shadow appeared beside him and Ray turned to find Tina staring at him with a bemused grin. "Didn't you hear me calling?"

Ray shrugged. "I was thinking."

"I guess the creaking of all those rusty gears must've drowned me out."

Ray arched an eyebrow. He never knew what to expect with Tina—strictly business or schoolgirl flirty. And even after all these years, he wasn't sure if she came by it naturally or if it was just something she did to keep him on his toes.

Ray motioned to Finkleton. "What do you make of this?"

Tina grimaced. "It's horrible. I can hardly look at it. And I work with dead bodies every day. But that?" she said, wrinkling her nose. "It's vulgar."

Ray chewed his lip. "Maybe that's what the killer wanted to convey. Maybe that's how he feels about Finkleton and he wants the whole world to see him that way."

Tina nodded. "It makes sense. At least, as much as a killer's motives can."

Ray followed her gaze and noticed a swarm of flies buzzing around the corpse. One landed on Finkleton's upper lip. Another touched down on his cheek. A few seemed to be stuck in the net at Finkleton's backside, wriggling in vain to break free.

"Those are blow flies," Tina said. "They lay their eggs in any open wound or orifice they can find."

Ray grimaced.

"What's the matter?" Tina said. "Is the big, strong detective afraid of flies?"

"I'm disgusted by them. There's a difference."

"A subtle one. So how should we do this? Just lower the body into the bag?"

"As soon as the crime scene techs are finished documenting this area. Half hour, maybe."

Tina nodded. "Then I guess I'll see you later." Her eyes lingered for a moment longer than was comfortable and he found himself caught in the same hypnotic stare she once reserved for the bedroom.

He turned away and signaled to Billy, but he could still see Tina in his peripheral vision as she ducked beneath the police tape and hiked down the path.

Billy appeared beside him, a crooked grin creasing his lips. "I could watch her walk away for hours."

Ray folded his arms. "That's because you're a dirty old man."

"You know she wants you, right?"

"I'm starting to get that vibe."

"I hear she and her boyfriend just split."

Ray nodded. It was the talk of the locker room.

"Then what the hell are you waiting for?"

"It's not happening, Billy."

"Because of Michelle?"

"Yes, Billy, because of my wife."

"Come on, Ray. You gotta tap that before the moment's gone. Know what I mean?"

"I know Mary kicked your ass to the curb because you couldn't keep it in your pants. Also, she took all your money, but somehow you managed to buy a new Corvette, so go figure."

"A *used* Corvette," Billy said. "I had to dip into my retirement fund, but it was worth it, because that car is a babe magnet."

"I'd love to hear more horrible advice, but we've got a homicide to investigate."

Billy wrinkled his nose and gestured to Finkleton. "Yeah, and he ain't getting any fresher."

Ray flagged down Gary, who had just dispatched a pair of techs to sweep the area below the ridge. Ray pointed to the spider web. "Seems like that net is coated with something sticky. Make sure your guys are careful bagging it up."

"We'll take the customary precautions," Gary said, his shoulders stiffening. "Just like always."

"Look," Ray said, "we've had too many bystanders trekking through here and that net's probably our only shot at discovering trace fibers from the killer. So give me a break if I'm stating the obvious."

"Fine," Gary said. "But if this guy was smart, then coating the net would've been the last thing he did. Which means unless the wind cooperated, we won't have anything."

Billy groaned. "This day's becoming a big pain in my ass."

"Any luck with those tire tracks?" Ray asked.

Gary nodded. "We found a usable print about twenty yards down the path. Perfect depth for a cast. Looks like a truck tire. Shouldn't be hard to identify."

"Good," Ray said. "I'll let you get back to it." He turned to Hector. "Where do we stand with that ladder?"

"I'm waiting on another truck," Hector said. "Should only be a few more minutes."

"Come find me. I want to take the first look."

"You got it," Hector said, and hurried to catch up to Gary.

"Any word on Coleman?" Ray asked, turning to Billy.

"Just that he's not home."

Ray furrowed his brow. "We've never seen that guy leave his house once, and now this happens around the corner and suddenly he's not home?"

"Quite the coincidence, isn't it?" Billy said.

Ray gestured to Finkleton. "You notice that he and Danny both had parts amputated?"

"Yeah," Billy said. "And both went missing before turning up dead."

"But was it the same offense?"

"What do you mean?"

"If Danny's murder was revenge for molestation, you'd think he'd stop there."

"So maybe Finkleton molested him too. I've heard pedophiles have a talent for profiling victims."

"Maybe," Ray said. "But something about this is different. I just can't get my head around it yet."

Billy shrugged. "I'm gonna check on those witnesses, make sure I'm comfortable with their statements before releasing them."

As Billy strode across the perimeter, Ray caught sight of Garrison's imposing figure approaching.

"We know where he rode in from," Garrison said. "Found an open gate at the southeast entrance. Padlock severed with bolt cutters. We've also got a clear footprint beside the gate. Men's size eleven sneaker. Nike. Gary's team is making a cast now."

It wouldn't do much to narrow the field, but sometimes a collection of small clues could crack a case faster than a couple of big ones. "Those gates aren't wide enough for certain trucks," Ray said. "Something bigger than an F-150 might not be able to squeeze through. You find any traces of paint on the gateposts?"

"Not that I could see, but we'll double-check. They're dusting it for prints as we speak. I'm headed back there now."

Ray drew a deep breath and soaked it all in. This was the part of the job he loved. Collecting the evidence. Assembling the story. Building a case.

Hector returned with a ten-foot aluminum stepladder. "Where do you want it?"

Ray pointed to a spot a few feet to the left of Finkleton.

Hector unfolded the ladder and snapped the hinges into the lock position. "It's a little wobbly. Want me to hold it?"

"I'll take my chances."

The sun had risen higher into the sky and a slant of light pierced the canopy, illuminating the right half of Finkleton's body. As Ray climbed the ladder, the nauseating stench of decay assaulted him and he had to turn his head and cough into the crook of his arm.

*Nothing like a corpse baking in the sun.*

He cleared his throat and swatted at the flies buzzing around his face. From somewhere on the path, he could hear Hector chuckling. "Don't go too far," Ray said. "We're gonna need your camera."

Finkleton's hairy stomach was grossly distended and blotched purple where gravity had pooled the blood. He knew from past discussions with Doc Death that the bacteria in Finkleton's body would already be feeding on his intestines and his digestive fluids would begin breaking down his organs, eventually liquefying his insides. After a few days, those liquids would begin leaking from his body, but Ray could see no evidence of that now. Which meant the body was fresh.

Ray's position on the ladder put him at arm's length from Finkleton, and from that vantage point, he had a clear view of a jagged purple wound on Finkleton's throat that evidenced the dark thread of stitches. Finkleton's groin and the stump of his arm contained small wounds consistent with an IV, like the ones found on Danny the Mule.

But unlike Danny, Finkleton's penis hadn't wandered to another part of his body. Instead, it dangled between two of the prosthetic spider legs that were implanted into the stumps of his real legs. Each spider limb measured about four feet long and curved downward at a forty-five-degree angle. They were made from a thick, black wire that was rigid enough to hold its shape against the pull of gravity, and the bristles covering each limb were made from hundreds of black pipe cleaners twisted around the wire. The pipe cleaners resembled the kind his kids used in art projects at school. He'd seen the kids use them to spell out their names, make a Valentine's heart, form the wings of a bat... or even the legs of a spider.

*Is that what Finkleton is to this guy? Some twisted idea of an art project?*

A fly buzzed around Ray's ear and he shooed it away, nearly toppling off the ladder in the process. He seized the top step to steady himself and looked up at the web. The killer had strung white wire along the edges of the net to hold its shape, with the upper half connected to the harness and the lower half connected to two of the spider legs.

The eggs—two yellow and two white—were attached to the net with a fine strand of wire threaded through the shells, and each of the eggs was the size of Ray's fist. They resembled the jumbo plastic variety that many stores carried around Easter time. One of the white eggs had a ragged hole torn into the top and was ringed by a red smear suggestive of blood. Lucky for

Finkleton, the egg protruding from his butt cheeks was smaller, although Ray guessed that was probably a minor consolation.

Something on the harness caught his eye and he craned his neck for a better look. A single word was written on the strap in black magic marker: *Bitsy*.

As in the "Itsy Bitsy Spider."

The killer's idea of a joke?

He descended the ladder and signaled to Hector. "Ready with that camera?"

Hector nodded.

"Make sure you get some close-ups," Ray said. "All the way around."

"You got it."

While Hector recorded voice notes to correspond with each of his photos, Ray spotted Tina walking up the path with Luis. They had donned blue jumpsuits with the word *Coroner* emblazoned in yellow across the back and Luis had a body bag draped over his left arm.

Luis froze in his tracks when he caught sight of Finkleton. "Damn," he said, turning to Tina. "You didn't say anything about all *that*."

"Where's the van?" Ray asked.

"We can't get it through," Tina said. "Crime Scene Services is still collecting evidence. But I need to do my field exam, so I was hoping we could lower the body into the bag and bring the van around once the path is clear."

Ray took a moment to consider it. "Alright, but we've got to let Gary's team cut down the net first." He called Gary over and explained what Tina wanted to do. Gary agreed, and five minutes later the net was bagged up and logged into the growing evidence inventory.

Ray walked over to where the killer had secured the rope to the tree trunk. "How do you want to do this?" he asked Gary. "Did your guys vacuum the rope for fibers yet?"

"Not yet." Gary said. He signaled to Hector. "Bring over the evidence vacuum. We need to prep the body for transport."

Hector brought over something that resembled a plastic toolbox and set it on the ground. He opened the lid, pulled out a hose attachment, and snapped it into the side of the box. He powered up the unit and began vacuuming the rope, starting with the section around the trunk and using the ladder to reach to within three feet of the harness. Then he switched the unit off and gazed down at them. "If you lower the rope slowly, I can get the last section before he's on the ground."

Gary gave Hector a thumbs-up and handed Ray a pair of latex gloves. "Hold the rope against the trunk," Gary said, "and I'll untie the knot. You ready?"

"Ready," Ray said. With the rope wrapped twice around the tree, the leverage allowed him to hold the position when the knot came loose. At Hector's signal, he began lowering the body.

Once Hector finished vacuuming the final section of rope, Luis unzipped the body bag and positioned it beneath Finkleton. With Finkleton hovering three feet above the ground, Gary clipped the spider legs with a pair of wire cutters, then carefully folded the legs in half and slipped them into evidence bags.

"Alright," Gary said, "set him down."

Ray let out a little more rope and Finkleton descended gently into the open body bag. Hector unbuckled Finkleton's harness and transferred it into another evidence bag, along with the coil of rope.

Tina donned a pair of latex gloves and crouched down over Finkleton, feeling around his neck and head. "Early stage rigor mortis." She shifted to his abdomen, poking the blotchy purple area with her fingertip. "Blood's fully clotted, manifested as livor mortis." She reached into her bag for a scalpel and made an incision on the right side of Finkleton's chest. Luis handed her a thermometer. She inserted it into the bloodless opening and took a reading. "Eighty-six degrees." Then she pulled back Finkleton's eyelids, revealing vacant blue eyes coated with a milky pall. "Moderate amount of ocular fluid."

She spent a few moments examining Finkleton's neck. "Recent surgical wound on his throat. Sutures still visible."

"What do you think that's for?" Ray asked.

"I can't be sure until the autopsy." Tina reached into the bag and maneuvered Finkleton's head, exposing the area beneath his chin that was normally hidden by his jowls. "Do you see that bruising?"

Ray nodded. There was a thin line across the top of Finkleton's throat. "Looks like he was strangled."

"The bruising seems consistent with rope," Tina said. "Maybe the same rope we just pulled down from the tree."

"So why bother with the harness?" Luis asked. "Why not skip a step and hang him by the neck?"

"Maybe that didn't fit the scene the killer wanted to portray," Ray said. "To him, Finkleton was a spider, and spiders don't kill themselves with their own webs."

"Yeah," Billy said, striding toward them from across the path. "You don't see a lot of spider suicides on the books these days."

Tina rolled her eyes. Back when she and Ray were dating, she referred to Billy as *"that misogynist pig you ride along with."* Ray had never come to his defense since she wasn't exactly wrong.

"What's your best guess for time of death?" Ray asked.

Tina glanced skyward, as if crunching some mental math. "Six to eight hours ago. Rough estimate."

"You think he was dead before the killer strung him up?"

"If he was," Tina said, "it wasn't for long. The purple blotching on his stomach wouldn't be concentrated in a single spot if he'd died in another position and then got moved later."

Ray imagined the killer staging the scene, taunting Finkleton about his fate before wrapping the slack length of rope around his neck and squeezing the life out of him.

"Should I zip him?" Luis asked.

"I'm good," Ray said.

Tina nodded and Luis sealed the bag.

Gary spoke to someone over the radio, then turned to Luis and pointed southwest. "My team has finished sweeping the path over there. You can drive the van through and load the body, but everywhere else is off limits."

"Got it," Luis said, then started off down the path at his typical unhurried pace.

Ray touched Tina's shoulder. "Call me when you've scheduled the autopsy. I want to be there."

"Me too," Billy said.

Tina smiled politely. "The more the merrier."

"Alright," Ray said, glancing at Billy, "let's get back to work."

Billy winked at Tina before turning away.

"You know she hates you," Ray said when they were out of earshot. "Pretty much on every level."

"That's why I like messing with her."

"You do realize you give off a creepy vibe around attractive women?"

"I like to think it's part of my charm."

Ray brayed laughter. "You keep on thinking that."

They crossed over to the opposite end of the crime scene, where a uniformed officer was questioning the last pair of witnesses.

"Anything interesting come out of the interviews?" Ray asked.

"Not really," Billy said.

"Who was first on the scene?"

Billy flipped open his pocket pad and scanned the pages. "Harry Deerfield. Seventy years old. Out walking his dog. He's the one who put in the 911 call."

"What time was that?"

"Seven thirty-six. About ten minutes before we arrived."

"Did he say anything about the other witnesses?"

"He knows most of them, either from his neighborhood or from passing them on the trails every morning. Said most people had a daily routine."

"You notice anything unusual about anyone? Dirty clothes? Bloodstains? Something sticky on their hands?"

Billy shook his head. "I didn't see anything suspicious. But we did get prints of their shoes. Gary's team is crosschecking them against the footprint Garrison found by the gate."

Even if they discovered a match, it wouldn't mean much. The witnesses had to enter the park somewhere. So, unless the investigation discovered blood, latent prints, skin cells, or hair samples, they pretty much had nothing but circumstantial evidence. And maybe enough information to build a psychological profile.

Ray and Billy ducked beneath the police tape and surveyed the scene from a distance, their eyes registering the whole operation. It was a habit Billy had ingrained in him when they first paired up, back before Billy had one foot out the door. Usually, the more holistic perspective helped Ray glean some new nugget of information, but this time nothing jumped out at him. "You get anything?" he asked.

Billy shook his head. "Let's check in with Garrison."

The words had barely left Billy's lips when Ray detected a blur of movement in the trees. "Hey!" he shouted, charging after a dark-haired man wearing jeans and a T-shirt.

Dead leaves littered the ground, everything slick from the earlier rain. Ray drew his gun and skidded down the slope, grabbing the trunk of a stunted pine to keep his footing.

The man scrambled behind a boulder covered with scrub brush.

"Stop! Police!"

The man halted with his back to them.

Ray raised his gun. "On the ground with your hands out!"

As the man sank to his knees and laid down on his stomach, Ray moved in and fished the cuffs off his belt. "Bring your hands together behind your back." When the man obliged, Ray slapped the cuffs on him and used his foot to turn him over.

"Coleman!" Billy exclaimed.

"This isn't what it looks like," Coleman said. "I can explain."

Ray grabbed Coleman beneath the arms and yanked him to his feet. "You'd better have some answers."

Billy holstered his gun. "I can't wait to hear this."

"What are you doing here?" Ray demanded.

Coleman let out a sigh, his shoulders sagging. "I heard the sirens so I came to see what was happening. When I saw the cruisers heading for Stony Brook, I thought that…"

"That what?" Billy asked. "That we found where you stashed your wife's body?"

"No," Coleman said, a defiant tone creeping into his voice. "Where someone else did." His eyes welled up. "Suzie is either hurt or dead, taken by some sick lunatic who framed me. And you know what? I don't care anymore if no one believes me. I know the truth."

"What is the truth?" Ray asked. "Aren't you tired of keeping it locked up inside?"

Coleman ignored the question. "Did you find Suzie? I couldn't get close enough to see."

"Look," Ray said, gesturing to Billy. "We've both been married. We get it. I bet she pissed you off, right? Probably nagged you to the point where you just snapped? Only now you can barely remember it. But you're sorry. And scared. Am I right?"

Coleman shook his head. "I didn't do it. I swear to you. I loved her."

"Is that why you banged some other broad on a business trip?" Billy asked.

"That was the biggest mistake of my life. I'd do anything to take it back."

"Why were you sneaking around a crime scene?" Ray asked.

"I never crossed the yellow tape. I didn't do anything wrong."

"Except for running from a police officer," Billy said.

Coleman shook his head. "It sounds bad, okay? I get it. But I had to see if you found Suzie. And since I'm still a suspect, I thought it was best if no one saw me."

Billy cocked a thumb at Coleman. "This guy's full of great decisions."

"Please," Coleman said. "Just tell me. Is it her? Is it Suzie?"

"What's next," Billy asked. "You carrying a weapon too? Maybe a book on getting away with murder?"

Coleman kept quiet—probably his best decision of the day—and Ray stared at him, trying to get a reading on his bullshit meter. "You're under arrest," Ray said. "And because my partner is a lazy sonofabitch, I'm gonna read you your rights."

# CHAPTER NINETEEN

It was after midnight when Ray staggered through the front door, a dull pain throbbing behind his eyes. He wanted nothing more than to tiptoe into the bedroom, slip beneath the covers, and pass out until morning.

But Sparky had other plans.

The hyperactive Boston Terrier raced downstairs, claws scrabbling against the hardwood, and leaped around Ray's ankles while letting out a series of whining barks.

Ray lost his balance and staggered against the wall, trying to avoid stepping on the stupid mutt. "Come on, Sparky, zip it." He crouched down to give the dog a few seconds of attention, but it only succeeded in ratcheting up Sparky's intensity level.

Michelle had left the kitchen light on for him, and after kicking off his shoes and distracting Sparky with a bowl of food, he switched off the light and trudged upstairs, trying to purge his mind of what amounted to the worst Monday in recent memory.

He'd spent hours debriefing with other investigators, comparing notes and assembling it all into a coherent report on Finkleton's murder. It would be days before the crime lab processed all the evidence, but Gary had shared what was available so far.

The fingerprint analysis identified forty-eight sets of prints on the gatepost nearest to the crime scene, which wasn't a surprise considering the number of people who frequented the walking trails. The more interesting analysis involved determining how many of those prints belonged to people with

116

criminal records, especially those with a history of violence. Gary promised to have those results by the following afternoon, but since neither the eggs nor the padlock contained any latent prints, Ray doubted the killer's prints were among the forty-eight. More than likely, the killer had worn gloves.

The most promising revelation had come from what they found inside the eggs—four slips of standard computer paper, each inscribed with a single name in boldface Helvetica 18-point font. Names that belonged to artists Finkleton had discovered.

He and Billy planned to meet with the artists in the morning, find out what their stories were, rattle their cages a bit to see how they reacted. Billy, for one, loved rattling cages. It was kind of his thing. Which was another reason why Tina hated him.

The thought of Tina conjured up an old memory of her slipping out of a cocktail dress and climbing into bed on all fours, telling him that he wouldn't be getting any sleep that night.

He shrugged away the memory as he padded down the hall, knowing nothing good would ever come of it. When he reached Allie's room, he leaned over her bed and listened to the easy rhythm of her breathing. Thankfully, no giant eyeballs plagued her dreams tonight. He drew the covers around her shoulders and kissed her forehead before creeping into the hall to peer into the boys' room.

Jason was sprawled across the top bunk at a forty-five-degree angle to the bed like a drunken frat boy, his mouth agape, one arm draped across his forehead. Petey's toddler bed was empty, and when Ray went downstairs to the master bedroom, he spotted the chubby animal snuggled against Michelle.

He squeezed in next to them and Michelle blinked at him sleepily.

"Rough night?" she whispered.

"Rough entire day."

"Can you take Petey back to his room? He keeps flopping around like Linda Blair in *The Exorcist*."

Ray scooped Petey into his arms and stood up. "What do you say we flop around together when I get back?"

Michelle rolled over and groaned. "Aren't you tired?" she asked, drawing the blankets around herself.

"What are you doing, building a wall?"

"Yes, and in case you can't read the sign, it says, *No Trespassing*."

"Are you sure it doesn't say, *Come inside, we're open*?"

Michelle threw a pillow at him. "It definitely does not say that."

"I'm pretty sure it does." He headed out with Petey dangling from his arms like wet spaghetti.

"Maybe you should visit the bathroom," Michelle said after he returned. "I hear they're serving up lotion for one."

Ray collapsed onto the bed and groaned. "Very funny."

"Sorry, babe. I'll get you next time."

A moment later, she was asleep.

***

Finkleton's death dominated the morning news. And while most networks glossed over the gruesome details, one channel with a reputation for sensationalism aired a cell phone video of Finkleton dangling from the tree.

"I can't believe they're showing that," Michelle said. "And what kind of sicko does something like that, anyway?"

"I'll let you know once I find him."

Michelle shuddered. "I hate knowing a monster like that is out there. It makes me want to vomit."

Ray wrapped his arms around her waist and kissed the crown of her head, where her hair was still wild from sleep. She snatched the remote from his hand and clicked off the TV. "I think that's enough bad news for one morning."

"Wait until you see that I used the last of the creamer."

Michelle slapped his arm. "You'd better be joking." When Ray nodded, she poked a finger into his sternum. "Don't mess with me in the morning. And aren't you going to be late for work?"

Ray grabbed his keys from the coffee table. "Probably, but I like giving Spinonni something to bitch about."

***

"Alright, listen up," Spinonni said, scowling at the officers gathered for roll call. "The warrant came through on the Finkleton case. Detectives Hanley and Devlin, I want you to turn Coleman's house upside down, search every goddamn nook and cranny. And don't come back until you find some real evidence, something that might actually stick in a court of law."

Spinonni paused for effect and directed a menacing glare at Ray. "I've been told the State Police will provide assistance on this case, so I don't want to hear anything about you two getting into any pissing matches. Understood?"

"Got it," Ray said. "No pissing on state cops."

"Too bad," Billy said. "I hear they're into that."

Spinonni exhaled sharply and glanced at his notepad. "Next up, we've got another missing persons case. Subject is Greg Cassidy, a twenty-eight-year-old construction worker. Detectives Duncan and Greene, come see me afterward for the file."

When the briefing ended, Ray and Billy trudged into the breakroom for a second dose of coffee. "We've got a lot of ground to cover today," Ray said. "I think we should divide and conquer."

"Good idea," Billy said. "There's a few more strip clubs I'd like to investigate."

"I'm sure there are," Ray said, "but I was thinking one of us could pair up with Garrison on the Coleman warrant, while the other works the Finkleton investigation."

"Fine," Billy said, "but I get first pick."

"How do you figure?"

"Because I'm the one who had to tell Finkleton's wife that we found him dangling from a tree like a dead spider."

"How'd that go?"

119

"She threw up all over my best sports coat."

"I've seen your best sports coat—she did you a favor."

"I'm taking Coleman."

"Fine," Ray said. "We'll meet afterward for lunch. My pick."

\*\*\*

The reception desk at the Finkleton Gallery of Art resembled molten glass oozing toward the floor in a swirl of reds, blues, and yellows. A middle-aged woman wearing a navy pantsuit with a pair of tortoiseshell reading glasses perched atop her head stood behind it. "Welcome to the Finkleton Gallery," she said with an easy smile.

Ray nodded a greeting and flashed his badge. "I'm Detective Hanley with the Boston Police. I'd like to ask you a few questions."

The woman brushed a lock of silvery hair behind one ear and stepped out from behind the desk. "Is this about Barry?"

Ray nodded. "I'm afraid it's not good news."

The woman's eyes misted over. "Barry's wife told me last night. I'm still in shock. I don't understand how someone could do that to another human being."

"We may never make sense of it," Ray said. "But you can help me figure out who's responsible."

The woman retrieved a tissue from the desk and dabbed her eyes. "You're not the same officer who was here when Barry first went missing."

"That was Detective Ridley."

"Then why do you look so familiar to me?"

"I think you know my brother," Ray said. "He does some accounting work for you guys."

Her face brightened. "You look just like him. He's such a nice man, and smart as a whip."

"Thanks," Ray said. "And I'm sorry, but I didn't catch your name."

"Veronica Daniels."

Ray scanned the gallery, his eyes sweeping past a trio of bronze sculptures and a maze of interior walls covered in artwork. "Is anyone else working here, Ms. Daniels?"

"Just Keiko. She's in the back preparing for our next exhibit. And, please, call me Veronica."

"I'm surprised you're open, given the circumstances."

"Barry's wife insisted. She said Barry would've wanted it that way."

"How long have you worked here?"

Veronica tapped a manicured nail against her lips and thought for a moment. "My goodness, could it be fifteen years?"

"And what's your role?"

"I manage the day-to-day operations, interact with customers, and advertise new exhibits—you know, help bring people in the door."

Ray glanced around. He didn't see a single customer. "It seems quiet now."

"We don't get a lot of traffic. A few people wander in every now and then, but most just breeze through without buying."

Ray nodded, his eyes settling on a painting of a sailboat moored beside a rustic boathouse, the weathered siding festooned with colorful buoys. "Thirty-five hundred dollars? No wonder you don't get a lot of traffic."

"It's not a volume business," Veronica said. "We target high net worth customers with an appreciation for fine art. When a piece strikes a chord with the right customer, you'd be amazed at how much they'll spend to possess it. And really, the only time this place is crowded is when we launch a new exhibit."

"How often is that?"

"Four times a year. We invite the area's largest collectors to a private viewing where they can drink expensive wine and mingle with the artists. On those occasions, this place is jam-packed with wealthy people itching to part with their money."

"I'm sure the booze helps with that."

"I'd be lying if I said it didn't."

"How often do you interact with the artists?"

"I'm their main point of contact once they've signed with the gallery."

"So what's that? Daily, weekly?"

"I generally touch base with each of our artists once a week."

"And do any of them strike you as strange?"

Veronica surprised him by laughing. "They're all a little strange, detective."

"I'm sure they are. But have you ever gotten the sense that one of them might hold a grudge against Finkleton?"

"Not that I'm aware of."

"Are you sure about that, Veronica? Because I heard Finkleton tended to rub people the wrong way. I find it hard to believe someone like that didn't have enemies. Or at the very least, a dissatisfied customer, a jaded artist, or maybe a jealous business rival."

Veronica's back stiffened. "I know everyone Barry dealt with in this business, and I just don't believe that any of them would kill him."

"But someone did, Veronica. Someone killed him in a very horrific way. And trust me when I tell you that I've seen the smallest of slights drive a disturbed person to murder. So I need you to be very honest with me."

Veronica exhaled sharply. "This is very difficult," she said, dabbing her eyes with a tissue. "Barry was a good man, but he wasn't an easy person to like. He tended to—as you say—rub people the wrong way."

"You mind elaborating on that?"

Veronica frowned. "It feels wrong to speak ill of the dead, but if it helps the case, then I suppose Barry could sometimes come across as condescending and dismissive. Also, he was a bit of a know-it-all."

Ray nodded. He'd heard something very similar from Jacob. "Do you recognize any of the names on this list?" he asked, handing her a slip of paper.

Veronica slid her glasses into position and held the paper at arm's length. "These are artists we've worked with extensively. In fact, Barry helped launch their careers. They're not suspects, are they?"

"We found the names with Barry at the scene of the crime."

"How do you mean?"

"I'm sorry, but I can't divulge those details. What can you tell me about the first name on the list?"

"Ryan Masters? He's been with us for five years. That's his painting you were admiring, the one with the sailboat. He's done very well for himself recently."

"And what type of guy is he?" It was a broad question, but that was by design.

"I'd say he's friendly, bright, introspective. Maybe a little on the shy side. Young man, about your age. Very clean cut."

"And what about Nathan Devoux?"

"Nathan's a sweet old man who looks like Wilfred Brimley from those Quaker Oatmeal commercials. He began painting after retiring from a long career as an engineer."

"And Dean Saunders?"

"He owns a tattoo parlor in Gloucester, does sculptures on the side. Those bronze pieces over there are his."

"How old would you say he is?"

Veronica pursed her lips. "Forty, maybe. It's hard to tell. He always wears sunglasses, even inside. He's kind of scary looking, has a bushy beard and is covered in tattoos, but he's actually a sweetheart."

"Did he and Barry get along?"

Veronica chuckled. "I think Barry was intimidated by Dean. I've never seen Barry treat anyone with more kindness or respect, and that includes his wife."

"And what about Don Martinez?"

"Don is young, ambitious, and very serious about art. He and Barry had a bit of a falling out."

Ray arched an eyebrow. "How so?"

"Don felt Barry was taking advantage of him. Charging too much commission, to be exact."

"And was he?"

"Barry charged higher rates than most, but he also had a reputation for discovering new artists and helping them break through. A lot of collectors flock to the Finkleton Gallery for that very reason and Barry felt it justified the premium."

"And what do you think?"

"From what I understand, Don had a difficult childhood. He had an unhealthy exposure to people who took advantage of others, so it was hard for him to accept that staying with Barry was in his best interest."

"He's not under contract anymore?"

"No. One afternoon he showed up with a truck and removed his artwork from the gallery. Barry could have sued him for breach of contract, but he allowed him to drive away."

"Did you see the truck?"

Veronica nodded. "He double-parked on Newbury Street."

"Do you remember the make and model?"

"A silver pickup. Maybe a Ford or a Chevy, I'm not sure."

"How did Barry react when Don started yanking his art off the walls?"

"He told Don that he was making a huge mistake, that if Don walked out the door, there'd be no coming back."

"And what did Don say?"

"He gave Barry the middle finger and stormed out without another word."

"Did Barry ever see him again?"

"Not that I'm aware of."

Ray chewed his lip. "Did Barry ever work with any female artists?"

"A few, yes. But none on display at the moment."

"Is there any chance he led a double life, like maybe having a relationship with one of his artists?"

"Are you asking if Barry was gay?"

"Was he?"

"That's a rather narrow-minded stereotype, don't you think?"

"I'm just trying to cover every angle."

"Trust me, Barry was straight. He had a habit of ogling women. He thought he was being inconspicuous, but in reality, he was so obvious it was almost comical."

"Yeah?" Ray said. "How's that?" It was meant to sound conversational, but the question was deliberate. Her ability to answer increasingly specific questions told him a lot about whether she was telling the truth. When people lied, they typically provided simple answers and appeared uncomfortable when pressed for more detail.

"One of his techniques was to hold up his phone and pretend to read, except that his eyes would be focused beyond the screen at whatever woman happened to be wearing a low-cut blouse. His other tactic was to scan the room as if looking for something, except that his eyes would freeze on a pretty woman for a few seconds before completing the sweep."

"Classic moves."

"Right?" Veronica said, wiping tears from her eyes. "Barry wasn't perfect, but I'll miss him. He had such a keen eye for art."

A twentysomething Asian woman emerged from the back room and studied Ray curiously. Veronica motioned her over. "Keiko, this is Detective Hanley. I was just telling him about some of our artists. He's interested in anything we can tell him that would help the investigation."

"I wish I could help," Keiko said, "but I honestly can't imagine any of our artists harming Mr. Finkleton."

"What about Don Martinez?" Ray asked.

Keiko shook her head. "He and Mr. Finkleton didn't see eye to eye, but Don is a good person. There's no way he could've done it."

"What makes you so sure?"

Keiko shrugged. "I've always been good at reading people."

"How about the artists Finkleton refused to exhibit?"

"Artists do wander in here from time to time wearing their hearts on their sleeves. But Barry didn't like giving them false hopes. If he thought their work was terrible, he'd say so."

"Any chance you kept records of the artists Finkleton rejected?"

Veronica shook her head. "Once Barry dismissed someone, that was it."

"Can you think of a time when someone got angry about being dismissed?"

Veronica pursed her lips. "We did have a walk-in about a year ago who took Barry's criticism very hard. It sticks in my mind because I got a very unsettling feeling about him."

"What happened?"

"Barry thumbed through the artist's portfolio and stopped on a certain painting. He said something sarcastic like, 'What's this supposed to be? Dante meets Dali?' The artist started to respond, but Barry held up a hand and said he'd seen enough. 'That's not art, that's a nightmare,' he said. The artist got defensive and began pulling out other pictures, but Barry told him not to waste his time. On his way out, the artist gave Barry the most hateful stare I've ever seen. I never saw him again."

"Did the artist make any threats?"

"Not verbally, but he pointed at Barry in a way that seemed threatening."

"What did he look like?"

"He was white, I remember that. I guess medium build with brown hair, or maybe dirty blond? It's been so long, I don't know if I can trust my memory."

"Can you describe the painting Barry mocked?"

Veronica nodded. "It was a baby crawling through a field of bleeding clocks."

Ray arched an eyebrow. "That seems unusual."

Keiko's eyes lit up. "I saw that painting just the other day!"

"Where?" Ray asked.

"In Cambridge. Hanging in a coffee shop."

# CHAPTER TWENTY

"Seriously?" Garrison said. "This place?"

Billy shrugged. "It was Ray's idea."

Ray watched them approach from where he sat at an outdoor table at Finnegan's Landing, where he'd been waiting for twenty minutes. It didn't feel right to call it a patio, since the weathered resin furniture was arranged in the parking lot adjacent to the restaurant, offering an unobstructed view of West Broadway, where traffic was snarled from the stoplight opposite the Red Line subway station.

"Thanks for being so punctual," Ray said.

"Are we seriously going to eat here?" Garrison asked.

"What's not to like?" Ray said. "I hear they've got the best corned beef in the city."

Billy cocked a thumb at the windowless brick building across the street. "You telling me your choice for lunch has nothing to do with keeping an eye on The Rock?"

Ray peeled a menu off the table. "That's just a happy coincidence."

"I call bullshit," Billy said.

Ray smirked at Billy and Garrison as they settled into their seats. "What happened with the search of Coleman's place?"

"We came up empty," Garrison said. "The only thing Coleman was up to was his eyeballs in filth. I mean, that place was disgusting."

"Yeah," Billy said, "except Spinonni refused to believe there wasn't anything incriminating. He and Sergeant Callahan drove out to see for themselves."

128

"I'm guessing the outcome wasn't any different?"

"Of course not," Billy said. "You think those two added any value? Talk about a pain in my ass."

"You think Coleman was telling the truth?" Ray asked. "About Finkleton at least?"

"Maybe," Billy said. "Unless some of the DNA we collected from his house winds up belonging to Finkleton, but I doubt it."

A middle-aged waiter with greasy, black hair and angular features emerged onto the sidewalk carrying a tray of drinks for a group of construction workers. After making the delivery, he turned to Ray's table and did a double take.

"Ready to order?" he asked, fidgeting with his pen and notepad. His eyes passed over Garrison and a ghost of a sneer appeared beneath his features before morphing into something more benign.

After the waiter disappeared inside, Ray turned to Garrison. "You see him give you the once-over?"

"Must be the trooper hat," Billy said.

"Yeah," Garrison said, "because there aren't any cop-hating racists in Southie."

"Course not," Ray said. "Not in this—"

The #9 bus roared past them on Broadway, drowning out his words as it barreled through the intersection to beat a red light.

*Just another angry Boston driver*, Ray thought.

When he turned back to the table, he noticed Jack Flaherty and one of his lieutenants striding toward them. When Flaherty reached them, he loomed over Ray's chair and glared down at him with glacier-blue eyes. "If I didn't know any better, detective, I'd swear you were stalking me. What's next, you want to taste my shit to see what I ate for breakfast?"

The burly man standing beside Flaherty howled with laughter. "Good one," he said, fingering a jagged white scar on his cheek.

Ray lifted an eyebrow. "If I wanted to know what you ate for breakfast, I'd just ask your mom. She and I are real tight."

Billy kicked him under the table but Ray ignored the warning. "What are you and Mad Murph up to today? Shaking down local businesses? Finding some new kids to hook on heroin?"

Flaherty pulled out a chair and sat down. He propped his elbows on the table and leaned forward. "Let me tell you a story, detective. When I was growing up in the Old Colony projects, we had this dog that used to lurk around the neighborhood. Mean-looking mutt, part Lab, part Rottie. Every once in a while some knucklehead tossed it a ham bone, and it always dragged it to the same place on the cement path near East 8th.

"You remember that dog, Billy? You must've seen it. I remember you trudging down that path as a kid, your face all swollen from where your old man liked to clock you for no good reason."

Billy clenched his jaw and nodded.

"Anyway," Flaherty said, "this dog didn't like people getting too close, but it was always gnawing a bone on the path. You'd come around the bend, minding your own business, and that dog would be right in your face, snarling like a wolf. I always gave it a wide berth, but that sonofabitch would still bark at me with its head raised high, staring me down like it was itching for a fight. One day, I came around the bend listening to a Walkman I'd lifted from some Back Bay prepster and I nearly stumbled over the damn thing. It lunged at me, jaws snapping, and I lost my balance and fell onto the path. There I was, sitting on the ground, that dog barking right in my face, so close I could smell the stink of its breath. I reached for the Walkman and smashed it against the dog's nose. It yelped in surprise and snapped at me, its teeth grabbing hold of my shirtsleeve. I yanked my arm back and the fabric tore free, leaving the dog with a tattered shred of hand-me-down flannel in its jaws.

"For a moment, it seemed unsure whether to attack or retreat, so I jumped on top of it and started wringing its neck. It twitched its legs and flailed around, suddenly looking like a sad little puppy instead of the mean mongrel that wanted to kill me just seconds before. I could've let go—I don't think it would've bothered me again. But it had threatened me. And underestimated me. Two sins I find unforgivable. So I kept on squeezing until that sonofabitch was nothing but a dead dog in the road."

Ray folded his arms and stared across the table as another bus roared down Broadway. "Well, that was a heartwarming story. You should consider writing children's books."

"You're missing the point, detective."

"Which is?"

"You're beginning to remind me a lot of that dog."

Ray lifted an eyebrow. "Is that supposed to be a threat?"

"You could arrest me for making a specific threat, couldn't you, detective? Why don't you just consider it a nice lunchtime story?"

"If we're doing story time," Ray said, "then you'll love this one. It's called, *A Beginner's Guide to Surviving Prison Rape*. I think it'll come in handy for where you're going."

A silver Infinity SUV lurched to a halt outside the restaurant. A dark-haired passenger in aviator sunglasses leaned out the window and sneered before leveling an AR-15 in their direction.

"Look out!" Garrison yelled.

Ray dove off the chair and took cover under the table, pressing his stomach against the ground as a staccato of gunfire rang in his ears and bullet casings jangled to the sidewalk like quarters spewing from a slot machine.

From the corner of his eye, Ray could see Mad Murph sprawled on his back in a pool of blood, his face blown half to bits. Billy lay to his right, flattened against the ground behind a barrier of railroad ties that separated the patio from the parking lot. Garrison was curled into a fetal position beneath the table, clutching his stomach and gritting his teeth. Flaherty crouched behind the trooper's hulking form, his head tucked between his forearms.

As the bullets continued to fly, a series of screams rang out from the table behind them and Ray caught a glimpse of a construction worker sprawled on the ground, the clover treads of his work boot stained a glistening crimson.

When the gunfire ceased, leaving a phantom echo ringing in Ray's ears, the Infinity peeled away down Broadway trailing an acrid plume of burnt rubber in its wake.

Ray scrambled to his feet and charged into the road, drawing his Glock and returning fire. One of his shots blew out the rear window, glass shattering in all directions. Another shot hit the rear passenger tire and sent the car fishtailing across the intersection, causing it to crash head-on into a concrete utility pole.

"Got you," Ray muttered.

The passenger door swung open and Vito the Cucumber staggered out, one side of his face coated in a mask of blood. Vito spun toward Ray with the AR-15 and opened fire.

Ray flung himself over the hood of a Jeep Wrangler parked on the street. He crouched behind an oversized tire as a barrage of bullets plunked into the chassis and safety glass rained down around him like glittering jewels. He waited for the dry click of the empty chamber before peering around the front bumper.

Vito pitched the assault rifle into the street and reached frantically to his waist for a handgun. He'd earned his nickname for being cool under pressure, but he certainly wasn't acting it now.

"Drop it!" Ray yelled, taking aim over the Jeep's hood as a warble of sirens rose in the distance.

Vito's fingers curled around the grip of his gun—he'd come too far to give up now—and Ray pulled the trigger without hesitation, hitting center mass. Vito's knees buckled and he collapsed to the pavement. The gun tumbled from his hand and skidded into the gutter.

Ray eyed the Infinity before venturing into the street. The concrete utility pole was buried two feet into its front end and steam billowed up from a busted radiator, partially obscuring the silhouette of a man slumped in the driver's seat.

Ray crept toward Vito, both hands on his Glock. But Vito was too far gone to make a move. "Did I get him?" Vito asked, a rivulet of blood running from the corner of his mouth. "Did I kill that mick bastard?"

Ray pointed his gun between Vito's eyes. "You shot a cop. You don't deserve to know."

Vito coughed violently, grimacing as he spat up blood. "He killed my brother."

Ray flashed back to Jimmy the Weasel's funeral. He'd seen Vito standing in the circle of mourners beside Jimmy's widow, his grief masked behind his aviator glasses. That's how it was with these guys. Violence begetting violence.

"Please," Vito said. "I gotta know."

A shot rang out in the street and Ray whirled around to see a man in a bloody dress shirt slump to the ground, a gun sliding out of his hand.

Billy holstered his Glock and crossed the street. "What the hell's wrong with you? You didn't think to check on the driver?"

Ray's legs went rubbery. "I was saving him for you."

"You're not even wearing a vest, are you?"

Ray shrugged. It was too goddamned hot on a day like this.

"You'd better smarten up," Billy said, thrusting a finger at him. "You keep charging into situations like that and you're gonna wind up dead. And who do you think they're gonna ask to notify Michelle that you're never coming home? I'd rather shoot myself than make that trip, so try using a little caution."

Ray holstered his Glock. "How's Garrison?"

"A whole lot smarter than you. He actually wears his vest."

"He's alright?"

"Might've cracked a rib, but yeah, he's okay."

"What about Flaherty?"

Billy frowned. "That sonofabitch has nine fucking lives."

*** 

A dozen units converged onto the scene, police flashers reflecting off the surrounding windows in stroboscopic bursts of red and blue. Paramedics charged toward Finnegan's Landing and triaged the victims, loading them into ambulances and speeding off toward the hospital with sirens wailing.

Finnegan's patio resembled a slaughterhouse floor. Blood glistened in every corner. Trails of scarlet footprints stained the sidewalk in all directions.

What was it Giabatti had said at Jimmy's funeral?

*I've got a feeling this is gonna be one hell of a bloody summer.*

Question was, had Giabatti ordered the hit, or was Vito acting on his own?

Ray stood with his hands on his hips and surveyed the scene. Broadway was closed to traffic in both directions, a pair of squad cars angled in a V at either end of the street. Uniformed officers rerouted motorists down A Street and Dot Ave, and judging by the distant blaring of horns, Ray imagined cars were backed up all the way to L Street, no doubt cursing their bad luck.

The Crime Scene Services team was already on site, snapping pictures of Finnegan's patio from all angles and bagging up bullet casings and debris from the gutter. Billy stood outside of the Dunkin' Donuts a few doors down talking to Sergeant Callahan. Judging from all the pointing and gesturing, Ray figured Billy was giving his report of the shooting. Unlike Lieutenant Spinonni, the sergeant was a real cops' cop. He trusted his men and managed by exception. And since Ray and

Billy were both seasoned detectives, Callahan didn't spend much time overseeing their work. Which was perfectly fine by Ray.

Callahan caught Ray looking and motioned him over. The sergeant had a slight build and a kind face, and although his thinning hair was still sandy blond, the deep lines at the corners of his eyes hinted at a more advanced age. Callahan shook Ray's hand, holding it for a moment longer than was comfortable, as was often his way. "Billy tells me you were quite the hero this afternoon. A little too brazen, maybe, but a hero nonetheless."

"I wouldn't be standing here if it wasn't for Billy."

Callahan nodded. "That's the kind of teamwork I like to see. I've gotta warn you though, the lieutenant is concerned about the fallout from all of this."

"What fallout?" Billy asked.

"The mayor held a press conference this afternoon about the escalating violence in the city. He spoke about partnering with the police chief and the FBI to implement new strategies to crack down on the mob." Callahan gestured to the scene behind them. "Unfortunately, all of this went down during the mayor's speech and he was completely in the dark. But the reporters sitting in the audience got alerts on their phones and blindsided him during Q&A, making him look like a fool."

Ray frowned. "So now the blame game starts."

"You got it," Callahan said. "The mayor blames the chief, the chief blames the captain, and so on down the line." He pointed to Ray and Billy. "But most importantly, we don't want it coming out that when Giabatti's goons opened fire you two were having lunch with Flaherty."

Billy's eyes widened. "That's a crock—"

Callahan laid a hand on Billy's shoulder. "I know. That's why we need to get ahead of this before anyone can spin it." He shifted his gaze to Ray. "I'll do damage control with the lieutenant, since you can't seem to have a conversation with the man without insulting him. Understood?"

"Yeah, Sarge, I got it."

"Good. And I'm sure I don't need to remind you of department policy, but you're both on administrative leave, effective immediately. Bring Detective Greene up to speed on anything you need investigated while you're out."

"Come on, Sarge," Billy said. "You're gonna put us on leave for this?"

"You know I don't make the policy," Callahan said. "But I expect you to follow it. Now, I can have an officer escort you to the psychiatrist right now in the back of a squad car, or you can do it on your own within the hour, but I'll be checking in with Doctor Stevenson."

"We'll take ourselves," Ray said.

"Good," Callahan said. "As long as he doesn't think you're cuckoo for Cocoa Puffs, I'd say you'll be back on the streets in a day or two. So why don't you take care of business and then get a stiff drink. You cheated death today. Let's hope it never comes back to even the score."

"Yeah," Billy said, "let's hope."

Callahan patted their backs before ducking beneath the crime scene tape and heading toward his unmarked Impala. When the sergeant was out of earshot, Ray said, "I wanted to interview those artists before calling it a day."

"I'd say that's off the table now."

"We take down two gunmen and the department yanks us off the streets? What the hell kind of logic is that?"

"Just take the free vacation and let it ride. We can give Detective Greene the less likely suspects and save the others for when we get back."

"Fine," Ray said. "Maybe Greene can also track down that stripper's last known address."

Billy grinned. "Can you imagine Greene at a strip club?"

Ray shook his head. Greene was as straight-laced as they came and was so socially awkward that Ray suspected he might have Asperger's.

Billy motioned toward Finnegan's Landing, where a patrolman stood talking to Flaherty and scribbling in a notepad. "Should we add our two cents?"

"Let him say what he wants," Ray said. "It's our word against his."

After a few moments, the patrolman flipped his notepad closed. Flaherty glanced in their direction, a grin tugging at his lips. He strode across the street and tipped them a wave before disappearing behind the battered green doors of The Rock.

Billy shook his head. "He doesn't seem too broken up about Mad Murph getting blown to bits."

"That's because Flaherty only cares about Flaherty."

Ray's eyes wandered back to the blood-smeared patio. It was a lot of collateral damage for a failed assassination attempt. Two of the construction workers had died and another was in critical condition. Only one had escaped with minor injuries. Even their waiter had gotten caught in the crossfire, cut up by flying bits of glass from the windows shattering.

Ray caught sight of Hector from Crime Scene Services taking pictures of the skid marks where Vito and his partner had peeled wheels in their doomed attempt to flee the scene. Gary Wong appeared beside Hector and exchanged a few words before heading over to Ray and Billy.

"Looks like this one's pretty clear cut."

"Yeah," Ray said. "Billy and I made sure you didn't have to work too hard."

Gary grinned. "It's nice to get an easy one every once in a while."

"You got anything new on Finkleton?" Ray asked.

"A few updates, yes. But I wanted to talk about Danny the Mule first."

"What do you got?" Ray asked.

"A pair of silicone elephant ears."

"What the hell is that supposed to mean?" Billy asked.

"My team found them floating in the quarry with a bunch of other trash. We bagged them up and flagged them for further analysis, not expecting anything to come of it. But after seeing Finkleton transformed into a spider and knowing that Danny had stitches in his ears and had experienced his own body modification, it got me thinking."

"It's supposed to be a trunk," Ray said. "The penis on his face. He made Finkleton into a spider and Danny into an elephant."

"That's what I think too," Gary said. "And we found strands of Danny's hair caught in the silicone."

Billy nudged Ray in the arm. "You remember what RJ said about Angie T's kid?"

"The kid warned him not to accept elephant rides from Danny. Christ, we've got to find that stripper."

Billy chuckled. "Now that's what I'm talking about."

"Did you find any other hair?" Ray asked. "Any DNA we can link to the killer?"

"Unfortunately, not," Gary said. "But maybe what we have on Finkleton will help."

"I'm listening," Ray said.

"It's not much, but we did get a few hits when we crosschecked the entry gate prints with the criminal records database—two DUIs and a serial shoplifter. All of them live near the park."

Billy shook his head. "Twenty bucks says that doesn't amount to anything."

"Maybe not," Gary said. "But we also got an ID on the tire tracks found by the path. They were made by a Goodyear Wrangler with a 265-millimeter width."

"What kind of trucks are we talking?" Ray asked.

"It's a pretty broad field," Gary said. "Class 1 and class 2 pickups, possibly a large SUV. Basically, anything from a Toyota Tacoma to a Ford F-150. It's carried as a replacement tire at a variety of auto parts stores, so it's not unique to a particular make or model."

"That's not exactly the breakthrough we were hoping for," Ray said.

"Sorry guys, I wish I had more."

"What about the testing of the rope fibers?" Billy asked.

"Came back negative," Gary said.

"What about that sticky substance on the web," Ray said. "Do you know what that was?"

Gary chuckled. "It was honey."

"What's so funny about that?" Billy asked.

"It's the killer's idea of a joke," Ray said.

"I must be the only one not getting it," Billy said.

"The killer made Finkleton into a spider," Ray said, "and Finkleton had a habit of rubbing people the wrong way. I think he's saying Finkleton could've caught more flies with honey."

Billy pursed his lips. "So this is all about teaching Finkleton a lesson? Putting him in his place?"

"Could be," Ray said. "And as twisted as this murder was, it was also very creative. And symbolic. So what does that tell you?"

Billy grunted. "We need to interview those artists."

# CHAPTER TWENTY-ONE

"How did it make you feel, Ray? Pulling that trigger, watching a man die?"

Ray stared across the desk at Doctor Stevenson and resisted the urge to go with his natural response. *One scumbag down, one million to go.* Instead, he sipped from a Styrofoam cup filled with watery coffee and scowled at Stevenson. "I felt like I had no choice. If I didn't pull the trigger, he would've shot me."

"But how did you feel *emotionally?*" Stevenson steepled his fingers and studied Ray with scientific detachment.

Ray wondered how it would feel to drive his fist into Stevenson's doughy face. But he knew how to play the game, so he gave Stevenson the response he was looking for. "I felt relieved at first. Glad the danger had passed. But as Vito lay dying, I also felt pity."

"For whom?"

"For the victims. For Vito. For the senselessness of it all."

Stevenson leaned forward and nodded, as if he'd been waiting for this moment all along. No doubt thinking his genius had guided yet another patient to an epiphany of self-discovery.

"And what of your father, Ray?"

"You tell me."

"I beg your pardon?"

"It seems to be your favorite topic of conversation whenever I'm sent here." He had veered off script, but he didn't care. Telling people what they wanted to hear wasn't his style and he could only stomach it for so long.

"Are you still searching for your father's killer?"

"I keep my eyes open."

"And before you shot Vito, did he remind you of the man who murdered your father?"

Ray clenched his hands into fists. "I know what you're doing, Doc. I don't suffer from post-traumatic stress disorder. I don't go around shooting people who remind me of my father's killer. And I don't use deadly force unless it's absolutely necessary. And anyone who thinks otherwise is full of shit. Do me a favor and put that in your report."

He pushed back his chair and stood up.

Stevenson's expression didn't change. He continued to observe Ray with his prying, gray eyes. "Is there anything else you'd like to say?"

Ray halted at the doorway and glanced over his shoulder. "Get some better coffee... or next time, I really will go rogue."

*** 

Ray stormed into the waiting area and found Billy lounging on a leather sofa, leafing through an issue of *Cosmo*. He wondered if Doc Stevenson made an experiment out of observing which magazines his patients selected.

Billy tossed the magazine onto the coffee table and stood up. "How'd it go?"

"He's not bleeding."

"Sounds like you passed. What do you say we get that drink now?"

Ray's phone chirped before he could reply. He fished it out of his pocket and glanced at the display. *Christ*. This was the third call in the last hour. He accepted the call and brought the phone to his ear, bracing himself for the inevitable.

"Ray? Is that you? Are you okay? Is everything alright?"

"Yeah, Ma, it's me. Why wouldn't I be okay?"

"They said your name on the news. I almost had a heart attack. They said it was a mob execution, bodies piled up in the streets."

Ray closed his eyes and sighed. "That's an exaggeration. And I'm sure the news didn't say I was injured."

"What do they know? They're always getting things wrong. Rushing to beat each other to the story, not taking the time to check facts. Do you really think I could trust that bimbo at Channel 7? If I put my ear to her head, I'm sure I could hear the ocean. And how can she even read the story with those fake boobs blocking her view of her notes?"

"I'm pretty sure there's a teleprompter, Ma. It's the 21$^{st}$ century, no one's looking down at a sheet of paper anymore."

"Well, I wish they were. When Walter Cronkite was sitting behind that desk, the world was a whole lot safer. I can tell you that."

"Okay, well, I'd love to talk more about newscasters with big boobs but—"

"So would I," Billy said.

"—I'm trying to wrap up this investigation."

"Okay, dear. But you're okay? I mean, really?"

"Yeah, Ma."

"You know, I wish you'd quit the force and go to law school. Your grades were so good in college. I know it was only criminal justice, but—"

"Okay, Ma, I gotta go. Talk later, okay?"

"I love you."

"Okay, same here. Goodbye." He ended the call and shook his head. "I knew I shouldn't have picked up."

Billy grinned. "But I find her so entertaining."

"Yeah, she's a blast."

"So, about that drink?"

"Let's make it a coffee."

"What're you pregnant or something?"

Ray lifted an eyebrow. "Wouldn't you like to know?" He reached into his pocket for the keys to the Explorer.

"We going to Dunks?"

Ray shook his head. "There's a place in Cambridge I want to check out. I'll tell you about it on the way."

***

Ray squeezed the Explorer into a metered spot across from the iconic live music venue, The Middle East. A fixture of Central Square since the '70s, The Middle East was painted an eclectic mix of purple, green, and yellow, and featured the golden head of a bull looming above an oversized mural of multicultural figures. It was a microcosm of the Cambridge neighborhood—diverse, artsy, and edgy. A place where new-age hipsters came for live music, good coffee, and ethnic restaurants, where students from MIT, BU, and Harvard came to kick back between classes, grab a drink, catch some live theatre, or drop in on an improv comedy show.

Billy stared out the window and scowled. "I've never seen so many man buns in my life. If I had a pair of scissors on me, I'd snip off every goddamn one."

"Just what this neighborhood needs," Ray said, "a cranky old man killing everyone's buzz."

Billy climbed out of the truck and gave him the finger. "Wait until you turn forty-five. See how funny it is then."

"I'll check back in thirteen years. Just let me know which nursing home you'll be at."

Billy adjusted his sports coat and gazed down the street. "I took Kelly here a few months ago to see a comedy show, but all we got was some freak wearing a doll around his neck while fighting furniture."

Ray chuckled. "I would've paid money just to see the look on your face."

"Come on," Billy said. "Let's get this over with. You're cutting into my drinking time."

They followed Brookline Street for two and a half blocks before arriving at the coffee shop Keiko had told him about. With an obvious nod to the MIT crowd, the sign above The Particle Bean displayed a glowing blue laser splitting a

143

coffee bean down the middle, creating a spray of grinds that fused together to form a heart. Inside, the café was bright and airy, furnished with distressed wood tables and cushioned chairs in eye-popping colors. Works of art hung from the slate-gray walls in an erratic arrangement that Ray found almost too dizzying to look at.

Billy strode up to the counter and ordered a small black coffee, but the pimply-faced barista shifted his weight and frowned. "Uh, we don't have a small."

"What the hell do you mean you don't have a small?"

"We have four sizes: electron, proton, neutron, and atom."

Billy fixed the kid with a withering stare. "Aren't all of those small?"

"They're arranged in order of subatomic mass."

Billy clenched his teeth. "I want a goddamn small."

"Just give him an electron," Ray interjected. It didn't help that the kid was sporting a man bun. "And I'll take a proton latte."

Billy shook his head. "I hate this fucking neighborhood."

"Why don't you find us a seat? I'm buying."

"You'd better be," Billy grumbled before stalking away.

When Ray delivered the coffee a few minutes later, he found Billy sitting in a velvet wing chair thumbing through a recent issue of the *Improper Bostonian*.

"Whatever happened to *The Phoenix*?" Billy asked, taking the coffee from Ray. "They used to have the best Adults Classified section. Anything you wanted, they had."

Ray shrugged. "I'm gonna check out the art."

"Alright," Billy said, turning to the local party scene photos. "I'll catch up with you in a few."

Ray walked along the nearest wall, his eyes scanning the paintings, each of which had a laminated tag listing the artist's name and a price that practically guaranteed it would be hanging in The Particle Bean forever.

Some of the works were modern—just a few splatters of paint or broad brush strokes, the kind of thing Jason or Allie could've pulled off in art class. But there was also a series of charcoal portraits featuring the city's panhandlers. The artist had captured their faces in such stark detail that they were, at once, ugly and hauntingly beautiful.

The opposite wall showcased an array of beach and nautical scenes, most of them oil on canvas. As Ray approached the back corner of the café, he spotted the painting Keiko had described. The title of the work was *The Suffering of Ages,* and it featured a desolate landscape of red rock desert baking beneath a blazing sun. On the right-hand side of the painting, a naked baby crawled through a field of bleeding clocks, his skin pocked with festering sores, his elongated scrotum dragging behind him on the cracked hardpan. Glistening tears ran down his cheeks, transforming into tiny scorpions that dropped to the ground and skittered off in every direction. Toward the top of the canvas, painted in miniature, a man in a suit shoved a toddler into a trash can. On the far left, painted half the size of the baby, an old man lay tangled in a nest of thorns, rivulets of blood seeping from wounds that showed glimpses of bone underneath.

The bottom corner of the painting was signed *The Artist*, followed by two intertwined infinity symbols in the shape of an "X". The same symbol appeared in the eyes of the baby and on the backs of the scorpions.

Something about the signature tugged at Ray's memory—almost like déjà vu—but he couldn't place it.

Billy moved in beside him. "Looks like death row art."

"How much you got on you?"

Billy eyed the price. "You gotta be kidding me."

"Just give me a hundred fifty and I'll cover the rest. The department will reimburse us."

Billy groaned. "That's all I got until we're reinstated." He pressed a fistful of bills into Ray's palm.

Ray pocketed the cash and pulled the painting off the wall. He brought it to the counter and laid it down in front of the barista who'd served them earlier.

The kid looked from Ray to the painting. "Uh, I only do coffee. Let me get the manager." He disappeared into the back room and returned with a well-dressed Latino man wearing designer glasses and a salt-and-pepper goatee.

"Find something you like?" the manager asked.

"This piece caught my eye," Ray said. "Do you know the artist?"

"I've had that painting up for over a year. You're the first person to show any interest."

"Yeah, well I collect surreal paintings. Do you have anything else by this artist? I'd love to see his portfolio."

"No, but I can get his contact information." The manager trudged around the counter and retrieved the tag from the wall. He flipped it over and studied the writing on the back. "Looks like he only included his email address. Not even a name, just *The Artist*. Like he's Prince or something." The manager chuckled. "Sounds like he's suffering from delusions of grandeur."

"Yeah," Ray said. "I bet he is."

# CHAPTER TWENTY-TWO

The kids mobbed Ray as he walked through the front door, racing into his arms as Sparky darted through his legs yipping excitedly. Mr. Snuggles—who until now had been sleeping beneath the foyer table—gave him a dirty look and stalked into the kitchen, flipping his tail in disapproval.

Ray scooped up the kids and threw them onto the couch. "Tickle attack!" he yelled, and descended upon them with a furious onslaught of belly tickling that left all three kids sweaty and panting for breath.

Michelle stood in the doorway to the living room, her arms folded across her chest. "I love how I bust my butt all day taking care of these kids and you're the one who comes home to a hero's welcome."

"What can I say, it's my magnetic personality."

"Is that what you call it?"

Ray slid his hands around her waist. "Don't worry, I saved some tickle time just for you."

She slapped his hands away and turned around in a huff. "What's the matter?"

Michelle stormed into the kitchen. "As if you didn't know."

Ray rolled his eyes and followed her. "Are we playing the guessing game again? Because I hate the guessing game."

"Figure it out, Ray. Aren't you supposed to be good at that?"

"Figure what out?"

Michelle whirled around. "Your mother called in a panic and said you were involved in a shoot-out. She couldn't reach you, and neither could I, so then *I* started to panic."

"You never called me."

"Are you saying I'm a liar, Ray? Check your phone."

He fished it from his pocket and looked at the recent call list, which showed Michelle's missed calls sandwiched between his mom's. Christ, how had he missed that?

"When you didn't answer, I checked the closet and saw you'd left your vest at home. How long have you been going without it, Ray? I mean, are you kidding me? Do you want the kids to grow up without a father? Or for me to wind up as a single mother?"

"I'm sorry. I promise I won't skip another day."

"That's it? You're sorry?" She cocked her head and glared at him, her ponytail slicing the air like a scythe. "There was a big shoot-out in the city. The least you could do is check in and let me know you're okay."

"You're right, I'm sorry."

It was ironic that he could stare down a murderous gangster like Flaherty but buckled so easily when it came to his wife—all five-foot-four inches of her.

"Go play with the kids," she said. "I can't talk to you right now."

He exhaled sharply and watched her storm off. How the hell was he supposed to know they mentioned his name on the news? Probably some crime beat reporter listening to a police scanner trying to get an inside scoop. Goddamn irresponsible reporting. He shook his head and slunk into the living room, where Jason and Allie were engaged in their own argument.

"What's this all about?" he asked.

Jason cocked a thumb at Allie. "She's afraid to go into the bathroom alone."

"Is that true?"

Allie nodded, her curly blond hair flopping over her eyes.

"What's there to be afraid of?"

Her eyes darkened. "Bears."

Jason pointed to his head and drew an air circle with his finger. "She saw a toilet paper commercial with a cartoon bear and now she won't go into the bathroom by herself."

"Allie," Ray said, "there's nothing to be afraid of. Kids are very hard to digest, so bears will only eat one every ten years or so."

Allie eyed him skeptically, her face scrunched up.

"That bear in the bathroom? He ate our first kid seven years ago. You've heard us talk about Mikey, right? Great kid. You would've liked him."

"Dad," Jason said, his face drawn in concern. "I know you're just teasing."

"Don't worry, you've got three more years before you need to worry about anything. Just don't pee on the seat, buddy. Bears hate that."

"And moms too," Allie said.

Ray shrugged. "That's what they get for not being courteous enough to lift the toilet seat when they're finished."

Allie and Jason started giggling, but Ray noticed Petey standing by the couch in an Elmo diaper, two fingers curled into his mouth, his eyes as wide as silver dollars.

Michelle stalked into the room and swept Petey into her arms. "Really, Ray? This afternoon wasn't enough? Now you have to scare the baby? Do you know how many months of potty training you just set us back?"

"I just—"

But Michelle wasn't waiting for an answer. She kissed Petey on the forehead and stalked out of the room.

Jason and Allie exchanged a glance and started chanting in a sing-song voice, "Daddy's in trouble, Daddy's in trouble."

Ray shook his head. "You ain't kidding."

***

Later that night, after tucking the kids into bed, Ray went downstairs to smooth things over with Michelle but found that she'd barricaded herself in the bedroom. He stood in the hallway with his hands on his hips wondering if he should force a discussion or leave her alone.

It was the classic husband Catch 22—damned if he did, damned if he didn't.

In the end, he decided the locked door probably meant she wasn't ready to talk, so he grabbed his laptop from the cluttered desk in the kitchen, took a Heineken from the fridge, and mounted the stairs to the roof deck.

Outside, the city lights twinkled against the gathering twilight, a warm breeze carrying the salty scent of the sea. He set the laptop down on the patio table and stared out toward the Bunker Hill Monument, which glowed blue against the darkening sky.

He raised his beer to the city.

*Here's to surviving. Whether by the grace of God or just dumb luck.*

He thought about the construction workers who'd died in a hail of bullets, leaving behind wives and children. Ray toasted them as well, remembering his own father's violent end and the cold shadow of his absence, which lingered like the phantom ache of a lost limb.

Had Ray sat in Garrison's chair that afternoon, the bullet that lodged into Garrison's Kevlar vest would've struck him instead, and he would've bled out on the pavement before the first ambulance arrived. It was a scary thought, but he refused to dwell on it. People spent too much energy focused on what might've been and not nearly enough time focused on the here and now. It's what kept some people stuck in a rut, while others conquered the world.

*If you're not moving, you're dying.*

It was one of his father's favorite sayings.

He hoisted the Heineken to the sky. "This one's for you, Dad."

His eyes welled up unexpectedly and he had to bite his lip to keep it from trembling. The raw emotion of his father's brutal last moments ran deep, and on nights like this it sometimes clawed its way to the surface. He set the Heineken on the table and touched a finger to his cheek, letting a tear roll over his hand like quicksilver, the city lights reflected in its depths. He imagined a thousand tears in a thousand households across the city, all shed for a thousand different reasons.

He drew a shuddering breath and flicked it over the railing.

*If you're not moving, you're dying.*

He powered up his laptop and drummed his fingers against the table, waiting for their stubborn Wi-Fi to connect. Once online, he created a new Gmail account with the username JP_Art_enthusiast99 and composed a message.

*Dear Artist:*

*I saw your painting at the Particle Bean today and just had to have it. The Suffering of Ages fits perfectly with my collection. I'm a big fan of Surrealism and I'm very impressed by your talent. I would love to see the rest of your portfolio and am willing to spend top dollar.*

*Can you meet me at the Particle Bean sometime this week? The day after tomorrow, if possible? I look forward to hearing from you soon.*

*Sincerely,*

*JP*

With that accomplished, he visited the website he'd discovered a few days earlier with the snide comments on Danny the Mule—deaddumbbizzare.com. This time, photos of Finkleton's death dominated the main page, and a trail of comments followed a shot of Finkleton hanging from the tree in full spider regalia.

Ray recognized some of the usernames from Danny's page. A profile picture accompanied each name, but because nobody wanted their real identity linked to such hateful comments, the pictures mainly consisted of sports logos, memes, or pet photos instead.

*BigRex: Hey look, it's Spiderman!*

*Reba99: Gross! Time to put back on the red and blue pajamas.*

*SoxFan: I guess being a second-rate superhero finally got to him... he had to put himself out of his misery.*

*Duff: That dude sure pissed someone off.*

*GothDiva: Revenge of Little Miss Muffet.*

*VinnyT: What's in the bowl, bitch?*

*GothDiva: That better not be directed at me, VinnyT!*

*VinnyT: It's from Andrew Dice Clay, but if the shoe fits...*

*SoxFan: The Dice Man Cometh!*

*Stiles44: WTF? I don't even know where to begin with this one.*

*TheArtist: It seems the Itsy Bitsy Spider climbed up the wrong waterspout.*

Ray's pulse quickened. Not only was The Artist the same tag name from the painting, but the logo in the profile picture also had the same interlocking infinity symbols. That explained his déjà vu at The Particle Bean. He'd probably seen the same name and symbol on the posts about Danny the Mule.

He toggled over to Danny's photos and found a post from the Artist about how expressive Danny's face was. He slapped the table and grinned. "I've got you now, you sonofabitch."

# CHAPTER TWENTY-THREE

It looked like something straight out of *The X-Files*. A ghostly-white humanoid without limbs sprawled across a steel table, the flesh around its shoulders and groin blistered from cauterization, giving it the appearance of something otherworldly.

Ray leaned against an adjacent autopsy table, clad from head-to-toe in a paper gown, mask, and booties. He was close enough to the body to see what he cared to see, but far enough to avoid the splatter as Tina cracked open Finkleton's rib cage with a pair of gardening shears.

Doc Death stood to her left, allowing her to take the lead on the procedure. Luis was positioned near Finkleton's head, manning a plastic cart stocked with a scale and a collection of biohazard containers. A second cart beside Tina contained a sinister array of cutting tools that seemed better suited to a medieval torture chamber.

The stench of death tugged at Ray's gag reflex, and it was through sheer determination that he kept his gorge down.

A wall-mounted video camera recorded the procedure as Tina presented the case for the record, giving a play-by-play account using a slew of medical jargon Ray didn't fully understand. After tilting Finkleton's head back and noting the degree of rigor, she examined the wound on his throat and the ring-like bruise they'd first noticed when they lowered him into the body bag. She projected her voice toward the camera.

"A dark red ligature mark measuring 2.5 centimeters wide encircles the anterior of the neck just below the laryngeal prominence. It appears to be consistent with strangulation by rope or cord."

Tina leaned over Finkleton and shined a light onto his face. "Evidence of petechial hemorrhaging in the conjunctival surfaces of the eyes and in the mucosa of the lips. Presence of needle marks on the jugular vein, possibly to administer medication or anesthesia. Both the superior and inferior extremities appear to have been amputated premortem, with each wound closed via cauterization around a length of 16-gauge stainless steel surgical wire. The wounds appear recent and well-tended."

Tina brandished her scalpel and sectioned a piece of cauterized flesh at Finkleton's shoulder, exposing the white gleam of bone where the limb had been severed. "The wire appears to be threaded through a hole drilled into the bone."

"Christ," Ray muttered.

Tina passed the sectioned tissue to Luis, who sealed it in a plastic container.

Doc Death leaned over the body. "No spurs observed. The cut appears to have been made with a professional-grade bone saw."

Ray craned his neck for a better look. "You sure about that?"

Doc nodded. "Using the wrong saw would splinter the bone and cause severe trauma. But this is clean. Whoever did this possessed the requisite knowledge and tools for the job."

"Where would someone get a bone saw?" Ray asked.

"I suppose you could pick one up online from a medical equipment company. It seems you can get anything online these days. But hospitals and medical schools would have them as well." Doc Death gestured to the tray of cutting tools. "We've got one right here. Tina will use it to open Mr. Finkleton's skull in a few minutes."

Ray felt his stomach flutter, but clenched his jaw against it. If he blew chunks in here, Doc would never let him watch from this side of the glass again.

"Hand me the 18-gauge needle," Tina said, turning to Luis. She removed the cap and inserted the needle into Finkleton's right eye, drawing fluid into the syringe. She repeated the process on the left eye. "Vitreous procurement yielded 8.5 milliliters of fluid."

She handed the syringe to Luis, who emptied it into a glass tube and held the contents up to the light.

"Remind me what that's for again," Ray said.

Tina blinked at him behind blood-speckled goggles. "Postmortem, the cells in the eyes release potassium at a constant rate. Measurement of the potassium levels helps to establish time of death."

Doc chimed in. "It's often more reliable than examining blood or other bodily fluids, since those can be affected by certain postmortem chemical changes."

Ray nodded, his eyes wandering to the white dome of plastic sandwiched between Finkleton's lower torso and the surface of the table. "Are you ever going to take that egg out of his ass? I'll bet there's a surprise inside."

"What was in the others?" Doc asked.

"The names of Finkleton's artists. People whose careers he helped build."

"Do you think one of them could be the killer?" Tina asked.

"It's possible," Ray said. "Right now, we've got a lead on an artist Finkleton refused to work with. Someone whose talent he insulted. From what I understand, Finkleton wasn't well-liked. He obviously pissed off the wrong person."

The egg was buried halfway into Finkleton's rectum and Tina strained to extricate it with a pair of surgical tongs. "This is a first for me," she said after the egg popped free.

Ray lifted an eyebrow. "If it ever becomes routine, it's probably time to call it quits."

Tina examined the egg in the light, gripping the larger end with the tongs. "It has a few pin-sized holes in the shell, but otherwise seems intact."

"Go ahead and open it," Ray said. "I'd like a peek before it's shipped to the crime lab."

"It's taped shut," Tina said, reaching for a scalpel. She swept the blade around the center line, turning the egg with the tongs. "I'm almost afraid to open it."

"Just don't touch the plastic," Ray said. "I want it dusted for prints."

Luis handed her another pair of tongs and she pried off the top half of the egg, revealing something black and bristly inside. Before Ray could even register what the thing was, it crawled out of the shell and scurried up Tina's arm.

She dropped the tongs and stumbled against the table, a screech escaping her lips.

Ray tore the goggles off his face and swatted the spider off her arm. It landed on the floor and skittered toward Luis, who nearly fell over the cart, screaming, "Holy shit! Holy shit!"

Doc Death grabbed a plastic container from the cart and brought it down over the spider, trapping it inside. He sank to his knees and studied it through the plastic. "It's a baby tarantula."

Ray let out a shaky breath, his heart thumping like techno bass. "I guess that's supposed to be the killer's idea of a joke."

"Well, it's not funny," Tina said.

Luis shuddered. "Man, I hate spiders."

"Do you think you can continue?" Doc asked.

Tina glared at him. "Just because I'm a woman doesn't mean I can't deal with a little spider."

Luis raised his hand. "I think *I* might need a minute."

For the next hour, Tina removed Finkleton's organs and placed them on a steel tray where Luis would take temperature readings, weigh them, and collect fluid and tissue samples for further analysis.

"Let's get a closer look at that neck wound," Tina said. She sliced open Finkleton's throat and peeled back the layers of flesh, as if fileting a fish. She leaned in for a closer look, her

156

face inches from the incision, her pale-green surgical mask rippling from her breath. "His vocal cords were severed."

"Finkleton was probably making too much noise," Ray said. "Which means the killer might've kept him locked up in his home."

Tina continued with the procedure, leaning over Finkleton's midsection. "I'm now examining the contents of the patient's stomach. Anyone want to guess what Finkleton's been eating?"

"What?" Ray asked, although he had a feeling he already knew.

"Flies. And by the spoonful, from the looks of it."

Doc Death clucked his tongue. "Imagine being propped up and force-fed like that."

"What do you mean 'propped up'?" Ray asked.

"When we were prepping for the exam," Doc said, "we noted bruising on Mr. Finkleton's back and buttocks, almost like bedsores. Except based on the position of the bruises, it appears he was kept vertical rather than horizontal."

"You mean like leaning against a wall?" Ray asked.

Doc Death nodded. "Precisely. And being kept in that position for an extended period would've been tantamount to torture."

"So he wasn't kept in the harness?" Ray asked.

"Based on the pattern and severity of bruises, it appears the harness was used solely for the hanging."

As Doc spoke, Tina made an incision behind Finkleton's left ear and swept the blade across the crown of his skull. She peeled back Finkleton's scalp and reached for the bone saw.

"You might want to step back," she said. "This could get messy."

***

Ray stared at his plate and cursed himself for ordering roast beef. All that pink meat leaking juices into the bun reminded him of Finkleton on the autopsy table. Tina, on the other hand, had already devoured half of her sandwich. "What's the matter?" she asked, blotting her lips on a napkin.

"I lost my appetite."

"When did that happen?"

"Around the time you fired up the bone saw."

"Judging by the look on your face, I'm surprised you didn't faint."

"I'd stab myself with a scalpel before I let that happen." He picked up his sandwich and took a bite.

"What do you think?"

He gave her a thumbs-up despite the wave of nausea that washed over him as he swallowed.

"I told you this place makes the best sandwich."

Ray took a swig of Coke and nodded, hoping the carbonation would settle his stomach. Tina watched him with a bemused grin, and he found himself wondering why she'd asked him to lunch in the first place. "I noticed Doc Weintraub's still looking over your shoulder."

"You'd think after ten years he'd stop micromanaging my cases."

"Try having Spinonni for a boss."

"Oh God, no thank you." She tucked a lock of hair behind her ear and laughed. "It's nice catching up outside of work. It reminds me of old times."

"Yeah," Ray said, not sure where this was going. "What have you been up to, anyway? You still doing triathlons?"

"I try to get in a few a year, but I haven't felt like training lately."

"Why not?"

"Mark and I broke up."

"Oh. Sorry to hear that."

"You already knew, didn't you?"

"I heard a rumor. What happened?"

"I finally realized he's a self-centered jerk who'll never change."

"I could've told you that."

"I should probably stop dating cops, right?"

"Bunch of assholes," Ray said. "You should try firemen. Everyone loves firemen."

"You were never like that. Beneath that macho exterior, you're actually a very sweet guy."

"It's brave of you to finally admit it."

She smacked his arm playfully, but the smile soon faded from her lips. "Is there something wrong with me?"

"What are you talking about?"

"What if I'm destined to be alone?"

"Come on, you're beautiful, smart, and interesting. What's not to love?"

"It wasn't enough to keep you around."

"Hey," he said, reaching for her hand. "That was a long time ago, and I've always regretted the way things ended."

"Really?"

"Really." Instead of being honest with Tina about meeting Michelle, he'd told her they were just too different and he wanted out of the relationship.

"So now what?" she asked.

"Well, if you decide to give cops another try, you might have a shot with Billy."

"I'd rather become a nun."

"I think that might be a fantasy of his."

"Gross. What happened with him today? Did he get locked in his cave again?"

"Technically, we're on administrative leave until tomorrow and he had no interest in working on his day off."

"Well, since you're off, you won't mind coming to my place to hang a mirror."

"Is that why you asked me to lunch?"

"You're the detective, you tell me."

"I don't know…"

"Come on, Ray. It weighs fifty pounds. I can't hang it by myself and I'm having trouble finding a handyman who'll accept a five-minute job."

"Tina—"

"Please?" she said, batting her lashes.

"Okay, fine. But stop giving me the Bambi eyes."

\*\*\*

Tina lived on a tree-lined street in the South End, halfway between the medical examiner's office and Huntington Ave. Her unit was on the second floor of a restored Victorian brownstone with bow windows and black shutters.

"What do you think?" she asked, opening the door. "Bring back any memories?"

He stepped into the foyer and looked around. The living room was furnished in a modern style that Michelle hated—a black and white motif with steel accents. An exposed brick wall balanced out the modern touches, along with a rustic wooden bookshelf crammed with medical texts.

Being in her condo felt strangely familiar, like finding an old pair of jeans in the back of the closet and discovering they still fit. He peered around the corner. "Did you get the kitchen redone?"

"I added some subway tile and refurbished the cabinet doors."

"It looks good."

"Thanks. Let me show you the mirror."

It was leaning against the exposed brick wall, more artsy than functional, with a series of interconnected squares that reminded him of a mosaic. Tina had already made marks for the screws, and once she brought over the toolbox, he drilled holes for the anchors.

She disappeared into the hallway as he searched for a matching pair of screws. A few minutes later, he attached the mirror to the wall and stepped back to ensure that it was level. With all the squares pitched at different angles, the mirror returned a distorted reflection of the living room, along with a blurred image of Tina standing beside the couch.

It wasn't until he turned around that he saw she was naked.

160

"I hope you don't mind," she said, "but I've got one more job for you."

Ray stood with his feet rooted to the hardwood, his eyes moving down the length of her body, from where her curly brown hair fell across her bare shoulders to the familiar shape of her breasts and the tattoo of a butterfly on her pubic bone.

She padded over to him, smiling coyly. "Do you remember how you could never get enough?"

"That was a long time ago."

Her hands slipped around his waist and her touch sent a shudder coursing through him. "I see the way you look at me in the field, Ray. I know you've thought about this."

She guided his hands over her breasts, and for a moment he couldn't pull himself away. But then he shook his head and let his hands flop to his sides. "I can't do this, Tina."

"Are you sure?" She inched closer, staring up at him, the light from the mirror dancing in her eyes. "Maybe this will change your mind."

She unbuttoned his jeans and sank to her knees, pulling his boxers down with her.

"Tina..."

He knew he should push her away, hike up his pants and run for the door, but the wet heat of her mouth closed around him... and all he could do was groan.

# CHAPTER TWENTY-FOUR

"How'd it go yesterday?" Billy asked. "I miss anything good?"

Ray sipped his coffee. "The autopsy was interesting."

"Yeah? Did Tina miss me?"

The mention of Tina filled him with self-loathing, but he played it cool to avoid arousing suspicion. "Not that I could tell."

"She'll come around," Billy said, "once I turn on the charm."

"You actually think you have charm?"

"Of course not, but I can fake it. Did I tell you what happened with Kelly?"

The last thing Ray wanted was to hear about Billy's love life, but Billy didn't wait for a response. "I'll tell you what, that chick was a freak in the bedroom. The things she did would make a porn star blush. Too bad she turned into a full-fledged psycho bitch."

"You don't think you had anything to do with that?"

"What the hell are you talking about?"

"You cheated on her, didn't you?"

"We weren't exclusive."

"Did she know that?"

"If she didn't, she does now."

Ray shook his head. As much as Billy behaved like a dirtbag, what Ray had done to Michelle was ten times worse, and there was nothing he could do to take it back.

Sergeant Callahan poked his head into the breakroom. "The lieutenant wants to see you."

Billy groaned. "What'd we do this time?"

Callahan motioned to the hallway. "Let's go."

Ray and Billy exchanged a glance before following Callahan to Spinonni's office, where the lieutenant sat behind his desk berating the station's janitor, Henry.

"How can we be out of cleaner?" Spinonni asked. "Isn't part of your job knowing when to reorder supplies? Were you planning to sit on your ass until the supplies magically appeared? Until a leprechaun shat out a bottle of Windex?"

Ray could only see the back of Henry's snowy-white head, but he knew the old janitor must be seething.

"It takes a special solution to remove that much graffiti," Henry said. "And the last time you only gave me enough money for one bottle."

"Are you saying this is my fault?"

"No sir, I just—"

Spinonni reached into his drawer for the petty cash envelope and threw a fistful of bills at Henry. "Get two bottles this time, and don't forget to bring me the receipt."

Henry stooped down to retrieve the bills before shuffling out of Spinonni's office with his shoulders slumped. He met Ray's gaze as he passed through the door. "He's all yours."

Ray patted the old man on the back. "Thanks for warming him up."

Spinonni waved them into his office. With his hair-trigger temper and monster beer gut, the lieutenant was a heart attack waiting to happen. But since only the good die young, Ray figured Spinonni would ride out the apocalypse with the rats and the cockroaches.

Spinonni smoothed out the bristles of his moustache and waited until they'd settled into the chairs opposite his desk. "Sergeant Callahan tells me you've got a lead on the Finkleton case."

Ray nodded. "We think the same guy did both Finkleton and Danny the Mule."

"Because they were both disfigured? I hope you've got more than that."

"He made them into things," Ray said. "Finkleton into a spider and Danny into an elephant. Plus, the autopsies showed Finkleton and Danny were kept alive for as long as possible by someone with medical training."

"What else do you have?"

Ray told the lieutenant about his conversation with Keiko and the painting they'd found at The Particle Bean. "It was signed *The Artist* and had a logo that looked like an X formed by two infinity symbols."

Spinonni folded his arms. "So?"

"So, I found someone using the same name and symbol on a website where people comment on bizarre deaths. The Artist posted comments on two different threads—one with photos of Danny and the other with photos of Finkleton."

Spinonni furrowed his brow. "I thought you said there was a medical angle. Now you're telling me he's an artist?"

"It's possible he's both, or that he's working with someone."

"Didn't you say he referenced the Itsy Bitsy Spider in his posts?" Billy asked.

Ray had almost forgotten. "That's right, and the harness securing Finkleton to the tree had the word *Bitsy* written on it. Almost like a pet name."

Spinonni tapped a meaty finger against his desk. "Have you established contact?"

"We've arranged a meeting at The Particle Bean to see the rest of his portfolio," Ray said.

"When?"

"This afternoon. Two o'clock."

Spinonni eyeballed Callahan. "I want four undercover units on site."

"If anything looks out of the ordinary," Ray said, "we risk spooking this guy."

Spinonni leaned forward. "Last time I checked, you don't get a vote."

Ray looked to Callahan for help, but the sergeant just shrugged.

"You get anyone from Computer Forensics to look at that website?" Spinonni asked.

"They're checking into it now," Ray said.

"Good. We'll meet in the briefing room at noon to discuss the logistics. Oh, and one more thing. Your buddy Coleman is due for release today. Why don't you see if you can prevent him from wandering around any new murder scenes, or is that too much to ask?"

***

When Ray arrived at The Particle Bean fifteen minutes prior to the arranged meeting time, three units were already on site. Detectives Greene and Pearce wore hardhats and orange reflective vests with *Department of Public Works* emblazoned across the back. They had set up cones around an open manhole cover and were standing to either side of it, pretending to take a coffee break.

Detectives Benton and Eisberg waited across the street in a white van with a vehicle wrap depicting a grinning Porky Pig holding a monkey wrench. It was one of eight logos the guys from the department had created, and when Spinonni first saw it, he nearly lost his mind over the derogatory insinuation. But due to budget constraints it remained in the rotation, and the guys used it as often as they could to get a rise out of the lieutenant.

Ray ordered a proton latte from the same man-bun-wearing millennial who'd served him before. He took a seat at a corner table facing the door and spotted Billy and Callahan across the café sipping coffee and pretending to be engrossed in conversation.

In his reply email, the Artist had said he'd be wearing jeans and a red T-shirt, but by 2:15 neither Ray nor the other units had seen anyone fitting that description. At 2:30, Ray approached the counter to speak to the manager.

"I bought a painting from you the other day."

The manager nodded. "You're not looking for a refund, are you?"

"I'm supposed to be meeting the artist here. Did you hear anything from him?"

The manager shook his head.

"You have any idea what he looks like?" Ray asked.

"I only met him once, about a year ago. He's a white guy, has dark hair. I don't think I could pick him out of a lineup."

Ray lifted an eyebrow. "That's an interesting choice of words."

"Well, you *are* a cop, aren't you?"

"What makes you say that?"

The manager gestured to the barista with the man bun. "When Kenny came to get me the other day, he said that a couple of cops were interested in a painting."

"How'd you know we were cops?" Ray asked.

The kid shrugged. "I don't know, you just looked like cops to me. Tough guys in sports coats. Bad attitudes. Plus, I saw your partner's gun when he sat down."

"Have you had any contact with the artist?" Ray asked.

Kenny shook his head. "I don't get involved in any of that. I just sell coffee, remember?"

"So you don't know the artist?"

"No," Kenny said.

Ray turned back to the manager. "I'll need your contact information."

The manager plucked a business card from a stack near the register. Ray glanced at the name on the card and handed him one of his own. "Okay, Mr. Baez. I'm gonna wait awhile longer. If you do hear from the artist, be it today or some other time, give me a call. And whatever you do, don't tell him I'm a cop."

# THE ART OF DYING

***

It was 3:00 before Ray left The Particle Bean with Billy and Sergeant Callahan. The entire crew met back at the precinct, with Lieutenant Spinonni grilling them in the briefing room, where the walls were plastered with crime scene photos, diagrams, and newspaper clippings.

"What the hell happened?" Spinonni asked.

"He made us," Billy said. "Too many goddamn cooks in the kitchen."

Spinonni eyed Callahan. "Is that true?"

"I don't see how he could've made us," Callahan said.

Ray didn't want to criticize the sergeant in front of Spinonni, but it wasn't in his nature to hold his tongue. "The Artist would've been on high alert, knowing that we might be able to trace his art through Finkleton. And with the van parked across the street and the dummy DPW crew loitering out front, it would've been a red flag to anyone who's seen a cop movie in the past twenty years."

"But nobody spotted a guy in a red shirt near the building," Callahan said, "which makes me think he never showed."

"Unless he wore something different," Ray said. "If he was worried about the art connection, he might've lied about the shirt to make himself invisible while he scoped out the scene."

"What about surveillance footage?" Spinonni asked. "Anyone think to check the security cameras in the vicinity?"

"Greene and Pearce are working on it," Callahan said.

"What about the manager?" Billy asked. "For all we know, he could've painted that picture himself."

"Run a background check," Spinonni said. "Do some reconnaissance work. Find some other goddamn way to crack this case."

"We're in the middle of chasing down other leads," Ray said. "Right now, Gary's team is checking the painting for prints and fibers. And I've still got that website to follow up on."

167

"Don't bother," Spinonni said. "I checked with Computer Forensics while you were out. Those posts were made from 700 Boylston Street, as in the Boston Public Library." He shook his head. "Your case has gone to shit, Hanley. And now I've got to let the captain know."

***

Ray climbed into the Explorer and swore. "Come on," he said, glaring at his phone.

"What is it?"

"I sent an email to the Artist after his no-show and it just came back undeliverable. He must've closed his account."

"He's covering his tracks," Billy said. "Can't say I'm surprised."

Ray slammed his fist against the steering wheel. "We just lost our only advantage. If he goes underground now, we can kiss this case goodbye."

"Maybe Greene will find something at the library," Billy said.

"You really believe that?"

Billy shook his head. "You know how many random prints they'll find on those computers? So far, this guy has left behind almost no trace evidence. He's like a ghost. Greene's not gonna find anything."

Ray heaved a sigh and tugged at his Kevlar vest, which he'd made a show of putting on before leaving for work. Even if they recovered surveillance video from near The Particle Bean or the library, it wouldn't be much use since they only had a vague description of the Artist from The Particle Bean's manager. And it certainly didn't help that both locations saw a ton of pedestrian traffic around lunchtime, so picking a suspect out of the crowd wouldn't be easy.

He could almost hear the phantom footsteps of the Artist slipping away. He drew a deep breath and stared through the windshield at the precinct's wall, where the orange block letters of RJ's weekly diss asked a perfectly reasonable question.

# THE ART OF DYING

*Why so many cops?*
*Because everyone needs an asshole.*

Ray had a flashback of Tina sinking to her knees, and he imagined Michelle in that same moment, fighting to change Petey's diaper, near tears because he wouldn't just sit in one place after keeping her up half the night. At least he'd finally come to his senses and pushed Tina away before it could go any further. But he never should've let it get that far in the first place.

*Just another asshole cop.*

"You okay?" Billy asked.

"Yeah, fine." He drew a deep breath. "I think we ought to talk to RJ again, see if he can remember anything else about that stripper or her son."

"I thought we were gonna interview Finkleton's artists," Billy said. "The ones with their names in the eggs."

"I meant after that."

"It's almost four o'clock. How many artists we got on the list?"

Ray reached into his sports jacket and withdrew a notepad from the interior pocket. "We've got four, but Greene met with two while we were on leave."

"The ones we agreed on?"

Ray flipped to a dogeared page near the end of his notebook. "He questioned Nathan Devoux, a retired engineer, and Ryan Masters, a younger artist who paints mostly nautical scenes."

"Anything worth following up on?"

Ray shook his head. "According to Greene, Devoux was a real grandfatherly type. Nice guy. On the heavy side. Too out of shape to be kidnapping men half his age."

"What about Masters?"

"He was soft spoken, kind of sensitive. Seemed pretty broken up about Finkleton's murder. Which makes sense, since

Veronica said his career had taken off under Finkleton. Also, he was in San Fran at the time of the murder."

"He could've hired it out," Billy said.

"What the Artist did to him was way too personal to delegate."

"He could've gotten Finkleton prepped and then had someone else string him up once he was in California."

"I think the Artist would've wanted to be there in the final moments," Ray said. "Part of his MO is psychological torture. He would've taunted Finkleton before killing him, just like he taunted us by putting that spider in the egg."

Billy ran a hand through his pompadour. "Did Greene show them the picture you took of the painting?"

Ray nodded. "Devoux and Masters claimed they'd never seen it before."

"And Greene believed them?"

"That's what he told me."

"What about the three prints Gary found on the gatepost, the shoplifter and DUIs? Greene get to them too?" Billy asked.

"Didn't amount to anything. Just like you said."

Billy held out his hand. "You owe me twenty bucks."

"I never took that bet."

"Sure you didn't," Billy said. "So who's the next artist on the list?"

Ray fired up the Explorer and shifted into reverse. "I'll tell you on the way."

# CHAPTER TWENTY-FIVE

Suzie Coleman faded in and out of consciousness, drifting between nightmare visions and a nightmare reality. She was lost in the cold embrace of the living darkness, where the slow drip of unseen water punctuated the quiet suffering of another restless night. In her dreams, she languished in the dark forever, with only the Artist looming over her to satisfy his urges. In her waking moments, the dank air of the gallery prickled her skin with gooseflesh, and the incessant whimpering of her cellmate grated against her already frayed nerves.

She once had high hopes for Greg, although she could no longer pinpoint when that *once* was. Time seemed to ebb and flow in this place rather than tick away in the traditional sense. Somewhere in that continuum, she recalled the Artist wheeling Greg into the gallery. He was strapped to a gurney and appeared unconscious, his broad chest chiseled with muscle.

The Artist hummed an upbeat tune as he pierced Greg's nose and fastened a golden ring through his nostrils. To complete the metamorphosis, he implanted plastic horns into Greg's shaved scalp and tattooed a red bull's-eye on his chest. Then, he hoisted his newly minted minotaur into the air with a rope and pulley and secured him against the wall, clothing him in nothing but a loincloth.

When Greg regained consciousness, he raged against his chains with such savagery that Suzie half-expected the iron ringlets to tear out of the wall.

The Artist watched his antics with quiet amusement. He clucked his tongue and said, "Let's play a game, shall we?" He stalked across the gallery and grabbed an old croquet mallet leaning against the wall. He walked back to Greg and brandished the mallet. "What do you say, Suzie? Think I can hit the bull's-eye?"

Before Suzie could reply, the Artist swung the mallet into Greg's stomach, making a sound like a fastball striking a catcher's mitt. Greg's face twisted into a mask of agony, his jaw dropping open in a silent scream.

The Artist flipped the mallet into the air and pumped his fist as if he'd just hit a homerun. He turned toward the far wall, where a camera was always rolling, recording everything with its unblinking red eye. He cupped his hands over his mouth and did a surprisingly good impression of a gameshow host.

"Tell the Artist what he's won!"

"Well, Bob, today's winner will receive the board game version of Whack-A-Bull, plus seven minutes in heaven with Mrs. C."

The Artist patted Greg's foot, which dangled shoulder-height above the ground. "Thanks for playing, Greg, but you should really work on those abs."

The Artist sauntered over to Suzie and caressed her thighs. "Call me crazy, but I feel like we both won." He unfastened his belt and wriggled out of his jeans, grinning as he exposed himself to her.

Suzie shrank against the wall as the Artist ran his hands over her breasts. He pressed himself against her and the scent of his cologne wafted into her nostrils—a pungent musk that only partially concealed an underlying stench that made her stomach turn.

"Seven minutes just doesn't seem like enough, does it?" He wrapped his hands around the small of her back and thrust himself inside her. "Do a good job," he groaned, "and I'll flip you over for the bonus round."

Later that night, after the Artist had locked up, Suzie and Greg plotted their revenge. Greg spoke confidently about escape, although Suzie didn't see how that was possible. Even if Greg managed to strangle the Artist with his legs, how would he break free of the chains?

She imagined them starving to death, their bodies progressing through various stages of decay until they were nothing but skeletons dangling from the wall, every grueling moment caught on video for some unknown audience.

But Greg kept ignoring this fact, instead boasting about how he could snap the Artist's neck in one jerk of his feet, or how he could knock the Artist unconscious with a kick to the head. Maybe it was just a coping mechanism.

But as time eked by in their windowless dungeon, the Artist taunted and beat Greg as punishment for his sins. Depriving him of food. Playing round after round of Whack-A-Bull. It took its toll. He stopped boasting about killing the Artist or finding a way to escape. And, after the Artist castrated him, he became a shadow of his former self, reduced to a blubbering man-child who whimpered around the clock, resigned to whatever horrible fate the Artist had planned.

She found it hard to pity him. He was weak-minded and mean, and he lacked the mental fortitude necessary for survival. While she'd rather not have eaten his Rocky Mountain oysters, she couldn't afford to refuse a meal. And if Greg had watched with betrayal as she dined—particularly when the Artist had clicked his oyster against hers following a toast—it eased her conscience to remember how his loincloth had swelled every time the Artist had his way with her.

She was on her own now. It was best not to forget that. Greg was as good as dead, and she had to assume the Artist had killed Bitsy and the man with the phallic trunk, the one he called the Elephant. She had to face facts. She was alone with a psycho, chained naked to the wall and kept on display like a living statue. A cushioned platform the size of a textbook supported her butt, leaving her legs dangling two feet above the floor in much the same way she once sat on the edge of her grandpa's diving board when she was a kid.

The position subjected her to frequent and painful cramps, which she could only partially combat by pulling herself upright on the platform. Standing allowed her arms the luxury of resting against her sides. It also alleviated the pressure on her butt, which had developed sores from prolonged sitting.

Suzie stretched her legs and gazed into the darkness. How long had it been now? Days? Weeks? Months? Would anyone ever find her? Was Jim beside himself with grief? Or was he already shacking up with that slut he met in New York?

They were dangerous thoughts, the sort that could drive a person mad. She'd seen it happen to the Elephant. By the end, he'd gone batshit crazy—giggling to himself, shouting at things that weren't there. If she wasn't careful, she'd end up just like him.

Escape was only possible if she kept her wits. Which was why she exercised her mind by remembering song lyrics, movie lines, and passages from books, recalling words lost to her for years, extracting them from the dark fissures of her brain where nothing was ever truly forgotten.

When she couldn't sleep, she composed her own poetry, reciting the verses in her mind, since speaking them aloud felt dangerously close to insanity. The poems were dark and terrible, but they were also cathartic and served to compartmentalize her fears so that she could lock them away where they wouldn't cripple her. Tonight's work was still fresh in her mind.

*The near-dead and the dying fear the sadistically lying,*
*Through torturous days of violence in waves,*
*And shivering nights spent praying for light,*
*Until dawn arrives and the red door yawns wide,*
*And the mad, sly grin of the one who tallies the sin,*
*Dashes the hopes of not yielding the ghost,*
*And though acceptance is surely the hardest,*
*In here, it's clear, we all belong to the Artist.*

# THE ART OF DYING

Her freshman year English professor would've flunked her for rhyming, but since Mr. Vaughn had never been tortured in a dungeon, he needed to cut her some slack. She was a survivor and she would do whatever it took to stay alive. The Artist could take her body. He could take her dignity. But he could never take her mind. And despite the gravity of her situation, she refused to go gently into the night.

Mr. Vaughn also would've frowned upon her failure to attribute that last thought to whatever author, poet, or war hero first coined the phrase. But it didn't matter. It was hers now. She owned it. Just like she owned the night. Like she owned the Artist.

It seemed strange to make such a bold claim, especially since she was chained to the wall, but it was the truth. The Artist had loved her once. She would see to it that he loved her again. Somewhere beneath the delusions of grandeur, the psychotic tendencies, and the warped perception of justice, was a sad little boy crying out for love.

So, for now, she would be the perfect inmate, the perfect prize. She would earn his trust. She would stroke his ego. She would use her feminine charms to tame the beast that raged inside of him.

And when he was finally calm—when that sad little boy at last felt safe and fulfilled—she would strike him down. And dance upon his grave.

# CHAPTER TWENTY-SIX

Salty Dean's Tattoo Parlor shared a wall with a bait and tackle shop across from the Jodrey Fish Pier in Gloucester. Behind the building, the Atlantic loomed ash gray under an overcast sky, the sound of rolling waves pierced by the angry squawk of gulls fighting for scraps left behind by fishermen.

Inside the shop, a weathered brunette with multiple face piercings sat hunched over a laptop, the wall behind her cluttered with framed photos of tattoo designs. Past the reception desk, a bearded tattoo artist with arms like pythons put the finishing touches on a tattoo of a black dragon coiled around the spine of an Asian customer with spiky orange hair. It was an intricate design that captured the dragon in motion, its iridescent scales reflecting the light, its sinewy wings flexed for takeoff.

The artist glanced over his shoulder at Ray and Billy, who had just entered the shop and triggered the door chime. "Be right with you," he said. A few minutes later, the artist stripped off his latex gloves and escorted the customer to the front desk for checkout. After a brief discussion about post-procedure care, the artist turned toward Ray and Billy.

He was an imposing figure—six-three or six-four—with tousled black hair and a bushy beard streaked with gray. He looked like he could've been the leader of an outlaw biker gang, except that his eyes lacked the requisite degree of malice.

"What can I help you with?"

"Are you Dean Saunders?" Ray said.

"That depends on who's asking."

Ray and Billy flashed their badges. "I'm Detective Hanley and this is my partner, Detective Devlin. We're with the Boston Police."

"You're a bit out of your jurisdiction, aren't you?"

"We want to ask you a few questions," Ray said.

Saunders eyed the door and waited for his customer to exit. "Is this about Barry Finkleton?"

"What do you know about him?" Billy asked.

"I'm one of his artists. Veronica told me what happened."

"How would you describe your relationship with Finkleton?" Ray asked.

"We got along fine. He helped launch my career. I've sold more than a hundred sculptures through his gallery."

"You ever paint?" Billy asked.

"Just on bodies."

"Does this look familiar to you?" Ray showed him a picture of *The Suffering of Ages*.

Saunders shook his head. "I don't know many other artists. I just do my own thing, you know?"

"What do you think of the painting?" Billy asked. "Is it good, or what?"

"It's not my taste."

"Would you say the artist is talented?" Billy asked.

Saunders shrugged. "I wouldn't hire him as a tattoo artist."

"Why did you say he?" Ray asked. "We never said the artist was a man."

Saunders raised his hands in a defensive gesture. "I just assumed. Maybe that means I'm sexist, but last time I checked that wasn't a crime."

"Oh, he's sexist alright," the woman at the front desk said. "Expects me to cook and clean when we get home, as if I wasn't here working beside him all day long."

177

Saunders rolled his eyes. "You spend fifteen minutes a day waiting on customers and about eight hours messing around on that computer."

"He's got a point," Billy said. "You barely looked at us when we came in. Not even so much as a hello."

The woman gave Billy the finger. "Maybe I don't talk to assholes."

"Sorry," Saunders said, "she's been in a mood today."

"Don't worry," Ray said. "He gets that a lot. Back to Finkleton. Do you have any idea who might've killed him?"

"Like I said, I don't get involved in that scene. I just do my sculptures and deliver them to the gallery. When something sells, he cuts me a check. Or he used to, anyway."

"Did he pay you fairly?" Ray asked.

"To be honest, I don't know. It always seemed fair to me, but I'm new to the business. Barry had all the connections to the rich buyers, so without him I'd just have hunks of bronze cluttering my garage."

"Do you have anyone who'll vouch for your whereabouts this past week?" Billy asked.

Saunders cocked a thumb toward the front desk. "Brenda."

Billy met her gaze from across the room. "Has he been around this week?"

"Yeah," Brenda said. "And I'd know, because he's a constant pain in my ass."

"Is there anyone else who can vouch for you?" Ray asked.

"I go to an AA meeting at the Methodist church on East Main every night at eight. Anyone there can vouch for me."

"What about last Sunday night?" Ray asked. "You go to a meeting then?"

"Yeah, and afterward I went to a buddy's house to play cards."

"How many people were there?"

"About five."

"We're gonna need names," Ray said. "What time did you leave?"

"It was a late night. I didn't get home until after one."

"Alright," Ray said. "One last question. Is that your truck parked in the lot? The silver F-150?"

"Yeah, why?"

"You mind if we take a look?"

\*\*\*

The tracks they'd discovered at Stony Brook Reservation were made by 265-millimeter Wranglers, which didn't match the larger variety Firestones on Saunders's truck. His girlfriend drove a yellow VW bug—perhaps to match her sunny disposition—but Ray doubted it would be an effective means of transporting a giant humanoid spider.

"Talk about coming up empty," Billy said as they rode back into the city. "We literally struck out on all counts."

Ray squeezed the wheel and said nothing.

Before interviewing Saunders, they'd visited Don Martinez, the artist who'd accused Finkleton of ripping him off. According to Veronica, Martinez had violated his contract by removing his works from Finkleton's gallery. He was also the artist whose name was inside the egg that appeared half-devoured, presumably by Finkleton.

Despite being a promising suspect, and the only one with a real motive, it turned out that Martinez had undergone knee surgery a couple days prior to Finkleton's murder. When Billy pressed him for proof, Martinez unbandaged his knee to reveal the wound, which was sufficiently nasty to support his claim. He also presented them with a stack of medical bills from Mass General that corroborated the date of his surgery.

When Ray and Billy arrived at the precinct, the weekly diss had vanished from the wall and Henry was standing in the parking lot, rinsing off a scrub brush. "Nice work," Ray said, patting Henry on the shoulder.

Henry flashed them his trademark grin, which erased years from his face. "It only took four hours, three bottles of cleaner, and a shit-ton of elbow grease."

Billy chuckled as he reached for the door to the building. "Too bad Spinonni will still find something to bitch about."

The 11th Precinct consisted of multiple units, including homicide, gang, and narcotics, and given its proximity to the rougher side of the city, the place buzzed with activity pretty much 24/7. The area known as the bullpen contained twenty-four desks, which were occupied by officers and analysts talking on the phone and pecking away at their keyboards, drafting incident reports in a two-fingered approach that would've made Ray's high school typing teacher cringe.

Ray spotted Trooper Garrison standing in the booking area talking to Sergeant Callahan. "Welcome back," Ray said, shaking Garrison's hand. "How you feeling?"

Garrison patted his stomach. "It takes more than a couple bullets to hurt these abs of steel."

Ray grinned. "Still as cocky as ever."

"A few inches lower," Billy said, "and his cocky would've gone splat."

Garrison winced. "Man, I don't even want to think about that."

"Come on," Callahan said, "let's head into the briefing room."

They followed Callahan through the bullpen and into the briefing room, where the back wall had been commandeered for the case. A whiteboard displayed the timeline of events, accompanied by names and dates of the suspects they'd interviewed. A poster-sized photo of *The Suffering of Ages* hung beside the whiteboard like a madman's nightmare, surrounded by dozens of crime scene photos depicting Danny's waterlogged corpse and Finkleton's freakish impersonation of a spider.

Ray studied the surrealistic landscape of the painting, which offered a rare glimpse into the killer's mind. "Did Gary find any trace evidence on the painting?"

Callahan shook his head. "The paint is too coarse to hold a print."

"What about fibers?" Garrison asked.

"They've got to shave the paint off one flake at a time," Callahan said. "It'll be like looking for a needle in a haystack."

"What about that egg I brought in?" Ray said.

"Came back negative."

"Christ," Ray said. "We can't catch a break." He studied the whiteboard and reviewed what they knew about the Artist, including what the department's profiler had inferred about his psyche.

–White male, aged 25-30, medium build, dark hair
–Aspiring painter, calls himself The Artist
–Call sign is two interlocking infinity symbols forming an X
–Painted *The Suffering of Ages* displayed in The Particle Bean coffee shop (Cambridge)
–Drives a truck with 265-millimeter Wrangler tires
–Medical training (med school, EMT?)
–Disfigures victims via amputation / body modification
–Makes victims into something new (spider, elephant)
–Leaves object in rectum (matchbox car, plastic egg)
–Keeps victims alive to prolong suffering
–Motive / choice of victims may be revenge based
–Danny the Mule (molestation) / Finkleton (rejection of art)
–Probable loner and past victim of sexual abuse
–Likely bullied as a child
–Likely suffers from delusions of grandeur / inflated ego
–Probable sociopath with high IQ
–Likely lives and works within city limits

–Mother may have been a stripper (Angie T) with ties to Jack Flaherty
–Might've grown up in East Boston

Ray folded his arms and stared at the board, hoping some new connection would jump out at him. But nothing did.

Callahan turned to Detective Greene, who'd just entered the room. "How'd it go at the library?"

Greene shifted his weight from one leg to the other, something he tended to do when all eyes were upon him. He spoke in a habitual monotone, reporting events in a just-the-facts Joe Friday sort of way. "We found two terminals with a browsing history that included deaddumbandbizzare.com. The site was last accessed on May 18 with the username The Artist."

"What's Gary say about prints?" Ray asked.

"His team is still analyzing prints lifted from the keyboards, monitors, and desks. So far, they've found twenty-seven prints that are usable, but Gary says those were likely from the most recent users. I'll review the results when they become available, but according to the librarian, a typical day draws several hundred users on those computers."

"Seriously?" Billy said. "That many people go to the library?"

"If the Artist last posted two days ago," Garrison said, "his prints would've gotten smudged off by now."

"Quite possibly," Greene said, "but if he touched somewhere other than the keyboard, like the chair leg or the monitor, then our odds increase."

"I wouldn't bet on it," Ray said. "This guy's been careful to a fault. I wouldn't be surprised if he wore gloves."

"That occurred to me as well," Greene said. "I asked the librarian if he observed anyone with gloves accessing the computers recently. He responded that they get so many weirdos and germaphobes wandering through the place that he hardly takes notice anymore."

Callahan shifted his gaze to Ray and Billy. "Anything promising come out of questioning those artists today?"

Billy folded his arms. "We struck out."

"One of them just had surgery," Ray said, "and the other one's got no motive and has a solid alibi."

"So more dead ends?" Callahan asked.

"Yeah," Billy said. "More dead ends."

Ray approached the whiteboard and pointed to a list of names under the heading *Competitors*. He turned to Greene. "You interviewed some of these guys when Finkleton first went missing. Any of them worth another visit?"

Greene shook his head. "Ridley spoke with them before he got called to active duty. I reviewed his notes and followed up with them, but I don't think there's anything there. They all appear to be upstanding citizens with solid alibis."

"Where do we stand on the surveillance video?" Callahan asked.

"There's no cameras within two blocks of The Particle Bean," Greene said. "There's a couple on Boylston Street with a limited view of people entering the library, but we can trace anyone of interest back to other cameras farther down the street."

"That's true," Garrison said, "except there's dozens of white guys in their mid-twenties coming and going around the time the Artist posted. And we've found no physical evidence that would help narrow the field."

Ray looked at Callahan. "I think our best lead is the painting. I say we release it to the media and open up the tip line."

"Did we show the painting to Finkleton's competitors?" Callahan asked.

Greene nodded. "None of them recognized it."

"Alright," Callahan said, "then I agree that releasing it seems like the next logical move. The Artist already knows we have the painting, so we wouldn't be showing our hand. What else do you guys have?"

"We've still got a lead on that stripper," Billy said.

Garrison chuckled. "You never forget a stripper, do you, Billy?"

"You should've seen him at the Puma," Ray said. "I was standing toe-to-toe with Flaherty, about to go a few rounds, his bouncers swarming around me, and there's Billy at the main stage chatting up some third-rate stripper."

"I happened to be conducting my own interview," Billy said. "And for the record, she had first-rate tits."

"I call bullshit," Garrison said. "On both counts. You and I have very different definitions of *first-rate*."

Greene folded his arms and frowned, uncomfortable with the banter.

"Let's get Clint in here," Ray said, referring to the analyst he'd tasked with tracking down the stripper. He reached for the phone hanging beside the whiteboard and punched in a four-digit extension.

Clint arrived a few moments later with a stack of papers. He was a soft-spoken man who bore a strong resemblance to George Costanza from *Seinfeld*, so the guys at the precinct naturally called him that. But since Clint didn't care much for the nickname or for the inference that he was short, balding, and overweight, Ray was one of the few people who called him by his real name.

"There he is," Billy said. "Georgie-boy."

Clint nodded in Billy's direction but said nothing.

"What did you find?" Ray asked.

"I ran the information through the database and identified twenty-three women who lived in East Boston in the past ten years with a last name beginning with T and a first name that might be associated with the name Angie."

"What's that cover?" Ray asked. "Angela, Angelina, Angelica?"

"I ran it wider than that," Clint said. "I included any woman whose name begins with a-n-g."

"And how many are dead now, but would've been around sixty if still alive?" Ray asked.

Clint shuffled his papers. "Just two, but one of them never had children and the other one only had a daughter."

Ray groaned. "What do you have on the woman with the daughter?"

"She was an elementary school teacher who also worked part time for the local church. Her records show pretty much constant employment."

"Doesn't sound like a stripper," Garrison said.

"And unless her daughter had a sex change, she's not the Artist," Callahan said.

"Can you refine the search?" Ray asked. "Widen the age range and look for first or middle names beginning with A?"

Clint nodded. "You got it."

Ray turned to Sergeant Callahan. "I'll also follow up with the FBI agents who raided the Puma. They're supposed to be checking payroll records to see if they can find any information on Angie T."

Callahan rolled his eyes. "Good luck with that."

The FBI had a long history of unresponsiveness to the Boston police, especially when a request wasn't directly tied to their case.

"I could go back to the Puma and interview more strippers," Billy said. "Maybe ask a few questions over dinner."

Callahan chuckled. "You've got a serious problem, Billy."

"I was thinking," Greene said, his eyes staring past them, "the Artist might have some victims we don't know about."

"Who do we have missing right now?" Garrison asked.

"Not counting runaways, we've got Suzie Coleman and Greg Cassidy," Callahan said. He gestured to Ray, Billy, and Greene. "And these are the guys working those cases."

"We've considered the link to the Coleman case," Ray said. "And there could be something to it. Suzie lives around the corner from where we found Finkleton. She also went to art school."

"And Greg is a construction worker who lives in Southie," Greene said. "He's a known womanizer who was last seen at the Bell in Hand Tavern. There are no obvious connections to the Artist, but I'll have another look at his file to see if anything intersects with Finkleton, Danny, or Coleman."

Callahan nodded. "That gives me enough to update the lieutenant."

Billy chuckled. "Have fun with that."

# CHAPTER TWENTY-SEVEN

Ray arrived home to the sound of Petey squealing with delight. It was damn near impossible not to smile at that sound, no matter how stressful his day. He kicked his shoes off and padded into the living room, where Petey sat on Michelle's lap like a chubby little Buddha.

Jason and Allie sat on either side of Petey, singing their own rendition of "The Wheels on the Bus," except in their version the babies on the bus went beep, beep, beep, and with every beep they poked a finger into Petey's belly. It was something they'd started when Petey was three months old, and they only had to sing the first two words before Petey went bonkers.

When Petey caught sight of Ray, he squirmed off Michelle's lap and toddled over to him with his arms raised above his head. "Da-da home, want up."

Ray lifted him into the air and gave him a squeeze. "Did you have a good day, buddy?"

Petey drew his lips together in an exaggerated pout. "Sparky poop my shoe."

"Sorry to hear that, buddy. Trust me, we've all been there."

Allie flung her arms around his leg. "Daddy, come see what we made. It's in the kitchen, hurry!"

He reached down and ruffled her hair. "Okay, honey, just give me a couple minutes to get changed."

"I made something too," Jason said.

Ray gave him a high-five. "Wait for me in the kitchen and I'll be right there, okay?"

As Jason and Allie scampered away, Michelle's clear blue eyes locked on his and he felt an inexplicable certainty that she could peer into his mind and ferret out his infidelity like a bomb-sniffing dog.

"Uh, how was your day?" he asked, bouncing Petey in his arms.

Michelle stood up and winced, stretching her back. "Tiring."

Ray set Petey down on the floor and watched him bound off toward the kitchen in a toddle-run hybrid that seemed to be less of a toddle every day.

Michelle folded herself into Ray's arms and pressed her cheek against his chest.

"That bad?" he asked.

When she glanced up, her face looked haggard, as if she hadn't gotten a good night's sleep in days. "They're my children," she said, "and I love them, but sometimes I feel like I'm being pecked to death by chickens."

Ray would've laughed if not for the grim expression on her face. Instead, he kissed her forehead and held her close. But in the back of his mind, he could hear Tina moaning. Christ, he was better than that, wasn't he? Not just another dirtbag cop? Or was that who he was all along, and he'd just never been tested? Why hadn't he bolted when she first reached for his pants instead of waiting until halfway through a blowjob?

He'd made a mistake. And whether Michelle knew it or not, he'd driven a crack into the foundation of their marriage. If he wasn't careful, everything they'd built would come crumbling down around them, because Michelle wasn't the sort of woman who'd forgive a sin like that.

Some secrets a man had to bury deep, and so he wrapped this one in chains and dropped it into the abyss of his mind, hoping to hell it never clawed its way out. And, in the meantime, he vowed never to betray her again.

"Is something wrong?" Michelle asked.

"No, just a lot happening at work."

"Do you want to talk about it?"

"Not really. I just need to get out of this monkey suit so I can decompress." He headed into the bedroom and changed into his standard lounge clothes—a pair of basketball shorts and a worn Red Sox T-shirt.

Michelle appeared in the doorway as he shoved his dirty clothes into the hamper. "I was thinking we could open a bottle of wine after the kids go to bed. You know, make it into a date night. I feel like it's been a while."

"Uh, yeah. That sounds good." But his stomach knotted at the idea. How was he supposed to make it through date night if he could barely look her in the eyes?

Allie yelled from the kitchen. "Daddy, what's taking so long? I wanna show you what I made!"

"Be right there." He glanced at Michelle and shrugged, relieved to escape the date night conversation. When he got into the kitchen, Allie unfolded a long chain of brown construction paper topped with a crown of green.

"Ta-da! Do you like it?"

"I love it," he said, petting her blond locks. "Is it a tree?"

She planted her hands on her hips. "Of course it's a tree, Daddy. What else would it be?"

"It's for the *Three Billy Goats Gruff* play," Jason said, coming around the island with his own artwork. "We're helping with the decorations. I made a rock," he said, holding up a patchwork of gray construction paper.

"Looks great, buddy."

"And that's not the only surprise," Michelle said.

"There's more?" Ray lifted an eyebrow in mock disbelief.

Allie waved her hands in the air and jumped up and down. "I got the part! I'm gonna be the baby billy goat Gruff!"

Ray swept her into his arms and kissed her forehead. "I'm so proud of you, honey. You'll be the prettiest goat in the whole school."

"Thanks, Daddy!"

He set her down and she skipped away toward the playroom with Jason and Petey trailing after her. "When's the play?" he asked.

"Friday at six," Michelle said. "Can you make it?"

"Yeah, I'll be there. I can't wait to see her in that costume."

"Me too. It'll be adorable. Oh, and just so you know, Jason tried out for the oldest billy goat but didn't get the part. He says he's not upset, but it looked like he was on the verge of tears when Allie told you her news."

"Should I talk to him?"

"Maybe later. He seems content playing with Allie and Petey right now."

Neither spoke for a moment, and the silence felt awkward. "Can I give you a hand with dinner?"

"Sorry, hon, but the kids and I already ate. There's a plate for you in the fridge. Chicken with pasta." She opened the fridge and grabbed the plate and a bottle of wine. "Would you like a glass? I decided I can't wait until the kids are in bed."

"Is it red or white?"

"I wouldn't put red in the fridge."

"My mom always did."

"Your mom is nuts. Normal people don't do that."

Ray shrugged and carried the plate to the kitchen table.

"You're not going to heat that up?"

"I like it cold."

Michelle wrinkled her nose and poured him a glass of wine. It was one of her trademark gestures and he loved how cute it made her look, even though it was her unspoken way of saying, *I think you're being an idiot, but whatever.*

She raised her glass and held it out to him.

"We're toasting?" he asked, lifting his glass. "To what?"

"To date night."

"Uh, okay. To date night."

They clinked glasses.

190

When he finished eating, Michelle got up to pour them another glass. "I almost forgot," she said, handing him a manila envelope from the counter. "This came for you today."

There was no stamp, no return address. Just his first name typed in all caps on a stick-on label. Simple, efficient, and untraceable. He set the envelope on the table and stared at it, his gut filling with dread. "Where'd this come from?"

"Someone rang the doorbell and left it on the porch."

"What time was that?"

"Around noon. The kids were still at school."

Ray reached beside his plate for a butter knife and wiped it clean with a napkin. He slid the blade beneath the envelope's metal fastener and pried up the prongs. If there were any prints on it, he wanted them preserved.

"What is it?" Michelle asked.

Ray peered inside the envelope and thumbed through a stack of photos, his heart thumping in his chest. Instead of another murder victim, the photos depicted Ray and Tina together, and although they weren't at lunch, she did have her mouth full.

He met Michelle's eyes over the table. "You didn't open this?"

She shook her head. "Why, what is it?"

"Crime scene photos. Grisly ones. You didn't see who left the envelope?"

"I was in the middle of changing Petey's diaper. They were gone by the time I got to the door. Do you think it was Billy?"

Ray shook his head.

"Then who?"

He clenched his jaw and stared down at the envelope. "Someone who's playing games with me."

# CHAPTER TWENTY-EIGHT

Sal Giabatti leaned against the rail and gazed at the track with a rolled-up racing program clutched in one hand. As usual, he was dressed to the nines in a designer suit and trendy sunglasses. Ray figured the whole getup must've cost him at least three grand.

A bugle announced the call to post and a group of diminutive jockeys led their horses to the starting gate as a voice like the great and powerful Oz emanated from the loudspeakers, urging everyone to place a bet. Giabatti flattened the program against the rail and made a few marks on the page with a Mont Blanc pen, then handed the program to one of his hulking enforcers, who climbed the steps to the grandstand to register the bet.

Ray gave Garrison a nod and they rose from their seats and descended toward Giabatti, who watched their progress with a knowing smirk.

"Beautiful day for a race, isn't it boys?" Giabatti said.

Garrison nodded. "Can't you tell I've been working on my tan?"

"How long have you known we were here?" Ray asked.

"Long enough," Giabatti said. "I've got eyes everywhere."

Ray wasn't surprised. Giabatti had a lot of dangerous enemies. He'd risen to power by pitting his rivals against one another, and those who'd survived still had an axe to grind. But the odds of anyone toppling Giabatti were next to nothing. The old man was a master manipulator who was rumored to think three steps ahead of everyone else.

"You believe they're talking about closing this place down?" Giabatti said. "With all this history?"

"What history?" Ray asked. "Race fixing?"

"I'm talking real history," Giabatti said. "Seabiscuit ran some of his best races here. And the Beatles, they played right over there in '66." Giabatti let out a nostalgic sigh. "I love this place—the sights, the smells, the excitement. You can feel it in the air like electricity."

Ray looked at the faces in the crowd, but the only emotions he detected were sadness and desperation.

"Who do you have in the next race?" Garrison asked.

"Thunderstud to win," Giabatti said, and winked. "I've got a good feeling about that horse."

"Yeah," Ray said, "I bet you do."

Giabatti chuckled. "What is it this time? The drive-by?"

Garrison nodded.

"I'm surprised you didn't come sooner."

"We've been busy," Ray said.

"So I've heard. Didn't I tell you it would be one hell of a bloody summer?"

"Did you order it?" Garrison asked.

Giabatti's face darkened. "Do you really think I'd authorize a drive-by shooting in a public place? Vito and Donny went crazy with revenge. End of story."

"Revenge for Jimmy and Mikey?" Garrison asked.

"Yeah," Giabatti said, "for Jimmy and Mikey."

"Let me get this straight," Ray said. "You're saying you would've killed Flaherty's guys a different way, but Vito and Donny jumped the gun."

"You know I'm not gonna answer that."

"But you know I've got to ask."

Giabatti's eyes narrowed. "I hear you're the one who shot Vito."

Ray nodded. There was no use denying it.

"I don't fault you for it," Giabatti said.

"I appreciate that," Ray said, "but I'm not in the business of staying in your good graces."

Giabatti let out a belly laugh. "That's what I like about you, Ray. You always stick to your principles. I respect that."

"So work with me," Ray said. "Tell me what you know about Jimmy and Mikey's murders. Give me something I can use to nail Flaherty. Because the way I see it, putting away that psychopath is in everyone's best interest."

"Like I told you before," Giabatti said, "it's a family matter."

Ray held Giabatti's eyes for a moment, but it was clear the old man wasn't going to budge. He and Flaherty had a long, sordid history, and if Giabatti ratted on Flaherty, Flaherty would drag the old man down with him. It was a classic Mexican standoff, and unless one of them got immunity from prosecution, the other would keep his mouth shut. And the odds of either turning state's witness were about as good as Michelle laughing off his indiscretion with Tina.

The ring of the starting bell caught them all by surprise. Giabatti's face lit up as the gates flung wide and the horses stormed onto the track, their hooves kicking up dirt. A ripple of excitement moved through the crowd and the entire grandstand shot to its feet.

Giabatti drummed his hands against the rail. "Come on, Thunderstud! Run, you sonofabitch!"

The announcer called the play-by-play, the words rolling from his lips so fast Ray could barely register their meaning. He focused his attention on the track and watched a trio of horses round the bend and break away from the pack. They thundered into the homestretch, jockeys bent over the saddles.

For a few moments, it looked as though there might be a three-way tie, but then a muscular gray horse surged ahead in the final yards, its mane flapping in the wind.

"I don't believe it!" the announcer bellowed. "It's Thunderstud by a length! A thirty-to-one payout. How do you like that?"

Ray looked at Giabatti and arched an eyebrow. "Now ain't that a coincidence?"

# CHAPTER TWENTY-NINE

Suzie Coleman stared into the darkness and cursed the interminable night. Sleep was a rarity that came in fleeting spells that were frequently interrupted by muscle spasms, nightmares, and vertigo. A raw and seeping chill permeated the air, combining with a gnawing hunger and excruciating cramps to form a trifecta of misery that was surely the envy of Satan, himself.

Eventually, night yielded to day and a halo of light materialized around the gallery door. Soon thereafter, the sound of footsteps emanated from the hallway beyond, and Suzie closed her eyes and listened to the Artist fiddling with the locks.

She'd heard it enough times to distinguish the sound of three separate locks—a spring-loaded deadbolt, a latch bolt, and a chain. When the jangling ceased, the door swung open with a reluctant screech of hinges like a stereotypical house of horrors, leaving Suzie to wonder if it was art imitating life or life imitating art.

The Artist wheeled a stainless-steel cart into the gallery and flicked on the light. "Rise and shine, my little ones. It's another beautiful day."

As he turned to shut the door, Suzie caught a glimpse of a small, metallic object gleaming on the ground, reflecting the light from the hall. She made a mental map of its location and watched the Artist push the cart into the center of the gallery. It was the same one that normally held his surgical tools, except now it held a ceramic bowl and a brown paper bag instead.

He leered at Suzie. "Don't you look ravishing this morning? Did you do something different with your hair?"

She forced a smile. "Just a finger comb."

"You did that for me?"

"Yes," she said, trying to sound sincere. "You're my caretaker now. I want to do what I can to please you."

*And manipulate you... and murder you.*

"I'm glad to see that you're finally coming around." He dragged the stepladder over to her. "How about a little handfeeding this morning? And no, I'm not talking about Bitsy. You finished off his pudgy little hand days ago." He climbed onto the stepladder and gazed into her eyes. "You know, Suzie, I always knew our paths would cross again one day. And here we are after all these years."

Suzie had a flashback of him sitting in the back of a police car, his brooding expression conveying a complex mix of emotions—anger, sadness, betrayal, surprise—as if he didn't think he'd done anything wrong.

Something cold pressed against her lips and she realized the Artist was trying to push a spoon into her mouth.

"Earth to Suzie," he said. "Are you thinking about old times?"

She could smell the yogurt even before tasting it and her mouth instantly watered. "So good," she said, and meant it.

"I remembered how much you loved Greek yogurt mixed with honey."

"Thank you," she said, and meant that too.

"You're welcome, darling."

"Hey," Greg said, suddenly perking up. "What about me?"

The Artist clucked his tongue. "Be patient, my insolent Minotaur. I've got a special treat for you." When he finished feeding Suzie, he tossed Greg the brown paper bag. "Bon appétit."

Greg tore open the bag and shoved a fistful of lawn clippings into his mouth.

The Artist turned toward the camera. "Grass-fed cattle," he said. "It's the responsible choice."

Greg ate several handfuls before throwing the bag to the ground. "I'm still hungry," he grumbled, and Suzie noticed that his teeth were stained green.

The Artist reached into his back pocket and waved a stick of beef jerky at him, as if offering to play fetch.

Greg lunged for the jerky, but the Artist yanked it away.

"Ah, ah, not so fast. You know what you have to do."

Greg's face darkened. "I don't want to."

"Suit yourself," the Artist said. "I'm sure Suzie will eat it. You know how this girl loves meat."

Greg heaved a sigh. "Fine," he said, and began to sing in a half-decent baritone.

> *I'm a big, strong bull*
> *On a little farm,*
> *And all through the years,*
> *I've been causing harm,*
> *'Cause there was nobody*
> *In the whole damn town,*
> *Who could put me in my place,*
> *Until along came Farmer Brown.*

The Artist rocked on his heels, clapping in time with the music. When the song ended, he slid the jerky into Greg's outstretched hand. "Now tell me, who is Farmer Brown?"

"You are," Greg said, gobbling up the treat.

"That's right, Greg. I'm Farmer Brown, and you've been a very naughty bull, haven't you?"

Greg nodded. "I'm sorry for bullying you when we were kids."

"The time for sorry has passed. Now is the time for atonement."

"I don't know what that means."

"Why am I not surprised?"

The Artist stooped down to retrieve the paper bag, and Greg's eyes lit up with the realization that he was within striking distance. Suzie glared at Greg and gave her head a violent shake. It wasn't the right time. Greg seemed to realize it too, and Suzie watched the tension drain from his muscles as he leaned back against the wall.

The Artist crumpled up the paper bag and tossed it onto the cart, oblivious to the fact that he'd nearly been choked to death.

Suzie's eyes shifted to the video camera. How often did he review the footage?

The Artist tapped a finger against his lips and stared at the empty section of wall beside Greg. "Does anyone else miss Bitsy? I never realized how much that fat little spider brightened my day. Oh well, he's living the good life now—hanging out in nature, catching all sorts of flies. Perhaps even a few worms."

A searing pain shot through Suzie's leg and she stumbled against the wall, nearly falling off the platform. She gritted her teeth and tried to massage her thigh where the muscle had contracted into a bulging mass.

"What is it?" the Artist asked.

She could barely talk through the pain. "Charley horse."

"Would it help to walk around? You've earned some loyalty points today, and I suppose it's in my best interest to keep you limber, if you know what I mean."

Suzie glanced up from her leg. Was he serious? Or was it another one of his cruel jokes?

The Artist climbed onto the stepladder and gazed into her eyes. "You won't try anything stupid?"

"Please, I just need to stretch."

The Artist regarded her for a long moment. "None of my exhibits has ever received this privilege, so if you even think about taking advantage of my kindness, you will be a very sorry goddess. Do you understand?"

"I understand," she said, and planted a kiss on his lips.

The Artist's face softened, and for a moment she caught a glimpse of the young man she once knew.

"I'll be back with the key," he said, and exited the gallery. He returned a few minutes later with a small black key, which he held before her eyes. "You promise to be good?"

"I promise."

He inserted the key into the slot of each shackle and her restraints fell away from her arms and jangled against the wall, the lengths of chain swinging behind her. She glanced at her bare wrists. For the first time since awakening in the Artist's gallery of horrors, she was free.

The Artist guided her down from the platform, her knees buckling on the stepladder. "Easy does it," he said, catching her in his arms and helping her to the floor.

Suzie's eyes welled up at the feel of solid ground. "I'll just walk in a circle, okay? I promise I'll be good."

"That's not fair!" Greg shouted. "Why does she get to stretch and I don't?"

"Don't worry," the Artist said, "you'll get your exercise soon enough. I'm planning a Whack-a-Bull marathon for later this afternoon." The Artist rolled his eyes and looked at Suzie. "Have you ever met such a crybaby?"

She shook her head and bent down to touch her toes, her eyes zeroing in on the metallic object she'd spotted earlier. It was a panel nail, and it lay a few inches from her outstretched hand. But with the Artist standing so near, watching her with a quiet intensity, how could she get it without him noticing?

And then she had an idea.

She returned to a standing position and smiled coyly at the Artist. "I think you'll like this move," she said, and made a show of bending over in front of him.

She could feel everything spreading apart down there as her fingertips brushed the concrete, and she prayed that his attention was focused on her lady parts rather than her hands. A moment later, she had the nail pinched between her thumb and forefinger. She stood slowly, sliding her hands along her thighs as she straightened, and tucked the nail into the fold of her labia. She sensed the Artist moving toward her and felt her stomach clench with dread. He'd seen what she'd done… and now he'd punish her.

But his face told a different story.

"Now, that's what I call stretching! I should've let you out of those manacles ages ago." He slid his arms around her waist and pulled her so close she could feel the wild thump of his heart against her chest. "I need you," he whispered, his breath steaming in her ear. "Lie down on that gurney."

But Suzie remained rooted to the floor, a wave of panic washing over her.

The Artist's face hardened. "You'd better not be toying with me."

"No, it's just… I'm sore down there from last time."

He was about to protest, but Suzie pressed a finger against his lips. "Can you think of anywhere else you'd like to put it?"

The Artist grinned. "Aren't you a dirty girl?" He took her hand and guided her to the stepladder. "Bend over this," he said, unzipping his jeans.

She forced another smile before gripping the top rung of the ladder with sweat-slicked palms and bending over it with her butt raised. When it was over, it hurt to straighten, but she still had the nail tucked into her secret place, and she considered that a victory.

The Artist hiked up his pants. "I suppose you've done enough limbering up for one day. Let's get you back to your station."

Greg's eyes locked on hers as she stepped toward the platform and she knew that he wanted her to lure the Artist to within strangling distance. But Greg's section was at least six feet away from hers. If she veered even a foot beyond her platform, the Artist would sense an ambush. It was too risky. It was her first time out of the chains and the Artist was on high alert. Better for her to bide her time, gain his trust, and wait for him to let his guard down.

201

She avoided Greg's eyes and climbed onto the stepladder, accepting a hand from the Artist. He guided her onto her platform and clamped the shackles around her wrists.

*Please, God, don't let this be a mistake.*

The Artist pressed his lips against hers and she nearly gagged on the hot stink of his breath. "I've got a feeling we'll be together for a long time, Suzie." He cocked a thumb at Greg. "But I'm not so sure about him."

"What do you mean?" Greg asked.

"I'm afraid you won't be around much longer. You lack the necessary skills for survival, and frankly, you just don't have the *balls*."

# CHAPTER THIRTY

"Well, look who got himself all cleaned up," Billy said, cocking a thumb at Coleman. "You got a new girlfriend already?"

Coleman held open the door as Ray and Billy stepped inside. "I decided it was time to get off the couch and do something to help bring Suzie back."

"What's different now?" Ray asked. "Why didn't you take charge when she first went missing?"

Coleman regarded him with an icy stare. "Do you have any idea how it feels for your wife to go missing and for everyone in the world to believe you killed her, including people you thought were your friends. I shut down, okay?"

"Better late than never, right?" Billy asked. "Except in a case like this, every second counts."

Coleman's face flushed crimson. "I know that," he said, an edge creeping into his voice.

"Then why the hell weren't you acting like it?" Billy asked. "You made it that much harder for us to do our jobs. And let's not even get into why you thought it was a good idea to go snooping around a crime scene."

"I told you, I was in a messed-up place. But I want to fix it now. I have something to tell you guys."

"What's that?" Ray said.

"I started thinking about this guy Suzie dated during freshman year of college. It was a long time ago, but maybe he's still holding a grudge."

"Go on," Ray said.

"She had been dating him for a few weeks when I first met her at a frat party. Suzie and I clicked right away, and for the next couple of weeks we were inseparable. But all that time, the guy—Brendan—kept calling and leaving her these pathetic messages like, '*I can't function without you*' or '*why won't you call me back*' or '*please, Suzie, I just need to hear your voice.*' She felt too bad to break up with him since it was obviously going to shatter the guy's ego. She said it would be like shooting a puppy, but I told her it wasn't fair to keep stringing him along. So, finally, she called him to break the news.

"We both expected him to get all weepy and beg her to reconsider, but instead he hung up without a word. About ten minutes later, while we were rolling around on her bed celebrating our newfound freedom, Brendan pounded on her door. He sounded like he'd gone completely unhinged, screaming and cursing and ramming his body against the door. I heard him yelling, 'Is someone in there with you? I swear to God I'll kill him!' Suzie managed to grab the phone and alert campus security before the doorjamb split and Brendan charged inside. He made a beeline for me as I rolled out of bed and pulled up my pants. He shoved me against the wall and grabbed a lamp off the bedside table. Smashed me in the temple and knocked me flat.

"Suzie had a little mop of a dog named Maddy, and while all of this was going on, Maddy was barking like a maniac. When Brendan grabbed Suzie by the shoulders and started shaking her, Maddy clamped her jaws around his ankle. She was just a tiny thing—and usually as sweet as could be— but she had a mouthful of needles. When Maddy refused to let go, Brendan grabbed the same lamp he'd used on me and drew it back over his shoulder to hit the dog, but Suzie threw herself in between them. For some reason that snapped Brendan out of his rage. He muttered something under his breath and let the lamp slide out of his hand before hurrying out the door. I started to go after him, but I barely made it into the hall before I got woozy and fell down. I didn't realize it then, but I ended up needing a half dozen stitches.

"Brendan got expelled and would've done jail time, but Suzie opted for a restraining order instead of pressing charges. I still can't understand why. Maybe she didn't want to confront him in court. I know she certainly never wanted to see him again."

Billy glared at Coleman. "How the hell is this the first time you're telling us about this guy?"

Coleman shrugged. "I was in shock. And then I was drunk. I mean, you saw me. I could barely get my pants on in the morning. And besides, it happened ten years ago and we haven't heard from the guy since."

"Her parents never mentioned the incident to us either," Ray said. "Why?"

"They didn't know. I think Suzie wanted to put it out of her mind, pretend like it never happened. We never talked about the attack. I mean, not once in ten years. Which is probably why I didn't think of it right away."

"You'd better hope it doesn't turn out to be this guy," Billy said, "because I don't know how you'd live with yourself."

Coleman's eyes welled up. "Please, just find her."

Ray and Billy exchanged a glance. "Come on," Ray said, heading for the door.

"Where are you going?" Coleman asked.

"We're gonna have a chat with campus police," Ray said.

***

Since Coleman was unable to recall Brendan's full name or the exact date of the incident, Sergeant Drescher of the New England College of Art and Design campus police ran the search under Suzie's name, which back in the day was Suzie Paragopolis.

A description of the incident popped up on Drescher's computer and the events matched Coleman's story, except the dog's name was Mandy instead of Maddy—a detail that spoke volumes about Coleman's attentiveness to his wife's feelings. They thanked Sergeant Drescher and left with a printout of the incident report.

Billy dialed the precinct from the car. "I need a full report on Brendan Taritello," he said, and gave Brendan's social security number to Clint.

Ray drummed his fingers against the steering wheel. This was exactly the break they'd been waiting for—an art student with a history of violence, someone with an old grudge against both Suzie and Jim Coleman. It meshed perfectly with the Artist's MO.

"Are you sure?" Billy said into the phone. "That's all you got? Alright, thanks," he said and hung up. He turned to Ray. "You're not gonna believe this."

"What?"

"Brendan Taritello died three years ago."

Ray slammed his fist against the console. "You've got to be kidding me."

"He was killed in a single car wreck on the Mass Pike."

Ray strangled the steering wheel. "Christ."

# CHAPTER THIRTY-ONE

RJ stood upon the footbridge overlooking the Public Garden lagoon. A pair of swan boats glided along the water beneath him, set against a lush backdrop of weeping willows, cherry trees, and tulips. Instead of his usual tank top and baggy shorts, RJ wore dress slacks with a button-down shirt and paisley tie. He'd even trimmed his facial hair into a respectably groomed goatee.

"What's with the getup?" Billy asked. "You fishing for yuppies?"

"This outfit just charmed a lady judge into dismissing my speeding tickets."

"I thought I told you to stay out of trouble," Ray said.

"What, you never got a speeding ticket?" RJ asked.

"It all adds up," Ray said. "Speeding tickets, vandalism, drug dealing."

"What are you talking about?"

"You don't think I've got friends in Vice? Your name came up the other day. So quit playing dumb and use your head. You're better than that."

"Yeah, well, maybe I'm not."

"Focus on the body shop and building those custom cars," Ray said. "Because if you keep dealing, you're gonna end up just like your old man."

RJ folded his arms. "I didn't come here for a lecture."

"You came here for whatever the hell we want," Billy said.

"So what is it then? You taking me on the swan boats?"

Ray squinted against the sun. "We want whatever else you've got on that kid you saw with Danny the Mule."

"You think he killed Danny?"

"It's the best theory we've got right now," Ray said. "Which is why I need you to tell us anything else you remember."

"I already told you what I know."

"I need you to reach deep on this," Ray said. "Anything you've got, even if it seems insignificant."

RJ rubbed his chin. "Well, there may be one other thing, but it'll cost extra."

"How much?" Ray asked.

"A buck fifty."

Ray fished out his wallet and peered inside. "All I've got is a hundred."

"Don't look at me," Billy said. "I'm tapped."

RJ held out his hand. "You can pay me the difference next time."

Ray slid five twenties out of his billfold and waved the money at RJ. "You don't get anything until I know what I'm buying."

"It's about who fathered the stripper's kid."

Ray handed him the cash. "Go on."

"Rumor around The Rock was that Flaherty knocked up the stripper."

Ray lifted an eyebrow. "Well, now we're getting somewhere."

"Why?" Billy asked. "Because Jack Flaherty banged a stripper? That's not exactly front-page news."

"Not Jack," RJ said. "Tom."

"Wait a minute," Ray said. "Tom Flaherty?"

"That's right," RJ said. "The honorable Thomas P. Flaherty, mayor of this fine city of Boston."

\*\*\*

"Do you believe him?" Billy asked.

Ray navigated the Explorer through the usual Back Bay gridlock. "Why wouldn't I? We've never known him to lie before."

"Maybe he's the Artist."

"Come on."

"Think about it, Ray. What if there wasn't another kid at The Rock? What if RJ was the one who Danny molested? We know he's into graffiti, so maybe he could've painted *The Suffering of Ages*. I know you like him and all, but he's not exactly a Boy Scout. He might have a dark side we don't know about."

Ray stared at the line of cars backing up near the Park Plaza hotel. "It doesn't explain the medical angle. I doubt RJ could perform an amputation and nurse someone back to health."

"You never know," Billy said. "You can learn a lot by watching YouTube."

"What do you know about YouTube?"

"I fixed my dishwasher by watching one of those videos. Saved me three hundred bucks."

Ray lifted an eyebrow. "What's an old dog like you doing learning new tricks?"

"You'd better watch yourself, or this old dog's gonna kick your ass."

Something about Billy's comment reminded him of the story Flaherty had told at Finnegan's Landing. "How come you never told me you grew up in the same complex as Flaherty?"

"I had a pretty shitty childhood. It's not something I like to talk about."

"What was Flaherty like back then?"

"He wasn't someone you wanted to mess with. And not just because he was violent, but because he was unpredictable and violent. And remember, I grew up with a lot of tough guys. Our neighborhood was full of them. But crazy beats tough every time."

"How well did you know him?"

"He's a few years older than me and he dropped out of school to work construction, so our paths never really crossed. Except for this one time at the park."

"What happened?"

"I was shooting some hoops, glad to be away from our shitty apartment and my dad's drunken fists. I was probably fourteen at the time. And I'd only been there for a few minutes before a couple punks showed up and started ripping on me for missing a layup. These guys—Pat and Brian—they had at least four years on me and were seasoned street fighters, so there was no way I could take them. But I also didn't want to run off the court like a pussy, so I tried my best to ignore them. They obviously didn't like the silent treatment, because when I went for another layup, Pat took out my legs while I was in the air and I did a belly flop onto the concrete. I rolled onto my back and tried to get up, but Brian hauled off and kicked me in the nuts. I could hear them laughing as I tried to crawl away. A few seconds later, they went dead silent and I looked up and saw Jack Flaherty striding onto the court with an ice-cold look in his eyes. He must've been on his way home from a job because he was carrying one of those steel construction worker's lunchboxes. I'll never forget the expression on Pat's and Brian's faces—they weren't sure if Flaherty was going to attack them or join in.

"That question got answered when Flaherty headbutted Brian and drove a knee into his stomach. Brian dropped to the concrete without saying a word, and he ended up being the lucky one. Pat put up his fists and smirked at Flaherty, like he'd been waiting a long time for a shot at the title. But Flaherty never broke stride. He tackled Pat at the foul line and started bashing his face with the lunchbox, swinging his arm like he was chopping wood with a hatchet. Pat barely made a sound—I think because he was choking on his own teeth—and all I could hear was the meaty thud of metal pounding flesh. I caught a glimpse of Pat's face as I ran away. It was a caved-in mask of blood, except for the few places where I could see the gleam of bone underneath. I thought for sure he was dead, but somehow he pulled through. In the end, he lost most of his teeth and half of his wits. I still see him from time to time wandering the streets of Southie with a spaced-out expression on his face."

"Christ," Ray said. "Was Flaherty ever prosecuted?"

"What do you think? Even back then, he was a master of fear and intimidation."

"What was his brother like?"

"Tom? He stayed out of trouble. I don't think he was squeaky clean, but next to Jack he was a golden boy."

Ray tapped a finger against the steering wheel.

"I know that look," Billy said. "You want to question the mayor."

"What other choice do we have?"

"We could lose our jobs."

"Come on," Ray said. "Coleman's lead about Suzie's ex-boyfriend is a dead end. We've gotten no credible tips from releasing the Artist's painting to the media. And Jack Flaherty's gonna give us jack squat. So why not see if we can at least squeeze a name out of the mayor?"

"Because I don't want to get fired. And you shouldn't either."

Ray clenched his jaw and steered the car into the precinct's parking lot. "You really are a sucker for fear and intimidation, aren't you, Billy?"

\*\*\*

"You're late," Agent Dearborn said.

Ray strode past the bullpen and motioned for the agents to follow him into the briefing room. "What can I say? Traffic's a bitch."

"What's all this?" Calhoun asked, eyeballing the photos of the Artist's victims. "You guys got a serial on your hands?"

"Starting to look that way."

He didn't like how the agents were studying the whiteboards. Dearborn, especially, wore a haughty expression, as if he thought everything they'd done on the case was amateurish.

"What's so important you two trekked all the way down here to talk to me?" Ray asked.

"We got the green light on the sting," Dearborn said, "but Larry's getting cold feet. Says he'd be more comfortable if you were there." He rolled his eyes. "Fucking prima donna."

"When is it?"

"Monday at noon."

"Where?"

"You don't need to know that right now."

"What, are you afraid I'll tip off Flaherty?"

"The less people who know the details, the better. Just show up at FBI headquarters at eleven."

"On one condition," Ray said. "You have that name for me by the middle of next week."

Dearborn furrowed his brow. "What name?"

Calhoun said, "He's been asking about a woman who stripped at the Puma a decade ago."

"What do you need that for?" Dearborn asked. "Billy looking for a new girlfriend?"

Ray gestured to the wall of victims. "She's a person of interest in this case. And, right now, all I've got is her first name and a stage name."

Dearborn looked at Calhoun. "Can we make that happen?"

"I'll get someone focused on the personnel records," Calhoun said. "If her details are in there, we'll find them."

Dearborn nodded. "So, what do you say, detective? Are you in?"

"Yeah," Ray said, "I'm in."

# CHAPTER THIRTY-TWO

Allie crawled across the stage wearing a furry gray costume with black horns, and after weaving around a handful of kids dressed as trees and rocks, she set foot onto a plywood bridge spanning a narrow river.

She made it three steps before a voice bellowed, "Who's that trip trapping across my bridge?"

"It's only me," Allie replied, "the littlest billy goat Gruff. I'm on my way to the hillside to where the sweet grass grows, and I am going to eat it all up until I am nice and fat."

Ray watched the scene unfold in miniature on his iPhone while recording Allie's acting debut. She'd barely slept the night before, terrified that she'd forget her lines. Thankfully, she'd nailed the first one and seemed to be settling down.

"Now I'm coming to gobble you up!" the troll yelled, leaping into view. It was just Ethan Morrison from next door in a rubber monster's mask, but Allie nearly jumped out of her skin.

Ray nudged Jacob, who was sitting to his left. "Either Allie's a great actress or I'm gonna need to take that costume to the dry cleaners."

From the stage, Allie said, "Please don't eat me. I'm much too little and will hardly fill your belly. You should wait for my brother, since he is much bigger than I."

When the play ended, the audience erupted in applause. The kids joined hands and took a bow, their faces beaming. Michelle blew kisses to Allie and to Jason, who'd landed a last-minute role as an oak tree.

Ray turned toward Jacob and Megan as the applause died down. "Welcome to Friday night after kids. You sure you want to go through with it?"

"Are you kidding?" Megan said. "That was adorable."

Jacob shrugged. "I'm just in it for the sex."

"Better not get used to that," Ray said, clapping him on the back.

When the lights came on, they filed out of their seats and shuffled into the main aisle, where Ray fell into step with his neighbor Tommy Morrison.

"Kids did good, huh?" Tommy said.

Ray nodded. "I don't know where they found that mask for Ethan, but Allie's gonna have nightmares for weeks."

Tommy motioned for Ray to slow up. "I don't know if you heard this or not," he said, lowering his voice, "but Darren Boyle made bail yesterday. Donnegan saw him getting liquored up at Quinn's. Apparently, he was telling anyone who would listen that you set him up."

"How the hell would he know that?"

"Beats me, but he says he's gonna make you pay."

Ray chewed his lip, calculating the odds a guy like Darren Boyle would risk more jail time for a shot at revenge. "It's probably just trash talk."

"That's what I figured," Tommy said, "but I wanted you to know."

Ray patted him on the shoulder. "Thanks, Tommy. I appreciate the heads-up."

"No problem. I gotta catch up with Pauline. See you later."

Ray watched Tommy push ahead through the crowd.

"You can't tell me you're not worried about that," Jacob said.

Ray shrugged. "Guys like that are all talk. All they care about is looking tough in front of their buddies."

"Shouldn't you file a report or something?"

"Don't sweat it, little brother. It's all part of the job."

214

"Still, I'd be nervous."

"That's because you've got soft hands and fancy socks."

By the time they reached the parking lot, Michelle and Megan had loaded the kids into the family car. "We'll meet you at the ice cream shop," Michelle said. "These kids are jonesing for a sugar fix."

Allie rolled down the window and stuck out her tongue. "Hurry up, slow pokes!"

"We'll see you there," Ray said.

As they approached Jacob's flashy sports coupe, a voice called out from behind them.

"Detective Hanley, what a coincidence."

Ray felt his hackles go up even before he turned around. "Go ahead," he said to Jacob. "I'll just be a minute."

After Jacob climbed into the car, Ray walked over to where Flaherty stood beside a vintage black Camaro. "What are you doing here?"

"It's not a good feeling, is it, detective? Someone breathing down your neck wherever you go?"

"Actually, you saved me a trip. I've got some questions about your brother."

"Is that so?"

"I hear he knocked up a stripper when he first made city council. Kept it real hush hush. I hear she used to bring the kid around while she turned tricks at The Rock."

"Now why would you dredge up such ugly rumors about my family?"

"Where's your nephew these days? I'd love to talk to him. I hear he's been up to no good."

"I don't know anything about that," Flaherty said. "Why don't you ask my brother? By the way, how'd you like those pictures I left you?"

Ray bristled. He should've known it was Flaherty. "Don't ever come near my house again. Do you understand?"

"I don't know who that girl was, detective, but she sure looked hungry."

Ray had a feeling Flaherty knew exactly who Tina was, but now wasn't the time to call him on it. "What do you want?"

"Some breathing room. I don't meddle in your business, and you don't meddle in mine."

"And if I say no?"

"Then it's bye-bye happy family."

Ray clenched his jaw, but said nothing.

"We all have secrets, detective. But I think the real measure of a man is how far he's willing to go to keep them."

# CHAPTER THIRTY-THREE

"That's the plan?" Ray asked, standing in the FBI briefing room. "That's the best you could come up with?" He shook his head. "I don't like it."

"Well, that's tough shit," Agent Dearborn said, "because your opinion doesn't matter."

Ray stared through the glass wall of the conference room to where Larry sat in the reception area with a magazine draped over his lap, one leg jittering so much that reading even a sentence would be impossible. But Larry wasn't focused on the magazine. His gaze was directed at the conference room, no doubt wondering what was being discussed inside. But all he'd be able to see was a vague shifting of shadows.

"Larry was briefed on the risks," Dearborn said, "and he's agreed to accept them, so unless anyone's got a tactical question, I'd say it's time to get this operation underway."

\*\*\*

Dearborn had selected a white box truck with MBTA decals for their surveillance vehicle. It was parked across the street from the Dunkin' Donuts on West Broadway behind a broken-down MBTA bus with its hazards flashing. It was a decent enough cover, but a bit more conspicuous than Ray would've liked, especially this close to The Rock.

Inside the truck, an array of high-tech electronics filled the back wall of the cargo area and a burly agent named Blackstone manned the equipment from a rolling desk chair. He wore a short-sleeved dress shirt with a paisley tie and was sweating as though he'd recently completed a 5K. As Blackstone leaned over the console to test the connection, Ray caught a whiff of BO and had to breathe into the crook of his arm to keep from gagging. He tilted his head toward the portable air conditioner in the corner and watched the monitor over Blackstone's shoulders. The screen displayed a clear view of Broadway looking southeast past the T-station, capturing both Finnegan's Landing and The Rock.

Ray cleared his throat and turned to Dearborn. "You said Larry's not wired. So where's the listening device?"

"That's none of your concern," Dearborn said.

"It is my concern. Larry asked for me because he doesn't trust you to look out for him."

Dearborn shook his head and turned away.

"It's with one of our agents inside the restaurant," Calhoun said. "Along with a couple of extenders placed in strategic locations. It's programmed to recognize both Larry's voice and Flaherty's. It can also filter out background noise or any conversations we deem irrelevant."

Ray lifted an eyebrow. That beat anything the police department had at its disposal. Just like the feds to keep the best technology for themselves. He shifted his attention back to the monitor and studied the flow of pedestrian traffic. After a few moments, he spotted Larry at the top of the screen. He had just exited the subway station and was walking south along Broadway wearing a backpack filled with $25,000.

It was a few days shy of the collection deadline, so Flaherty wouldn't be expecting him. Normally, Flaherty's henchmen would come knocking, rather than the other way around. The plan was for Larry to deliver half of his debt to Flaherty and ask for a three-week extension on the rest.

Somewhere behind Larry, an undercover agent was supposed to be disguised as a businessman, which likely just meant he was carrying a copy of the Wall Street Journal. Ray scanned the crowd for a moment and then pointed to the screen. "Is that your guy?" he asked, gesturing to a medium-built man in a charcoal suit.

Dearborn frowned. "How the hell did you know?"

"Because you all have that same cocky swagger. They teach you that at Quantico, or what? Right after Advanced Hair Gel Mechanics?"

"Fuck off," Dearborn said, "or I'll bounce you from the van."

"During the middle of a sting? Probably not the smartest idea. And let's not forget who arrested Larry in the first place."

Dearborn poked a finger into Ray's sternum. "Just shut your mouth and stay out of my way."

"What did I tell you about that finger?"

Calhoun grabbed Dearborn's arm and drew him back. "We can't afford to get distracted."

Dearborn grunted and turned back to the monitor.

Blackstone motioned them over. "Larry's headed into the restaurant."

"Get me the audio," Dearborn snapped.

Blackstone clacked away at his keyboard and the van filled with the bustling sounds of a lunchtime restaurant crowd. The monitor displayed a chart with a dozen sound waves in various colors. Blackstone clicked on a series of them, adjusting the settings up or down. After a few moments, they could hear Larry's voice.

"I'm looking for Jack Flaherty."

"And who the hell're you?" replied a man with an Irish brogue.

"Larry Reynolds. You can tell him I have his money."

"He expecting you?"

No answer, which probably meant that Larry had nodded, something he'd been coached not to do.

"Wait here."

Ray concentrated on the video. He could make out several tables through the plate glass windows of Finnegan's Landing, but he couldn't see all the way to the bar where Larry was supposed to be.

Agent Dearborn picked up a headset from the equipment console and spoke into the mic. "Morgan, do you have a visual?"

"Affirmative," Agent Morgan replied. "Suspect is approaching the bar."

Suddenly, Flaherty's voice filled the surveillance vehicle. "You've got a lot of balls coming in here. Or maybe just half a brain. So which is it?"

"I have a proposition for you," Larry said.

"I already don't like it. And I asked you a question, so I'd say you're off to a bad start."

"I'm sorry," Larry said. "What was the question?"

Ray grimaced. Flaherty was going to eat him alive.

"You're not very smart, are you, Larry?"

"Maybe not street smart."

"You're out of your element."

"You could say that."

"How'd you know where to find me?"

"I heard you often come here for lunch."

"Who told you that?"

"A friend of mine. He said everyone in Southie knows you eat here during the week."

"What's his name?"

Larry answered just as they'd rehearsed. "Patrick."

"And does Patrick have a last name?"

"I don't want to get him into trouble. And besides, he moved out of Southie a few years ago."

"You know, Larry, the more you say, the less I believe you. And if there's one thing I can't stand, it's being lied to. So what I want to know is, why would you disrespect me during my lunch?"

"I didn't... I mean, I—"

"Who sent you, Larry?"

"Nobody sent me. I've got half your money. I just need a little more time to—"

"I don't know what you're talking about, Larry. But if you want to discuss business, then let's go somewhere more private."

Ray looked at Dearborn. "It's time to call it off."

"Relax, Hanley. He'll probably just check for a wire. And we've got all the exits covered."

"What if he kills Larry in the storeroom?"

"Then we'll nail him for murder."

"You sonofabitch."

"What happened to the audio?" Calhoun asked.

Blackstone turned a dial and the sudden roar of the restaurant crowd made them all wince. "Hang on," he said, adjusting the settings.

But all they heard was silence.

"Maybe they're not talking," Calhoun said.

Dearborn spoke into the mic. "Morgan, what's happening in there?"

"They went into the kitchen. Should I pursue?"

"Negative," Dearborn said. "Give it a minute."

"Do you have a blueprint of the restaurant?" Ray asked Blackstone.

Blackstone keyed something into the computer and a diagram of Finnegan's Landing appeared on the monitor. Behind the dining area and bathrooms, they could see the kitchen, a walk-in refrigerator, a storeroom, and an office.

"Can you pick up conversations in those other rooms?" Ray asked.

"Let me tap into the extenders," Blackstone said. He fiddled with the settings and they heard the clamor of pots and pans and men shouting at each other in clipped Spanish.

"Go to the office," Dearborn said.

But all they got was the sound of someone typing while Neil Diamond sang in the background.

"Can you zero in on the walk-in freezer?" Ray asked.

Blackstone shook his head. "Too much insulation."

"Try the storeroom," Calhoun said.

Blackstone adjusted the settings and they heard a faint shuffling that might've been someone stocking the shelves.

Dearborn spoke into the mic. "Carter, do you have a visual on the back door?"

"Affirmative. No movement so far."

Ray headed for the exit. "I'm going in."

"Like hell you are," Dearborn said. "Calhoun and I will check it out. You stay here."

"I'm coming with you."

Dearborn drew his weapon and flung open the rear door. "Stay put," he said, leveling a finger at Ray. "That's an order."

Ray smacked the ceiling of the truck and swore. "I told you this was a bad idea!" He pulled the door shut and studied the monitor. A few moments later, he could see Dearborn and Calhoun storming through the entrance to Finnegan's Landing.

"FBI!" Dearborn shouted. "Nobody move!"

A collective gasp rippled through the crowd, a sea of heads turning toward the front door in a synchronous swivel. Some of the diners were associates of Flaherty's, but most were just regular citizens getting a bite to eat on their lunch break. If the situation erupted into a firefight, it would be a bloodbath.

Ray watched the monitor as Agent Morgan moved in to cover the entrance.

"Where's Flaherty?" Calhoun shouted.

"How the feck should I know?" the man with the Irish brogue said.

A pair of agents charged into the restaurant and escorted diners outside, handing them off to other agents who whisked them away to a safe zone a block and a half farther down Broadway. As the last of the diners exited the building, a contingent of state police cars converged onto the scene with their lights flashing. A team of troopers unrolled a spool of crime scene tape and cordoned off the area.

Ray clenched his hands and listened to the agents conduct a room-to-room sweep. After a few minutes, the search went quiet.

"Where the hell are they?" Dearborn shouted. "Did anyone go through the back door?"

"Negative," Agent Carter said.

"Maybe they're holed up somewhere," Calhoun said. "Let's sweep it again."

"Christ," Ray said, reaching for the door.

Agent Blackstone shot to his feet. "Dearborn told you to stay put."

"Dearborn can kiss my ass."

Ray jumped into the street, where a swarm of federal agents and state troopers worked against a backdrop of flashing blue lights erecting sidewalk barricades and rerouting pedestrian traffic down Dot Ave.

Ray gazed diagonally across the street from Finnegan's Landing to The Rock. Flaherty was rumored to be a silent partner in the restaurant, and regardless of whether he bought in or muscled his way in, he'd be the one calling the shots. He'd done it before with strip clubs, liquor stores, and bookmakers, so why not his favorite restaurant?

A pair of state troopers stood guard near The Rock, facing toward Finnegan's Landing, where a heavily armed SWAT team stormed out of an armored truck.

Ray couldn't help but feel like they were all missing something. Flaherty was too smart to get trapped inside of his own restaurant. He thought back to the day of the drive-by shooting when Giabatti's goons had gunned down Mad Murph and those construction workers.

He suddenly remembered that Flaherty owned a construction company—it was the nearest thing he had to a legitimate business. Ray glanced from Finnegan's Landing to The Rock, then back again. The two buildings stood approximately 150 feet apart. He lowered his eyes to the pavement.

*Christ!*

He darted across the street toward The Rock and caught a glimpse of Trooper Garrison coming toward him.

"Where are you going?" Garrison asked.

Ray signaled for him to follow and Garrison fell in beside him. They arrived at The Rock's front door and Ray threw his weight against the battered green steel, but it wouldn't budge.

Garrison looked over his shoulder at Finnegan's Landing. "What's going on? You think he's got a tunnel or something?"

Ray kicked the door in frustration, leaving a scuff mark against the emerald green paint. "That's my theory."

Garrison hurried over to the nearby troopers. "Get someone from SWAT. Tell them we need to bust down this door right now."

Ray glanced up at the closed-circuit camera mounted into the brick above the entryway. If Flaherty was inside, he'd already be headed for the back door. Ray drew his gun and stalked to the side of the building. He hopped a chain-link fence and squeezed through a thick row of hedges, Garrison following closely behind.

A parking lot with room for a dozen spaces abutted the rear of the building. It only had three cars at the moment, none of which he recognized as Flaherty's. Another security camera peered at them from above a reinforced garage door serving as the sole point of entry into the rear of the building.

Ray extended his middle finger to the camera.

"You think he's in there?" Garrison asked.

"I don't know," Ray said, his eyes sweeping the grounds.

The neighboring building was a paint supply shop that had gone out of business years ago, the storefront windows shuttered for as long as Ray could remember. He'd always assumed that nobody in his right mind would set up shop next to Flaherty, but when he registered a blur of movement in the store's parking lot, it dawned on him that Flaherty might actually own the place.

Ray and Garrison charged across the parking lot and barreled through the hedges in time to see Flaherty closing the trunk of a gray Chevy Impala before jumping into the driver's seat.

"Get down," Ray whispered, pulling Garrison into the hedges.

Flaherty exited onto Silver Street, then made a quick left onto A Street.

A US Postal Service truck idled at the curb a few yards away. Ray could see a heavyset mailman farther down the street waddling toward the door of a nearby business.

"Let's go," Ray said. He scrambled into the truck and stomped on the accelerator as Garrison squeezed between the passenger door and a mail crate and braced himself against the dash.

"He's headed south," Garrison said. "He knows the other end of Dot Ave is crawling with cops."

"You got your radio?" Ray asked.

Garrison unclipped it from his belt.

"Let's not call in the cavalry until we've got him in our sights."

"You got it," Garrison said.

Ray edged the mail truck up to fifty miles per hour and Garrison grimaced as they blew past parked cars with less than an inch of clearance. Garrison was the type of guy who wore his seatbelt even when parked on the shoulder of the road, and right now he didn't even have a seat.

"What's the matter?" Ray asked. "You don't like my driving?"

"If you get me killed, I swear I'll haunt you for the rest of your life."

They caught sight of Flaherty as he turned onto Old Colony Ave. Ray eased up on the gas and kept the tail at a safe distance. Flaherty appeared to be doing the speed limit, trying not to call attention to himself, which meant he didn't realize anyone had followed. At least not yet.

Garrison brought the radio to his lips. "This is Trooper Garrison requesting backup. We've got a visual on Jack Flaherty. He's headed south on Old Colony in a gray Chevy Impala, approaching Morrissey Boulevard. We believe he's got Larry in the trunk."

Morrissey Boulevard was a three-lane highway that led into the neighboring city of Quincy. It was also where Flaherty could pick up the interstate and disappear for good.

"Roger that," the dispatcher responded. "Alerting all units."

When Flaherty reached the traffic circle, he surprised them by bypassing Morrissey Boulevard and turning left along the waterfront past the Old Colony projects and Carson Beach, where Ray had once witnessed two homeless people having sex.

Ray leaned over the steering wheel. "Where the hell is he going?"

Garrison spoke into the radio again. "Flaherty is now on William Day Boulevard headed toward L Street. We are pursuing him in a US Postal Service truck."

A voice blared through the radio. "This is Special Agent Dearborn. Is Flaherty aware of your presence?"

"Negative," Garrison said.

"Do not engage," Dearborn said. "Do you understand? We're setting up a blockade. He's not making it out of Southie."

"Copy that," Garrison said. "Suspect is turning onto L Street."

"Who's with you?" Dearborn asked, more of an accusation than a question.

Ray leaned toward Garrison and directed his voice into the radio. "How's it going, Dearborn? Your boys find that tunnel yet?"

"Hanley? I thought I told you to stay in the truck."

"You're lucky I didn't listen."

"You'd better not fuck this up, you hear me?"

"I'm pretty sure you already took care of that," Ray said.

"Crossing the bridge onto Summer Street," Garrison said.

The Black Falcon cruise terminal came into view on their right, a Norwegian Cruise Line ship towering over the docks.

"Stay on him," Dearborn said, "but not too close."

"We know how this works," Ray said.

Garrison released the talk button and looked at Ray. "Now's probably not the time to get into a pissing match with the feds."

"Why don't you tell him that?"

Ray gazed down Summer Street to where the steely peaks of the Financial District rose into the sky. If Flaherty kept the Impala on course, he'd pass South Station and take Atlantic Ave to I-93.

Instead, Flaherty turned right onto D Street.

"What the hell is he doing?" Garrison asked.

"He's got a boat," Ray said. "I bet he's headed for the marina so he can avoid the dragnet and sail out of here. Drop Larry off for a swim in the Atlantic."

When Ray steered the mail truck onto D Street, the Impala surged ahead and veered left onto Congress Street.

"He sees us!" Garrison shouted. "He sees us!"

"Move in!" Dearborn yelled.

Another voice came through the radio. "This is Unit 217. We're headed south on Congress Street, approaching your position."

Ray slammed on the brakes and did a U-turn, cutting off a white SUV and forcing it to swerve onto the shoulder, where it teetered on two wheels before coming to a rest on all four.

Garrison braced himself against the dash. "What the hell are you doing?"

227

"When Flaherty sees that cruiser, he's gonna turn back onto Summer Street and I want to be there waiting for him." He cut the wheel hard and stomped on the accelerator, emerging from the turn with tires screeching. The mail truck shuddered as he pushed it over sixty, the plastic bins in the back sliding all over the floor.

As they approached the Convention Center, the Impala barreled back onto Summer Street a hundred yards ahead. Garrison drew his gun and leaned out the window, aiming for the tires. "Hold it steady."

"I am holding it steady. Just take the shot."

"There's too much vibration. If I put a bullet into the back of the car, it might hit Larry."

"We're losing him," Ray said, the Impala picking up speed. "Do it now!"

Garrison anchored himself against the door and took aim.

The warble of sirens rose in the distance.

Garrison fired. The bullet struck the pavement and drew sparks. His next shot plunked into the bumper, but the one after that blew out the rear passenger tire and sent the Impala fishtailing across the road.

"Got him!" Garrison yelled, pumping his fist.

The Impala sideswiped a car, jumped the curb, and flattened a fire hydrant, sending a geyser of water shooting into the air. The door swung open and Flaherty staggered out, a trickle of blood running down his forehead. He raised his gun and aimed it at their windshield, but Ray cut the wheel and slammed on the brakes, turning the truck sideways.

Ray shifted into park and hopped out of the truck as Unit 217 rolled up behind them and a pair of squad cars closed in from the opposite end of Summer Street. South Station loomed to their left, towering five stories over the street with its mammoth arched doorways, granite columns, and curved façade.

Flaherty was already halfway to the station, waving his gun in the air and sending a crush of pedestrians scattering in all directions.

Ray and Garrison weaved through the fleeing crowd, losing sight of Flaherty as they entered the concourse. Garrison locked eyes with an elderly flower vendor wearing wrinkled chinos and a red apron. "Where'd he go?" Garrison asked.

The man pointed toward an electronic train schedule suspended from a vaulted ceiling.

"Amtrak or subway?" Garrison pressed.

"I don't—"

Ray didn't wait for the man to finish. He plowed ahead into the station, holding his badge in one hand and his Glock in the other. Flaherty had a narrow window of time before the transit police shut everything down, but he had plenty of options—buses, commuter rail, subway, or Amtrak.

Ray scanned the crowd as he cut a path toward the escalators, making a quick read of their expressions. A brunette in a blue sundress met his eyes as she rode the escalator up from the lower level, her brow wrinkled in concern.

Ray waved his badge at her. "Did you see something?"

"A man with a gun just ran past me."

"Where'd he go?"

"Toward Alewife."

Ray signaled to Garrison and raced down the stairs, following the Red Line signs to Alewife. He emerged onto a crowded subway platform, flashing his badge and keeping his gun aimed at the ground. "Police! Where is he?"

Several people pointed to the tracks.

"You've got to be kidding me," Garrison said.

Ray ran to the edge of the platform and peered into the tunnel. The signal light glowed white in the darkness. It would remain lit until a train was approaching the station.

Ray jumped onto the tracks, his heels striking loose gravel. When he stood erect, he was eye level with the platform.

"What the hell are you doing?" Garrison asked.

Ray gestured to the wall separating the Alewife side of the station from the Braintree side. It contained a series of cutouts large enough for a man to squeeze through. Beside one of the cutouts, a red sign with white lettering read: *Danger Third Rail!*

"He might've crossed over," Ray said. "Check the other side and get Transit to shut down the trains."

"Okay," Garrison said. "But be careful."

Ray stalked along the tracks, keeping his body close to the edge of the platform. He heard Garrison running toward the stairs, his fleeing footfalls reminding him of the night of his father's murder. The killer's footfalls had sounded just like that, echoing through the tunnel as his father's last breath ended in a liquid gurgle. By then, the coppery scent of blood permeated the air, mingling with the musty heat of the tunnels and the pungent odor of urine wafting off the tracks.

That same subterranean stench filled his nostrils now, and for a moment, he felt like a fifteen-year-old kid again—frightened and helpless and alone.

He reached the end of the platform and the tunnel yawned before him like a gaping, black mouth. If Flaherty was lying in wait somewhere in the darkness, Ray would be the perfect target, standing as he was beneath the last of the overhead lights.

He cocked his head to listen for Flaherty, but all he could hear was the squeaking of rats. He tightened his grip on his gun and crept forward until the shadows consumed him. Something scurried over his foot and he jerked backward, almost stumbling into the third rail, which would've injected 600 volts of electricity into his body and fried him like a hot-oiled turkey.

A snickering emanated from somewhere ahead. "What's the matter, detective? Afraid of a little mouse?"

Ray strained to see through the darkness. "Drop your gun, Flaherty."

"I don't think so, detective. I grew up running these tunnels, so I know my way around. Just like that gangbanger who killed your father."

Ray recoiled as if slapped. "What do you know about that?"

"I know a lot of things, detective. Right now, I've got you in my sights. If you make one wrong move, I'll shoot you full of holes and these hungry rats will mistake you for swiss cheese."

"Give me a name, Flaherty, if you've really got one."

"The scent of your blood will draw them out of the shadows. They'll sniff the air, whiskers twitching, and once they sense your helplessness, they'll swarm over you, squeaking and skittering as they chew your face off. I've seen it happen, detective. They'll fight each other just to feast on your eyes."

Something about the tunnel had changed, and it took Ray a moment to realize the signal light had gone dark.

"I said give me a name."

"That's not how this works, detective. You let me walk away and a package will arrive with all the details you could ever want."

The rails awakened with an ominous hum.

"I'm not letting you go."

"What about our secret, detective? It would be a shame if that pretty wife of yours discovered your betrayal."

A hot breeze wafted through the tunnel and swept Ray's hair off his brow. The rumble of an approaching train soon followed, its wheels screeching as it rounded an unseen bend.

"I know where to hide," Flaherty said. "But the question is, do you?"

By now, Ray's eyes had adjusted to the darkness and he could discern Flaherty's silhouette in the distance. As Ray raised his Glock, a rat scurried between his legs and he tripped over the rail and fell onto the tracks.

The sound of the train grew steadily louder, drowning out the mocking echo of Flaherty's laughter. A bright light

231

washed over him and he lunged forward on all fours, his hands scrabbling for purchase in the loose gravel. The train sounded as if it was accelerating into the station. Would the conductor be able to see him so low to the ground?

He staggered to his feet and the train's brakes squealed in response, but how much track would it take to stop a forty-ton train?

A horn blared and Ray could feel the wind at his back as the train parted the air. The beginning of the platform came into view and he could see the horrified expressions of the commuters gathered at the scene.

A moment later, almost in unison, the crowd shielded its eyes.

*Christ*, Ray thought, *it's gonna be close.*

# CHAPTER THIRTY-FOUR

*When I was a child, I was afraid of creatures,*
*Spawned by nightmares, books, or features.*
*And as I lay awake in bed,*
*And stared into the darkness with dread,*
*I could sense them in the shadows,*
*With claws and fangs like arrows,*
*Lapping up my fears and sapping me of tears,*
*While patiently waiting, their fangs salivating,*
*For a taste of my flesh or to hasten my death.*

*But as I aged, I grew not to be afraid,*
*For no monsters did hide beneath my bed or beside.*
*But fleeting were the days of fearless wonder,*
*Between the savage beasts of a child's mind torn asunder,*
*And the sobering age of wisdom,*
*That ironic twist beyond the schism,*
*When man is unmasked as the monster at last,*
*And I can't close my eyes or crawl beneath the blankets to hide,*
*For man has ample numbers to rape and kill and plunder.*

*And so now I long for those bygone days,*
*When all the world's monsters could be slayed,*
*With the creatures of the night—*
*An entire legion of evil,*
*Vanquished by the flick of a light.*

Suzie's poems had grown longer and more intricate, but that didn't mean they were any better. Given her current situation, she knew it shouldn't matter, but it was one of the few things she could control, and she drew a certain power from shaping the words in a way that gave life to her feelings.

A couple of days had passed since Greg's aborted attempt to strangle the Artist, and since the Artist hadn't retaliated, Suzie figured he wasn't in the habit of reviewing the video footage. If anything, he might be watching a live feed to check on them before entering the gallery. Of course, she could be wrong, but if she was ever going to escape from the gallery, she had to start taking risks.

The first step had been hiding the nail from the Artist, but that was only the beginning of a long and dangerous road. It had taken some delicate maneuvering to retrieve the nail from the fold of her labia and poke it into the drywall behind her. She'd managed not to cut herself during the initial insertion, but extracting it was another story. When the Artist made his rounds the next day, she blamed the blood on her period, and thankfully he accepted the explanation without question.

Last night, she made her first attempt at picking the locks and found that if she pinched the nail between her thumb and forefinger and stood on her tiptoes, she could reach across her body and angle it into the keyholes.

The shackles resembled oversized cast-iron handcuffs, and judging from the rudimentary construction and the coarse layer of rust, they seemed like a relic of a bygone age. Sometimes, in the dead of night, she couldn't help but wonder who had last worn them and what fate he or she may have suffered. If there was a silver lining to any of this, the shackles probably lacked the enhanced security features of a modern lock. And maybe it was her imagination, but after a few hours of practice, she felt as if she might be close to springing one of them.

If she did manage to escape, the Artist would be in for a shock come morning. In case he was checking the monitor prior to entering the gallery, she and Greg would remain against the wall with their shackles on, but the locks opened. And when the Artist approached them to offer breakfast or to hose urine off the floor, they would leap down from their posts and attack.

Sometimes, she imagined bashing the Artist's head against the concrete until his blood gurgled into the center drain. Other times, she imagined Greg stomping on his windpipe while she pulverized his balls with the croquet mallet.

If the Artist happened to be watching the monitor in that moment, he would see Suzie grinning in the dim glow of the picture lights and might wonder if she was going insane. And if he kept watching, he would see her fiddle with one of the locks for nearly twenty minutes, her calves trembling from being on her toes for so long.

And if the sound quality was especially good, he might even hear the distinct click as the ancient lock, at last, sprang open.

# CHAPTER THIRTY-FIVE

The last thing Ray saw in those final moments was Garrison charging toward the edge of the platform with his teeth bared and the muscles of his neck bulging. Ray could sense the train bearing down on him as he emerged into the station, and he was momentarily blinded by the bright lights and a gut-wrenching wave of panic.

His foot snagged beneath a railroad tie and he stumbled forward, his arms pinwheeling for balance. A moment later, a crushing force squeezed his back and chest and he experienced a dizzying sensation of weightlessness.

It wasn't until he crashed down onto a jarring slab of concrete that he realized Garrison had hauled him off the tracks and pulled him onto the platform. He rolled onto his back and turned in time to see the Red Line train draw to a screeching halt midway into the station.

Garrison leaned over him, beads of sweat glistening against his brow. "Damnit, Ray! What the hell were you thinking?"

"Who said I was thinking?" He pulled himself into a sitting position and winced at a twinge of pain in his ankle. "You're not going to ask if I'm okay?"

"You're a crazy damn fool."

"I might've sprained my ankle."

"Do you have any idea how close you came to being roadkill?"

"Are you lecturing me? After what I just went through?"

"Damn right I'm lecturing you. That was reckless. And stupid."

"I might've gotten a little overzealous."

"You think?"

Ray draped an arm around Garrison's shoulders. "I owe you one, buddy."

"You owe me more than one."

"Yeah," Ray said, "thanks for having my back."

Garrison grinned, and Ray could feel the tension drain from the big man's shoulders. "That was way too close," Garrison said. "One for the highlight reel."

"I'll pay you back one of these days."

"You damn well better."

A thunder of footfalls echoed through the station as several transit officers charged down the stairs. "Where'd he go?" the lead officer shouted.

Ray pointed to the tracks.

"We'll take it from here," the officer said. "We know these tunnels better than anyone. He won't get away."

\*\*\*

Except Flaherty did get away, and Ray spent the remainder of the afternoon camped out in the FBI's situation room. He would've preferred to be out looking for Flaherty, but Dearborn and his superiors kept grilling him about what happened in the tunnels.

Meanwhile, Captain Daniels of the MBTA Police displayed a map of the Red Line subway system on a screen at the front of the room. He traced a series of lines using a laser pointer. "My teams have swept the tunnels here, here, and here with no sign of Flaherty. These represent active subway and commuter rail lines, but since we're dealing with a system dating back to 1897, we've also got several abandoned tunnels to contend with."

He highlighted the areas with the pointer.

"Some of these tunnels are clear, but others are littered with rubble and rusted equipment, which could provide Flaherty with ample opportunities to hide. My team is moving into these areas as we speak, accompanied by a state police SWAT unit and a half-dozen federal agents. Unfortunately, there's a chance Flaherty is no longer in the tunnels, since there are several exits between stations."

"What kind of exits?" the special agent in charge asked.

"Emergency hatches, vents, even a few stairways leading to abandoned maintenance buildings. I've sent officers to the major locations, but if Flaherty knows his way around as well as he claims to, then it's possible he beat us there."

The special agent in charge glared in Dearborn's direction. "You'd better hope he doesn't get away."

"We couldn't have anticipated the tunnel at Finnegan's Landing," Dearborn snapped.

The room fell quiet and Ray noticed that Agent Calhoun had retreated to the far wall, putting as much distance between himself and Dearborn as possible.

"If you'd done the proper due diligence," the special agent in charge said, "we wouldn't be standing here, but instead you got upstaged by a city detective."

Dearborn's face flushed crimson. "If Detective Hanley had shared his suspicion of the tunnel, Flaherty never would've reached South Station."

The special agent in charge looked at Ray. "Is that true?"

Ray shook his head. "There wasn't any time. Flaherty was probably halfway through the tunnel before it even occurred to me. And if I'd stopped to run it up the chain of command, we never would've seen him get into the car."

"So you didn't tell anyone?" the special agent in charge asked.

Garrison raised his hand. "He told me outside of The Rock and I asked SWAT to break down the door. But that was before we spotted Flaherty in the parking lot."

"That's right," Ray said. "And as soon as we commandeered the mail truck, Trooper Garrison radioed in with Flaherty's location."

"Then I guess your asses are covered," the special agent in charge said. He motioned to Captain Daniels. "Sorry for the interruption. Please continue."

Dearborn shot Ray a dirty look.

If the agent wasn't such an arrogant prick, Ray would almost feel sorry for the guy. He nudged Garrison in the shoulder. "Thanks for backing me up."

"Don't worry," Garrison said. "I'll just add it to your tab."

# CHAPTER THIRTY-SIX

"You can't just drop in unannounced," Mrs. Granderling said, her face puckered up as if she'd bitten into a lemon. "Doctor Weintraub has a very busy schedule."

Ray strode past the reception desk without slowing. "I don't think his patients will mind."

He spotted Luis exiting the tissue storage room, his dark hair tied back in a ponytail, headphones pulled down over his neck. He pointed at Luis's chest. "Watch out for that spider."

Luis chuckled, not falling for it. "Are you any closer to catching that guy?"

"I'm beginning to think he's an evil genius."

"Maybe he's just lucky."

"I don't know," Ray said. "You saw how he staged Finkleton's murder. That's not luck, it's planning."

Luis slid the headphones over his ears. "He's bound to make a mistake one of these days. And if I know you, you'll be right there when he does."

"Let's hope." Ray continued down the hall and found Doc Death in his office, engrossed in paperwork. "Must be some good reading," Ray said. "Anything to do with my case?"

Doc adjusted his glasses. "It's the toxicology report for Mr. Finkleton."

"What's it say?"

"Mr. Finkleton had traces of Amobarbital in his system."

"Which is what, exactly?"

"It's a barbiturate commonly used for general anesthesia. I imagine the killer used it when performing the amputations."

"At least Finkleton was out cold for that, but can you imagine the shock when he woke up?"

"He also had elevated levels of amoxicillin in his system."

"That makes sense," Ray said. "He wanted to keep Finkleton alive for as long as possible."

"If you recall, Danny McDougal died from a blood infection, so perhaps our killer went heavy on Finkleton's antibiotics out of an abundance of caution."

"Which again points to some medical training," Ray said, "though maybe not a full-fledged doctor."

"Exactly."

"What else you got?"

Tina appeared in the doorway. "I thought I was supposed to be debriefing this case."

Ray folded his arms. "Haven't you done enough debriefing?"

Doc Death shot him a puzzled look. "Did I miss something?"

"I'm just giving her a hard time."

"Would you like to tell Ray what we found in Mr. Finkleton's hair?" Doc asked.

"Plaster of Paris," she said. "The exact same chemical composition as the piece we found on Danny McDougal."

\*\*\*

A few minutes later, Ray stood outside of the ME's office watching the flow of traffic on Albany Street. He heard the door open behind him and knew without turning that it was Tina.

"What the hell was that?" she asked. "Were you trying to get me in trouble with Weintraub?"

"The other day at your apartment, that never should've happened."

"Then why were you flirting with me at the restaurant?"

"I wasn't flirting with you. I was trying to be sympathetic. You're the one who threw yourself at me."

Tina's cheeks reddened. "I misread the signals, okay? I thought you wanted me to surprise you the way I used to."

"I'm married, Tina."

"Then why didn't you stop me as soon as I came out of the bedroom? Why'd you let me go through with it?"

"I don't know. I guess seeing you like that brought back too many memories."

She buried her face in her hands and shook her head. "I'm so humiliated."

"It's not your fault. I should've stopped it like you said."

"Can we please pretend like it never happened?"

Ray nodded. "Let's bury it deep."

# CHAPTER THIRTY-SEVEN

"I hear you had fun playing in the subway the other day," Billy said.

"Yeah," Ray said, checking the rearview mirror, "you should've been there."

"No one invited me."

"How was court yesterday?"

"Waste of time. Waited all day to testify for two minutes." It was a domestic homicide they'd investigated a year earlier, and about as open and shut as they came.

"At least you didn't get raked over the coals like I did for the Coleman hearing."

"That's right," Billy said with a chuckle. "You got your ass reamed on that one." He sipped his coffee. "What's the word on Flaherty?"

"He's gone. Literally dropped off the face of the earth."

"And Larry?"

"Last I heard, Larry's in protective custody in the not so capable hands of Special Agent Dearborn."

Billy snickered. "I hear he almost got canned."

"Probably should've," Ray said. "You got any idea where Flaherty might be?"

"Somewhere we won't find him. He's probably halfway to South America by now."

"Unless he's holed up in a local safe house, waiting for the heat to die down."

"He's a crafty sonofabitch," Billy said. "He could be anywhere. What else happened while I was out?"

"Clint came back with the refined search for Angie T, but it didn't help."

"What about the Puma's payroll records? Any word from the feds?"

"Dearborn won't return my calls and Calhoun claims they've been backed up since Flaherty went on the lam."

"Sounds like he's blowing smoke. Any other developments? Or did you just sit at the precinct and twiddle your thumbs all day?"

Ray gave him the finger. "I drove to Gloucester and followed up on Dean Saunders's alibi."

"And?"

"Everyone I talked to vouched for him. On the night of Finkleton's murder, he attended an AA meeting and then went to a friend's house to play cards. Nearest I can tell, he left the friend's house around 1:30 a.m. and went straight home. A neighbor saw him go inside and said she would've heard the truck start up if he left again since it's obnoxiously loud and she's usually up all hours of the night."

"What if Saunders took his girlfriend's VW bug?" Billy said. "He could've driven to wherever he was holding Finkleton, switched to a truck, and then headed to Stony Brook Reservation."

"It's possible," Ray said, "but his girlfriend claims Saunders was there for the rest of the night."

"She could be lying."

"His cell phone location data corroborates their story."

"He could've left the phone at home before heading out again."

"True," Ray said, "but it's more than an hour drive to Stony Brook. By the time he got there and strung up Finkleton it would be after three in the morning, which seems too late to jibe with Tina's estimated time of death."

"It would only be off by a couple hours, which is within the margin for error."

"My gut says it's not him, but you're right—we can't completely rule him out."

"What about the background check on The Particle Bean's manager?" Billy asked.

"Came back squeaky clean. The guy's a Boy Scout."

"So what you're saying is I missed jack shit."

Ray nodded. "I think the trail's gone cold."

"No more posts on deaddumbandbizzare.com?"

"Nothing," Ray said. "The best we've gotten is a handful of calls to the tip line with people claiming to recognize *The Suffering of Ages*."

"Let me guess," Billy said, "the usual kooks?"

"You got it."

"What about Gary? He come back with anything on the library computers?"

"Not anything we can use."

Billy drew a deep breath and frowned. "We could hit a few more coffee shops and galleries, see if anyone recognizes the painting."

"We've covered that ground already. It's a waste of time."

"You got any better ideas?" Billy asked.

"Yeah, I'd like to have a chat with the mayor."

"I'm sure the feds have already spoken with him."

"About Flaherty maybe, but not about the Artist."

"Spinonni will shit a brick."

"So we don't tell him."

"You don't think it'll get back to him?"

"I'll be very tactful," Ray said.

"I think it's a terrible idea."

"I'll take that under advisement," Ray said, and turned off at the Government Center exit.

***

Boston City Hall was a concrete monstrosity that appeared to be part beehive, part space invaders mothership, and looked as though it had been relocated—block-by-hideous

245

block—from a former eastern European nation's communist headquarters.

Ray strode across the sprawling brick courtyard of City Hall Plaza with Billy trailing a half-step behind. "I thought you said this was a bad idea."

"Not a bad idea, a terrible idea."

"So why are you following me?"

"Because you'll never get a meeting without me."

"Oh yeah," Ray said, "because you're such a pillar of society."

"Don't be mad just because I've got connections."

Ray smirked. "Connections? We'll see about that."

They entered the lobby and waited in line for the metal detector. When it was their turn, Ray handed his ID to the security officer. "Detective Hanley, Boston Police." He cocked a thumb at Billy. "And of course, Detective Devlin, who I'm sure needs no introduction."

"You carrying?" the guard asked.

Ray and Billy opened their sports coats to show their guns.

"Just a minute," the guard said while a colleague verified their credentials. "Alright, you're clear."

They proceeded to the fifth floor, which housed a reception area dedicated to the mayor's office. It had two reception desks and Ray chose the one attended by a bookish brunette with pretty eyes, figuring he had a better chance of charming her than the dour-looking old man at the other desk.

She greeted him with a smile and listened attentively to his spiel. "I'm sorry," she said when he finished, "but the mayor's schedule is full. I can put in a request for tomorrow, but I can't make any promises. You might have better luck coordinating your meeting through the police chief."

"I would," Ray said, "but it relates to an investigation that's time sensitive, and sometimes the police bureaucracy is even worse than the government bureaucracy."

Billy muscled up beside Ray and leaned his forearms on the desk. "Could you just tell the mayor that Billy Devlin needs five minutes of his time? We grew up together, he knows me."

The receptionist did a poor job of hiding her skepticism, but she passed the message along to one of the mayor's aides, a sandy-haired ex-frat boy type in an expensive suit. The aide disappeared through a door behind the reception desk. When he returned a minute later, he motioned to a leather sofa in the waiting area. "Have a seat, detectives. The mayor will see you as soon as his meeting ends."

Billy planted his hands on his hips and stared at Ray. "I think someone owes me an apology."

\*\*\*

The mayor's office featured floor-to-ceiling windows that offered stunning views of Faneuil Hall and the yawning blue vista of Boston Harbor. The interior walls were drab by contrast, constructed of slate-gray concrete that seemed better suited to a prison than the office of the city's most powerful man. The mayor was seated behind a mahogany desk with a hand-carved seal of the city, and as Ray and Billy entered the room, the mayor rose to greet them.

"Billy Devlin, how the hell are you?"

"Doing good," Billy said, crossing the room to shake the mayor's hand. "I'd ask how you're doing, but shit, you're the mayor. I don't even know what to call you anymore—your honor, your highness, Mr. Mayor."

"Just Tom," the mayor said, flashing them a grin. "Still just the same old kid from Southie."

*Yeah,* Ray thought, *except now you live on Beacon Hill.*

Billy gestured to Ray. "This is my partner, Detective Ray Hanley."

The mayor shook Ray's hand. "You keeping Billy in line?" he asked, regarding him with the same penetrating gaze as his mobster brother.

247

"It's a full-time job," Ray said, returning the mayor's squeeze with equal force.

"Have a seat," the mayor said, motioning to a pair of leather wing chairs opposite his desk. "I'm afraid I can only spare five minutes."

"That's all we need," Billy said. "I'll cut right to it. We're investigating a serial killer, and right now our primary suspect is the son of a former stripper we know only as Angie T."

"What's this got to do with me?"

"The stripper used to frequent Jack's bar years ago," Billy said.

"What makes you think I would know anything about that? You know I don't have anything to do with my brother."

Billy shrugged. "We were hoping you might know of her through the grapevine. I don't need to tell you how word gets around in Southie, especially back in the day."

The mayor scowled. "If talk about Jack doesn't relate to throwing his ass in jail, then I tune it out. You understand? My brother's dead to me."

"Look," Ray said, "I understand why the question might make you defensive—"

"I'm not getting defensive."

"—but your brother wouldn't tell us," Ray continued, "and now he's a fugitive."

"Why don't you ask his associates?"

"We have," Ray said, "but they're not a very talkative bunch. Also, none of them is rumored to have fathered the stripper's son."

The mayor folded his arms. "I'm sure she's not the first stripper Jack knocked up."

"Actually," Ray said, "we don't believe Jack is the father."

"Then who is?"

"Well, Mr. Mayor," Ray said, "that would be you."

\*\*\*

Later that afternoon, Ray and Billy found themselves sitting in a much less luxurious office, one that was devoid of windows and permeated with the unsettling aroma of tuna fish wrapped in sweat socks.

"What the hell were you thinking?" Lieutenant Spinonni barked.

Ray and Billy exchanged a glance. "We just asked the mayor a couple of simple questions," Ray said.

Spinonni's face flushed. "What gave you the idea that it was okay to talk to the mayor?"

"First of all," Ray said, "anyone can request an audience with the mayor. And second, Billy knows him from when they were kids."

"I don't care if Billy and the mayor held hands during the neighborhood circle jerk. You violated department policy and pissed off the mayor. And maybe you're having trouble understanding cause and effect, but when you piss off the mayor, you piss off the chief. And that makes me look like I can't control my men, which pisses *me* off."

Ray folded his arms and shifted in his seat. "We've got a lead that the mayor might be the father of a serial killer, and neither the chief nor the captain acted on it. The way I see it, we did them a favor by playing bad cop with the mayor."

"A favor? You got a secondhand tip from a source with a questionable track record and you think the department's going to stake its reputation on that? Next time, try corroborating a fact or two before asking the chief to commit political suicide. Are we clear?"

Billy nodded, but Ray went on as if he hadn't heard. "He lied," Ray said. "As soon as we brought up Angie T, the mayor's eyes just about popped out of his head."

"You're missing the point," Spinonni said. "We're not here to discuss the case; we're here to discuss disciplinary action. And my recommendation is for a two-week suspension without pay, which I personally think is getting off easy. But for reasons I don't understand, the chief wanted to let you go with a warning."

Ray breathed a sigh of relief. Two weeks without pay would've been like a donkey kick to the wallet. Private school tuition was stretching his paycheck to the max.

Spinonni leaned across the desk and fixed them with a menacing stare. "Before you two run out of here celebrating, be advised that if you pull something like this again, you can kiss your jobs goodbye. That's a promise."

# CHAPTER THIRTY-EIGHT

Ray sensed something was off as soon as he set foot on his porch. Normally, when he arrived home at this hour, the TV in the front room would be blaring the latest seizure-inducing glut of cartoons, and either Allie or Jason would be bickering or Petey would be crying. And that was on a good day.

But right now, everything was quiet. And with Flaherty still at large, he found it unsettling. He glanced into the street where Michelle had parked her Corolla beneath the ancient oak that was constantly dropping pollen or acorns or leaves. In the winter, he swore it dropped sticks just to piss him off. So that meant the family was home, but the house was serene. Which might make sense in some households, but not in his.

He turned the key in the lock and stepped inside. The only sign of life was Mr. Snuggles, who lay on the arm of the couch like a narcoleptic sentinel, raising one eye half-mast before deciding Ray wasn't worth the trouble.

As Ray closed the door and set the keys on the foyer table, Sparky bounded downstairs with his tongue lolling. When he reached Ray's feet, he spun around in spastic circles, unable to decide whether he wanted to be petted, picked up, or chased. Ray bent down and scratched Sparky behind the ears. "What's the matter, boy? Where is everyone?"

A moment later, Michelle stormed into the family room waving a manila envelope in the air. "Care to explain this, Ray?"

But instead of handing him the envelope, she smacked him across the face with it. She hit him three times before he managed to wrestle it out of her hands.

A picture slid out of the envelope during the scuffle and glided to the floor between them. In it, Ray's head was tilted back in ecstasy and Tina was on her knees with her lips pursed around him. Ray snatched the picture off the floor and shoved it back inside the envelope, as if covering the image could somehow erase the deed.

"How could you, Ray?"

He laid a hand on her shoulder but she slapped it away.

"Don't you touch me! Don't you *dare*!"

He'd only seen that look in her eyes once before, and that was when the neighborhood bully sucker-punched Jason at the playground. He never imagined the same horrified expression would one day be directed at him.

"Let me explain."

"Explain what, Ray? I think these pictures are pretty self-explanatory, don't you?"

"It's not what you think."

"Really, Ray? Is it a new way of performing the Heimlich?"

"Michelle, please—"

"Shut up, Ray. Just *shut up*! How long has this been going on?"

"It was just that one time, I swear."

"Is that supposed to make me feel better? Like one time doesn't count?"

"I pushed her off me. It didn't go any further than that."

"Give me a break, Ray. It doesn't look like you put up much of a fight."

"I told her to stop, that I was happily married."

Michelle slapped his face. "*Were* happily married, Ray. *Were*!" She stalked into the bedroom, retrieved a prepacked duffle bag, and shoved it into his chest. "Get out!"

"Michelle, wait."

"Go! Before the kids get back from my mom's."

"Please, just listen."

"What makes you think I'll believe a word you say?"

"I made a huge mistake. I'm sorry."

Michelle pushed him toward the front door and herded him onto the porch.

"Just give me a chance to work this out. It'll never happen again, I prom—"

She slammed the door in his face.

# CHAPTER THIRTY-NINE

Lily Reynolds heard a tinkling of glass, followed by the shuffle-stomp of footsteps. She barely had time to sit up in bed and slip on her glasses before a man appeared in her doorway, standing in the shadows and regarding her with a leering grin.

For a moment, she was paralyzed, unable to draw the bedsheet over her frayed nightgown. She'd heard enough stories of home invasions to know the intruders sometimes raped old ladies, so there was a chance that this could be more than just a robbery.

"Take whatever you want," she croaked, "just don't hurt me."

The man in the doorway tilted his head, as if considering her offer. "We're not here for your money, Mrs. Reynolds. And as long as you cooperate, we won't harm you."

"What do you want?" She was afraid of the answer, but even more afraid of the silence. She drew a shuddering breath and tried to slow her racing heart.

"Let's move into the kitchen, shall we, Mrs. Reynolds? And do us all a favor and grab a robe. No one wants to see your saggy old tits."

Lily climbed out of bed and draped the robe over her shoulders, her body trembling as she followed the man past his hulking associate.

The man switched on the kitchen light and motioned for her to sit down, making no attempt to hide his face and leaving her to wonder if that was a good sign or a bad one. She guessed him to be in his late forties or early fifties, although he lacked the typical softness of middle age and carried himself with the brutal confidence of a man who hurt people for a living. His associate was twice his size, but considerably younger and had a buzz cut paired with a shaggy goatee.

"What do you want?" Lily asked, although now that the fog of sleep had dissipated she had a feeling she might already know.

"I'd like to talk about your son."

"What about him?"

"Larry and I have business to discuss, but I'm afraid he's done a disappearing act."

Lily shook her head. "I don't know where he is."

"I'd like very much to speak with him, Mrs. Reynolds. We have a lot of catching up to do."

Lily shifted her gaze to the hallway. After her husband had passed, she bought a gun for protection and kept it in an old shoe box in the bedroom closet. If she could make an excuse to go into the bedroom, she might be able to shoot her way out of her current predicament and solve yet another one of Larry's problems.

"If you're thinking about running," the man said, "I wouldn't advise it."

Lily's eight-year-old tabby cat padded into the kitchen and rubbed herself against the man's leg.

"What do we have here?" He scooped the cat into his arms and stroked her head. "Now, isn't she a pretty kitty? What's her name?"

Lily swallowed the lump in her throat. "Muffin."

The man scratched Muffin beneath the chin and the tabby tilted her head and purred like a motorboat. "What do you think, Muffin? Is your mama telling the truth about Larry?"

The man leaned his ear close to Muffin's muzzle and raised an eyebrow, as if the cat were speaking to him. He looked at Lily and clucked his tongue. "Muffin says you're lying, Mrs. Reynolds. And I'm afraid if you don't start telling the truth, I'll have no choice but to hurt this pretty kitty."

"Please," Lily said, standing up. "Leave her alone."

The associate seized her by the shoulders and forced her back into the chair.

The man sniffed Muffin's fur and looked at Lily. "I don't think this muffin is fully cooked."

The associate's lips curled into a grin. "Maybe we should put her in the microwave for a few minutes."

"Exactly what I was thinking." The man opened the microwave and shoved Muffin inside.

"No," Lily moaned. "Don't!"

"Tell us where Larry is," the man said, "or I'll cook your *fucking* cat."

Lily jumped to her feet. "Wait! He... the FBI has him."

The man fixed her with a menacing glare. "Where?"

"I don't know. He said he wasn't supposed to tell anyone."

The man pressed a button and the microwave came to life with a minute on the clock.

Lily lunged for the microwave and screamed, but the associate wrapped her in a bear hug and threw her to the ground. As her head smacked the linoleum, she could see Muffin through the glass, the tabby's yellow-green eyes opening wide as the console began to rotate.

"Where is he?" the man shouted.

Muffin, they were killing Muffin!

"Where is he?"

Lily's mind raced. If she gave them what they wanted, she could save Muffin and warn Larry after they were gone. The FBI would move him somewhere else and everything would be okay.

"The Park Plaza Hotel," she blurted.

"What room?"

"Nine twenty-three."

The man opened the door with fifty-five seconds remaining on the clock. Muffin bolted out of the microwave and scrambled into the den, scared but otherwise okay.

256

The man grinned at her. "We were never here, Mrs. Reynolds. Do you understand?"

Lily tried to speak, but could only manage a sob.

"If you go to the police or mention our visit to anyone, we'll come back to finish cooking Muffin. And when she explodes like a furry meatball, it'll be your fault. Understand?"

She nodded.

"And if that's not incentive enough, I know where your grandkids live. So if the feds move Larry to another hotel, it'll be their blood on your hands."

Lily felt her lower lip quiver. "I won't say anything, I promise."

The man glared at her. "That's a wise decision, Mrs. Reynolds. We'll be on our way in a moment, but there's something we need to borrow first."

# CHAPTER FORTY

Despite the alluring power promised by its advertising, Ray was pretty sure that an ice-cold Heineken wouldn't win Michelle back, although it was doing a hell of a job dulling the pain. Ray drained his pint and flagged down a tattooed barmaid with a pixie haircut. She took his empty with a flirty smile and weaved skillfully through the crowd toward the bar to bring him another.

He draped an arm around his duffle bag and watched through the open windows as pedestrians strolled past Quinn's. A warm breeze swept through the bar and stirred up a pungent cocktail of beer, sweat, and cologne mixed with the salty scent of the sea.

Jacob approached Quinn's from the east end of Main Street, looking all buttoned-up in a fancy suit and tie. He entered the bar and scanned the crowd, looking a bit like a kid lost in the mall. Then his eyes locked on Ray and he shook his head before plodding over.

"I had a feeling I'd find you here," Jacob said, settling into the seat across from Ray.

Ray gestured to his duffle bag. "I had nowhere else to go. Megan tell you what happened?"

"Is it true?"

"Depends on what she said."

"She said there were pictures."

"Yeah, it's pretty hard to argue those."

The barmaid returned with Ray's beer.

Ray cocked a thumb at Jacob. "Put it on his tab, will you? I'm saving up for a divorce attorney."

Jacob ordered a Heineken and waited for the barmaid to leave before asking his next question. "Did Michelle actually mention a divorce?"

"You should've seen her face. It was like I was dead to her." He took a long pull of beer.

"Who was it?"

"You remember Tina?"

"The woman you were dating when you first met Michelle?"

Ray nodded. "She still works at the ME's office."

"You want to tell me what happened?"

When Ray finished his story, Jacob regarded him with a skeptical gaze. "You had no idea what she was up to?"

"It crossed my mind that she might make a move, but I never meant to act on it."

The barmaid handed Jacob a beer and he took a sip before setting it on the table. "Come on, Ray. You know better than to put yourself into a situation like that. You should've made an excuse to avoid going to her place."

"I know what I should've done, Jacob. But I can't change it now. I can't ever take it back."

"So why did you go?"

Ray heaved a sigh. "Tina's always had a way of getting me to do exactly what she wants. That's why I ended things the first time—I got tired of being manipulated." He thumped his fist against the table. "I ruined everything."

He was hoping Jacob would contradict him, but instead his little brother remained silent. Ray finished his beer and exhaled sharply. "She won't return my calls. Or my texts."

"She needs time to process this," Jacob said. "The best thing you can do right now is give her some space. Just let her know you're sorry and that you won't bother her for a while."

"What if she doesn't want me back? What if she won't let me see the kids?" He could hear panic creeping into his voice and hated himself for it.

"You guys have a strong foundation and that counts for something. But you hurt her, Ray, so she's going to make you sweat it out. And when she's ready to talk, she'll goad you into a fight, but don't fall into that trap. Just shut up and take it. And when she's done yelling, you'll need to grovel for forgiveness. That's your *only* move," he said, pointing a finger at Ray. "And even then, there are no guarantees."

Ray folded his arms. "You're doing a piss-poor job of cheering me up."

"I'm not here to cheer you up. What you did was shitty. And if you want Michelle back, you'll need to earn back her trust, and that'll take a lot of time and a lot of humility, so you'd better check your ego at the door."

"I can do that," Ray said.

"I assume you'll want to crash at my place?"

"If Megan doesn't mind."

"Well, right now, she's with Michelle, but when she gets home, I'm pretty sure she'll want to tear you a new one."

Ray grabbed his duffle bag. "Great, I'll get to practice my humility."

# CHAPTER FORTY-ONE

After two days in a hotel room with these arrogant pricks, Larry half-wished that Flaherty had put him out of his misery. Between Dearborn's condescending attitude and Calhoun's passive aggressiveness with everything from the thermostat to his shower routine, Larry was one frayed nerve away from flinging himself out of their ninth-floor window.

The only problem was the damn thing wouldn't open.

In their short stay together, Larry already knew more than he cared to about the agents' personal lives. Dearborn had a nagging wife who cursed like a sailor and was a manic depressive who'd recently went off her meds, and Calhoun was a metrosexual bachelor who was so anal retentive that the women in his life only lasted a few weeks before fleeing his litany of rules, which bordered on obsessive compulsive.

As Larry sat on the sofa, he could hear Calhoun humming in the shower, and he watched with escalating malice as Dearborn monopolized the remote control from the chair beside him. Not only was Dearborn forcing him to watch commercials each time he clicked to a different news channel, but he was also talking to his wife on the phone, and because her only two volumes were loud and louder, Larry could hear every word.

Had it gone on another minute, Larry would've ripped the clicker out of Dearborn's hands and beat him over the head with it. Fortunately, Dearborn's wife launched into a string of obscenities and Dearborn got up, his cheeks reddening, and headed for the privacy of the bedroom.

Larry waited a few seconds before rising from the sofa and tiptoeing to the door. He glanced over his shoulder to make sure no one was watching, then he eased the door open and slipped into the hallway. He'd been waiting for a chance to escape ever since seeing his mom's text at six that morning. She'd called twice in the middle of the night, but his phone was on silence and it went straight to voicemail. Her text said that she wanted to talk in person, so he'd responded that he could probably escape for a few minutes after seven when the agents were busy with their morning routines.

He boarded the elevator and sent her a text saying that he was headed downstairs, chuckling to himself in the empty cabin because he wasn't even supposed to have his phone, let alone any contact with the outside world. When the agents had brought him to his apartment to pack a bag, he surrendered his old phone and smuggled the active one in his duffle bag and the morons still hadn't caught on.

When the elevator came to a halt, the doors rolled open to reveal the Park Plaza's opulent lobby with its coffered ceiling and crystal chandeliers. He hurried toward the exit, afraid that Dearborn might already be after him, and he almost barreled into the doorman as he charged outside. A moment later, his phone buzzed with a text alert.

*Meet me at the corner of Arlington and Columbus.*

Larry chuckled at his mom's cloak and dagger routine and wondered what second-rate spy movie she'd gotten the idea from. He doubted that she had anything important to tell him, but he was grateful to escape the hotel room, which agent Calhoun refused to allow above a frigid sixty-four degrees.

Larry allowed himself a moment to relax, relishing the warmth of the morning sun and inhaling the fresh air wafting toward him from the Public Garden. After getting his bearings, he headed toward the rendezvous point, weaving through a stream of businesspeople racing toward work like lemmings to a cliff.

When he reached the corner of Arlington and Columbus, he turned in a slow circle but didn't see his mom anywhere. He looked at his phone and noticed the voicemails she'd left in the middle of the night were from her landline. He hadn't bothered listening to them earlier, but wondered now if he should.

*I'm here,* he texted. *Where are you?*

Triple dots appeared in a message bubble as his mom slow-pecked a reply.

Larry glanced at the signpost to confirm his location, and when he looked back at his phone, the dots had been replaced with, *Coming in an Uber.*

Larry wrinkled his brow. An Uber?

A black SUV with tinted windows turned the corner and screeched to a halt. The back door swung open and Larry stepped toward the curb. "Mom?"

A pair of muscular arms seized him by the shoulders and dragged him inside. As the door slammed shut and the SUV accelerated down Columbus Ave, Larry found himself wedged between a rough-looking trio of thugs.

A man with silvery-blond hair turned toward him from the front passenger seat. "What's the matter," Flaherty asked, holding up his mom's cellphone. "Were you expecting someone else?"

# CHAPTER FORTY-TWO

Like many cafés in the North End, Molto Bene served up great food in a cramped space, with just a few small tables arranged in a single file against the wall and only a narrow walkway separating the front door from the seating area. Behind a glass counter loaded with pastries, a middle-aged barista with a thick accent and a perpetual scowl served up cappuccinos and espressos to a line of people snaking out the door.

Ray was lucky enough to snag a table in the corner, where he could keep an eye on the back door while sipping from the best cappuccino he'd had in years. With Billy and Garrison sitting on either side of him, they each had less than six inches of table space to call their own, and Garrison was at a clear disadvantage since he couldn't quite squeeze his giant's legs beneath the table. Billy had just devoured a chocolate croissant and was licking globs of chocolate off his fingers.

Garrison grimaced. "Didn't your mama teach you any table manners?"

"It's finger food," Billy said. "It's meant to be eaten with your hands."

"That doesn't make it okay to put your fingers in your mouth," Garrison said. "It's gross."

"Stop being such a neat freak," Billy said, "and maybe it won't bother you."

Ray shook his head. "You guys bicker more than my kids, and one of them is still in diapers." But a traitorous voice in his mind whispered, *How do you know that hasn't changed since the last time you saw them?*

He clenched his jaw and tried to focus on the task at hand. Molto Bene was Giabatti's go-to place for breakfast, and like many of the restaurants in the North End, VIPs like Giabatti dined in secret rooms that were off-limits to the public. And while they hadn't seen him enter the back room, they knew from recent surveillance patterns that he'd be passing their way any moment.

Ray set down his cappuccino and thought about the morning's briefing. "I still can't believe Larry would slip away from the feds like that."

"Dearborn will go down for it," Garrison said.

Ray nodded, but didn't take any pleasure from it. Without Larry's testimony, there'd be no chance for a double murder conviction. At most, they could get Flaherty for kidnapping at Finnegan's Landing, but with Larry absent and a lack of eyewitnesses, a good lawyer might be able to get him off.

"What'd you guys hear?" Billy said, turning to Garrison. "All we know is that he went missing."

"That's the official line," Garrison said, "but a buddy of mine at the bureau said the hotel security cameras showed Larry glued to his phone as he was leaving the hotel. And the feds must have a better relationship with the telecom companies than we do because they already obtained his phone records. Seems he was planning to meet up with his mom. Only problem is that his mother says she misplaced her cellphone a couple days ago and hasn't seen it since."

"Any witnesses come forward?" Ray asked.

"Not that I've heard."

"Somebody had to see something," Billy said. "And my money's on Flaherty's guys."

"If so, what's Flaherty's next move?" Ray asked. "Does he kill Larry, or does he cancel the debt and persuade him not to testify?"

"Maybe he waits," Billy said. "Sees what leads the feds have, what gets published in the press, and then decides."

"I don't know," Garrison said. "If Larry stays gone and there's no evidence that Flaherty took him, then Flaherty could walk."

"How do you figure?" Billy said.

"Because Larry's wanted for armed robbery," Garrison said. "It wouldn't be hard to convince a jury that Larry fled to avoid prosecution, as well as the risk of testifying against Flaherty."

Ray caught a blur of movement from the corner of his eye and sat up straight. "Here comes Giabatti."

The elder mafioso emerged from the back room in a perfectly tailored gray suit, flanked by a pair of bodyguards. "What a coincidence," he said, gesturing to their table. "I didn't know you came here for breakfast."

"We just happened to be in the neighborhood," Ray said.

Giabatti nudged Billy in the arm. "How'd you enjoy that croissant? I asked Pauline to take special care of your order."

Ray glanced up at the camera behind the counter. He'd had a feeling Giabatti would be watching. "We need a few minutes of your time."

"For you, yes. For him, no."

Billy folded his arms. "Still holding a grudge?"

Giabatti cocked his thumb at the front door and eyed his bodyguards. "Why don't you escort Billy to the curb? And see that he doesn't touch anything on the way out."

Billy stood up, and for a moment it looked as if he might blurt out something they'd all regret. Ray glared at him, and thankfully, he clamped his mouth shut.

"We've got to stop meeting like this," Giabatti said, taking a seat once Billy left. "I know you've got a job to do, but this is bordering on harassment. And I'm a very busy man."

"We'll make it quick," Ray said. "You got any idea where Flaherty's hiding?"

Giabatti chuckled. "I thought that might be what you were after."

"Why's that funny?" Garrison asked.

"Because he disappeared right under the noses of a hundred cops and made the entire law enforcement community look like a bunch of morons. It's good to know that when my time comes, I can just take off my glasses and waltz through the dragnet without being recognized."

Ray and Garrison exchanged a glance. If they said anything in their defense, the conversation would likely be over. "I can see how you'd find that amusing," Ray said. "But you didn't answer my question. Do you know where Flaherty is?"

"Flaherty doesn't make a habit of involving me in his business."

"But you must want to see him go down," Garrison said. "After all he's done to you."

"And what happens when he's behind bars?" Giabatti asked. "Who will the cops focus their energy on then?"

Ray tried a new direction. "You ever hear of a stripper named Angie T? She danced at the Puma under the name Amber, probably quit the business ten years ago."

"Doesn't ring any bells. How's this relate to Flaherty?"

"She used to frequent The Rock and had a son who might've been fathered by the mayor. We think it's her kid who killed Danny. Only we can't find the mom or the kid."

Giabatti pursed his lips and nodded, as if debating whether to reveal what he knew. "Maybe this is related," he said, "or maybe it's not, but a couple years ago I heard that someone was making trouble for the mayor's reelection campaign. Someone who claimed to be his son."

Ray lifted an eyebrow. Nothing like that had ever hit the papers. "What kind of trouble?"

Giabatti grinned. "What's it worth to you?"

Garrison fixed Giabatti with a steely gaze. "If you've got something that could damage Flaherty or the mayor, I'd call it a win-win for all of us. And let's not kid ourselves—if Jack Flaherty goes down, that's a big boon for your business."

"Maybe so," Giabatti said. "But should the day ever come when I need your help, I'd want you boys to remember my generosity."

"We'll keep that in mind," Ray said, "but you know we can't promise anything outside of the law."

Giabatti shrugged. "You expect me to accept such a terrible deal?"

"It's not meant to be a deal," Ray said.

Giabatti stared at the table and nodded slowly. And just when Ray thought he was going to clam up, Giabatti leaned forward and whispered something that broke the case wide open.

# CHAPTER FORTY-THREE

"What is it?" Garrison asked as they exited the café. "And don't tell me nothing, because I saw the way your eyes popped out of your skull back there."

Billy fell into step beside them and gestured to Garrison. "What's he talking about?"

"Giabatti says some guy claiming to be the mayor's son blackmailed the mayor during his reelection campaign," Ray said. "The mayor allegedly got him a new identity in exchange for not going public with some damaging secrets."

"What secrets?" Billy asked.

"Giabatti didn't know," Garrison said, "but I think Ray might have a hunch."

"Do you?" Billy asked.

"It just so happens I do," Ray said. He led them across the street to the tow-away zone where he'd parked the Explorer. He fished his phone from his pocket and dialed the precinct before climbing inside.

Billy eyed the number as Ray placed the phone on the console and hit speaker. "You calling Costanza?"

"You know he hates that nickname," Ray said.

Clint picked up on the third ring. "What can I help you with?" he asked after a brief exchange of greetings.

"Remember that search you ran on Suzie Coleman's college stalker?" Ray asked.

"Uh, yeah," Clint said, rustling paper in the background. "Brendan Taritello."

"You said he died in a car crash three years ago."

"That's right."

"What else do you have on his background?" Ray asked. "Any priors?"

"Uh, let's see… a couple citations for drunk and disorderly, a DUI, and an assault charge against his college professor."

"Coleman never mentioned anything about that," Ray said. "This happened at the College of Art and Design?"

"No, the BU School of Medicine."

"Wait a minute," Ray said. "He was a student there?"

"Looks that way," Clint said. "After the incident with Suzie, he transferred to BU. I guess he did well enough to get into their medical program after undergrad."

"Did he finish med school?" Garrison asked.

"He got expelled for assaulting the professor."

"Do me a favor," Ray said. "Check to see if the professor is still alive."

Clint clacked away at his computer. "He was found dead last April. Looks like he hung himself in his office."

"Suicide?" Ray asked.

"Yes, although friends and family said they didn't believe it. But do they ever?"

"Anything unusual about the professor's body?" Ray asked.

"Hang on, let me read the rest of the report."

The line went silent for over a minute before Clint returned. "The professor was found swinging naked from a rope with a rolled-up diploma shoved up his ass."

"A suicide?" Garrison asked. "Really?"

"There were no signs of forced entry," Clint said, "no evidence of a struggle."

"Maybe he had a gun to his head," Billy said.

Ray nodded. He was thinking the same thing. But without proof, it went on record as a suicide, and he knew from experience that people sometimes killed themselves in bizarre ways. "Hey, Clint," he said, "what do you show for the name of Brendan's mom?"

"Uh, let's see. Evangeline Taritello."

"I'll be damned," Billy said. "Angie T."

"Was that your hunch?" Garrison asked.

Ray nodded. "It clicked for me after Giabatti mentioned the new identity. What do you show for Angie's address?"

"Um, didn't I tell you? Angie was in the car with Brendan the night of the crash. Neither survived."

"Not on paper, they didn't," Ray said. "Just out of curiosity, who does Brendan's birth certificate list as the father?"

"It's blank."

"Do you have a last known address?" Ray asked.

"All I show for Brendan is his BU campus address, so I assume he moved back with his mom after getting expelled."

"And where was that?" Ray asked.

"Wait," Billy said, "let me guess. Somewhere in East Boston?"

*\*\**

The Taritellos last known address was a low-income housing complex near East Boston's Maverick Square. Ray, Billy, and Garrison climbed out of the truck and gazed up at the five-story brick building on the corner of Chelsea and Emmons streets, where the entire block was boxed in by a wall of buildings that trapped pedestrians like rats in a maze of concrete. A few gangly trees attempted to brighten the landscape, but they were so stunted and sparse that they only succeeded in making the street seem more depressing.

As they headed for the front door of the complex, a low-flying plane roared overhead on its approach to Logan Airport, so near to the ground Ray could see faces peering out of the windows.

"Better hope no one flushes a toilet," Billy said. "I'd hate to get killed by a hunk of brown ice after twenty-five years on the force."

"Don't worry," Ray said. "Ten-to-one you'll die of a heart attack instead."

"I always pictured him choking on his own vomit in a seedy motel room," Garrison said, "while a hooker rifles through his wallet."

Billy rolled his eyes. "You guys are a riot."

"Just for the record," Ray said, opening the door to the apartment building, "that plane's not high enough to freeze a turd."

As Ray crossed the threshold, the stench of urine wafted toward him and he wrinkled his nose in disgust. "Christ," he muttered. "How do people live like this?"

"Reminds me of Billy's place," Garrison said.

Billy shrugged. "I'd be insulted if it wasn't true."

"Maybe you shouldn't have spent all your money on a flashy car," Ray said.

"Are you kidding? The ladies love the Corvette. And by the time they see my place, it's already too late."

"Do you realize how creepy that sounds?" Garrison asked.

"It's all part of my charm," Billy said. "Besides, we can't all have a perfect family like some cops I know."

"I think that's supposed to be a dig at you," Garrison said.

"Yeah," Ray said, "I'm feeling the burn. What's the matter, Billy? I thought you loved the bachelor life."

Billy shrugged. "When your kid and your ex hate your guts, you do what you can to fill the emptiness."

"Tyler doesn't hate you," Ray said. "He's a twelve-year-old boy. That's just how they act."

Garrison nodded. "I was the same way with my old man, but we're good friends now."

"If you say so." Billy pressed ahead, finished with the conversation. He motioned to the elevators at the end of the hall. Someone had spray-painted a grinning skull and crossbones over the doors. It was smoking a joint and had a black swastika scrawled on its forehead.

"Not exactly what I'd call inviting," Garrison said. "Why don't we take the stairs."

"As long as Billy's old ticker can handle it," Ray said.

Billy gave him the finger and headed into the stairwell.

A light was out somewhere, and it took a while for Ray's eyes to adjust to the darkness. He reached into his sports coat and drew the Glock from his shoulder holster. Billy and Garrison did the same, and they ascended in silence.

The odds of the Taritellos still living in the same apartment were pretty much zilch, but a place like this wasn't exactly cop friendly, so there was no telling who they'd find in apartment 431. And while he hoped they were ready for anything, sometimes you just never knew.

When they reached 431, Ray rapped his knuckles against the door. "Boston Police. We want to ask you a few questions."

Garrison pressed his ear against the door and gave Ray a thumbs-up, indicating he'd heard movement inside.

"We know you're in there," Ray said. "Open up. We just want to talk."

When they got no response, Billy pushed Ray aside and pounded on the door. "We can do this all day!" he shouted. "So open the goddamned door or get used to hearing this sound. I get paid either way."

"Hold your horses," an elderly voice said from inside the apartment. "Give an old lady time to put on a robe."

They could hear shuffling feet approaching the door.

"Now step back so I can see your badges."

They took turns holding their badges up to the peephole, and a few moments later, they heard chains jingling and locks clicking. The door swung open to reveal a heavyset woman in a tattered pink robe. She had stringy gray hair and milky blue eyes. Judging by the wrinkles on her face and the spidery veins on her calves, Ray guessed her to be in the vicinity of eighty years old.

"Now, what's so damn important you're disturbing an old lady's afternoon nap?"

"I'm sorry about that," Ray said. "My partner is not what I'd call a patient man."

The old lady scowled at Billy. "No wonder everyone hates cops."

Billy shrugged. "I'm not in it to make friends."

"Mind if we come in?" Ray asked. "We want to ask you a few questions."

The woman motioned them inside and locked up behind them. "A lot of degenerates in this building. You ought to go door-to-door and put a bullet through their heads."

Billy chuckled. "I'm starting to like this lady."

"Ma'am," Garrison said, "I'm Trooper Garrison with the State Police, and this is Detective Hanley and Detective Devlin from the Boston Police. Would you mind telling us your name?"

"Greta Buntzman. Now come on and grab a seat. I'm not as young as I used to be." She led them into a small kitchen, where every inch of shelf space was cluttered with knickknacks, ceramics, or old photos. A collection of recently washed pots sat in a drying rack beneath the vines of a Devil's Ivy, which grew wild from a planter hanging from a ceiling hook.

Ray gestured to the old man sitting on the couch in the TV room. He was hooked up to an oxygen tank and had his eyes glued to the TV. The man had yet to glance in their direction. "Is that your husband, Mrs. Buntzman?"

"Going on sixty years. Except now he's half-mad with dementia and just sits there soiling his pants and staring at the tube. Watches the daytime soaps, mostly. Gets his rocks off ogling the young women."

"Mrs. Buntzman," Ray said, "how long have you and your husband lived in this apartment?"

"Oh, I'd say about three years now. Would you care for some tea?"

"No thanks," Ray said. "Did you know the previous occupants?"

"Got some nice tits on that one," Mr. Buntzman said, cackling from the couch.

"Zip it, Hank, we've got company." Mrs. Buntzman shook her head. "I'm sorry, what was the question?"

"I asked if you knew the previous occupants."

"The Taritellos?"

"That's them."

"We lived across the hall from them for years."

"You moved into this apartment when they left?" Ray asked.

Mrs. Buntzman nodded. "A place like this doesn't open up every day. The bedroom's got a wonderful view of the harbor."

"Do you have any idea where the Taritellos went?" Garrison asked.

"I'd imagine straight to hell. Angie was a sex worker, after all, and her boy—what was his name?"

"Brendan."

"Yes, that was it. Brendan. He was an odd duck. Never said much, but he gave me the creeps. Anyway, they died in a car crash."

"Mrs. Buntzman," Ray said, "we have reason to believe the Taritellos are still alive."

"Alive? How?"

"We think they faked their deaths."

"Why would they do that?"

"They got into trouble," Garrison said, "and were looking for a new start."

"That's right," Ray said, "and it's very important that we find them. Do you have any idea where they might be?"

Mrs. Buntzman frowned. "I can't say that I—"

"Check the morgue!" Her husband cackled, and ripped a wet fart.

Mrs. Buntzman shot him a dirty look. "I'm sorry, officers, but I'm afraid I can't help you. Even if the Taritellos are alive, I wouldn't know where to find them."

***

After making the rounds with the Buntzman's neighbors, they returned to the precinct and gathered in the briefing room.

"We should've taken the old lady's advice," Billy said, "and spread a few bullets around."

Ray was about to respond when Captain Barnes strode into the room with Spinonni and Sergeant Callahan. "What's this breakthrough?" the captain asked.

Ray brought them up to speed on Brendan Taritello. "We can link him directly to Danny the Mule and Suzie Coleman. And with his stint at art school, it's not much of a leap to connect him to Finkleton. We also know that he completed a couple years of medical school, so that explains how he could mutilate his victims and keep them alive for so long."

"Plus," Sergeant Callahan said, "there's no formal police report on the accident that allegedly killed the Taritellos, and the death certificates look like forgeries."

Captain Barnes nodded thoughtfully. "We need to make a full-court press on this. I want you to interview former colleagues and any known associates. Get the phone records, see who they were in the habit of talking to before they went off the grid."

"What about the mayor?" Ray asked. "Giabatti said—"

The captain cut him off. "We'll engage the mayor once we've exhausted all other avenues. We can't risk career suicide on the word of a mafia boss. Until we can prove otherwise, it's just as likely that Taritello went to Giabatti for help with obtaining a new identity. Could be that killing Danny was part of the bargain."

"Captain, I think you're making a mistake."

Spinonni glared at Ray. "You're out of line, Hanley."

276

Captain Barnes ignored the outburst. "Detective Hanley, your opinion is noted but overruled. You did great work today—all of you—but it's important not to let impatience cloud your judgement. Go home and get some rest. There's not much more that can be done tonight."

# CHAPTER FORTY-FOUR

Ray lurked outside of City Hall Plaza, cloaked in the shadows of a broken streetlight, and kept watch on the mayor's private entrance. At nine o'clock, the light in the mayor's office winked out and a black Chevy Tahoe pulled up alongside the building. A security officer climbed out of the SUV and greeted the mayor at the exit.

They made it halfway back to the car before Ray stepped out of the shadows. "Mr. Mayor, Detective Hanley from the Boston Police. I'd like a word with you."

The security officer thrust himself in front of the mayor and drew his gun.

The mayor whispered something to the officer and then called out to Ray. "I didn't expect to see you again so soon, detective. I thought you'd learned your lesson."

Ray shrugged. "I guess that makes me a slow learner. Can we speak privately for a moment?"

"No, detective, we may not." The mayor continued toward the car.

"It's about Brendan Taritello."

The mayor stopped dead in his tracks. "Am I supposed to know who that is?"

"From the way your jaw just dropped, I'd say you know exactly who he is."

"Give us a minute," the mayor said to the officer.

"I wouldn't advise it, sir."

"Just wait for me in the car."

The officer lingered for a moment and glared at Ray before trudging to the SUV.

"Just who the hell do you think you are?" the mayor asked.

"Someone who's not afraid to do his job."

"Really? Or are you just a dumb cop with a conspiracy theory?"

Ray handed the mayor a copy of Brendan's student ID photo. "Call me crazy, but I think this kid looks an awful lot like you. Same blue eyes, same sandy brown hair, same—"

"You ought to get your eyes checked. I've never seen this kid before in my life."

"You helped him fake his own death and get a new identity."

"You're crazy."

"There's two ways we can do this, Mr. Mayor. One, you tell me Brendan's new identity, or two—"

"There is no *two*, and you know it."

"Here's what I do know. We've got the Taritellos' falsified death records and we'll chase that paper trail wherever it leads. And I can guarantee it's only a matter of time before we find something that points back to you. In the meantime, if Suzie Coleman turns up dead and the press learns you withheld evidence that could've saved her life, then you can kiss your political career goodbye. But if you give me a name, and I happen to forget where I heard it from, then nobody needs to go after the paper trail. So, last chance, Mr. Mayor... what's it going to be?"

\*\*\*

Lieutenant Spinonni pulled Ray aside as soon as he arrived at the precinct the next morning. "My office. Now."

Ray wasn't sure if the hyena-like smirk plastered to the lieutenant's face qualified as a smile, but as he settled into the chair opposite Spinonni's desk, he decided it probably wasn't a good sign.

Spinonni folded his hands and studied Ray. "I want to savor this moment."

"Are you going to tell me what this is about?"

"I always knew you were trouble, Hanley. But the captain and chief always gave you the benefit of the doubt. But not this time."

"What are you saying?"

"Quit playing dumb, Hanley. You disobeyed a direct order and harassed the mayor. The captain is pissed. He doesn't even want to talk to you. Which is why I get to do the honors."

Ray clenched his hands into fists. The mayor had promised him a name by the afternoon.

*That's the last time I trust a politician.*

"I've been waiting years for this," Spinonni said, rubbing his hands together. "Detective Hanley, you are hereby ordered to turn in your badge and your gun. You've been suspended without pay, effective immediately. And pending the outcome of an internal review, you'll likely be terminated. So do yourself a favor and dust off that resume. And for the last time, get the hell out of my office."

***

The first beer felt good going down, so Ray followed it with another. And then another. Later, when it felt like his bladder might burst, he staggered toward the bathroom and stumbled into a barstool, catching the edge of the bar in time to avoid a faceplant.

He muttered an apology to Quinn's daytime bartender—Jimmy or Jerry or Johnny—and to the handful of professional drunks sitting hunched over the bar, frowning into their drinks.

*Christ, is that where I'm headed?* he thought, catching a glimpse of his haggard reflection in the mirror behind the bar. He needed to pull himself together. Right here. Right now.

After a visit to the bathroom, his head felt clearer, and he took a seat at the bar and forced himself to drink a few pints of water. By the time he left Quinn's two bathroom breaks later, he felt certain he could pass a field sobriety test. Not that it mattered, though. Spinonni had confiscated the Explorer and he had to take a cab over to Quinn's. So now he could add the car to the growing list of things he'd lost.

Christ, was he turning into Billy? Or Larry?

And where the hell was Larry, anyway? His mom wasn't talking, which could either mean Larry was on the run or that Flaherty's men had coerced her into keeping quiet. For Larry's sake, he hoped it was the former, but he had his doubts.

He ambled along Main Street with his fists thrust into his pockets. It was a perfect afternoon for a walk—bright sunshine, low humidity. But with everything on his mind, he couldn't enjoy it.

He'd committed career suicide, and for what? Because he was impatient? Because he wanted to run the investigation his own way? Maybe, but also because the captain and the chief didn't have the balls to do their jobs. All the evidence suggested that Suzie Coleman was alive. Otherwise, they would've found her by now since the Artist's MO was to discard bodies in a sensational fashion in full view of the public—a pattern that also fit the professor's hanging.

Maybe, at first, the Artist wanted to frame Jim Coleman for murder as revenge for stealing Suzie away from him. That would explain the bloody bed, the missing body, and the planting of evidence in Coleman's car. But now that Jim was out of jail with no charges filed, Suzie's days were probably numbered. Which meant they couldn't afford to waste time chasing their tails when the mayor was the quickest path to finding the Artist. Maybe Ray was guilty of being brash, but he'd done what was best for the case, so no matter what recommendation the internal review board made about his job, at least he'd stayed true to his values. Whether that paid the bills or not was another story.

He'd left Quinn's with no plans other than to wander around the block to clear his head, but his subconscious must've had its own agenda because he suddenly realized he was right around the corner from home.

Michelle was just pulling up to the curb as he reached the front walk, and when Jason and Allie spotted him, they flew out of the car. "Daddy's home!" They raced into his arms and almost bowled him over.

"I missed you guys so much." He hugged them tight, his eyes stinging with the threat of tears.

"We missed you too, Daddy!"

Michelle lifted Petey out of the car seat and he toddled over to Ray, each step sending a tremor through his chubby cheeks. "Da-da home!"

Ray lifted him above his head and flew him around the sidewalk like Superman. "I flying!" Petey squealed, "I flying!"

He set Petey down on the porch and fumbled in his pocket for the keys. Allie moved in beside him and gave him the stink eye. "I don't like it when you work so much. Will it be over soon?"

Michelle joined them on the porch, her arms loaded with the kids' backpacks, a diaper bag, and her purse. "Sorry, honey," she said, "but Daddy's still got a lot more work to do."

"Why don't you guys go inside?" Ray said. He slipped the key into the door and turned the knob, relieved to discover Michelle hadn't changed the locks.

After herding the kids inside, Ray pulled the door shut and turned to find Michelle glaring at him with her arms folded across her chest.

"What are you doing here, Ray?"

"I wanted to see you."

"You should've called."

"You don't answer your phone."

"Send me a text."

"You don't respond to those either."

"At least I'd know you were coming."

"Come on, Michelle. Are we really going to do this?"

"Do what?"

He drew a deep breath. What could he say that wouldn't piss her off? "I know how angry you must be."

"Do you, Ray? Do you really?"

"What I did was terrible. And I wish I could take it back. But these past couple of days have been the worst days of my life."

"Am I supposed to feel sorry for you? Is that what you're looking for, Ray? Pity?"

"That's not what I'm saying. I know you hate me right now. And I won't stand here and tell you that you shouldn't. I'm sorry for what I did and I hate how it's changed the way you look at me. But I will do anything—literally anything—for the chance to earn you back."

A tear trickled down Michelle's cheek and she swatted it away. "I don't know if I can trust you anymore."

Her words landed like a sucker punch. "I promise it won't happen again. Please, you're the best thing that's ever happened to me.

"It won't be the same, Ray. It will always be in the back of my mind. *Always*."

"We can go to counseling."

"You hate counseling."

"I don't want to lose you, Michelle. I don't want to break our family apart. That can't be what you want, is it?"

But Michelle didn't answer.

"Promise me that you won't give up on us," he said.

Michelle drew a shuddering breath, and for a long time didn't say anything. "I'll think about it," she said and reached for the door.

\*\*\*

Ray said a heart-wrenching goodbye to the kids before heading toward Monument Square, where he'd arranged for Jacob to pick him up after work. As he passed Monument Liquors on his way to the park, he waved to Sam Martinez through the window.

The last time he'd seen Sam was the night Larry robbed the place, which had been, what, over two weeks ago? A lot had changed since then, and he wished he could go back and undo the damage. But no matter how much mental energy he expended, he could never change the past. And while he could theoretically shape his own future, right now the outlook seemed bleak.

When he arrived at Monument Square, he made a conscious effort to clear his mind. He gazed up at the towering obelisk commemorating the Battle of Bunker Hill, which, ironically, stood on Breed's Hill, where most of the battle had taken place. The granite used to construct the monument had originated from the same Quincy quarries where they'd found Danny the Mule's mutilated corpse nearly two centuries later. How was that for irony?

As he reached for his phone to check the time, a spray of granite flew off the monument and struck him on the cheek. An instant later, a tiny hole the size of a .22 caliber bullet appeared in the granite, accompanied by more bits of flying rock. He dropped into a crouch and reached into his sports coat for his missing Glock, but not before a bullet slammed into his Kevlar vest.

He rolled onto his side with a groan and caught a glimpse of a black-clad figure withdrawing into the trees on the east end of the park. Wincing, Ray staggered to his feet and hurried across the park, charging down the grassy ridge leading toward the ritzy brownstones lining Monument Square. He was unarmed—Spinonni had made sure of it—but the shooter didn't know that and would be focused on retreat rather than engaging in a firefight.

So far, his knowledge of the shooter was limited to medium build and black shirt. It'd happened so fast, he never had the chance to register hair color, sex, or ethnicity. Potential suspects ran through his mind—the Artist, Flaherty, Giabatti, the mayor, Darren Boyle. The shooter had used a silencer, but missed the kill shot, so that meant he wasn't a contract killer. Or at least not a good one.

Ray scaled the wrought iron fence at the end of the park and scrutinized the street in both directions. Nothing about his surroundings appeared out of the ordinary. The sidewalks bustled with pedestrians headed home from work and no one seemed alarmed, which meant the shooter had likely blended into the crowd and disappeared.

He walked up and down the block to ensure that he didn't miss anything, and then headed back to the park to collect the bullet casings. Afterward, he called Billy to tell him what'd happened.

"Good thing you had on your vest," Billy said. "You want me to get someone down there?"

"For what? Other than the casings and the slug in my vest, there's no evidence and no eyewitnesses. I just wanted to warn you."

"You think it's the Artist?" Billy asked. "Could be he's trying to take us out before we get too close."

"For all we know, it could be the mayor."

"That seems too risky for someone in his position."

"Why don't you ask him about it? See if you can get Brendon Taritello's new name while you're at it."

"What, so I can get suspended too? I'm not risking my pension over this case. I'm not even supposed to be talking to you."

"So, you're just going to roll over, is that it? Let the mayor get away with obstruction of justice? You know it could cost Suzie Coleman her life, don't you?"

"I can't, Ray. My hands are tied."

"What's the matter, Billy? You too old to grow a pair?"

"Not everything is black and white, Ray. I want to keep my job and I don't think there's anything wrong with that, so screw you for asking."

# CHAPTER FORTY-FIVE

Jacob stared at Ray from across the front seat and shook his head. "Are you sure you're okay?"

Ray rubbed his stomach and winced. "Yeah, I'm fine."

"But you could've been killed."

"I could've been a lot of things, Jacob."

"I don't understand how you can be so calm."

"I don't waste time worrying about things that didn't happen."

"If only it was that easy."

Ray pointed a finger at him. "Don't you go telling Ma about this. I'll never hear the end of it."

"Do you think I'm crazy?"

"I don't know, little brother. Are you?"

"You're crazy enough for both of us."

Ray brayed laughter. "Now, ain't that the truth?"

"Do you really think you'll lose your job?"

"If the mayor comes out clean, then I'd say it's a strong possibility."

"What if he doesn't?"

"Then the department can't afford to fire me. It'll look like they were on the mayor's side. People will whisper about corruption."

"What are the odds the department goes digging into the mayor's business?"

"Not very good."

"What are you going to do?"

"Don't worry, little brother, I've got a plan. But first I'll need to borrow your car."

# THE ART OF DYING

***

The next morning, Ray met Frank Eastman at the dilapidated Victorian that served as Frank's private investigator's office. They sat across from each other at a conference table marred by coffee stains and cigarette burns. Frank cast a sidelong look at Ray, a gnarled toothpick pinched between his lips. "You wanna tell me what you plan to do with this information?"

"Probably better that you don't know."

Frank slid a sheet of paper across the table. He was a man of few words, yet he communicated a great deal by his expressions, and even just a subtle variation in the twist of his lips yielded intricate differences in the pattern of lines cutting across his face.

Ray lifted an eyebrow as he examined the page. "Christ, Frank, are you still using a dot-matrix printer?"

"Can you read it or not?"

Ray scanned the list of addresses. "Barely."

"Not all of those are in the mayor's name," Frank said, "but he controls Clover Realty Trust just the same."

Ray nodded. "I owe you one."

"Second favor in two weeks. Must be desperate times."

"Yeah," Ray said, "something like that. But since I'm here, how about an advance on the next favor?"

Frank rolled the toothpick from one side of his mouth to the other. "What do you mean?"

"I need to borrow a gun."

# CHAPTER FORTY-SIX

It looked like a normal suburban home. Beige split-level with wood shingles and a stone chimney running up the left-hand wall. It was set back on a quiet cul-de-sac in West Roxbury, bordering the wooded preserve of Stony Brook Reservation, the nearest neighbor half a football field away.

Ray stared at the property from the side of the road, studying it through the windshield of Jacob's Lexus. The longer he examined it, the more flaws he found—flakes of paint peeling from the eaves, the wood beneath dark with rot. A rusted weathervane twirled on the roof, the head of the arrow broken off.

It was one of the properties owned by the mayor's trust, and it happened to be located within a mile of both Coleman's house and the jogging trail where they'd found Finkleton dangling from a tree.

If Ray's theory was correct, Taritello had extorted the mayor for a place to stay in addition to a new identity, since he would've had to vanish from his previous life and had no job or degree to fall back on. Which meant the charcoal-gray Chevy Silverado parked in the driveway might belong to the Artist. And because it was a Saturday morning, there was a good chance that whoever lived here was still at home.

He pulled out his phone and drafted a text to Billy.

*Found the Artist. 32 Oak Circle Drive, West Roxbury. Come as soon as you can.*

But instead of sending the message, he locked the phone's display and killed the car's engine. He couldn't afford a mistake, not with his career on the line and not with how he'd left things with Billy. He had to be sure. And that meant confronting whoever lived here.

After a final check of his Kevlar vest, he climbed out of the Lexus and positioned himself on the left-hand side of the driveway, keeping the Silverado between himself and the house. He crouched down and examined the truck's tires. Goodyear Wranglers, 265-millimeter. The same make and model as the tracks they'd found on the trail near Finkleton's body.

He peered into the flatbed. Empty. But he'd bet Billy's pension that it contained forensic evidence that could be traced back to Finkleton. The Artist probably attached the harness in the back of the truck, threw the rope over the branch, and then hoisted him up. Maybe even tied one end of the rope to the trailer hitch to make it easier to lift him.

A blur of movement caught his eye, and he turned to see a figure approaching from the backyard—Caucasian male, medium build, wearing jeans and a black T-shirt. Dark hair pulled back into a ponytail. The man halted at the sight of Ray and did a double take. Despite the distance, something about him struck Ray as familiar, and maybe it was just his imagination, but the man's shoulders seemed to relax as he came forward.

"Ray? Is that you?"

A strange sense of déjà vu washed over Ray, prickling his skin with an electrifying tingle of goose bumps. He suddenly understood how the Artist had succeeded in leaving behind almost no trace evidence.

He knew this man. Luis Durgin. Doc Death's forensic autopsy technician.

As Luis approached, Mr. Buntzman's words echoed through his mind.

*Check the morgue.*

Maybe the old man wasn't as senile as they'd thought.

"What's going on?" Luis asked. "Is something wrong?"

Ray fumbled for an excuse to justify his presence. "Do you remember when we found Finkleton hanging in the woods?"

"How could I forget?"

"We discovered a fingerprint on the harness used to string him up."

Luis flinched at Ray's lie. "You did?" It was slight, but it was there. And Ray was trained to notice.

"But it's not the big break we were hoping for," Ray said.

"Why not?"

"Because the print we found was yours." He let the words sink in, registering the panic on Luis's face. "Obviously, you must have touched the harness when you zipped up the body bag, so now I need to ask you a few questions."

Luis nodded, looking relieved. "Okay, sure."

"Don't worry, it's just a formality."

"I get it," Luis said, uttering a nervous laugh. "You've got to do your job, right?"

"That's right," Ray said, slapping at a phantom mosquito. "Mind if we go inside? These bugs are brutal."

"Uh, sure." A vein ticked at Luis's throat. His eyes seemed unable to focus.

*Christ*, Ray thought. *All this time, right under our noses.*

Luis led the way across his scraggily lawn.

"Looks like it's time for a mow," Ray said, keeping the conversation light as he followed a few paces behind and reached into his pocket for his phone.

As Luis climbed the porch stairs and fumbled with the lock, Ray sent the text he'd drafted earlier to Billy and returned the phone to his pocket.

The front door opened onto a small landing with a flight of stairs extending in either direction. The upper level had hardwood floors and crown molding throughout, and the living room featured leather furniture and a big screen TV. A surrealistic painting hung over the mantle, situated to the left of a bay window overlooking the backyard and the wooded expanse of Stony Brook Reservation beyond.

Luis motioned to a recliner. "Care to sit?"

Ray settled onto the edge of the chair, ready to spring into action if necessary.

"How about a drink?" Luis asked, walking into the kitchen without waiting for an answer.

Ray reached into his sports coat and unsnapped the holster securing Frank's SIG Sauer 9mm pistol. He had an obstructed view of the kitchen and could only see the refrigerator and sink beyond the half wall separating the rooms.

Luis opened the fridge. "You want a beer?"

"Sure."

Ray gazed down the hall to where several closed doors loomed in the shadows. "Nice place. What do you have, three bedrooms?"

"Four."

"And you live here alone?"

"A bachelor's paradise, my man."

"I'll bet." Ray strained his eyes for a better look at a painting displayed at the end of the hall, which from this distance resembled a replica of *The Suffering of Ages*.

Luis returned to the living room carrying a Sam Adams in each hand. Ray took the bottle—slick with condensation—and set it down on the coffee table.

There were two ways Luis could play this—answer the routine questions and send Ray packing, or make Ray disappear and hope no one else came knocking. Either way, Luis would need to purge the house of evidence, and if he was keeping Suzie alive somewhere, that meant getting rid of her too.

Which was why Ray couldn't leave without making an arrest. And while his lie had succeeded in getting him inside without a warrant, it also left no time for the normal precautions.

Luis sat on the sofa and took a long pull of beer. "What's the matter? Don't you like Sam Adams?"

In truth, Ray didn't care much for the hops, or the prospect of being poisoned. "I probably shouldn't drink while I'm on duty. But since you're already halfway finished, why don't you have it?"

Luis slid the bottle to the other end of the coffee table. "I'll save it for later."

Ray made a mental note to enter the beer into evidence. Odds were, it would test positive for the same barbiturate found in Finkleton's bloodstream. "You ready for those questions?"

"That depends," Luis said. "Are you going to play good cop or bad cop?"

Ray locked eyes with Luis. "I don't like to commit. Now," he said, "were you wearing gloves on the morning you prepped Finkleton's body for transport?"

"You were there, you tell me."

"Answer the question, Luis."

"Fine. I was wearing gloves."

"So how do you suppose your prints got onto the harness buckle?"

"I must've caught my glove on the body bag's zipper and ripped one of the fingers."

"And then what?"

Luis groaned. "Do I really need to spell everything out for you? I obviously brushed a finger against the harness buckle when the body was lowered into the bag."

"Did you report the contamination?"

"I didn't think I'd touched anything."

"So that's a no?"

"I didn't report it because I didn't think it was necessary. Will I get in trouble for this?"

"I can't make any guarantees."

"Who else knows about the print?" Luis asked.

"You mind if I have a look around?"

Luis blinked at him. "Didn't I just answer all of your questions?"

"Only the ones I asked."

Ray rose from the chair and gestured down the hall. "That's an interesting painting you got there. You mind telling me about it?"

Luis stood up. "I don't appreciate being made to feel like a criminal."

"You're not really afraid of spiders, are you, Luis?"

"What are you talking about?"

"During Finkleton's autopsy, you practically clawed your way through the wall to get away from a spider. But when I saw you a few days later and said there was a spider on your shirt, you didn't even flinch."

"Are you serious? You're going to draw that conclusion from a bad joke? When there obviously was no spider on my shirt?"

"I don't buy it, Brendan. You're not afraid of spiders."

"Why the hell is that even relevant? And why are you looking at me like that?"

"Because I just called you by the wrong name and you didn't even notice."

"What are you talking about?"

Ray reached into his pocket and showed him Brendan Taritello's mug shot. "That's you, isn't it?"

Luis shook his head. "I don't know that person."

"First time I saw that picture," Ray said, "all I could see was the resemblance to the mayor. But this kid looks a lot like you. You may have packed on a few pounds, grown your hair out and dyed it black, but it's you, isn't it, Brendan? Or do you prefer to be called *The Artist*?"

Luis reached behind his back, but Ray grabbed his arm and slammed him against the wall. Ray drew a .22 caliber pistol from the waistband of Luis's jeans and waved it in his face. "Is this what you shot me with yesterday? Lucky for me, you've got terrible aim."

He pulled a pair of handcuffs off his belt and clicked them around Luis's wrists. "I'm placing you under citizen's arrest, seeing as your crooked father had me suspended."

Luis glared at him. "This isn't over. You haven't won."

"Oh yeah?" Ray asked. "What makes you say that?"

The words were barely out of Ray's mouth before something crashed against the back of his head and the world went dark.

# CHAPTER FORTY-SEVEN

Ray awoke to a whining in his ears—almost like a mosquito, but bigger... angrier. His eyes felt like they were glued shut, his lids so heavy he had to strain just to move them. His head throbbed near the base of his neck, his pulse pounding in what felt like a nasty knot.

He tried to reach for the wound but found that he couldn't move his arms, his legs, or his torso. His eyes snapped open and saw a rocky ceiling. He was lying down, strapped naked to a gurney. In some sort of a fallout bunker.

The room drew slowly into focus and he had to bite his lip to stifle a scream. He was in the Artist's lair, and the Artist's victims were on full display. One man had a pair of horns fused to his head, a golden ring pierced through his nose, and a red bull's-eye tattooed on his chest. His arms were secured by heavy shackles, and a sign below his feet read, *The Minotaur*.

Suzie Coleman stood on an elevated platform beside the minotaur. She was chained naked to the wall, wearing a gold leaf headband above a sign reading, *Aphrodite*.

Another man's head was mounted to the wall like a hunting trophy. At first, Ray thought it was severed, but then the man's eyes shifted toward him and Ray realized the rest of his body was hidden behind the wall. The sign for the exhibit read, *The Rat*, and Ray could see that the Artist had shaved the man's head, blackened his nose, and attached whiskers to his cheeks. A ring of plaster surrounded the man's neck—probably to prevent him from pulling his head through the wall—and Ray suddenly understood why they'd found traces of plaster embedded in Danny's throat.

The man's lips parted and he spoke Ray's name in a gravelly voice. Ray shuddered at the sound and locked eyes with the freakish stranger, searching for a spark of recognition. And then it hit him: Larry.

The mosquito-like whine suddenly emanated on his left and Ray turned to see Luis standing beside him, revving the blade of a bone saw. "I told you this wasn't over, Ray."

"Why are you doing this?"

"Why did Da Vinci paint the *Mona Lisa*? Or Van Gogh *The Starry Night*? Because they were visionaries, Ray. Artistic geniuses who were ahead of their time."

"Is that what you call this, Luis? Art? Because it looks a lot like torture to me."

"Maybe to the untrained eye. But if you look closely, you'll see the art of human suffering is real, visceral, and four-dimensional."

"Four-dimensional?"

"It changes over time."

"So, you're watching them die."

"Now you're getting it."

"But haven't they suffered enough? Isn't it time you let them go?" Ray knew he had no chance of changing Luis's mind, but he had to stall until Billy arrived, assuming Billy was coming at all.

"They deserve to be here, Ray. They must atone for their sins. And the beauty of their suffering will rival the greatest masterpieces of all time."

"Let me go, Luis. People know where I am. If you hurt me, you'll only make it worse for yourself."

Luis shook his head. "You tried making a citizen's arrest, remember? You're on suspension and thought you could be the lone hero. No one's coming for you, Ray. We both know that."

The door to the bunker creaked open and a bubble of hope rose in Ray's chest.

But it wasn't Billy who walked through the door.

# THE ART OF DYING

Jack Flaherty dumped an armload of supplies onto a plastic cart and grinned at Ray. "You must be shitting a brick, detective. I mean, get a load of this place! I had no idea any of this was happening until you started asking questions about my nephew. So thanks for the tip, because we've had a hell of a time catching up." He nudged Luis in the shoulder. "Have you decided what you'll do to him?"

"Isn't it obvious?" Luis asked. "This little piggy went to market, while that other piggy stayed home."

Flaherty howled with laughter. "I like where you're going with this! Why don't you tell the detective how you'll do it?"

"Well," Luis said, shifting his attention to Ray. "First, I'm gonna shave your head and paint your body pink. Then, I'm gonna use this bone saw to shorten your limbs into stubby little pig's legs. Lop you off right here above the knees and elbows. Cauterize the wounds so you don't bleed out."

Luis switched on the bone saw and brought it within an inch of Ray's face. The mosquito-like whine filled his ears. "I can't wait for you to see it, Ray. It's gonna be a bloodbath. Which is why I brought my safety goggles and surgical scrubs. I wonder if you'll cry when your arms fall away from your body and strike the floor. Finkleton did. He was drugged, but, my goodness, he bawled like a baby."

Despite the raw chill permeating the bunker, sweat seeped from Ray's pores and coated the gurney's vinyl cushion in a slippery sheen. He glanced toward his feet and observed a series of industrial-strength Velcro straps stretched across his body, holding him so tightly that he couldn't draw more than a shallow breath. For added measure, his wrists and ankles were secured to the frame of the gurney by reinforced fabric cuffs, limiting his range of motion to less than an inch.

"Do you know where I dispose of the bloody scrubs?" Luis asked.

"I don't know," Ray said, stalling for time. "Where do you dispose of the bloody scrubs?"

"I bring them to work and dump them in the biohazard trash in the autopsy room. Isn't that genius?"

Ray grunted, testing the strength of the restraints. Maybe he could use his sweat as a lubricant to wriggle out of them. "What do you want, Luis? A merit badge for criminal insanity?"

Luis clucked his tongue. "I usually sedate my subjects when I'm hacking off their limbs, but Uncle Jack requested that we go natural this time, and who am I to say no?"

Ray drew a shuddering breath and prayed that Luis was bluffing, but a part of him knew better. Christ, was this how it was going to end? Would he never see his kids again?

Luis grabbed something off the cart and showed him a handheld instrument resembling a giant thermometer with a microphone at one end. "Do you know what this is?"

Ray shook his head. Where the hell was Billy?

"It's a sound meter. And if it registers more than 120 decibels, I start to worry about disturbing the neighbors. I'd hate for one of them to call the police. You know what I mean? So how about we make a deal—if you promise to keep your screaming to a minimum, I won't sever your vocal cords."

Flaherty picked up a croquet mallet that was leaning against the wall. "Have him bite on this handle to keep quiet."

"Good idea, Uncle Jack."

Flaherty loomed over the gurney. "Pretty soon, you'll be living on that wall, detective. And I'll get to watch you die a slow and horrible death. So let me hear you oink like a piggy, or I'll smash your nuts with this mallet."

"Sorry, Flaherty. I don't take requests."

Flaherty hoisted the mallet over his shoulder. "Maybe this will change your mind."

Ray clenched his legs and turned away, but the sudden creak of the bunker door froze Flaherty in place.

Billy stormed inside with his gun drawn and Ray let out his breath in a gust of relief.

"Drop it!" Billy shouted.

Flaherty lowered the mallet slowly, dropping his hand behind his back before releasing his grip on the handle and letting it clatter to the floor. Flaherty's hand returned lightning-quick from behind his back, clutching a gun he'd drawn from the waistband of his jeans. Before Billy could react, Flaherty pressed the muzzle against Ray's forehead.

"You drop it," Flaherty said. "Or your boyfriend dies."

Billy's face went dark. "If you kill him, I'll kill you."

"No, you won't," Flaherty said. "You remember the arrangement. If I die, my attorney will release a certain video and your dirty little secret will be broadcast to the world."

"What's he talking about?" Ray asked, a cold dread stealing over him.

"Go ahead, Billy. Tell him."

Billy's shoulders sagged. "Remember that night we busted Danny at the docks? I stumbled across a shipping container filled with cash. Had to be over a million bucks. And that kind of money... I mean, holy shit, right? It was around the time I was going through my divorce. All that cash is just sitting there, and you know it'll only end up going to the state to buy new cruisers or remodel the station. And guys like us, we put our lives on the line for peanuts. Where's the justice in that? So I grabbed a few stacks of bills thinking no one would ever miss it."

Ray glared at him. "You made a deal, didn't you? You do favors for Flaherty and he keeps quiet about the money."

"Just small things here and there."

"You tipped him off about the sting operation, didn't you?"

"I was hoping it would make us even."

"Christ, Billy, how could you?"

"What the hell was I supposed to do, Ray? He had me by the balls. I would've lost everything."

"You should've told me."

"What good would that have done? If you didn't turn me in, you would've been complicit."

"Great," Ray said, "so now here we are."

"I might have a way out of this," Billy said. "A win-win for everyone."

"Go on," Flaherty said.

"You drop the gun and walk out of here," Billy said, "and we pretend like we never saw you. And then Ray and I arrest Luis and look like heroes."

Flaherty nodded slowly, as if mulling it over. "Tell you what, Billy, you put your gun down and I'll think about it."

"We do it at the same time," Billy said, "or not at all."

"Alright," Flaherty said. "On the count of three, we point our guns at the floor, lay them down, and take a step back."

"Deal."

But it wasn't a fair one. Because as soon as both guns were on the ground, Flaherty reached behind his back and drew another one from the waistband of his jeans. Before Billy could register the double cross, Flaherty shot him in the face. The exit wound blew out the back of Billy's skull, and Ray screamed as his partner's brains splattered against the concrete. Billy's body seemed to fall in slow motion, like a tree toppling in the forest.

Flaherty's laughter echoed throughout the bunker. "I guess Billy and I had different ideas of a win-win. For me, it was *two* dead cops."

Luis snickered. "Clean up on aisle five."

Flaherty pulled a handkerchief from his pocket and wiped off the gun before handing it to Luis. "I think this one's yours."

Luis placed it on the cart beside him, oblivious to the fact that Flaherty's backup plan seemed to involve framing him for murder.

Flaherty stooped down to retrieve the second gun. "If you hear anyone coming, kill them all," he said, gesturing to Ray and the other exhibits.

"Where are you going?" Luis asked.

"I need to make sure Billy came alone." He glanced over his shoulder as he reached the bunker door. "Remember what I said. Anyone comes, you kill everyone."

"I will," Luis said.

Flaherty pulled the door shut and disappeared into the hallway beyond.

Luis grabbed a pair of hair clippers from the cart and switched them on. He leaned over the gurney and began buzzing Ray's hair down to the scalp.

"He's not coming back," Ray said. "Don't you get it? Billy would've called for backup. More cops are on the way."

"Then let them come. It's time to reveal the art of dying to the world, and you'll be my pièce de résistance." Luis set the clippers aside and slathered Ray's head with shaving cream. He reached onto the cart and brandished a straight blade speckled with blood. "I've been waiting a long time for this moment."

As Luis shaved Ray bald, his victims watched from their positions on the wall. Although they'd each experienced their own personal suffering, Ray was the center of attention now—the latest attraction in the Artist's gallery of horror.

And while Ray had survived dozens of life-threatening situations in the past, he couldn't recall ever being in a position so bleak. He was physically incapacitated, his captor planned to mutilate him and leave him for dead, and there wasn't a damn thing he could do about it.

He'd told Luis the cavalry was coming, but what were the odds Billy had called for backup? Doing so would've sealed Ray's fate at the department, since it would prove he'd continued to investigate while on suspension. Billy might've tried to protect him by coming alone.

*Christ.*

He thought about Jason, Allie, and Petey. They didn't know it yet, but yesterday was probably the last time they'd ever see their daddy alive. He recalled their bittersweet goodbye on the porch and cursed himself for getting into this mess. He'd put his ego before common sense, and now they would all pay the price.

Luis set the razor down on a tray of gleaming surgical instruments. "It's almost time for your transformation, Ray. Are you excited?"

"Let me off this gurney and I'll show you."

"Did I mention I'll be cutting your nose off? I'm going to reshape it into a snout before sewing it back on."

"I know you were abused, Luis. I know people did horrible things to you. But you don't have to do this. It's not your fault."

"You're right, Ray. I don't have to do this. I *want* to do it."

"Your father and uncle let this happen. They allowed Danny to abuse you. All the pain, all the failures in your life, it's their fault, Luis. If anyone should be on this gurney, it's them. Let me out of here and I'll help you get revenge."

"No," Luis said, shaking his head. "You're the little piggy, Ray. You're the little piggy who'll cry *wee wee wee* all the way home." He picked up a scalpel and cut tiny circles into the air. "Do you know what I'll use to make your piggy's tail? I'll give you a hint. It rhymes with Venus."

Ray swallowed a lump in his throat and Luis tossed his head back and cackled. "That's right, Ray. I'll cut off your penis and twist it around a wire. And then I'll attach it to the crack of your ass with surgical staples. But first I need to get my torch so I can cauterize your wounds. And I need to tell Uncle Jack that it's time to slice the bacon."

Luis snatched the gun off the cart and strode across the room, sidestepping the puddle of blood congealing around Billy's head. He exited the bunker, closing and latching the door behind him.

After the echo of Luis's departure faded into oblivion, Ray shifted his weight on the gurney, wrenching his body from side to side. But the restraints held fast.

"Get us out of here!" Larry cried, his rat's head protruding from the wall.

"I'm working on it," Ray said. He tried to wriggle the gurney in Suzie's direction. If he could get it close enough, she might be able to use her toes to unfasten the Velcro straps.

"It's no use," the Minotaur said. "We're all gonna die."

Ray didn't want to believe it, but the gurney refused to budge. Luis must have locked the wheels. Christ, they were running out of time! There had to be a way out of this. He had to think, damnit!

A rattling of chains drew his attention and he turned to where Suzie was fidgeting with her shackles, trying to pick the lock. Within seconds, she managed to free her left hand and the chains on that side went slack against the wall.

Ray could hardly believe his eyes.

"I can only get one," she said. "The other one never opens."

Ray studied the shackles from afar, his eyes focused on the gap between the metal and Suzie's slender wrist. "Can you pull your hand through?"

"No."

"What did you use to pick the lock?"

"A nail."

"I need you to listen to me, Suzie. Can you do that?"

She nodded.

"I need you to cut your wrist. Just deep enough to draw blood. Do you understand?"

"Yes."

"But you've got to be quick."

She moved her hand over the opposite wrist and made a sweeping motion beneath the iron cuff, exposing a thin ribbon of crimson.

"That's it," Ray said.

She worked her wrist against the edge of the metal, causing rivulets of blood to run down her forearm.

A thumping emanated from beyond the bunker.

A door slamming? Someone coming?

"Hurry!" Ray said.

"It's working!" Suzie said.

The shackle slipped off her wrist and banged against the wall, rattling the chains like the ghost of Jacob Marley. She stared at her bloody hand for a moment, as if marveling at her newfound freedom, before hopping off the platform and rushing toward the gurney.

Another sound emanated from beyond the walls of the bunker. Unmistakable this time. The thud of footfalls, and someone whistling an upbeat tune.

Suzie unfastened the gurney's restraints and Ray jumped to his feet and hugged her, forgetting for a moment that they were naked. "Go back to the wall," he whispered. "Pretend you're still locked up."

She shook her head, her eyes brimming with terror.

"You've got to trust me."

At first, he didn't think she would listen, but then she whirled around and darted back to the wall, climbing onto the pedestal and slipping her arms behind the chains.

Ray grabbed the croquet mallet and scrambled to the door, positioning himself in the corner, where he'd be shielded by its opening arc. He pressed his back against the wall and waited.

The sound of whistling continued as someone fumbled with the locks and metal clanged against metal. A bolt slid back and the door creaked open.

Luis stepped inside carrying a blowtorch and a jar of pink paint. He drew to a halt two paces into the bunker and gaped at the empty gurney. "What the—"

Ray kicked the door shut and swung the mallet, striking Luis in the face and sending him stumbling forward. The paint jar flew out of his hand and struck the ground, a puddle of pink oozing onto the concrete as Luis sank to his knees with the torch.

Ray wound up to hit Luis again, but the first blow had knocked him out cold. Ray tossed the mallet aside and grabbed

Luis by the foot, dragging him across the room. He scooped Luis into his arms and laid him flat on the gurney, fastening the restraints before he could regain consciousness.

The gun Flaherty had murdered Billy with protruded from the waistband of Luis's jeans. Ray snatched the gun and grabbed his own pants, which were balled up on the floor near the wall. He pulled them on and turned toward Suzie.

"I'm going after Flaherty. Free the others and wait here. If I'm not back in ten minutes, take my car and drive to the nearest police station." He fished Jacob's car keys from his pocket and handed them to her before rushing out of the bunker.

He emerged into a shadowy hallway devoid of windows. It had a subterranean feel, concrete all around, and sloped upward to a door leading into the basement. He passed through the door and navigated around a maze of obstacles— riding mower, patio furniture, golf clubs, and low hanging pipes—before exiting into another hallway inside the first floor living area. Tiptoeing barefoot across the hardwood, Ray conducted a room-to-room sweep of the bathroom, guestroom, and bonus room, all of which were unusually clean for a bachelor pad.

Still no sign of Flaherty.

Ray doubled back down the hall and crept upstairs with his finger resting against the trigger guard of Luis's gun. When he reached the top of the landing, he peered into the living room where he'd questioned Luis earlier. The room was empty. Even the beer bottles had been cleared away. The only evidence of their meeting was a half-dried ring of condensation gleaming on the coffee table.

He padded farther into the room and glanced into the kitchen, but Flaherty wasn't in there either. He must've hightailed it out of town. So, why did Ray have the feeling he wasn't alone? Just his nerves… or something more?

He peered out the window overlooking the front yard. A state police cruiser had just pulled into the driveway and he could see Garrison's shiny brown head through the windshield.

Which meant Billy had called him on his way over. But Billy was dead now, his body sprawled on the floor of the bunker, the back of his head blown apart. And it was all Ray's fault. How had he let things spiral so far out of control?

Outside the window, he detected a blur of movement near the house. Flaherty ducked behind a massive oak on the front lawn, holding a gun fitted with a silencer and preparing to ambush Garrison.

Ray whirled toward the door and froze as an older woman approached the landing from the hall. She pulled the trigger before he even registered the gun in her hand. The bullet grazed his shoulder and sent him stumbling into the recliner, his own gun clattering to the floor.

"You better not have hurt Brendan," she growled, adjusting her aim to his chest. Her gun was fitted with a silencer. Just like Flaherty's.

As Ray lifted his hands in surrender, he realized that he was staring at Doc Death's icy receptionist, Mrs. Granderling. "Christ," he said, "you're Angie Taritello."

"No shit. What have you done to Brendan?"

Ray shifted his gaze to the stairway behind her. "He's right over there."

Mrs. Granderling started to turn, but then thought better of it.

Ray seized on the momentary distraction and dove to the ground, somersaulting toward her as she fired an errant shot into the floorboards. He launched himself at her before she could adjust, tackling her at the waist like a linebacker leveling a quarterback. Except instead of landing on soft grass, they tumbled down the stairs with Ray riding on top.

When they crashed into the door at the bottom of the landing, Mrs. Granderling lay moaning, her body bent askew. Ray rolled off her and snatched her gun from the floor. As he sprang to his feet, the bullet wound in his shoulder radiated a shockwave of pain, but he gritted his teeth against it and charged outside.

"Garrison, look out!"

The sudden outburst threw off Flaherty's aim, and instead of a kill shot, the bullet struck Garrison's Kevlar vest.

Flaherty whirled toward Ray, but it was too late.

Ray had already pulled the trigger.

A blooming rose of crimson soaked Flaherty's shirt, his eyes wide with shock. The gun slipped from his hand and tumbled into the grass. He clutched his abdomen, blood seeping between his fingers. "I need an ambulance," he croaked.

Ray descended the porch stairs, keeping his gun trained on Flaherty. "You don't deserve an ambulance. And since we both used silencers, I doubt anyone called 911."

Flaherty's face was ashen. "I'll tell you who killed your father."

"You don't know who killed him. Billy told you the story, didn't he?"

Flaherty didn't answer, but the silence spoke volumes.

Garrison staggered across the front walk and fished Flaherty's gun from the grass. "Where's Billy?" he asked, holding a hand to his chest and wincing.

Ray swallowed a lump in his throat. "Billy didn't make it."

Garrison closed his eyes and shook his head slowly. "*Shit.*"

"You can't do this," Flaherty said, panic creeping into his voice. "It's against the law." He leaned against the oak and slid down the trunk until he was sitting in the grass.

"The law?" Ray said. "That's pretty ironic, coming from you. The world's better off without you, Flaherty. If you die, there's no trial, no chance of some dirtbag lawyer getting you off on a technicality. And the city gets what a friend of mine once called swift justice. I didn't appreciate what that meant before, but I do now."

Flaherty's lips pursed as if he was about to respond, but a wracking cough seized him and a dark rivulet of blood oozed from the corner of his mouth.

A warble of sirens rose in the distance, but it was too late for Flaherty. He slumped forward and pitched face-first into the grass.

Ray glanced down at the wound on his shoulder.

Garrison said, "Looks like you're the one who needs that ambulance. I guess a neighbor called after all."

The door creaked behind them and Ray whirled around, expecting to see Mrs. Granderling wielding the gun he'd dropped in the living room. Instead, it was Suzie Coleman staggering down the steps, her naked body covered in a glistening sheen of blood. She wore a strange expression, and when her lips parted, Ray saw that even her teeth were stained red.

Ray rushed toward her. "Suzie! Are you okay?"

She stared past him, her eyes vacant. "He won't hurt anyone ever again."

"The Artist?"

"I cut it off," she said, and cackled. "And then I fed it to him. And cut him. And watched him die."

Ray felt his knees go weak. "Get her a blanket."

Garrison ran to the cruiser and retrieved a blanket from the trunk. He draped it around Suzie's shoulders and sat her down in the grass. Ray sank to the ground beside her, no longer able to support his own weight.

"I'm sorry," he said, "I shouldn't have left you."

*Christ, what had she done?*

She hugged her knees and rocked herself, repeating the same words over and over. "I'm okay. I'm okay. I'm okay."

As if willing herself to believe it.

# CHAPTER FORTY-EIGHT

The city honored Billy with a hero's funeral for his role in taking down Flaherty and the Artist, complete with flag bearers, bagpipes, and hundreds of officers attending from states as far away as California. If surveillance video existed of Billy pocketing drug money, Flaherty's attorney failed to produce it.

Although it was customary for the mayor to speak at high profile funerals for officers killed in the line of duty, Mayor Tom Flaherty was in jail (along with Mrs. Granderling), so the governor stepped in to take his place. Billy's ex-wife was also in attendance, standing before the flag-draped casket with her arms around Tyler, who cried throughout the ceremony.

It was heart-wrenching to watch, but Ray wouldn't allow himself to look away. Doc Stevenson kept assuring him that Billy's death wasn't his fault, that he wasn't the one who'd pulled the trigger, but it was his own recklessness that had put Billy on the receiving end of Flaherty's gun.

Captain Barnes had lifted Ray's suspension and welcomed him back onto the force with a promotion to sergeant detective. But Ray didn't feel like he deserved the job, let alone the accolades or the media blitz. And as much as Billy sometimes got on his nerves, he realized that he loved him like a brother.

After his discharge from the hospital, Michelle had allowed him to come home. While he knew that things may never be the same again, at least they were together as a family. And he would spend the rest of his life making it up to her—not because he felt guilty, but because he loved her and she deserved better.

The kids were surprised to see his newly shorn scalp and made no secret about how much they hated it. Petey had taken one look at him and said, "Da-da, why you look like Humpty Dumpty?"

Four days had passed since Billy's death, but Ray had barely slept a wink. Whenever he closed his eyes, he was haunted by the slow-motion memory of Billy's head blowing apart. And during those rare moments when sleep did overtake him, he'd inevitably jolt awake drenched in sweat as the blood-soaked image of Suzie Coleman faded from his consciousness and her words echoed through his mind.

*I'm okay. I'm okay…*

But he didn't see how that was possible.

Not even with the best therapy money could buy.

Only Sal Giabatti had emerged from the chaos for the better. With the mayor in jail and Flaherty's gang without leadership, he would soon control the city's entire underworld and become richer than he'd ever imagined. Maybe the dapper old mobster had outsmarted them all. Maybe he'd even played them from the beginning. Either way, he was right about one thing.

It had turned into one hell of a bloody summer.

# Author's Note

If you enjoyed **The Art of Dying**, please consider rating it on Amazon or Goodreads. And if you're interested in another thrilling read, turn the page for a preview of **The Righteous and the Wicked**, a suspense thriller with elements of sci-fi, urban fantasy, and police procedural.

And as always, thanks for reading! I appreciate your support and welcome your comments and questions, so please don't hesitate to reach out to me at dcavignano@hotmail.com.

# THE RIGHTEOUS AND THE WICKED

The dying man staggered into the restaurant with such a clamor that Jacob Hanley dropped his menu and knocked over his drink. A stream of ice water surged toward his lap and Jacob jumped to his feet in time to see the old man lurch into the dining area.

Wild tufts of ivory hair crowned the man's scalp, his skin pale gray and liver-spotted. His features were so gaunt that Jacob imagined an invisible force might soon collapse his eyes, nose, and lips into the hollows of his skull.

The man stumbled toward Jacob, his arms pinwheeling for balance. He would've hit the floor face-first had Jacob not caught him around the waist and eased him into an empty chair. Jacob held one hand against the man's chest to keep him from falling.

The old man gasped for breath, his vibrant blue eyes locked on Jacob. "Beware the Order," he whispered. "The plane of the Symbios. The Great Elder... he will destroy—"

And then the old man drew a broken breath and died. Just like that.

As Jacob reflected on it later, sitting slouched on his living room sofa, he couldn't help but wonder how you could be alive one minute, so utterly there, and then be gone the next. It had to be a joke. Some sick cosmic prank to keep God amused.

# THE ART OF DYING

He pulled off his glasses and rubbed his eyes. It was getting late and he was thinking about Megan again. It seemed these days, all thoughts led back to Megan.

He stood up, suddenly itching for movement, and found himself at the bookshelf by the TV. He reached for a photo taken on the coast of Maine two summers before. Megan stood on the rocks by the shoreline, a weathered lighthouse rising up in the distance behind her. She held her arms outstretched and struck a pose for the camera, trying to ruin the picture with a goofy grin and a scrunched up nose.

It was classic Megan. So free-spirited and full of life. It was such a perfect picture, such a perfect day. Who would've guessed she'd be dead within a year?

A tear rolled down his cheek and splashed onto the frame, triggering a memory of that rainy March morning at the funeral parlor, the cloying scent of lilies and eucalyptus invading his nostrils as he stood beside Megan's casket while friends, family, and strangers patted his clay-cold hands and assured him that it would get easier as time wore on.

She'd been dead fifteen months now, but it seemed an eternity. Sometimes it was hard to remember that he was happy once, that laughter had filled this house. All he had now was the faint echo of her memory, a teasing reminder of her absence like the lingering scent of perfume on her clothes.

Footfalls shook the porch. The bell rang—a ding without a dong. It hadn't worked properly since he first installed it, which wasn't a surprise considering Megan had long ago declared him to be more handicap than handyman. She loved ribbing him about it, and it soon became part of the secret lexicon of their marriage. Every time it voiced its lonely ding, she would arch an eyebrow in that way of hers and ask, *What's wrong with your dong?*

Jacob opened the door to find his brother standing on the worn welcome mat with his fists thrust into his pockets. At six foot four, Ray stood five inches taller than Jacob, although both had the same liquid brown eyes, same wavy brown hair, and the same pale skin with a spattering of freckles around the bridge of the nose.

"I thought you were playing cards tonight," Jacob said.

Ray shrugged. "I was. But you sounded upset. I wanted to make sure you were okay."

"You didn't have to do that."

"What are big brothers for?"

Jacob held open the door. "You used to give a mean wedgie."

Ray grinned. "Remember that time in the mall? When I lifted you off the ground and ripped the underwear out of your pants, showed all your friends you were wearing Mighty Mouse Underoos?" He chuckled. "You bawled like a little girl."

"I thought you were here to cheer me up." He walked into the kitchen. "You want some coffee? I just brewed decaf."

"Sure." Ray sipped from the mug Jacob offered and winced. "You put Drano in here or what?"

"It's my secret ingredient."

Ray cleared his throat. "So tell me again what happened at the restaurant. Some old guy started spouting gibberish and then keeled over dead at your feet?"

Jacob nodded, recalling the look of desperation in the old man's eyes. "It was weird, you know? I was just sitting there, waiting for a client, and in walks Father Time."

"Sounds to me like the guy was nuts."

"I don't know, it just got to me—watching him die. I don't see the point."

"What point?"

"In dying."

"Everyone dies, Jacob."

"But it seems like such a waste. We're born, we grow old, we die. How can you live with that constantly hanging over your head?"

"Are you listening to yourself? Christ, Jacob. I know you loved her, but you've got to move on."

Jacob felt his face flush. "Do you think I can just flick a switch and forget I ever knew her? What if Michelle died—would you be able to just move on?"

"I don't know what I'd do, Jacob, but you've got to face facts. You're thirty-two years old. Megan's dead. You've got to stop acting as though you are too."

Jacob sighed. "A part of me died with her, Ray. Something inside me shriveled up and turned to dust. And now… now I just feel empty." He shook his head. "Maybe I need more time."

"Why? So you can continue to lose yourself in your work, come home and sit here all alone, cut off from the rest of the world? You can't live in the past, Jacob. The past is a graveyard, nothing but ghosts and shadows."

"You don't understand, Ray. You've got your life together, you've got Michelle and the kids, all of you healthy."

"Yeah, but any one of us could get hit by a bus tomorrow, get killed just like that." He snapped his fingers. "Death's everywhere, Jacob. Always lurking around the corner, waiting for its chance. But you don't see me moping around the house, feeling sorry for myself, getting depressed over things I can't change. It's not worth it. What you need to do is get out of the house, meet new people. Find yourself a hot little blond. The world's not over, Jacob. Not if you don't want it to be."

"It's not that easy."

"It'll only get harder if you keep shutting everybody out."

Jacob stared out the window. "Maybe you're right."

"Course I am." Ray clapped him on the back. "When have I ever been wrong?"

"You want a list?"

"Don't get wise, little brother. You're not too old for a wedgie. By the way, you owe me forty bucks."

"For what?"

"You bet against the Sox."

"That wasn't a serious bet."

Ray folded his arms. "You welching on me?"

"What are we, eleven?" He dug his wallet out of his pocket, and what he found inside prickled his skin with gooseflesh.

Ray furrowed his brow. "What's wrong?"

"This license. This... it isn't mine."

"Let me see." Ray snatched it out of Jacob's hand and tilted it into the light. The man in the picture was thirty years old, clean cut, with spiky blond hair and ice-blue eyes. "Charles J. Riggs III. Thirteen North Broadway, South Boston." He glanced at Jacob. "Where'd you get this?"

"I don't..." But then he remembered—the old man at Victoria's. After the ambulance had pulled away, no flashers, no sirens (he was pronounced dead at the scene), Jacob went back inside, forced down half a turkey club, and paid the bill when his client didn't show. He'd assumed the license on the table was his, figured it had fallen out of his wallet when he pulled out his credit card. And so he'd picked it up without a glance and slid it into his wallet behind a dog-eared business card.

He peered at the license over Ray's broad shoulders. "He's got the same eyes as the old man in the restaurant."

"Maybe it's his son."

"Grandson, maybe; the guy looked older than Methuselah."

"I wonder if they were able to ID the body. This happen in the city?"

Jacob nodded. "Post Office Square."

Ray tapped his thumbnail against the license. "If you want, I can bring this to the precinct with me tomorrow, help locate his next of kin."

But Jacob didn't answer.

"Jacob?"

"Yeah?"

"You alright?"

"Yeah, I was just... I don't know. I watched him die, Ray. I watched the light wink out of his eyes."

"He was an old man."

"I know." He set down his coffee. "I think I need to get out of the house for a while, go for a walk or something."

Ray lifted an eyebrow. "You kicking me out?"

"I want to clear my head, think about what you said."

Ray studied him a moment, liquid brown eyes filled with concern, and Jacob wondered, not for the first time, how much worse things would be if he didn't have his big brother to lean on.

Ray nodded slowly. "I'll walk you out."

The screen door banged shut behind them, wrested from Jacob's grasp by a gust of wind. The sun hung low in the sky like the last bloody ember of a dying fire. From the street came the clattering roll of a kicked can, followed by the excited cries of children scattering to find a hiding spot.

Ray climbed into his truck—a black Ford Explorer he bought after his promotion to detective sergeant earlier that year. He twirled the keys in his hand. "You gonna be all right?"

Jacob nodded. "Don't worry."

"All right, but watch out for those roving gangs of rich kids."

"I'll be extra careful."

Ray loved to rib him about living in Stonefield. It was a haven for young professionals, a quaint suburb with ornate Victorian homes, expensive cars, and manicured lawns. It seemed everyone there was a doctor, a lawyer, or a banker. Jacob, who was none of these, had always thought it would be the perfect place to start a family.

He and Megan had been trying for a year before she died. He used to love the way the ritual began. Megan would come into the living room and tap him on the shoulder. *Wanna make some babies?*

He would scoop her into his arms, carry her upstairs, and drop her onto the bed. Then he'd pretend like he'd thrown out his back and point to her belly. *Sure you don't already have one in there?*

"See you later," Ray said.

"Huh? Oh." Jacob lifted a hand. "I'll call you tomorrow."

"Forty bucks," Ray said, and pulled away from the curb.

Jacob stared after the Explorer, watching as it crested the hill at the end of his street and disappeared.

*Move on.*

What kind of advice was that? Ray meant well but, God, he had such a habit of oversimplifying. How could he possibly replace Megan? And why was everyone always pressuring him to forget her?

He walked to the end of the street and turned the corner, glancing up as he approached Stonefield center. Light glowed in the windows of the boutiques on Main Street, their awnings illuminated by the old-fashioned gas lamps that lined the streets. A granite obelisk commemorating the Revolutionary War loomed over the landscaped rotary ahead where Main, Summer, and Central streets intersected.

The Stonefield police station sat at the junction of Central and Main. It was a monster of a building—a concrete beast guarded by stone lions. It was set back from the road, the rear of the structure dissolving into the shadows that draped Kennedy Park and Whitecap Lake. Had it been midday, the lake would've been teeming with windsurfers skipping across the rough amber swells. But the water was dark now, the lake silent.

Crickets chirruped in the gathering twilight, the sound of Jacob's footfalls eliciting a momentary hush from the grass near his feet. He gazed at the sky through the canopy of trees and could see the first stars piercing the velvety darkness like pinpricks.

The scuff of a shoe snapped him to attention. He glanced over his shoulder and caught a glimpse of a stocky kid in his early twenties closing the gap between them. It was difficult to tell in the failing light, but it seemed as though the kid was staring right at him.

*Stop being so paranoid. He's probably just in a hurry.*

But the seed of anxiousness that had taken root in his brain and flowered these last fifteen months begged to differ. Something about the kid unnerved him, and the need to dart across the street and seek refuge in the bright lights of the boutiques gripped him with a maddening sense of urgency.

He could hear the kid's feet grinding sand against the pavement, could hear the whisper of fabric as the kid's legs scissored in what he imagined to be a jog. He held his breath and waited for the kid to pass.

A hand clamped onto his shoulder and spun him around. "Gimme your wallet." The kid's grip was like iron, their faces so close they might've been lovers. The kid's broad features were almost mongoloid in appearance. He had a chalk-white complexion and the thin purple lips of a corpse.

For a moment, Jacob was certain he'd seen the kid before... but where? And then he spotted a man climbing into a car across the street.

The kid followed Jacob's gaze. "You scream, you die."

Jacob noticed a butterfly knife clutched in the kid's hand. Mugged! He was being mugged.

"You deaf or something?" The blade whisked before his eyes.

Jacob thrust his wallet into the kid's hands. "Take it."

The door to the police station creaked open. A middle-aged man in police blues lit a cigarette and froze on the steps, his gaze angled in their direction. "Hey!" the cop yelled.

The kid's jaw dropped open. He shoved Jacob to the ground and fled into the street.

The cop pitched his cigarette and raced down the stairs.

A black Lincoln swerved around the corner and screeched to a halt. The kid dove into the backseat and the car peeled away from the curb, leaving a cloud of burnt rubber pluming out behind it.

Jacob rolled onto his side and caught a glimpse of the first two numbers of the license plate before a tinted panel of glass slid over it and everything faded to black.

**For more information about the author, visit:**

www.amazon.com/author/cavignano

www.derikcavignano.com

dcavignano@hotmail.com

Twitter @DerikCavignano

Southwest

Made in the
USA
Columbia, SC